BOOK 2: BENCHMARK LEGACY SERIES

EDD JORDAN

BookBaby Publishing

For questions about usage, please contact info@bookbaby.com or 877-961-6878.

Visit author's website at www.eddjordan.com.

First Edition

No animals were harmed in the making of this novel.

Content guidance: This novel contains references to posttraumatic stress disorder (PTSD), panic attacks, depression, anxiety, abortion, racism, violence, abduction, child abuse, sexual assault, and homicide.

If you or someone you know is in crisis, call **988** to reach the **Suicide and Crisis Lifeline** 800-273-TALK (8255) or **Text HOME to 741741** (U.S.); 686868 (Canada); 85258 (UK).

Visit **SpeakingOfSuicide.com/resources** for additional information and resources.

If the cover is missing from this novel, it has been picked from a dumpster, possibly the same dumpster Ubu was discovered in. Do yourself a favor: throw it away, wash your hands, and buy a new copy to support the author and charities listed on www.eddjordan.com. That way, he can buy more coffee to continue writing stories for the Benchmark Legacy Series.

ISBN 979-8-35090-929-6
eBook ISBN 979-8-35090-930-2

PROLOGUE

EIGHT YEARS AGO

Bright rays of sunshine pierced the morning fog as John strolled through his garden oasis behind his 1800s mansion. He held his morning coffee in one hand and his cell phone in the other, following the stone-paved path through the blackjack oak trees lining his spacious well-manicured back gardens. The black trunks stood out in contrast to the white morning mist.

As he rounded a corner, his wife Peri was several strides ahead, facing away from him. She wore a flowing white dress that blended in with the surrounding haze, making her invisible except for her luxurious black hair. She was admiring a red cardinal flower, delicately cradling it in her hands.

He creeped silently along the path, a good-natured game he has played with her since the day they met. Two hummingbirds flitted on either side of his wife. Graceful in flight, they inaudibly dashed off in opposite directions as he approached.

"If you think you can sneak up on me in the fog, you're kidding yourself," she said, not looking up.

"The thought never crossed my mind."

"Liar," she lightheartedly said. "I know you too well, my love." She finished caressing the flower and turned to face her husband. "This garden is so beautiful in the rising sun."

John smiled and said, "It pales compared to your beauty, my dear."

"Oh, oh. What did you do?" She tilted her head and with a half-smile said, "You only butter me up when you've spent another fortune on something I might not approve."

He didn't answer right away.

She said, "Well, out with it, dear."

To stall for time, he pretended to observe the lifting mist to his right, pondering how much of his plan he should reveal. He knew eventually she would learn everything. Throughout their time together, he shielded her from the stress of day-to-day business decisions, but she had a certain way about her. She would inevitably uncover the entire story.

Any attempt to keep parts of the plan from her would be futile. He said, "I've decided we should expand our operations."

For several seconds, Peri remained silent, pretending to analyze a flower near her. Without looking at her husband, she asked, "How do the shareholders feel about that?"

"Well, I've only begun the initial discovery stages so it's too early to bring them into it, but I think we can grow our fleet nationwide." She turned toward him. He looked her in the eye and said, "We can be larger than any airline."

She sighed heavily. They had gone through this before. "With big expansion come big headaches. Are you absolutely certain you want to proceed?"

"I know, dear. We will continue to bring in the right people. I am certain we will grow into the finest airline that has ever flown. It'll take time and won't happen overnight." He paused, gazing at the sunshine creating rainbows in the fog and searching for the words he wanted in the vibrant colors. "Through meticulous planning, it took us two years to complete this garden. We can build our airline using the same fortitude." As he said this, he made an arc with his left arm across the expanse of the backyard, spilling some of his coffee onto his fingers and the walkway below.

With coffee dripping down her husband's hand, Peri said, "Well, before you get your morning coffee all over my dress, why don't we sit down? You can try to convince me why we should have more stress in our lives." She softly grasped her husband's hand, guiding him with a gentle touch to a bench several steps up the pathway.

He said, studying the antique before sitting, "I believe this is the last bench we placed in the garden. Unlike the other ones we had to hunt down across the states, this antique came to us from that fellow out of the blue. I don't think I have even sat on it yet."

"Neither have I. The bench does look inviting with its smooth polished seat." She sat down, adjusting her dress beneath her so it didn't wrinkle. She continued, her hand tracing the lines of the wood beside her, "Strange how it's not damp from the morning dew."

"Perhaps the sun has already taken care of it," he said, not giving it much thought. He shifted to face her as he spoke. "Look, dear, if you tell me no, I won't proceed with the expansion, but I feel it's the right way to go."

The excitement in his voice was unmistakable as he spoke about the project. She had witnessed the fire of passion in his eyes many times, and it usually meant that his dreams would become reality. Nonetheless, when they failed, they caused them a significant financial setback. She never let those downfalls interfere with the steady rise they had. Over the course of their thirty-eight-year relationship, they had saved up a fair amount of money and established a renowned airline business.

Others would have been satisfied to keep the status quo, but not John. He was ever pushing higher. Her view was the opposite. She felt it was time to enjoy life without the corporate stress.

"Honey, perhaps we should take things slower. We're getting closer to retirement every day. Wouldn't you rather spend your days here in our backyard enjoying this garden than sitting in a concrete building surrounded by stress?"

John was disheartened by his wife's words. Occasionally, she had played the devil's advocate for his eccentric ideas. Most times, he could glean when she was on board with an idea. However, he could see in her eyes this time she didn't share his vision.

He locked eyes with her for a second more and then had to turn away, gazing at their beloved garden for a quiet moment. He set his phone down on the bench, regained eye contact, and held her hand in his. "Peri, there is nothing in this world I would do to cause you pain. If you believe this to be the wrong decision, then I will abide by your judgment." He tenderly squeezed her hand in a sign of his love.

To cheer her husband's mood, she said, "Why don't we sit here for a spell? Let's enjoy this beautiful garden, the sunrise, and each other's company."

As they were awed by the swirling mist dancing through the sun's rays yards away, John's phone buzzed with an incoming call. At first, he ignored it, continuing to hold his wife's hand. She worked her hand from his and said, "You should answer that. It may be important, dear."

His gaze lingered on his wife, a gentle smile on his face. Her face was composed, giving nothing away. He eyed the phone, heard the buzzing, and felt its vibrations as he picked it up. "Hi, Anders. What can I do for you?" He rose to his feet, silently telling his wife something and gesturing to his phone. He carried on his conversation as he walked through the fog, the sun's rays creating a kaleidoscope of colors.

Peri watched her husband walk away. As the distance grew and the sound of his voice faded into nondescript words, the mist encircled him in an unrecognizable blur. She contemplated what he had said about expanding their airline and wasn't entirely opposed to the idea. Over the years, she came to rely on his acute business acumen.

Despite the happy times, their life together had seen its fair share of struggles. When they were married, money was tight and the smell of cooking beans and hot dogs lingered in the air most nights. She smiled as she remembered him saying, "As long as I have you, nothing else matters."

Her parents, especially her father, had other thoughts about John. They had called him a dreamer and someone who would never amount to anything. Much to her parents' chagrin, she was in love, and they begrudgingly gave their blessing to the marriage. That was undoubtedly what drove John to his success.

He not only wanted to provide for his wife and his family, he steeled himself to show to her father that he was worthy of his daughter's hand.

He exceeded expectations in every way.

In their first decade together, John successfully climbed the corporate ladder, squirreling away the money he made. Just seven years into their marriage, he began his own business delivering packages in the Carolinas and Georgia via a vintage plane he had purchased after obtaining his pilot license. This grew into a regional shuttle for business clients and ultimately Benchmark Air.

Now he had his sights set on expanding the business from coast to coast.

Peri pondered that. John not only had built his business, he built a team who followed the mantra of the golden rule, striving to act with kindness and empathy. Treat others with the same warmth and compassion you hope to receive. His resolute philosophy had allowed the business to thrive.

Thirty years later, she desired to turn the business over to them so she could have more quality time with her husband. This brought other thoughts to her. Was she being selfish? Would this deprive John of what he truly enjoyed doing? He had become more than her father had ever thought possible, albeit he had not seen how high John had progressed.

The day before she lost him, her father told her in a raspy voice. "Peri, I realize now that I was mistaken in my opinion of John. He has given you so much more than I ever could have hoped for. He's been a wonderful husband to you and father to my grandchildren." A coughing fit came upon him, preventing further comment.

She answered when the coughing subsided. "Thank you for saying that, Daddy. I know it would mean a lot to John if you would tell him."

The day never came. He passed before he had the chance.

Peri thought all this while she watched the swirling mist dance through the black trunks and red flowers. Her eyelids drooped and within moments, she drifted off to sleep.

* * *

When John returned thirty minutes later, he found his wife sitting on the bench as he had left her. With her arms wrapped around herself as if to ward off a chill, she stared at a flower not too distant from the bench.

She said she had a strange dream, her voice trailing off as if it had left her with a feeling of unease.

John closed the distance to the bench and sat down next to his wife. He was startled when she turned to face him. She was pale and in stark contrast to how he had left her a short time ago. He asked her, "Peri, my dear, are you okay? Are you chilled? You look white as a ghost!"

She released her self-hug.

He reached out, taking hold of her left hand. "Your hands are as cold as ice." He brought up his other hand, clasping hers between them. "Let's get you back to the house before you catch a chill."

Not moving, Peri said, "It's not the air that has me chilled." She placed her right hand over his and guided them down on to her lap. She took a deep audible breath, finally saying, "We need to talk."

When she had finished recounting her dream-like narrative, she urged her husband to expand his business. In an uncharacteristically somber voice she said, "Fear clenches my stomach when I think of what our grandchildren's children will have to go through if we don't do something!"

John was speechless. He let go of Peri's hands as they warmed, and he embraced her. He was uncertain what to make of the dream she had, but he was pleased she had changed her mind and supported his airline's expansion.

However, all too soon, he discovered what had caused her reversal on the expansion. Within a week, he returned to the garden. It was a scorching summer evening after a long day of work. With a brandy in hand, he sat upon the bench. Within minutes, he let his eyelids drift down, his body feeling heavy and relaxed.

Later that evening, he did not call it a dream when he built up the courage to share with his wife what had occurred. He called it a vision.

It was the first of many. Peri had several as well, and on two occasions they had joint visions.

John's last revelation was crystal clear. Humanity's urgent need demanded the bench be relocated. After this vision and the alarming images encompassed within it, he never sat on the bench again, not admitting this to anyone, even his wife; he lacked the courage.

On the day the bench was crated to be shipped to New England, he felt a chill run through him. He had endured visions so shocking he could feel his pulse quickening in terror at just the thought of them. He closed his eyes and prayed on behalf of the people he had seen while on the bench, the very souls he had been tasked with assembling at the terminal.

As the bench was loaded onto the truck, he prayed they had greater strength than himself.

PART 1
PRESENT DAY

1

THE PARTY

The Silverado's radio played a soothing country tune in the dimness of the immaculately clean cab. Jack and Kourin, submerged within their own thoughts, traveled toward the party venue while the dashboard monitor displayed the artist and song title, lighting the subdued expressions on their faces. Neither heard the words being sung about alcohol, patriotism, love, and heartache. The latter was the emotion they both had freshly shared, bonding their love to each other.

With both hands on the steering wheel, Jack, owner of Roberts Construction, drove through the day's twilight, watching the road ahead while in deep thought of recent events.

Kourin, his date and owner of KCA Kourin Cosmetics & Accessories in the newly built Manchester Airport terminal, sat staring at the same road and immersed in remembrances from her teen years.

If a snapshot was taken of this moment in time, the observer may make the mistake of thinking they had a disagreement and were at odds with each other. Quite the opposite was the reality. They were very much in love. If life around them was normal, they would not be struggling with their thoughts and emotions. However, as they reflected on the previous two days, their lives were anything but ordinary now.

The Benchmark Air terminal garden caused them distress with memories of life-transforming past events that were reawakened when they sat on the antique bench. Jack had to confront the loss of his marriage to Kim, while Kourin was grief stricken, reliving a teenage pregnancy and placing her newborn for adoption.

Together, they shared and faced these heartrending events. After two years of grief and with Kourin's recent compassion, Jack let go of his failed marriage, placing the past behind him. Kourin, suffering the unspeakable rupture of her childhood that had haunted her as an adult, had shared part of her innermost anguish with Jack. Each were apprehensive of what lay ahead.

Jack kept his eyes forward on the road. He was tempted several times to peek at Kourin, even with the dim light, to check how she was holding up after opening her heart to him. He had never lost a child, but he had seen first-hand how much it had changed Harry, his best friend and foreman, and Christine, his now deceased wife.

This was never more obvious than how Harry had conducted himself in the last two days. Jack cut him some slack though, since his friend's experiences with the bench were shocking by anyone's standards. As a child, Harry had an abusive alcoholic father. The bench caused him to relive that terror. With a baffling twist, he was saved from harm by the unlikely appearance of a dog, Ubu. Harry, having learned from this and other's bench encounters, attempted to see his deceased Christine in happier times. He instead traveled back to his grandfather's childhood and literally saved his daideó from a surging river.

Jack kept these thoughts to himself, not wanting to upset Kourin further. He struggled to get a grip on what the hell was going on. At a red light, he risked a sideways look at the beautiful woman sitting next to him. She remained quiet.

From her blank expression, Jack could not tell what thoughts were going through her head. She had disclosed no further details beyond what she had tearfully and painfully shared with him. Jack felt there was more to the story, more agonizing than having to let her baby go. He couldn't fathom what could be worse, but he had a lifetime of experience telling him now was not the time to dig deeper. When Kourin was ready to disclose what was troubling her, she would. He would have to be patient. In his thoughts, he said. *When you're ready, I'll be here for you.* The light turned green, and he returned his eyes to the road.

Kourin's mind strained with controlling her emotional state. It was difficult with the raw emotions she had just experienced relating half of her history to Jack. There was comfort in having confided in him about her baby and allowing that hidden truth out in the open. In her chest, she could feel a heat building she hadn't experienced before. Her hands felt ice cold, as if the buildup of heat inside her was being drawn inward through her extremities. On the outside, she kept a placid face. A lifetime of hiding behind a false bravado mask was involuntary to her now. Fortunately, the cab was dark, with only the soft ambient light from the onboard computer system. She read the monitor and glanced out the window at the homes they passed, distracting her thoughts to bring herself under control. She dared not look at Jack, fearing her emotions would spike again. As the truck rambled down the city streets, the inner heat subsided and returned to her hands.

For well over a decade, she had not spoken to anyone about the trauma she had dealt with thirty-two years ago. The last time was fourteen years ago to her therapist the week her baby turned eighteen. Upon returning home that afternoon from what became her last session, she stored the gold locket containing a lock of her baby's hair in her jewelry box. It was a symbolic gesture of letting her now adult daughter, wherever she was, go. In the years that followed, from time to time, she did have uncontrollable crying fits. These occurred on her daughter's birthday, occasionally on a holiday, and several times when she saw another's daughter enjoying life with her mother, a joy she was never able to experience.

The conflicted emotions from thirty-two years ago came rushing back when Jack uncovered the well-worn locket from its hiding place. With all that had occurred with the bench, she wove her thoughts around the kismet of him finding the very thing from her past she had locked away. What had her thoughts in turmoil was, as the old radio host used to say, the rest of the story.

Someday she would have to tell Jack. Until then, though, it was her cross to bear as it always had been.

Jack pulled into the nearly full banquet hall parking lot. Many of the attendees had arrived ahead of them. He parked in a space that would provide an open spot on the passenger side. As he circled behind his truck to the other side, he scanned but did not see Miguel's Ford in the lot. There was a car pulling away near the entrance, and two of his workers were entering the hotel. Jose was with his wife, holding hands as they came to the circular doorway. Joneal was a few steps behind him. From this distance, Jack couldn't tell who he was with, but she had red hair. She was familiar to him, but he couldn't place her.

Jack was relieved some of his crew had accepted his offer of covering Uber rides to the venue. In his last call with Beth, his assistant, she assured him she would take care of it. He hoped Miguel had taken him up on his offer. Mandy's vision of the future from her bench encounter came to his mind, but he didn't want to dwell on that right now. Instead, he opened the passenger door and was greeted with a curvaceous leg.

Kourin waited in her seat for Jack to open her door, knowing he would prefer being chivalrous. She let him play his part, as getting in the jacked-up truck had been a challenge in her new dress and high heels. The midi-length black dress had a dangerously high slit that, with some maneuvering, had enabled her to step into the truck. This added benefit also fully exposed her right leg up to her hip. She normally preferred more modest outfits. However, when shopping weeks before with her friend Paige, she had convinced her to try on the off-shoulder dress. The designer dress exposed her skin in all the right places and hugged her curves nicely as if it was made for her.

Anders' blue eyes momentarily flashed into her thoughts as she recalled she had made the purchase with him in mind. She pushed him and his blue eyes out of her head. That relationship was over.

She turned her attention to Jack's brown eyes when he had arrived to pick her up. Upon opening her front door, he was tongue tied when he saw the dress. His honest reaction, in contrast to the bullshit she had dealt with from Anders, caused a spontaneous flow of emotions in her, resulting in kissing him to release it. He responded with a passionate kiss of his own, melting her heart with his soft lips. She felt heat building once again inside her as she relived the kiss.

Kourin was brought out of her musing when she heard her door open. The cool spring New England air against her bare skin helped to tone down and control her thoughts as she tempered down her inner fervor. She thought, *Control yourself, Kourin.*

She watched Jack's gaze linger on the gentle contours of her sculpted thigh and calf. His eyes progressed slowly from her bare skin up to her face. She swiveled her legs around to step out. He guided her onto the step rail down to the pavement. They were inches apart, and he held her just a little longer than necessary.

Kourin said close to his right ear, "Thank you, Mr. Roberts. You are always such a gentleman."

He replied, "You're more than welcome, Ms. Sanders." He noticed the locket hanging around her neck and debated saying something, choosing not to.

As she stood in front of him, she felt his gaze fall upon the locket that lay against her chest, nestled close to her heart. She did not want it to be an elephant in the room. "I wore the one you picked out."

"Kori, if it's too much . . ."

"No. I think it's time I work to put the past in the past." She cradled the locket in between her thumb and forefinger. "I still have a lot of work to do on that, but I need to start somewhere."

Jack gave her a hug. "I'll support you anyway I can."

"I know you will." She released herself from his embrace and turned around. "Now, Mr. Roberts, let's enter, shall we?"

"As you wish." He extended his arm, locking them together as they walked the short distance to the revolving doorway.

* * *

Laurel arrived at Mandy's condo ten minutes early to pick her up for the party. She knocked once on the door, and it swished open before she could land her second knock. Her best friend greeted with a warm smile.

"Hi, Laurel. Wow! You look amazing." She looked around Laurel for Ubu, asking, "Where's my friend?"

"Hi. He's waiting for us in the car."

Ubu was peering out of the rear passenger window of the Jeep. She waved and called out to him, "Hi, Ubu! Be there in a jiffy."

While this was happening, Sarah came up behind Mandy. "Laurel, this is my new friend, Sarah. She's my plus one tonight."

"Hi, Sarah. A pleasure to meet you." Laurel looked over the dress she had on. "That dress looks awfully familiar."

Sarah answered before Mandy could, "Mandy was kind enough to share her dress with me for the party. I wasn't prepared for a night out when I flew in."

"It looks like it was made just for you!" Laurel said. She turned to Mandy and asked, "Are you ready for tonight?" Laurel knew her question had many connotations because of Mandy's bench encounter, with Miguel getting drunk and causing a horrific accident tonight.

Mandy said, "As ready as I can be. I filled in Sarah a bit."

Laurel didn't need to ask what she was referring to.

Mandy's new friend stood in silence, still trying to wrap her head around the unbelievable story of a time-traveling bench.

Laurel spoke up when Sarah did not. "Well, we better get to the party, then." She wanted to ask what her thoughts were about the bench, as any knowledge she gained could contribute to changing the death of her friend Breckin when they had served together. Instead, she held her tongue, thinking she would have ample opportunities to speak with her during the evening.

Mandy insisted Sarah ride shotgun, as Ubu didn't mind sharing the back-seat with her. The half-pit half-lab, to his credit, stayed on his side of the seat facing Mandy so she could pet him. Ubu wore a black and white bandana around his neck and over his front shoulders. Laurel had decided that he needed to be fashionable tonight, so the service vest he normally wore stayed at home.

Mandy said to Ubu as she petted him, carefully avoiding where he was injured behind his ear, "My, you look dapper tonight in your bandana."

Ubu wagged his tail, hitting it against the door behind him, making a whap-whap-whap sound.

Backing out of the driveway, Laurel smiled at her two best friends' reflection in the mirror, knowing how much her dog loved Mandy.

Owing to the season, the Jeep's hard top ensured everyone's hairstyle remained intact. However, the three ladies would likely have more than a few black dog hairs on their dresses. That was life with a dog that Laurel and Mandy had accepted long ago.

As Laurel traveled toward the venue, she realized she could not wait to have Sarah's thoughts about the bench. "Sarah, now that you've heard what Mandy had to say about the bench, what do you make of it?"

At first, Sarah said nothing. Several seconds passed before she answered. "Well, it certainly is an interesting story."

Laurel asked, "So, I take it you don't believe Mandy saw the future?"

Sarah glanced at the Jeep's backseat passengers and said, "It seems a little far-fetched."

Mandy, pausing mid-pet between Ubu's ears, looked up at her with a neutral expression.

Sarah continued, "But I think Mandy believes it happened." She broke her gaze with Mandy and looked at Laurel beside her, who had her eyes ahead, watching the road. "I think there has to be another, simpler, explanation. However, what that is, I have no idea."

Laurel looked into her rearview mirror at Mandy when she next spoke. "It is fantastical for sure, but having had a similar experience, it all seems so real."

Mandy gave Laurel a smile and said, "I think it's hard to understand and accept if you haven't had it happen to you. Even then, it's . . . it's surreal."

"That's putting it mildly," replied Laurel.

Sarah said, "Well, whatever it is, I hope I never go through it. I have enough drama in my life at home. Thank you very much." All three laughed.

For the balance of the brief ride, Sarah chatted about her job and family. Mandy knew some of the story, but she and Laurel learned more about their new friend. They avoided any further discussion of the bench. Before long, the Jeep turned into the venue parking lot.

Laurel announced, as she pulled into the space next to her uncle's Silverado, "And we're here, ladies."

Mandy stepped out of the Jeep and surveyed the parking lot. Ubu leaped down from the seat, landing beside her.

Sarah asked, "Are you looking for Miguel's truck?"

"Yes. It's not here."

Laurel took the lead to the entrance, and they followed, the sound of their footsteps echoing in the air. Ubu stayed close to Laurel, his tail wagging eagerly as he followed.

Sarah said, "Maybe he's not coming."

"Oh, he'll be here," replied Mandy. "He's been talking about this night every day for the last couple of weeks, but that would prove the whole bench theory wrong if he didn't show up."

From ahead of them, Laurel said, "I don't think it'll be that simple."

As if on cue, Miguel pulled into the parking lot in his blue Ford pickup truck. He parked on the other side of the lot.

* * *

Kourin removed the matching black shawl she had worn against the chill of the spring evening as she entered the venue's lobby. Jack hadn't worn a coat over his suit. Kourin handed the shawl to him when he prompted her for it, and he walked over to the coat check several feet ahead on the right.

A young woman, with highlights of purple in her hair and wearing a very short black dress, was at the counter. With sad lips she greeted them, "Hey."

Jack noted her white lettered name on her oval tan name badge: Chessa. The badge was in stark contrast to her black dress. "Hi," Jack replied with a big smile to raise the spirits of the young lady. "Chessa. That's an interesting name. I don't think I've seen that before."

Chessa answered, maintaining her somber expression, "It's the name my mother gave me." The dour young woman gave him a numbered ticket stub and walked away with the shawl, not saying anything else.

Jack noticed a multicolored tattoo on the back of her neck. Colorful wings rose from her shoulders, with the tips ending behind each ear. Most of the tattoo was covered by her dress. He spotted, before she was out of view, another tattoo on her right leg. This one was vibrant like the other, a rainbow with a melting rose and heart.

When Chessa was out of view, he directed his attention to the beautiful blonde he was with. Their eyes met, thinking the same thing yet neither wanting to voice that this may be the "C" girl Mandy had spoken about earlier in the day.

Not wanting to go down the rabbit hole discussing what ifs about the bench, Jack instead said to Kourin, "Shall we?" He again held out his bent arm. She smiled, placing her arm within his. He escorted her toward the sound of music filtering through the hallway.

* * *

Laurel, with Ubu at her side, Mandy, and Sarah, walked to the venue's entrance. From the opposite side of the parking lot, they heard Miguel call out, "Hey, lovely ladies, how ya' doin' tonight?" They turned as one toward the voice. Miguel doubled timed it to catch up to them. He was alone. "Hi, U, M, L, and . . ." Miguel said upon arriving.

Mandy spoke up. "Miguel, this is Sarah. She's my guest tonight."

"All good with me, M! Nice to meet you, S."

Sarah looked at Mandy, who explained as she entered the revolving door, "Don't mind him. He shortens everyone's name. It's just his thing."

Sarah replied, following behind in the next-door wing, "Pleasure to meet you as well, Miguel."

Mandy froze in place after entering through the slowly spinning doors. Although she had driven by hundreds of times, she had never been to this hotel. She scanned the entrance. There were bathrooms to the left, music filtering down the elaborately decorated hallway in the middle, and the coat check room to her right. No one was at the coat check counter. She felt as if she just stepped into her dream.

Sarah and then Laurel stopped to either side of Mandy as she paused just inside the doorway. Miguel nearly bumped into them when he came through.

He peered down the hall where he thought they were looking and said, "Sounds like the party is underway. Shall we?" He moved two steps down the hallway and noticed Chessa appear at the coat check station. He stopped short.

Miguel, with a big smile, said to the dark-haired girl behind the counter, "Hello, there. Damn, I wish I had worn a jacket to check in!"

Sarah removed the coat she had borrowed from Mandy and walked the few steps to the coat check desk, as did Laurel and Mandy.

Chessa kept her apathetic expression. She handed each a ticket stub for their coats. In the twenty seconds for this to occur, she hadn't spoken a word.

As Laurel moved away from the counter, Miguel moved over to it with a smile as wide as his cheeks would allow. "Hi, my name's Miguel. What's yours?"

Chessa didn't answer. She pointed at her name badge. Miguel noticed her nails were painted black. He placed both elbows on the counter, as if he wanted to have a long conversation with her. He said, "Chessa. That's a beautiful name for a beautiful girl."

Mandy saw Miguel move toward the counter. She had to step around Laurel to get beside him. By the time she acted, Miguel had already dropped his pickup line to Chessa. Mandy clutched his left arm to steer him away from the counter.

He let Mandy lead him but not before he turned back toward the coat check desk with a big smile and exclaimed, "I'll be back, Chessa!"

Mandy held on to Miguel's arm, and Laurel walked beside him on the other side toward the music. Ubu followed as usual. Sarah, who was on the other side of Mandy, glanced back at Chessa. The young lady added to her melancholy with a furrowed brow and a disdainful stare directed toward Mandy.

The quartet plus one dog entered through propped open double doors that revealed a vast hall beyond. On the left side, a cover band performed against a backdrop of multicolored lights on a raised platform. The unoccupied dance floor stretched out before them with the parquet floor surrounded by small bar-height tables without chairs, offering a place to set down drinks while dancing. Most of these were occupied. Three of them, front and center, were commandeered by Jack's crew and their significant other or date, including Jack and Kourin. The rest of the grand hall contained tables for dining, with most of them occupied.

Three bar areas were positioned on the sides of the hall, the largest one at the farthest end from the band. Several guests were at each one. Next to the bars on either side were elaborate displays of cheese trays and other pre-dinner snacks. Both had stylish well-designed ice sculptures adorning the center. The closest one was an airplane in flight. The other, on the far wall, was difficult to discern from the quartet's vantage point. Wait staff weaved through the hall, the smell of hors d'oeuvres wafting through the air. The soothing sounds of soft rock music filled the room.

Miguel turned toward the nearest bar on their right. Mandy still had hold of his arm, so she followed him this time. Laurel and Sarah did as well. As always, Ubu followed Laurel. Miguel asked Mandy what she would like to have. She ordered a Manhattan. Sarah said she'd have a glass of pinot, adding that she had to fly tomorrow. Laurel ordered a Sam Adams and Miguel a suffering bastard. Upon receiving the drinks, Miguel told him he'd be back and left a tip.

They weaved through the tables to the construction crew near the dance floor. Mandy released Miguel from her grip when he joined the rest of the group on the right. Laurel stopped here as well when a female guest commented on how cute Ubu was with his tuxedo-like bandana. Mandy and Sarah continued two tables to the left where Jack was chatting with Kourin.

When Kourin turned her way, Mandy said, "Hi, Kourin, Jack. This is my friend, Sarah."

"Hi, Sarah. Pleasure to meet you. Are you and Mandy long-time friends?"

"Oh yes," she said, smiling. "We go way back to this morning when I met her in the coffee shop." They all started laughing. "Seriously though, we started chatting, and it's like we've already known each other for years."

"That's understandable. Mandy has that way about her," Jack said, tipping his mostly full beer in her direction. "Are you enjoying yourselves?"

"Actually, we've just arrived," Mandy said as she glanced around to see who was close by. Everyone outside their little circle was engaged in their own conversations. "But I want to ask you a question, if I may?"

"Fire away," said Jack, taking a sip of his beer.

Mandy took a long sip of her drink before asking, "Did you notice the coat check girl when you came in?"

He didn't answer right away. Kourin, standing beside him listening to the conversation and sipping her Tom Collins, remained silent. He looked at Sarah.

When Mandy noted him looking at Sarah, she added, "She's been clued in on what's going on."

Jack's eyes widened in alarm, but he quickly regained his composure. He glanced in Kourin's direction. "Well, I saw a rather interesting young lady check Kourin's shawl when we came in." He didn't want to add fuel to the fire by adding more.

Mandy asked, "And did you notice her name?" She paused. When Jack didn't offer it up, she said, "Chessa, a C. But more than that, the entrance is exactly how I saw it in my dream."

"Mandy, a lot of venues have that appearance when you walk in. Perhaps it just seems to be the same?" Jack knew what response was going to follow, but he had to downplay where Mandy was going with this.

"It's not just similar," she answered in a low but determined voice. "Every detail, including Chessa, is the same. It can't be a coincidence. She's the person I saw. And let's face it—she's not a run-of-the-mill coat check girl. She's unique."

Jack said, "I'll give you that. She is unique, but there are a lot of kids out there today that have that look." Mandy crinkled her nose, displaying her dis-satisfaction with his response. "Also, I think it's best if we don't speak about our dreams to too many people."

Mandy was about to answer when Laurel, with Ubu at her side, joined them, interrupting Mandy's comeback.

Laurel asked, "How's everyone doing over here?" From the dour expres-sions on everyone's faces, she had a good idea.

Kourin answered, while the others stared at each other. "Mandy's dream may have been more than just a dream."

Mandy said, "Laurel, you saw the coat check girl when we came in."

"Yes, I saw Miguel already hitting on Chessa as soon as we arrived, but he does that with everyone. That's not proof positive," said Laurel. She saw Mandy's imploring expression and added, "However, it might not be a bad idea to keep Miguel occupied elsewhere to prevent the potential outcome Mandy saw in her dream."

"How do you propose we do that?" Jack asked. "He's a kind of free spirit, if you know what I mean."

Mandy answered, "I'll stick with him. If I can keep him from going back to see Chessa, that might change everything."

Sarah chimed in, "It may take two of us. I'll give you a hand with that."

"Thanks, Sarah, but I don't want to tie you down when I've invited you here to have some fun."

"No prob. We've got this, *M*," Sarah said, using Miguel's signature abbreviation method. They all laughed, despite the uneasiness they all felt.

Mandy and Sarah left the group to join Miguel at the other table, leaving Laurel with Jack and Kourin. Jack asked his niece, "Are you handling all of this okay?" All knew he wasn't talking about the party.

"I think I'm doing as well as can be expected, considering the circumstances of how the day went." Laurel reached down to pet Ubu. "As long as I have my friend with me, all is good."

They looked down at Ubu. He turned his head toward the entrance door, causing the trio above him to do the same out of curiosity to what had caught his attention. Seconds later, John entered with his wife, followed by a few of his entourage. Kourin and Jack looked at each other. Without saying a word, both wondered how Ubu knew they were coming since the band was playing, drowning out any other noise.

John made his way around the hall with his wife, Peri, by his side, meeting everyone in attendance. His entourage located their reserved tables in the center of the dining area, taking their seats and not completing the pleasantries through the rest of the hall.

John eventually arrived at the dance floor and Jack's crew. He thanked each with a handshake for the superb work they had done on the terminal. At Jack's table, John acknowledged Ubu first, commending him as a loyal companion while accepting his paw into his when Ubu presented it. Next, he took Laurel's right hand into both of his and said, "He's a terrific animal, Laurel."

Laurel replied, "I'm fortunate to have him by my side."

"He'll protect you, my dear."

Jack and Kourin glanced at one another when he said this. Neither spoke, but Kourin raised her eyebrows.

"He's already proven himself more than once. Some days I'd be lost without him," Laurel stated.

"Keep him by your side. He'll always pull you through," John said, releasing her hand and turning to Jack and Kourin. "And how's my favorite contractor doing tonight?"

"As I've said before, I'm your only contractor, but I appreciate the sentiment. We're doing well, thank you," replied Jack.

Kourin said to John's wife, "Peri, that's a beautiful gown you're wearing."

Peri replied with her Southern accent, "Thank you, Kourin. There's a little shop in Charleston I buy all my dresses from. A couple of years back, John helped them out with some things. I became friends with the lovely owner, Sadie. Whenever I need a special dress for whatever occasion that's coming up, she always comes through for me."

"Well, she did this time as well," Kourin said with a smile, impressed she had remembered her name after only meeting a short time ago.

"You look beautiful as well, dear," Peri said. "Your dress maker did a wonderful job."

Kourin said, "Honestly, it's off the rack from a shop near here in Bedford."

"You look enchanting, Kourin," John reaffirmed. "Doesn't she look lovely, Jack?"

Jack, drinking his beer, froze mid-sip. He uttered in a soft voice as he gazed into Kourin's eyes, "Um, yes, she's gorgeous. I mean, yes, the dress is great."

John started laughing, as did Laurel, and even Peri was smiling. "Jack, you are the man of understatements." To Kourin he said, "Under that gruff exterior is a top-notch guy. Don't let him get away." John turned to his wife and said, "Excuse me one second, my love. I need to speak to the band."

Peri watched her husband walk toward the platform and said with her Southern accent charm, "Please excuse my husband if he's embarrassed y'all. Sometimes he speaks before he thinks."

Kourin said, "No need to apologize. Sometimes a man needs a good kick in the pants."

"Or what's right in front of his nose pointed out to him," Laurel added.

"You all know that I'm standing right here," Jack said.

The three ladies had a hearty laugh at Jack's expense, but he took it in stride.

* * *

Before playing another song, the lead vocalist, Liam, introduced himself and the other four band members. After each name, the audience erupted with clapping and cheering, showing a clear sign of enjoyment of their talent. He additionally announced that John would say a few words after the next song and asked everyone to come closer to the dance floor. Since Jack and the crew were already on the edge of the dance floor, they stayed where they were as others filed around them.

Harry arrived at the table during the next song. The contusion on his knee made him limp as he walked. He wore a traditional navy-blue suit and a white shirt with a red tie and looked more himself than he had in weeks. Everyone at all three tables greeted him. Bob went to the nearest bar and brought him back a beer.

As the song ended, Liam introduced John. John removed the mic from the stand, saying, "Let's hear it for Presage! Aren't they a great band?" Everyone in the hall applauded. "Don't worry, everyone. They'll be back shortly." The band members thanked him and went on a break. John surveyed the people before him, waiting until they all settled down.

The speech started with thanking everyone for coming. He thanked each group from the terminal: construction crew, shop owners, security, pilots, stewards, bag handlers, airplane support team, counter agents, Benchmark home office, and others. Not all were present, but there were many people in attendance that Jack did not recognize so he assumed these were some of those individuals. He hadn't realized the number of personnel involved in making the terminal opening a reality, as he had focused on his part of it.

Before going further, John gave an update on Phil's condition, stating he was recovering and in good spirits. He added Phil's disappointment he was going to miss tonight's party and tomorrow's soft opening. John proposed a toast to Phil's speedy recovery. All joined in and raised their respective beverage.

The owner of Benchmark Air then went into nitty-gritty details about the expected volume that was forthcoming in the weeks and ensuing months as more plane routes were added, bringing the terminal to full capacity operations within sixty days.

Jack was inattentive, as he knew he would not be around for the events of the future, while Kourin remained focused. Jack used the time to survey his crew, their respective dates, and especially Harry. He noted Harry kept his head down, analyzing the table in front of him. Mandy and Sarah watched John, listening to his speech, while Miguel, who was between them, scanned the hall. Jack saw Joneal with the redhead and realized who she was: Wren from the restaurant. He smiled, recalling the conversation at lunchtime when Kourin asked for a summary of Joneal's qualities. Jack thought, *He's a good guy. I'm glad you two found each other.* Shannon and Diric were a couple of tables over. He made a mental note to say hello to them afterwards. After Jack had finished surveying the people present, he heard John speaking about the garden.

"I would like to give my deepest thanks to Jack and his entire building crew for bringing my dream to life with the awe-inspiring garden in the terminal. I am overjoyed at the inclusion of our company's services to New England, yet I am even more rapturous about the garden area. Travelers will now have a mini haven to relax before, after, and in between flights. I am confident this garden will bring our customer service to the next level in the air industry. Again, thank you, Jack and the entire Roberts Construction team, for bringing this to fruition."

John placed the microphone under his arm, holding it against himself and allowing him to clap his hands. The entire hall joined in. After half a minute of clapping and the hall was once again quiet, John continued. "In conclusion, I want all of you to enjoy this evening. Benchmark Air appreciates your hard work and dedication. I look forward to working with all of you in this endeavor." As he concluded, the hall clapped once again.

After John completed his speech, he returned to Jack's table. Jack greeted him, "John, thank you for those kind words."

"No, thank you, Jack. You and your crew did a spectacular job. Besides the fact that you were on time in every aspect of the project and, more importantly, on budget, your team was a pleasure to work with. Your professionalism, eye for detail, follow through, and high standards made this project enjoyable. That's not just from my viewpoint. The feedback I've received from the Benchmark team bears proof to all of that."

Jack said, "Well, it's been a pleasure and an honor working with you on this."

John scanned the surrounding tables. "Now there is one person who I don't see here that I'd like to thank. Where's Beth tonight? Is she here?"

Jack was embarrassed. With everything that had happened with the bench and when he picked up Kourin, he had not noticed his admin wasn't there. "I'm not sure where she is, John. I know she was looking forward to tonight." He looked over at Harry. "Harry, have you seen Beth tonight?" Harry raised his gaze. He had an odd befuddled expression and cleared his throat before speaking. He said, "No, but she was planning on coming."

Jack looked back at John and promised, "I'll let her know you're looking for her when I see her."

"Thanks, Jack. I'd appreciate that. She did such a wonderful job coordinating everything with my team. I want to make sure I thank her properly." John turned to his wife asking, "Now, my dear, shall we join our table for dinner?"

Peri said, "It was a pleasure meeting y'all again." To Ubu she said, "And to you, my little friend. Take care of everyone." She lightly petted the top of his head, obviously avoiding the injured area hidden under his hair. She exited the table with John by her side, heading toward the center of the hall.

"Well, that was interesting," Kourin stated.

Beside her, Jack said, "Yes, I didn't expect John to say all those nice things."

"That's not what I'm talking about," she said to Jack. She turned to Laurel asking, "Did you notice what Peri said to Ubu?"

Laurel nodded her head but didn't answer.

Kourin saw Jack was puzzled by what they were talking about. She said, "Peri told Ubu to take care of everyone. Why would she say that? Shouldn't she have said to take care of Laurel? Doesn't that seem odd, or is it just me?"

Jack was going to speak, but Laurel beat him to it, saying, "Stranger still, how did she know not to touch Ubu where he was injured this morning? The injury isn't visible now. No one outside our little circle even knows it occurred." She looked down at Ubu and asked, "What's going on, my friend?"

Ubu rested his head against Mom's shin, his steady breathing a sign of his unwavering devotion. He didn't understand her words, but he kept their bond secure, letting her know he would always be there for her.

2

INVESTMENT FOR THE FUTURE

The Roberts Construction crew located the dining tables designated for them. Jack was going to sit with them when Laurel discovered a table nearby two over from John with a reserved sign and name plates for their group: Jack, Kourin, Laurel, Mandy, Harry, Beth, two blank name plates, and two others, Vasud and Niyati. The latter were not yet seated, and none in the group recognized the names.

Kourin said, as Presage played softer music to a crowd sitting down to eat, "Is it just me, or does it seem odd that our table has this assortment of name plates?"

Jack answered, "I'm thinking Beth had something to do with that."

"Perhaps," Kourin said as Jack assisted her with her chair and then took his seat.

Laurel and Mandy shared a smile after they saw the interaction between Jack and Kourin. They could tell something special was blossoming with them.

Mandy and Sarah sat next to each other. They had invited Miguel to sit with them when they arrived at the table, but he declined their offer. He naturally wanted to hang with the crew. Not wanting to make a scene, they let him go, but they positioned themselves so they were facing toward his table.

While name plate locations were being adjusted, Beth arrived wearing a long black dress with an exquisite pearl necklace. She was alone. As she neared the construction crew tables, she said hello to everyone. All three construction tables greeted her as if she walked into the Cheers bar. A loud "Beth" was called out and coincided with a momentary pause from the band between songs. Heads throughout the hall turned toward the boisterous gang. She stopped by each table, saying hello and meeting a few people she didn't know, including Wren.

Harry couldn't help but make a comparison to his first bench encounter when he relived grabbing Christine from under the water. All heads had turned when she shrieked as he rose from the water and embraced her in a kiss.

As he watched Beth with the crew, he saw Christine in her. Their physical features couldn't be more dissimilar, but their affable personality and charm had comparisons. As Beth approached, a powerful memory of her close-up smile and twinkling eyes took hold in his mind, a remembrance he desperately sought to expunge from existence.

When Beth arrived at Jack's group, she excused herself for being late. Beth asked Harry if she could sit next to him.

He uttered, "It's a free country."

Beth glanced at Jack as she sat down, a concerned expression on her face. To Harry's credit, though, even with his injured leg, he held the chair and guided it in when she sat. She thanked him. He did not reply and seated himself.

* * *

An empty chair remained between Laurel and Niyati's vacant seat. Ubu found his spot next to Laurel in the space. She slid the chair out of the way, providing him ample room. An attentive staff member noticed and removed the chair. Another staff member removed the dinner setting, leaving the area between Laurel and Niyati bare.

The first staff member returned to take their dinner and drink orders. All ordered another of what they had been drinking except Sarah ordering a glass of water with lemon. After taking the orders, she asked Laurel if she would like something for the dog as well. Laurel said yes and thanked her, as Ubu would eat just about anything. She assured her it would be dog appropriate.

Jack started up the conversation once the staff member had departed with their food orders. He asked Beth if she assisted with the table name cards and if everything else was okay.

She replied things were fine, but she was running late all day following up on a few potential projects. She said she had nothing to do with the party other than to let the Benchmark team know how many would attend. This caused Jack and Kourin to glance at each other. Beth noticed and inquired why he had asked.

"Well," he replied, "I think it's odd we have a table laid out with all our names. I mean," looking at Kourin as he spoke, "and please don't take offense. How would anyone know to place me and Kori next to each other? I can see everyone else at the table together since we work together, are related, or might bring a plus one." He looked at Mandy and his niece when he said the last. He added, "But even I didn't know yesterday that I'd be here with Kori."

"That is odd for sure," said Kourin. "Maybe they changed some names around when John and Peri spoke to us a few hours ago."

Jack said, "That's making a big assumption. I mean, what if we weren't coming together? I didn't even know we were until a short time ago."

Laurel spoke up. "That seems weird to me, unless they know more than they're letting on."

"Perhaps," Beth said. "Or they're matchmakers." Laurel and Mandy smiled as Beth added, while looking at Kourin and Jack, "You two look good together."

Jack and Kourin locked eyes.

His cheeks turned a rosy shade of red while gazing into her green eyes. For a moment, he thought he saw a flicker of gold around the pupil. He dismissed it as the hall lighting playing tricks on him. Several seconds passed, and he felt his flushed face subside.

Kourin smiled at the attractive man she was with and sensed a gentle heat deep inside as she had on the drive to the venue. She rubbed her hands together as her fingers seemed to be suddenly chilled while her inner self had a warm feeling.

When she broke eye contact with Jack, she chanced a glance in Harry's direction, curious if he would become irrational as he had the day before. She was relieved he was calm and staring down at the table, apparently oblivious to the conversation.

Mandy felt a warm sensation, witnessing the interaction between Jack and Kourin. It reminded her of a recent movie she watched with her cat Autumn. As the movie drew to a close, the woman finally realized her soul mate had been right in front of her all along, and they embraced beneath a red-and-yellow-leaved oak tree. She thought of the supermarket manager she had met with earlier and remembered the warmth in his smile. Miguel's rowdy laughter in the distance brought her daydream to an abrupt end.

Jack said, "Well, for whatever reason we're all together, I'm glad it worked out the way it has. In some ways, I'm sad this project is wrapped up."

At that point, Harry, who had been silent the entire time staring at the contents of his half-filled beer, spoke up. "I wouldn't say we're wrapped here at all."

Beth asked, "Why do you say that, Harry? What's left to do on the punch list?"

Harry looked around the table before speaking, eyeing each person. "You know what I'm talking about. There's something not right in the garden."

All the faces around the table turned to each other, except for Mandy's, which stayed pointed at Miguel a couple of tables over. It was Sarah who broke the silence at the table, asking, "What do you think should be done in the garden?"

Harry directed his attention at her, not maliciously, just with a vacant stare. After a moment of sizing her up, he answered, "If you had experienced what I did, you'd be sayin' the same thing. Something's not right there." He paused, keeping his gaze upon her. "That bench . . . that bench is . . ." he trailed off, not completing his train of thought.

Sarah finished Harry's statement for him, saying, "That bench is just a bench, like all the others." She halted and was uncertain whether to continue. She looked at Mandy before speaking, witnessing an anguished expression on her face as she monitored Miguel. For Mandy's sake, if not for everyone else's, she had to say what was on her mind. "It's inconceivable an inanimate object such as a bench could do anything that I've been told. It defies every law of science and reasonability." She paused, sizing up her audience who, to this point, remained quiet while the surrounding party went on. She completed her thoughts. "There has to be a logical explanation, one that doesn't sound like an episode of the *Twilight Zone*."

Harry let her finish before he spoke, looking into her eyes across the table. "You haven't sat on it. You haven't experienced it. Until you do . . ."

Sarah didn't speak, but she diverted her eyes from his stare.

Harry, noting her eye deflection, said, "Wait a minute. You have sat on it! I can see your expression. You've sat on the bench!"

This grabbed everyone's attention. They turned toward Sarah.

She felt them all gazing upon her. "No, I haven't sat on the bench. I haven't even been into the garden."

Harry didn't let it go, asking, "But something happened, didn't it?" When Sarah didn't respond, Harry shouted and banged a fist on the table, "Didn't it?" Several people at the surrounding tables turned in Harry's direction.

Beth spoke up, placing a hand on Harry's arm. "Harry, calm down. No need to shout."

Harry, breaking his gaze at Sarah to look around half the table, said, "I don't give a shit about them. They have no idea the magnitude of all this!"

Sarah had a bewildered expression.

Mandy asked, "Sarah, is there something you're not telling us?"

Before she could answer, Vasud and Niyati arrived at the table, saying, "Hello, everyone. So sorry that we are late."

* * *

Miguel was outwardly enjoying his bantering with the crew. Conversations drifted from incidents at work to the anticipation of the upcoming camping trip to antics from parties past to escapades yet to come. Miguel contributed to the conversation, joking and laughing as usual, but as he took another sip from his second suffering bastard, his mind wandered back to Chessa.

He studied Joneal, who sat across the table from him, interact with Wren from the restaurant. They sat close together, laughing and enjoying the banter between the crew members. How had Joneal been so lucky to find such a wonderful girl while he sat here alone?

Mandy said she would be his date tonight when they met up in the parking lot, but he knew she didn't mean it. She was just being nice, like she always was. What he needed tonight was someone special, a person who wanted to have fun and be wild, who wasn't afraid to be different, a person precisely like Chessa!

* * *

Mandy watched Miguel, who was enjoying himself, so much so that she could hear laughter coming from their table even above all the other conversations ongoing throughout the venue. Concerned he hadn't stayed with her so she could monitor him, she'd have to do what she could from this short distance away. Half listening to the conversation going on at her table, she was brought out of her melancholy state when she heard Harry yell at Sarah and slam his fist onto the table. She looked at Sarah and saw the stricken expression on her face. She had to ask, "Sarah, is there something you're not telling us?" But before Sarah could answer, the last two table guests arrived, shelving any further conversation.

* * *

Vasud and Niyati introduced themselves by first name only, not stating what part of Benchmark or the terminal they worked for. Kourin took the lead for the table and introduced everyone. All said, "Hello," "Hi," "Welcome," or

"Pleased to meet you," except Harry who did a quick head nod. As soon as the pleasantries were completed, the drinks arrived. The waiter took Vasud's and Niyati's drink and food order, saying he'd get that in right away.

Vasud asked Jack about the terminal project. He seemed to be very well versed in the overall scope of the project, including the budget, making Jack wonder if he was part of the Benchmark accounting department. Jack answered his questions, since nothing was proprietary information from his point of view. He did not mention the bench.

Kourin sipped her drink while Jack answered Vasud's questions. After a few minutes, Vasud turned his attention to her. He asked what goals she expected to achieve in her business. Kourin thought about it before she spoke, not wanting to insult the guest at the party. Instead of answering, she asked, "Excuse me for asking, but what is it you do for Benchmark?"

Niyati, who had not said a word since the initial introductions, spoke up. "Please forgive my husband's impoliteness. Sometimes work interferes with his sensitivity." Vasud gave his wife an annoyed look. She continued, "We've invested in Benchmark Air and very much want it to succeed."

"My wife understates the situation greatly."

"Vas, we have had this discussion many times already. What's done is done," Niyati said, somewhat annoyed.

Kourin took the several seconds of silence that followed as an opening to speak. "I'm sorry if I've offended you. I was curious about all the questions."

John's voice came from behind her. "No need to apologize, Kourin. I'm glad you've finally met Vas and his lovely wife, Niyati. Welcome, my friends! I'm so glad you could make it." John walked around the table as he said the last to shake Vas' hand and give Niyati an unpretentious hug and kiss on her left cheek. "I was hoping you could join us this evening."

"With everything we've gone through to get to this point, there wasn't too much to decide," Vasud stated. Niyati now gave him the annoyed look. He saw it and added, "But I am sure it will all prove to be well worth it in the end."

"And it will be, Vas. It will be," said John. He felt he needed to give some context to the conversation with everyone listening. "As you can see, there were some disagreements about building this terminal here in Manchester."

"I think calling it disagreements is stating it lightly," said Vasud.

"Well, perhaps," John replied. "Yet everyone eventually conceded to my way of thinking."

"Yes, we did," Niyati answered while she patted Vasud's hand that was resting on the table. "Some were a little more stubborn than others, but they came around."

"Let's hope it pays off," Vasud declared. "If you'll excuse me, John, I should say hello to Victoria and the others I see are here." He turned toward his wife and said, "Come, Niy. Let's give our hellos." He walked off, not waiting for his wife to join him.

"Please forgive my husband. He means well," Niyati said. With that, she followed her husband a few tables over.

"I'm sorry about that," John said. "What Vas lacks in civility, he more than makes up for with his business acumen."

Kourin asked, "John, what is he to the building of this terminal?"

John explained, "Vasud's agreement to back this terminal financially made the project possible. Well, actually, it is Niyati's family's money. He manages it. She's the one that holds the purse strings, though."

"But it was my understanding this project was a sure win in traffic and business profitability," stated Jack.

John said, "Don't get me wrong, Jack. It absolutely is! This terminal will be very busy with more traffic than it probably can handle."

"I don't understand why Vasud has hesitations about it."

"Well, since the cat's out of the bag, you might as well know," John said. "Besides Manchester, the Benchmark eggheads had three other locations where the terminal could have been built. All three had a greater ROI, so Vasud and many others argued to build in one of those locations before this one. However, there are things much more important than money. One must confront and battle for what they firmly believe in."

John appeared to notice Beth for the first time and walked over to her, thanking her for the wonderful job she did with the Benchmark team.

Beth thanked him. She said it was a pleasure working with everyone, although she had to twist a few arms to get what she needed from some people in operations.

John laughed and told her he appreciated her tenacity in getting the job done. He told her if she ever needed a new job to contact him. He would find a place for her on his team.

Beth appreciated his overture but told him she was quite happy working with Jack and Harry.

After this exchange, John excused himself from the group to join Vasud and Niyati where they were speaking with several Benchmark corporate executives three tables over.

The group gawked at each other without speaking while the cover band played a soft nineties love song in the background.

The moment was broken when they heard loud laughter come from a table nearby. Miguel was enthralling his table with one of his stories, and all were laughing. Mandy watched Miguel, satisfied he was okay for now. She looked away from him when Laurel broke the silence at the table. "Well, if confronting and fighting for what you believe in didn't sound ominous, I don't know what else would."

"Let's not read more into it than what it is," said her uncle.

Harry was about to speak when Mandy beat him to it. He deferred to her. "His statement can be taken any number of ways, but knowing what we now know, it seems there's more going on here than we thought."

Jack said, "Or John was simply referring to his battle within his company to place the terminal here in Manchester for some personal reasons he has."

"Or he has a hidden agenda that involves the bench," Harry said without malice.

More laughter came from Miguel's table, causing Mandy to look in that direction.

Jack said, "All we know for sure is that we all had something happen to us today." Laurel, Harry, and Mandy each began to say something. Jack put his hands up to near shoulder height and continued. "Hold on. Let me finish. I'll be the first to admit that it's been one helluva day for all of us. Is it a coincidence? That seems unlikely given what we all experienced. What is it? I don't know." He looked at Beth. "I'm guessing you're confused about what in the world we're talking about?"

All turned toward Beth who had been sitting quietly since John spoke with her. She looked at the eyes upon her, ending with Harry's. He asked her in an uncharacteristically calm voice, "Beth, what is it?"

"Well," she said, looking at Harry and turning away to analyze her water glass. All waited for her to continue.

When she didn't, Jack asked, "Beth, did you go into the garden today?" When she didn't answer, he added, "Beth?"

She looked up from the glass. The music played around them with laughter and undecipherable conversations from the surrounding tables. "I . . ." She looked at Harry. "I went into the garden yesterday when I was searching for Harry." She stopped again and looked at the glass. This time, she continued. "I saw my Tom."

"Oh, Beth!" Harry exclaimed and gave her a hug.

The others at the table were taken aback by Harry's out-of-character response.

"It's okay. We're here for you now," Harry said to her as she placed her head on his shoulder. To her credit, though, she did not cry.

Most at the table knew what had happened to Beth's husband, now over ten years in the past. Sarah did not. Laurel whispered to her, "I'll fill you in later." She nodded in acknowledgment.

Jack watched Harry holding Beth, giving her a reassuring hug. He was at a loss for words. He knew well the anguish Beth had been through when Tom was killed at a construction site, along with the ensuing pain she suffered from the lawsuits that followed.

* * *

Kourin had kept her thoughts to herself since John made his declaration and watched the interactions of those at the table. She had watched Beth and Sarah, who also remained quiet. She understood Sarah being quiet as she was new to the group and, from an earlier comment, she had something occur. None knew what that was. Beth knew most of the people at the table. After a few comments after arriving, she remained oddly quiet and reserved. When John had made his odd statement, Kourin saw something in Beth's expression that led her to believe there was more there. As John interacted with her, she appeared to have a mask on hiding something. Because Kourin had spent her whole life behind a mask of her own, she could tell when others appeared to have one as well. Beth had a story to tell.

Kourin was certain Beth was going to say something when Jack made his comment that something had happened to all of them. She just as quickly stopped herself and studied her glass of water when Jack continued. Kourin kept an eye on her as the conversation continued around them.

When Beth stated she had sat on the bench, Kourin saw the anguish wash over her face. She herself had a similar pain and felt the need to help Beth through hers even though she didn't know her story with Tom.

"Beth?" Kourin said to her while she rested her head on Harry's shoulder. "Beth, would you accompany me to the powder room?"

When Kourin asked her the question, Beth looked up from Harry's shoulder. Her mind had been elsewhere, but Kourin stating her name had brought her back. She looked at Harry who gave a half smile and nodded to her. She turned to Kourin. Without a word, she gave a brief nod and rose from her chair.

Kourin gave Jack's hand a squeeze when Beth nodded to her. He stood as well when Kourin got up. Together, Beth and Kourin weaved through the tables to the restrooms on the side of the hall.

Jack sat back down and surveyed the table. He found all eyes were upon him, except for Mandy who was watching Miguel. He was about to ask Sarah what had occurred with her when the salads arrived.

Vasud and Niyati returned to their seats, so all conversation about the bench ceased to a more conventional discussion of the terminal, Jack's construction business, Benchmark's aspirations from Vasud's viewpoint, and, of course, coffee talk from Laurel and Mandy. The dinner entrees appeared, as did Kourin and Beth.

Beth remained quiet, but she seemed to be a little brighter than she had been. Kourin whispered in Jack's ear that all was as well as it could be under the circumstances. Beth just needed time to deal with what she had experienced.

After the entrees, Vasud and Niyati once again left the table to mingle with other party guests. Jack was about to ask Sarah about her occurrence when Mandy rose from her chair and said to all, "Excuse me."

All eyes followed her as she walked past the crew's table. Jack followed her trajectory and saw Miguel at the closest bar. Sarah witnessed this as well and excused herself, saying, "I should give her a hand." She followed Mandy's path to the bar area. This left Jack, Kourin, Harry, Beth, Laurel and, of course, Ubu.

Ubu had enjoyed a nice chopped up dinner of steak and vegetables. He felt Mom was safe, but he kept alert, watching all the unknown people around him. People stopped and spoke with Mom, with all of them looking in his direction. She had a smile and seemed at ease during these meetings. He was about to lie down and relax after having just eaten a second dinner when John walked by the table. He perked up when someone said something, and he stopped right beside him.

Kourin saw John heading from his table to walk by theirs. She asked, "John, may we have a minute?"

John stopped behind Ubu and turned toward the table. "Yes, Kourin, what can I do for you?" John looked down at Ubu and pet his head.

"John," Kourin began as she looked at Jack and then up at John. "I think there's more about the bench you're not telling us. Would you like to share?"

John, to his credit, kept the same expression he had and answered, "I'm not sure I follow?"

Kourin said, "The center bench in your garden is more than it seems to be."

John saw all at the table were staring at him, awaiting an answer. He said, "It's just a bench I had in my backyard, as they all were."

This time Laurel spoke up before Kourin could reply. "John, that bench is more than just a bench." John didn't respond right away, so she added, "Take, for instance, what you're doing right now."

"And what is that, Laurel?" he asked, while still petting Ubu.

"I notice that, as you pet Ubu, you're very careful not to touch the area where he got hurt this morning. How do you explain that?"

"Well, I'm not—" John began.

Kourin added, "And earlier, when Peri was petting Ubu, she too avoided the injured area. I'm fairly certain no one ever mentioned to either of you he had a recent injury."

He paused and looked down at Ubu, asking, "What do you think, Ubu?"

Ubu enjoyed John's head pets. He had a good feeling about him. When John spoke to him, he gave a tilted head answer, not knowing what was being asked of him.

John received a non-answer from Ubu, not expecting anything else other than a few seconds' delay to think of a response to Kourin's and Laurel's inquisition. He had known this day would come eventually. He did not know it would arrive so quickly. After all, it had taken him a full year with the bench in his backyard before he realized it was not just a bench.

After stalling as long as he could, he gave an answer. "Perhaps there are a few things you need to know. You seek answers. Hell, I was clueless about it for over a year myself. However, here and now is not the time to have that discussion."

Laurel was about to interject when John added, "I know. You have questions and feel I have answers." John looked at each person at the table before continuing while soft music continued filling the hall. He looked down at Ubu, halting his petting. "How about this? We have the ribbon cutting for the soft opening at eight in front of both your stores by the garden. Let's meet at nine once all the hoopla has subsided. How's that sound?"

Laurel was about to reply when Jack spoke first, saying, "John, that sounds reasonable. There's been a few strange occurrences that need explanation."

"That's putting it mildly!" Harry spoke up. Harry glanced at Beth who returned his look with pleading eyes while she had a hand over his on the table, so he added, "But we need to get to the bottom of this." Beth squeezed Harry's hand and smiled.

"Okay. So, nine it is," Jack said.

"Yes," John confirmed. "Until then, everyone, why don't you enjoy this wonderful party? Jack, I'd say Kourin is going to want a dance before too long, and Laurel, set aside your worries tonight. Enjoy!"

John looked at Beth, seeing her concerned face. "Beth, again thank you for all your help with tonight's party and especially all you've done throughout the terminal process. In the end, it will all have been worth it."

Beth said in a subdued tone, "Thank you, John. I've been fortunate to work with wonderful people like Jack and Harry."

John smiled and said, "Now, if you'll excuse me, I need to locate my lovely wife. I promised her a dance." With that, he exited the table before anyone could add another word.

* * *

Sarah approached the bar where Mandy and Miguel were standing. She heard Miguel say, "You're not my mother." Sarah thought. *Oh, that doesn't sound good.* Miguel was holding another drink in his hand, at least the third suffering bastard since he arrived.

Mandy answered him, as Sarah arrived beside her, "No, Miguel, I am not, but I am someone who cares very much about you. I just want to be sure you're safe."

Miguel, eyeing Sarah when she arrived, said, "I'm fine, M. I'm just having a good time, is all." He took a healthy sip of his drink to punctuate his point. "And they make great drinks here! Can I get either of you one?"

"Not right now, thanks," Mandy replied and followed up with her own question. "How about we head back to the table for dessert?"

He replied, holding up his drink, "I have all the dessert I want right here!"

The band started playing a dance song. Sarah opted to assist Mandy before the conversation took a downward turn. She asked, "Hey, Miguel, why don't you join me for a dance? It's been a while since I've been out dancing, and I don't have a partner." Sarah smiled at Miguel and held out her hand to him, asking, "What do ya' say? Care to show a new girl in town a good time?"

Miguel couldn't help but smile, and Sarah's blue eyes were captivating.

Based on the tone he had with her, Mandy thought he was going to say no. However, he yielded when Sarah did a head tilt and doubled down on a wide smile. She led him by the hand from the bar toward the dance floor.

Sarah caught Mandy's gaze as they approached the tables Roberts Construction was using. Mandy mouthed a silent "thank you" to her while Miguel wasn't looking. She responded with a silent "you're welcome."

Miguel dropped off his drink on the table he had been at and followed Sarah. There were two other couples on the dance floor, and two more joined in. Sarah was happy other couples were on the floor. It had been several years since she had been out dancing with her husband, Jerry.

Mandy stopped at her table and sat down. She didn't have her usual Mandy smile on.

Laurel was the first to say something. "At least he's occupied." All knew what she was implying. Occupy Miguel and keep him far from Chessa to prevent Mandy's vision from occurring.

"Yes, but for how long?" Mandy questioned.

Kourin said, "Let's all work together to keep him distracted. We can switch off after a little while. Is that okay with you, Jack?"

"We need to do whatever it takes," he responded. "By the way, while you were gone, Mandy, John set up a meeting for tomorrow morning at nine after the soft open ceremony. He definitely knows more about the bench."

Mandy was intrigued and momentarily distracted from thinking about Miguel. She asked, "Like, what does he know?"

Laurel spoke up first. "He wouldn't say, but he made it seem like he knew more."

Kourin added, "And he was surprised that we already knew something was up with the bench. Remember? He said he didn't know about it until . . . What did he say? Oh yeah, a year after he got it! How could you have the bench that long and not have had weird things happen?"

"Maybe he didn't sit on it in that year," Jack said.

"Or the bench didn't reveal itself to him until then," Harry interjected. All eyes went to him. He continued. "Look. Who knows what the hell that bench is up to? Maybe it bides its time until the moment is just right before it acts."

Beth spoke up first, asking, "Harry, you're suggesting the bench is alive?" Harry looked at her but said nothing. "I find that hard to believe. It's just a bench."

"Beth, you don't understand what that thing is capable of!" He paused and looked into her eyes before continuing in a softer tone. "I know what you experienced was painful." He reached out and held her right hand between both of his. "But I believe it is trying to tell us something. It wants me to . . . to do . . ." Harry paused and looked around the table as all waited for him to continue. "Well, I have no fucking idea what it wants. I've relived episodes of my life that . . . and one that . . ." he trailed off, not finishing his thoughts.

Beth replied in a soft voice, "Harry, I know the pain you've been through, what we've been through." She placed her left hand on top of his. "We can make it through this. Whatever the heck is going on, I'll be there with you."

Harry peered into Beth's eyes. He saw sincerity. He saw caring. He saw . . . He removed his hands from Beth, not saying a word. With a nearly empty beer in front of him, his thoughts returned to Christine and how he had betrayed her.

Beth let Harry withdraw his hands from hers. She watched his facial expression change from one of questions to a deep sorrowful sadness. She had witnessed this before. It brought a tear to her eye.

The other four at the table witnessed the interaction between Harry and Beth. They could not hear the last exchanges between the two, but they saw Harry pull into himself and away from Beth. They glanced at one another. Without saying a word, they worried Harry was returning to the dark place he had been earlier in the day.

"Harry makes a valid point," Laurel said after each held their silence for several heartbeats. "I think we may have been looking at this all wrong."

Mandy asked, "What do you mean?"

Before Laurel could answer, Sarah returned with Miguel.

3

VISION ASPECT

John departed the table with his thoughts roiling through his mind. He knew the day would arrive when someone would probe about the bench, but he had not expected it to happen so quickly. He thought he had more time.

He spied his wife near the far wall ice sculpture. She was speaking with Dafina and Amir who worked in the operations department of Benchmark Air. Without dedicated individuals such as them, he would not have an airline.

He moved toward them, thinking about the brief conversation he had with Jack, Laurel, and Kourin. They were unnerved by something. Beth and Harry were, too. He did not know the latter very well, having only spoken with him in passing on his visits. The others, though, he felt he knew them well from his own experiences in his backyard.

Peri was laughing as John joined her from behind. "Hello, everyone," he said. "How are you enjoying the party?"

Dafina answered, "Very well, John. It seems everyone is having a great time."

Amir added, "The food has been excellent!" He looked at the table spread before them, filled with a variety of cheeses, crackers, and vegetables. "There's certainly enough to choose from." As he made this statement, he reached down to pluck a purple grape from a vine. "Delicious too," he added.

"I'm glad you're enjoying it. Everyone worked hard on this project, including both of you. I just had a nice compliment about your department." Both Dafina and Amir waited in anticipation for John to continue. "I was just chatting with Beth from Roberts Construction. She had very positive things to say about your assistance and the work your group did to make this terminal come alive."

Peri's attention perked up at John's choice of words but did not comment.

"Well, that's great to hear," Dafina said. As she said this, she gave Amir a sideways glance. "She was good to work with."

Amir said, "She was persistent." Dafina's eye caught his. He added, "In a good way."

John started laughing. "It's all good. She told me that there was . . . How should I say this? There was some back and forth that occurred, but all worked out in the end."

"There was plenty of that for sure," said Amir.

Dafina added, "But in the end, it all came together."

John nodded his head in agreement. "You both should take a moment to connect with her. She's in the middle of the room at Jack's table. I think she'd appreciate a little positive feedback as well."

"We'll definitely do that," said Dafina. "And no time like the present." She asked Amir, "Shall we?" They excused themselves from John and Peri and headed toward the center of the room in search of Beth.

John said to his wife, "We need to have a word, dear."

Peri, at first, was going to comment about John's phrasing that the terminal came alive. However, when she saw his expression, she instead asked, "They said something about the bench, didn't they?" She glanced at the appetizer table while asking her question. Set on top of the impressive appetizer spread was a slightly melting ice sculpture—a beautiful replica of the bench set in a garden oasis.

John followed her sight to the mockup of his vision. He replied, "Yes." He reached out to hold his wife's hands in his. As she turned to face him, he added, "It has begun."

* * *

"So, is Miguel as good a dancer as he claims to be?" Jack asked Sarah.

"He gave me a run for my money," Sarah laughed.

"She's just being modest," Miguel added. "S is an excellent dancer."

Mandy said, as she stood up and took Miguel's hand, "I think you owe me a dance now." With a smile on his face, he let her lead him away to the dance floor.

After they departed, Sarah said to no one in particular, "We cannot keep him on the dance floor all night. I could barely keep up with him after just two dances." She plunked herself down in the nearest chair.

Kourin surveyed the room and said, "Well, maybe if we can solicit more help, we can keep him corralled." She honed in on Jack's crew. "Perhaps they'd be willing to help?"

Jack answered, "Perhaps, but more likely they'd just contribute to his delinquency." He saw Kourin's expression as he turned away from his crew and back to the table. Her facial expression conveyed the message that, "if you have a better idea, let's hear it."

He added, "It's worth a try."

After Jack and Kourin exited the table in search of help, Laurel asked Sarah, "What did you experience with the bench?"

Sarah shifted her gaze from Laurel to Harry and Beth who were sitting across the table. They returned her gaze. From their demeanor, she could not discern if she should share her odd experience with people she just met.

Harry was eager to hear what had happened to Sarah, hoping it would aid his knowledge to control the bench to return to his Christine. Not having met Sarah before tonight, Beth was still curious if she had experienced something similar to herself. Regardless of their feelings, they kept their innermost thoughts to themselves.

"As my flight was taxiing past the Benchmark terminal . . ." Sarah began. Just as she was saying "Benchmark," a couple were passing the table and stopped. Sarah paused her story and looked up at the newcomers. The others at the table did as well.

"Excuse us for intruding," said the young black woman. "I'm Dafina, and this is Amir. Are you by chance, Beth?"

Beth, upon hearing her name and recognizing the names, said, "That would be me. It's a pleasure to meet you both."

"Oh no, the pleasure is all mine, I mean ours," Dafina replied, adding a sideways glance at Amir. To Laurel and Sarah, she said, "Please excuse our interruption."

Laurel held a blank expression on her face, as she was annoyed at the intrusion and wanted to know what had happened to Sarah. On the other side of the table, Harry did not hide his annoyance on his face. It was Sarah who responded, though, "No problem. We're just chatting. Please have a seat."

"I don't want to intrude," Dafina said.

"Think nothing of it. Laurel and I were just heading to the bar for another drink," Sarah said and rose. Laurel, taking the hint, stood as well.

Laurel added, "Please sit. We'll be right back." She said to Ubu, accompanied by a hand gesture, "Come, Ubu."

Sarah exited the table, with Laurel and Ubu following. They headed toward the entrance they had arrived through.

* * *

Ubu guarded Mom. This place was loud and unfamiliar. Although Sister and friends were also here, he was anxious. Mom stood and spoke to him. She directed him to follow, which he would have done even if she hadn't commanded him to do so. He was in a strange place surrounded by deafening noises, overwhelming smells, and many faces he did not know. He remained vigilant for the evil dark man he had seen earlier today in the hot place.

* * *

Perturbed and wanting to hear Sarah's story, Harry watched her leave their table, replaced by the newcomers. For the time being, her story would have to wait as he remained by Beth's side. He could sense she was acting off from her usual self. Although he wouldn't admit to it if asked, he needed to be with her as well. A reassuring hand upon his own reminded him of the countless times Christine had held his hand.

As he reminisced, he heard Beth conversing beside him with Dafina and Amir. He ignored the conversation. With the band playing a slow love song, his mind wandered to his own backyard where he saw his smiling wife holding his infant son as she swayed to a now distant song and happier days.

* * *

Just beyond the threshold of the hall's double door entrance, Laurel caught up with Sarah in the garishly decorated hallway. She motioned Laurel to one of several seating areas away from the open doors. It was a little quieter down the hall. She sat in a wingback chair covered with a large colorful red flower pattern. Laurel sat in a matching one beside it. They were at an angle positioned toward each other, with two other chairs unoccupied. Ubu sat on the carpet beside Laurel, watching Sarah, with a clear view of the doorway they had just come through.

"So why did we have to come out here?" asked Laurel.

"Sorry. When the couple came by the table, I realized what I had been about to say wasn't appropriate with all the ears around," Sarah answered, looking up and down the hall. They were alone.

"Sounds ominous."

"Well, it was weird," Sarah said as she looked down at her hands. She hadn't realized she was holding one with the other. She separated them and looked at Laurel. "Maybe it was just my imagination or the afternoon light playing tricks on my eyes." She paused. "I don't know."

Laurel said, "It's been a day of oddities for sure. But one thing I've learned from it all is it is better to say it out loud. I've found it kinda helps to deal with it. Then you can decide if it is something or not."

Sarah was about to speak when they heard Mandy from the doorway. "There you are!" As she walked over to them, she said, "I was wondering where you guys ran off to."

Miguel was not with her.

When she saw their unasked question, she added, "He's dancing with Wren. I'm not sure how it all happened, but when I got back to the table, a couple were talking with Harry and Beth. I saw Kourin two tables over, and she motioned for me to come over. Miguel followed, and the next thing I knew, Wren was taking Miguel back to the dance floor, followed by Jack and Kourin. I did a quick scan of the hall and didn't see you. Why are we out here?"

Laurel answered, "Sarah was just about to tell us what she experienced today."

Mandy asked Sarah, "At home when I told you about my experience with the bench, why didn't you tell me you had sat on it?"

"Oh, I didn't. Honestly, I'm not sure if something happened or not. When you told me about your experience and some of what happened with other people, I didn't know what to think. Frankly, I still don't." She paused, glancing from Mandy to Laurel and back to Mandy, questioning if she should share what she believed she saw. Neither of the ladies appeared to be judgmental. She said, "Let me tell you what I experienced. Maybe it's nothing." Subconsciously, she clasped her hands tightly together.

Laurel and Mandy waited in anticipation. Music continued playing in the background while Ubu kept his eyes on the hall entrance doorway.

Focused on a red swirling pattern in the floor carpeting, not wanting to make eye contact with either lady, Sarah related her story. "As my flight was landing this afternoon, there was a blink in the instrument panel when we touched down." She paused, looking up at the two ladies, who remained stoic with blank expressions. "That's not supposed to happen, ever."

"A system glitch?" Mandy offered.

"That's what Brad said when we began taxiing toward our terminal. He said he'd have maintenance check it out."

"Who is Brad?" asked Mandy.

"The pilot I flew with, but the glitch is not the weirdest thing that occurred." She paused, collecting her thoughts. "As we were passing by the new terminal and I was thinking about contacting you to see if you wanted to have dinner, I had the strangest vision." She stopped. Her body shuddered.

Laurel and Mandy exchanged glances. Laurel asked, "Sarah, what did you see?"

Sarah hesitated several heartbeats before answering. Both Laurel and Mandy gave Sarah the time she needed to relate her story at her own pace. The music continued playing on in the background.

"As I was passing the new Benchmark jet with the sun reflecting off the brilliant white exterior shell, for a second, maybe two, it changed to . . . I'm not sure how to describe it." She paused and looked at Mandy. "You know how with old film when you used to have to bring it to a store and have it developed? You would get back the film in little strips with the developed pictures. When you looked at what was on the strips, it looked like a ghost image of the actual picture. That's what I saw, the plane as a ghost image."

Mandy said, "That sounds horrible, but maybe it was just the sun playing tricks on you. You said there was a reflection off the plane."

"True. That's what I told myself," Sarah answered, "but . . ." she paused, not saying anything more.

Mandy finished her thought for her. "But when I told you what had happened with me and you heard all the other stories . . ."

"Yes. When everything is added together, I'm thinking maybe what I witnessed was more than just sun reflection." She looked Mandy in the eye, adding, "I think I saw a doomed plane."

4

SUFFERING BASTARD

Miguel felt the drinks he had scoffed surging through his system. The first one wasn't the strongest drink, but heavy tipping to the bartender, Nigel, had reaped the reward he had hoped. By the third suffering bastard, each sip packed a plus! His mind was a little fuzzy, but he was enjoying himself. The crew were having a great time at their tables, laughing and joking about anything and everything.

As he sat at the crew's table, he thought about how the night had progressed. He had danced with several lovely ladies: S, M, and R. He figured Sarah and Mandy were just being nice to him. Both were beautiful, but Sarah was married so he knew that was a non-starter already. Mandy—although he would like to get to know her better—had always seemed not at all interested in him. Not that he hadn't tried on every opportunity visiting the coffee shop each morning and often a second time later in the morning or early afternoon. Ultimately, he just went through the motions with her, never expecting to achieve the result he desired. Until today when, out of the blue, she had displayed more attention than he had received from her ever.

He thought about Wren and the dance he had with her after M. He called her R since the "W" was silent, and R seemed to suit her more with her red hair. He found her quite attractive and would like to get to know her better. However, even in his current inebriated state, he knew he would not break the

Bro Code since she was at the party with his friend Joneal. After two songs, he returned her to her date.

More laughter came from Jose and Bob to his right, breaking him out of his melancholy memory search. He swallowed the last two inches in his glass. It was a bit too watery for his liking, but he didn't want to waste the rum. Most bars made a suffering bastard with rum, which he preferred. Last year, on a date, he went to a bar in Exeter that had made it with bourbon and gin. He drank it anyway, even though he preferred the rum version.

An image of the girl he dated that night came to him, and the hollow void he had felt in his chest when she ghosted him. In the subsequent weeks, he had asked himself what happened during the date that resulted in the brush off. Not coming to any conclusion, he chalked it up to her just not being into him. Too bad because he had enjoyed being with her.

He asked everyone at the table if they wanted another round. All answered they were all set, so he set off on his own to get another of the deliciousness he craved.

Nigel, who was Miguel's age or somewhat older, saw him approaching the bar and greeted him with, "Would you like another, my friend?"

"Yesss, pleassse," Miguel slurred his words.

Within a couple of minutes, Nigel returned with his drink. "Will there be anything else?"

"No, thanksss," Miguel replied and left a five-dollar bill on the counter that Nigel scooped up. He said thank you, but Miguel was already on the move away from the bar. On his return trip near his table, he glanced at a few alluring women. He recognized Leah, the bubbly young girl from the electronics store. He was going to make a detour to her table when he heard a familiar voice behind him.

"There you are," Kourin said as she and Jack intercepted him from his intended destination. "We were wondering where you had gone off to."

"Just refilling my glassss."

"I see that. Would you like to get something to eat? There are some great smelling treats on the table right over there," she said, pointing at the table with the bench ice sculpture.

"No, thanksss, K. I'm good with thisss," he replied, holding up his drink and spilling some of it out. He looked in Leah's direction and said, "I'm just looking for a dance partner," with a mischievous twinkle in his eyes.

Laughter came from the Roberts Construction table, and all three looked in that direction as Jose and Bob did a high five and laughed. This distracted Miguel from the other table, giving Jack the opportunity to say to Kourin, "Kori, why don't you keep Miguel company while I go in search of Mandy?"

"That sounds like a wonderful idea," she said, holding out her hand to Miguel. "Come with me. Let's see what we're missing over there." Once again, he allowed himself to be led away. Kourin turned so that Miguel couldn't see her face. She mouthed to Jack, "Find Mandy."

Jack gave a thumbs up as Kourin turned away. He went in search of Mandy and his niece. He hadn't been too concerned with Mandy's vision, thinking that, since it hadn't happened, they'd be able to control the situation to ensure it did not come to pass. After this encounter with Miguel, seeing his intoxication level, he was having doubts.

Kourin guided Miguel back to the place where the group had now combined three tables into one so they could all sit together. All were laughing, talking, singing, and having a grand time. Miguel released from Kourin's grasp and joined right in as if he had never left.

Kourin stepped back and surveyed the room as thoroughly as possible. Where was Mandy? As she gazed out upon the party goers, her eyes landed on John and Peri who were looking right at her from far across the hall. The cheerful expressions they had worn previously and whenever she had seen them before were now absent. A thought came to her as she held their gaze in hers. *I think something has changed.*

* * *

Jack scanned the hall and could not locate Mandy or Laurel. He had the notion they went to the coat check area to confront Chessa and decided to check there. As he walked between two groups of people, he spotted Vasud and Niyati in a third group, as well as some other familiar Benchmark employees.

As he attempted to walk past them, he heard Vasud call out to him. "Jack, we were just talking about you. Please, if you have a moment, I have a question for you."

Jack wanted to say no and exit the hall, but his persona wouldn't let him just pass by. He stopped and said, "Sure. What can I do for you?" As he spoke, his gaze wandered to the open hall doors just a few feet away. Out beyond, he could not see Mandy or Laurel. He hoped they weren't where he thought they were.

* * *

Kourin stood to Miguel's left, facing the dance floor and the band. The music was far louder now than during dinner. The dance floor was nearly full, as people had consumed enough alcohol to believe they could dance.

Presage belted out a decent rendition of Lady Gaga's "Edge of Glory." As they played, she did not see Jack sidelined from locating Mandy. However, she did see Miguel take a long sip of his drink. At this pace, she knew he was going to be beyond drunk. She thought, *Maybe if I get him to dance more, he can work it out of his system. At least he'll be away from his drink.*

As Presage completed Gaga, they began "Live It Up." She said to Miguel, "Miguel, I love JLo. Let's dance!" She grabbed his left hand. "What do ya' say?"

Miguel gave it half a thought before replying, "Sssure, K." He let Kourin lead the way to the dance floor.

Kourin watched him keep the rapid beat. She knew his alcohol level had to be extremely high, but she had to give him credit. He danced far better than most of the other people on the floor. Despite the tempo being too rapid for her, she did her best to make it appear she knew what she was doing. As she moved around the floor, she continued to search for Mandy, to no avail.

As the song ended, Kourin took a step to exit the dance floor when a slower song began. Miguel grabbed her hand to pull her in close to dance. She hadn't danced with him like this before and was apprehensive about it. As Miguel held her inches from his own body, she kept thinking, *It's to save him.*

When the song ended, Miguel released her, and he headed back to the table. Kourin followed as another slow song began. A man with piercing blue eyes appeared at her side and said, "May I have this dance?"

Anders—her first instinct was to decline and keep walking. She watched Miguel continue on to the group without her, so for now, he was safe.

She turned her attention to Anders. As part of the Benchmark operations team, he had been assigned to assist with her shop opening. In those few weeks, their relationship had progressed beyond that, far beyond that. Kourin had hoped he would not be at the party tonight.

Miguel laughed with the crew a short distance away. Against her better judgment, she turned to the blue-eyed man, forced a smile, and took his hand to dance.

"It is a pleasure to see you again, Kourin," he said as he held on to her, swaying to the music. "You have returned none of the messages I left you since our last meeting."

"I thought I had made it clear to you the last time we spoke that our interactions going forward would be professional only, if at all."

Anders looked into Kourin's eyes and said, "I think we both want more than that, don't you think?" Anders held Kourin in his arms, dancing as if they had never been apart.

As Kourin moved her feet, she was thinking, *How in the hell did I get myself into this situation?*

While Kourin fretted over her predicament, she did not notice Miguel down his drink and proceed back to his favorite bartender for another.

* * *

In the distance behind Kourin, Jack made small talk with Vasud, answering a few questions about the terminal. He finally could excuse himself and exit out the hall entrance, not noticing Miguel arrive at the bar to his left.

Up the hallway, near the venue entrance and coat check area, were two people talking. Even from this distance, he could see neither was Mandy nor Laurel. He looked down the hallway to the right and saw more people seated and talking—no one he knew. The other way, he saw a trio of women and a black dog. He sighed in relief and hurried over to them. As he approached, Ubu stood up with his tail wagging.

* * *

Miguel's bartender delivered two drinks to him. At first, Nigel had refused serving two at once, but Miguel had assured him the second one was not for himself. After a little back and forth, Nigel gave in. Miguel gave him a ten-dollar tip and took a sip from a cocktail. He picked up the other drink and headed for the hall entrance.

* * *

Jack arrived at the trio plus one black dog, simultaneously with Miguel picking up his drinks. As Jack did a quick pet on Ubu's head, he said to the trio, "So what's going on out here, ladies?"

All three looked up at Jack as one, having not noticed his approach. Mandy and Laurel sprang up, with Sarah following a little behind the two. All three spoke at the same time: "Sarah had an experience passing by the terminal," "Wait 'til you hear what happened to Sarah," "I'm not sure what I saw."

While they overwhelmed Jack, Ubu watched Miguel unsteadily amble through the hall doors up the hallway, out of sight.

* * *

As the music ended, Kourin pulled away from Anders to put distance between them. As she turned, he grasped her elbow. She whipped her head around in a panic, the vision of Harry's hold on her the day before abruptly coming to her mind. She caught Anders' blue eyes in her own.

He asked, oblivious to her panic attack, "May I get you a refreshment?"

His blue eyes were like a magnet, and she found it almost impossible to resist looking at them. She answered, as her alarm subsided, "Um, no thank you. I'm good." She could feel the heat building inside her. It felt different from what she had experienced with Jack. Her hands felt ice cold even though the rest of her was hot from dancing. She said, "I need to find my friends."

Anders replied, "I hope we have another dance before this night is through."

Kourin did not respond as she strode off the dance floor back to the crew's table. She chided herself for not saying no when he had asked her to dance. The last thing she needed right now was to go through everything again with him.

She brought a picture of Jack to her mind as she scanned the table for Miguel or Jack. Not spotting either, she looked outwards through the hall. She did not look back toward the dance floor. She did not want Anders to think she was interested in him for a second time.

Had she looked, she would have seen a pair of blue eyes at the edge of the dance floor glued to her every move.

* * *

Miguel held a drink in each hand as he made a zigzag line through the brightly colored hallway toward the exit. However, the exit was not his intended destination. As he passed two gaudily colored chairs with a large plastic plant behind them on his right, two women walked toward him on his left. He said to them, "Good evening, ladiesss," raising the drink in his left hand in a mock salute. He ignored the liquid spilling onto his fingers. The ladies ignored the inebriated man passing by them. He continued on.

The ladies were forgotten as he came upon his destination on the left. There was no one else in the hallway as he approached the counter. Before him stood the object of his trek up the hallway: Chessa.

Miguel offered a courteous "Hola, señorita," while Chessa silently watched him. "I brought you something." He handed the drink from his left hand to her, placing it on the counter between them. He took a sip of his own drink. "Mmm. Delicious. Try it. You'll like it."

Chessa eyed the drink and then sized up Miguel. She pondered the scene and her options.

He maintained his smile, and his brown eyes locked with hers.

She finally said, "Oh, what the hell." She had a long sip.

As she set the glass down on the counter, a sly smile etched the corner of her lips. With lavender smokey eyeshadow surrounding bewitching eyes, Chessa held Miguel's attention. She knew the effect she was having on him. She used the tip of her tongue to separate her matte dark violet lips from one side of her tepid smile to the other.

She repeated his words to her in a beguiling voice, "Mmm. Delicious. I will try it." The ends of her lips changed to a half smile. She purred, "But you'll be the one who likes it."

* * *

The three ladies calmed down after Jack listened to half a minute of non-stop clamoring. Ubu wasn't concerned in the hallway among friends and lay down on the red design of the carpet. For the next two minutes, Sarah apprised Jack about what she had beforehand revealed to Mandy and Laurel. With the second telling, she controlled her emotions.

Jack listened intently as Sarah related her story. When she finished, he glanced at Mandy and Laurel. "That's certainly a frightening vision."

"But . . ." Laurel said, knowing her uncle.

He looked away from Laurel to Sarah. "But it may not be related at all to the bench."

Laurel made a face of disapproval.

Before she could say anything, Jack continued, "That being said, the last couple of days have been bizarre. I'll give you that. Before we say every odd thing that happens is related to the bench, we should take a breath and analyze it." He looked at each of them before continuing. "Sarah hasn't even sat on the bench. As I understand this, the closest she came was having coffee in your café. I'm not sure it is connected or just a freak occurrence." Jack did not volunteer his own experience while sitting at the gate waiting for John's plane to arrive, but the connection was not lost on him.

His niece spoke up first, her voice rising with each word. "A freak occurrence? What the hell is that supposed to mean?"

Sarah answered for Jack. "He's right. It's a stretch to say it was anything more than an optical illusion."

Laurel was about to rebut when Mandy chimed in, "Jack, where's Kourin?"

He replied, "She's with Miguel. Which reminds me, she sent me to find you for help with him. I think we should . . ."

Without letting him finish his statement or saying another word, Mandy turned and dashed toward the hall entrance. The three were left standing, watching her rush away. Jack turned to Sarah and said, "I hope I didn't offend you."

"Not at all. I'm still trying to wrap my head around what Mandy told me earlier."

"As are we all," Jack said. "Shall we?" He reached out his hand with a palm up in the direction of the hall's entrance. "Miguel has been drinking more. She's going to need help." With Ubu at Laurel's side, they all followed Mandy who had already disappeared into the hall.

* * *

Mandy scanned the bar area to her right as she entered the hall: no Miguel or Kourin. She hurried to the crew's table, spotting Kourin looking in her direction. She was not with Miguel. Mandy panicked and made a beeline to Kourin. On her way, Carlos intercepted her.

"Hi, Mandy!" Carlos stood between the two tables she was weaving through to get to the crew's table. "I was hoping to bump into you."

Mandy was going to reply that this place wasn't that big, but even in distress, she remained the amiable person who she was. Instead, she said, "Oh great to see you, Carlos." As she spoke, she peered around his left shoulder, trying to locate Miguel.

He asked, "Would you like to dance?"

This brought Mandy back to Carlos' attention. "I would, but I need to find someone at the moment." She looked to the right of him, scanning her eyes across the hall in that direction before coming back to Carlos. "You haven't seen Miguel, have you?"

"Miguel?" Carlos thought about it for a few seconds. "Can't say that I have." He paused, trying to think of something witty to say as usual. "But I'm here. What can I do for you?"

Mandy gave a half-hearted smile. "No offense, Carlos, but I need to find Miguel."

Carlos was smart enough to not push that any further, but he didn't take the hint that she wasn't interested in hanging with him. He said, "Okay. I'll help you find him."

"Great," Mandy responded. When Carlos didn't move, she added, "Let's check with Kourin to see if she's seen him." Mandy looked in her direction and moved that way. Fortunately, Carlos let her pass, following behind.

From three steps away, Mandy asked, "Kourin, where's Miguel? Jack said he was with you."

"I lost him," Kourin replied. She saw Mandy's facial expression change to anguish. "I'm trying to find him."

"How could you lose him?"

"We got separated. He couldn't have gone far. We were just together a few minutes ago."

Carlos stood directly behind Mandy, wondering why these two women were fixated on finding Miguel.

Jack arrived with Sarah and Laurel in tow. Ubu brought up the rear. Jack stood beside Kourin, while the others stopped beside Carlos. Laughter rose from the crew's table, and voices grew louder as Presage began a rock song.

Mandy shouted, "We need to find him, pronto! Where could he have gone?" She scanned the hall again, not seeing him.

Jack spoke up. "Maybe he went to the bathroom?" He looked around the hall and noticed a restroom sign beside a doorway opposite the hall entrance they had been using. "He's probably in there." The others looked in the direction Jack was. "I'll go check."

As Jack walked away, Mandy said, "If he's not there, where else could he be?" She was looking at Laurel. They both got a serious expression on their faces. "You don't think he's . . . But we were in the hall. We would have seen him go past us!"

Laurel said, "Probably, but what if we didn't?"

Carlos did not know what the two ladies meant. He kept silent.

Mandy said, as she turned toward the exit, "I'm going to go check."

"I'll go with you," said Sarah.

Carlos, not wanting to lose his opportunity with Mandy, followed behind them. He wondered why everyone was so interested in finding Miguel. What did he have that they wanted? And how could he get some?

5

DREAMS DO COME TRUE

Kourin and Laurel stood watching after Mandy and Sarah exited the hall with Carlos in tow. Kourin directed her attention toward the restrooms to watch for Jack, and hopefully, he would have Miguel with him.

As she observed the restroom area and with the music blasting, Laurel moved closer to her. Ubu stayed by her side, matching the distance they moved. Laurel asked Kourin, "How did Miguel go missing?"

"I got distracted." She looked at the restroom door, hoping Jack would appear so she could avoid this conversation. He did not. She turned back to Laurel. "I was dancing with Miguel, and we were leaving the dance floor when," she checked the restroom doors again—no Jack—"a man asked me to dance."

"So, you let Miguel wonder off alone?"

Kourin answered, "Well, he was headed back to the table. I tried to decline, but it was one of the Benchmark guys." She did not expand on who the person was, not wanting to get into all that right now, especially with Jack's niece. She averted her eyes from Laurel, gazing off to the right, as if searching for Miguel, but in truth, she was masking the humiliation she felt for dancing with Anders and not remaining with Miguel. As she regained her composure, she said, "I didn't want to be rude."

Laurel was about to reply when Kourin said, "There's Jack!"

Jack hastened back, alone. As the two women watched him weave around party guests, he shook his head from a few tables over. Upon arrival, he said, "He wasn't in there. Now, where do we look?"

* * *

Mandy was almost running up the hallway, with Sarah and Carlos several steps behind. As they came upon the coat check desk, they found it abandoned. Mandy looked around and said, "Hello." No reply. She looked across at the restrooms and started toward them.

Carlos gently caught Mandy's arm as she was passing by him and said, "Mandy, maybe I should go check?"

Mandy came to a sudden stop and gazed at Carlos. Abruptly, the bench dream engulfed her. Instead of Carlos standing before her, she saw Declan. Her mind swirled, and her chest became heavy. She couldn't catch her breath. Declan's image distorted with the darkness surrounding it. She collapsed.

Carlos saw Mandy fainting and caught her in his arms. He led her over to the two red chairs behind her.

Sarah, a few steps behind Mandy, saw her collapsing. Thankfully, Carlos was right there, and he guided her to the seat. She said to Carlos, "See if you can find a damp cloth in the bathroom." As he ran into the men's room, she sat in the other chair and held her friend's hands, which were cool to the touch. She said, "Mandy, are you okay?" She squeezed her hands slightly tighter. "Mandy?"

Mandy's eyes opened and blinked several times in rapid succession. She glanced around, bringing her eyes to focus on Sarah sitting in front of her. She couldn't recall sitting down and looked away at the empty coat check counter. Music was playing down the hall. Her bench dream came back to her, but this time she kept her composure. She heard a door to her right open. Carlos appeared next to her, holding a folded-up damp paper towel.

Sarah reached for the paper towel. It would have to do. Without asking Mandy, she placed it on her forehead and held it there. She looked up at Carlos and said, "Please get her a drink of water." As Carlos sprinted toward the sound of the music, she added, "And try to find Laurel or Jack!" Sarah turned her attention back to her friend asking, "Mandy, are you okay?"

Mandy raised her hand, taking the damp cloth from Sarah. She patted her forehead once and both cheeks before answering. "I . . . I think so." She looked at the counter again. "I was hit by the dream I had. I saw Declan standing before me and was overwhelmed."

"But it wasn't Declan. It was Carlos." She examined Mandy's eyes, trying to determine if she was okay. Her pupil dilation was normal, but the eye color seemed greener than she recalled them being. "You seem more yourself now. Do you feel okay? Should I find a doctor?"

"No, I'm alright. I was just lightheaded for a moment." She glared at the counter. "I know where Miguel is."

* * *

Jack, Kourin, and Laurel visually scanned the hall in desperation to locate Miguel. With no success, they abandoned their search, having concluded he must have left the hall. They shifted their gaze to the exit and noticed an animated Carlos near the bar signaling in their direction.

* * *

As if on cue, the coat check door opened and out stumbled Miguel, adjusting his shirt in the waistband of his pants. He saw Mandy and Sarah sitting across from him in the hall. "M, S, what a' you doin' sittin' out here?"

"Oh no," Mandy said. She looked at Sarah with a panicked expression. "It's happening!" She rose, still unsteady on her feet from her fainting spell.

Sarah stood when Mandy did, and luckily, she noted her unsteadiness. As she grabbed Mandy's arm, she could feel her body shaking, and she asked, "What's happening?" Sarah looked at Miguel who was walking awkwardly toward them.

"M, 're you okay?" Miguel asked as he got closer. "You don't look so good." He stood next to Mandy, himself swaying on his unsteady legs. "Can I get you a drink?"

As he said that, Chessa appeared at the coat check counter, adjusting a strap on her black dress. The object of her desire was speaking with the two blondes he had arrived with. She asked, "Miguel?"

Miguel turned to her. "These 're my friendsss, M and Sss," he slurred, and as he declared and stumbled, "Ladies, thissss is C," they could smell the rum on his breath. "We were just getting to know each other."

Mandy was uncertain what to say, recalling what had occurred in the bench dream.

Sarah said to Miguel, indicating the chairs beside them, "Maybe you should sit down."

"No, thanksss. I'm good," he replied. "I was just on my way to get C and me another drink."

"I think maybe you've had enough," said Sarah.

Mandy's eyes went wide, not wanting the same outcome to happen as her dream. She reached out and held on to Miguel's arm, saying, "Why don't you stay here and keep us company?"

Across the hall, Chessa's eyes also widened but for a very different reason than Mandy's. While Mandy sought to coax Miguel into the chair beside them, Chessa went through her door and bounded across the hall. "Hands off him, bitch. He's mine!" Within seconds, Miguel was being tugged in two different directions.

Mandy was surprised by Chessa's sudden outburst and let Miguel's arm go. She stated in what she hoped was a calm voice, "I'm not trying to take him from you."

Sarah was now behind Miguel, flanked by Mandy and Chessa. Miguel swayed, so she extended her arms to make certain he didn't fall back onto her.

Chessa observed Sarah reaching out to Miguel and presumed the blue-eyed blonde intended to embrace him. She guided Miguel, unsteady on his feet as he was, away from the two women. "Come on, Miguel. We're leaving." She led him farther away.

Mandy closed the few steps they had made and grabbed Miguel's hand. "No, Miguel. Don't go!" She was no longer composed. "Please, I need you to stay!"

Sarah was a step behind Mandy.

Chessa perceived the two ladies were trying to keep Miguel away from her. She screamed at the green-eyed blonde, "Stop! He's mine!" The purple-haired girl yanked on Miguel's hand, pulling him unexpectedly away from Mandy's grasp. They headed to the glass exit door to the right of the revolving door.

Mandy was taken off balance when Chessa pulled Miguel away from her. She stumbled, twisting her ankle, and fell to the floor. Sarah tumbled forward as well, attempting to hold Mandy up. Off balance, she too fell, landing on top of Mandy.

Chessa reached the door and asked Miguel, "Do you have your keys?"

The last Mandy saw of the man she was attempting to protect was him removing his keys from his pocket and answering, "I've got them right here, C." She lost sight of them as they exited through the door.

* * *

Jack, Laurel, and Kourin raced up the hallway, with Carlos and Ubu close behind. At the end of the hall, they found Sarah helping Mandy to sit in a chair near the restrooms. As they arrived, Laurel asked, "What happened? Did you find Miguel?"

Mandy looked up. They could tell from the tears streaming down her face what the answer was.

6
PARTY AFTERMATH

Jack sprinted to the exit door with Laurel a few steps behind. Ubu naturally followed, not knowing what danger lay ahead. Jack bolted out onto the walkway, hoping Miguel would be there.

Laurel paused at the door opening when she saw her uncle scanning the parking lot. She shouted to him, "He's parked over on the left near the lot entrance." Jack ran in that direction, well ahead of Laurel and Ubu behind him.

Kourin waited by the entrance, checking the other direction in case Miguel went that way. When she scanned back to her left, she saw Jack by the lot entrance, peering up and down the street. The slump in his shoulders confirmed what they all already knew. Miguel's truck was gone.

Jack continued to survey the parking lot as he walked back toward Kourin, hoping to spot an overlooked Ford. His niece and her dog walked with him. Upon reaching Kourin, all knew they were unsuccessful in preventing Mandy's vision.

"We failed, Uncle Jack. We knew what was going to happen, and it happened anyway." Laurel looked down at Ubu. "Maybe destiny cannot be changed." She wasn't thinking about Miguel.

Jack said, "We don't know that the outcome is still going to be the same." He glanced at Kourin who had a concerned expression. "Maybe they just drove down the street a couple of blocks and went to her place or something."

With nothing they could do about Miguel leaving, Kourin said, "Let's check on Mandy." She led the way through the door, with the others following.

They found her still on the chair, her shoulders shaking with distress. Sarah remained by her side, attempting to console her. Mandy's head hung low, and she was weeping uncontrollably.

As Kourin approached, Sarah shifted her attention away from her distraught new friend. With concern clearly visible on her face, she said, "We tried to stop him."

Laurel stayed a few feet away so as not to crowd Mandy, but Ubu trotted on to sit next to her. He nudged her leg with his head. When Sister didn't react, he repeated his prodding with more force.

Mandy, with eyes bloodshot from crying, looked up enough to see Ubu at her side. The black dog placed his entire head onto her lap. His soulful brown eyes made contact with hers. She instinctively placed one hand between his ears and pet him, avoiding the injured area. Her sobbing subsided.

Carlos came out of the restroom with tissues, handing them to Mandy. She wiped away the tears and dried her nose. Crushing the tissues in her palm with her other hand, she resumed patting Ubu.

Laurel broke the awkward silence. "Uncle Jack, Carlos." She glanced at Kourin without saying her name and continued, "Why don't you go back to the hall? I'll stay here with Mandy and Sarah for a bit."

Jack looked at Kourin, and she gave him a slight nod. He said, "Sure. We'll not be far away if you need us."

Carlos observed Mandy, wanting to help her, but he knew he wasn't what she needed right now. With a glance toward Jack and Kourin, he excused himself and headed down the hall.

The two ladies remained to care for Mandy. Ubu's head stayed on her lap.

Mandy's mood improved after several minutes of stroking Ubu's hair between his ears. When Laurel saw her more like her normal self, she asked if she wanted to rejoin the others at the party. She was pretty certain what the answer would be.

Mandy said in a low voice, "I'm not in the mood for a party." She continued lightly petting Ubu. "I just want to go home."

"No prob," Laurel said. "I'll take you."

"I don't want to ruin your night. I'll call for a ride."

"Nonsense. We came together; we leave together."

Sarah nodded, not saying a word.

Laurel eyed the abandoned coat check desk and said, "But we need to get our coats." She found the door was not closed all the way and retrieved their coats.

As the trio plus one dog stepped onto the walkway outside, Laurel told the others she needed a moment to text Jack they were leaving so they didn't wonder where they had disappeared to. Laurel pulled her cell phone out of her coat pocket and sent a text.

When Laurel used her cell phone, Mandy realized she had hers in her coat pocket as well. She retrieved it and saw she had two messages.

Mom: *You didn't call me back after the cat incident. Is everything ok? Have a good time at the party.*

Mandy's fingers hovered over the keyboard, but then she chose to see what the second message said.

Emry: *Mission accomplished as you requested.*

Laurel and Sarah had started toward the Jeep when they realized Mandy wasn't walking with them. Sarah asked, "Mandy, everything okay?"

Mandy looked up from her phone, a big smile on her face. "It's better than okay."

* * *

Jack and Kourin returned to their table as Carlos drifted off on his own after entering the hall. Harry and Beth were engaged in an intimate conversation and placed some separation between themselves when they were no longer alone. Kourin glanced at Jack but kept her comments to herself. Their relationship appeared to be more familiar than just coworkers. Jack had no reaction and seemed oblivious to what was so apparent to her.

Beth asked, upon seeing their somber expressions, "Everything okay?"

Kourin answered, "No, not really." She looked at Jack and continued when he didn't pick up the conversation. "Miguel just left with Chessa."

Harry and Beth looked at each other, not saying a word.

Jack said, "Mandy tried to stop them, but . . ." His cell phone vibrated in his pocket. "Excuse me." He took the phone out, welcoming the distraction from having to talk about what had just occurred.

Laurel: *we're heading out mandy wants to go home*

Jack told the table Mandy and Laurel were heading home. As he was putting away his phone, it buzzed again.

Laurel: *mandy had a backup plan miguel should be ok. fill you in once we're sure. might not be til morning*

Jack was completely surprised.

Harry, who had been observing him, asked, "What is it?"

"I'm not entirely sure, but Laurel says Mandy had a backup plan and Miguel should be okay. They'll let us know when they know for certain, but it may not be until tomorrow."

"That's great news!" said Kourin.

"But what the hell does backup plan mean?" Harry asked.

Jack said, "I have no idea, but let's hope whatever it is, it worked."

* * *

Miguel drove his Ford toward his home in Bedford. Chessa had told him her mother would be home, so going to her place wasn't an option. On the way, he stopped at a packie to pick up a bottle of rum and a two-liter Coke.

When he returned to the truck, the overhead lighting highlighted the deep purple of Chessa's hair and made her dark purple eyeshadow sparkle. He felt exhilaration when she half smiled at him.

He placed the bag holding the two bottles onto the floor at her feet. When his hand came up, he caressed the inner side of her left thigh at the edge of her dress.

Chessa intercepted his hand before it went higher and under her short dress. "Hold your horses there, big guy. We've got all night." She gently lifted his hand off her thigh but held on to it.

Miguel gazed into her eyes and kissed her. He knew he was drunk, but he also felt an intoxication from the girl sitting next to him. As his lips left hers, the cab was shrouded in darkness as the timer on the overhead light expired.

Normally, about now on past dates, he would say something witty, perhaps even charming. Instead, a moment of lucidity came to him through the fogginess of the alcohol he had consumed. He thought, *She's amazing, the girl you've been searching for.* He gently kissed her on her cheek and moved into position to drive. As he started the truck, he glanced her way and thought, *Don't fuck this up.*

He drove through the night, keeping the truck between the yellow and white lines. However, his mind was swirling in thought of the beautiful girl sitting next to him. As he came to the intersection of Donald Street and Old Bedford Road, he was thinking about the kiss they had just shared. He drove straight through the stop sign he forgot was there.

Several minutes later and a few miles down the road, he pulled into his apartment complex driveway and found his parking spot. He retrieved the bag from the passenger side floor as Chessa opened her door and exited the truck, her purple hair streaks once again standing out in the light. Miguel felt a spark of electricity as she turned to him, their eyes meeting and her lips curving into a full smile. He thought, *I'm the luckiest man alive.*

* * *

Jack and Kourin danced three more times before deciding to call it an evening. They hadn't heard from Laurel, so they hoped everything was alright. Jack texted Miguel and asked him to let him know when he made it home safely. No reply was returned then or the rest of the evening.

Harry never moved from the initial spot he had sat in because of his injured knee. Beth stayed with him the entire time.

Kourin noticed them speaking closely, with their heads just inches apart several times, but whenever she and Jack returned to the table, they separated. Through the evening, Kourin kept one eye on Harry. She was still apprehensive about the way he had grabbed her and the memories it recalled. She maintained her distance from him.

As she watched Beth and Harry interact, she glimpsed a more gentle side of Harry that he quickly concealed when it appeared. She thought, *There's something there, but why are they trying so hard to hide it?*

Several yards away from Kourin, a man with steel-blue eyes watched her dancing, laughing, and enjoying herself with Jack. Anders kept his distance, but his desire didn't fade. In reality, it swelled with each sparkling smile she donned, highlighting her bewitching face. He craved holding her intimately for another dance. That moment never came. His blue eyes stalked her until all at the table rose, located John several tables over, spoke to him briefly, and exited the hall.

The evening had not progressed the way he had hoped. He resolved to rectify that in the days ahead as he downed the last of his Macallan. The burning sensation in his throat did little to quell the thirst he possessed for Kourin.

7

ADAM MCAFFREY

Mandy awoke to the sound of her shower running. She glanced at the nightstand clock: five thirty-three. It took her a moment to recollect who was in her shower—Sarah. Her new friend had stayed the night after attending the party. She pushed the memory of the party aside, not wanting to relive the evening and all that went awry.

Her white tank tee-shirt had ridden up to her breasts as she tossed and turned all night, and her pink shorts were in similar disarray, giving her an uncomfortable wedgie.

With a quick adjustment to her sleepwear, she hurried into her living room and clicked the TV on. She pressed the back arrow four times to zoom to the top of the five o'clock hour. She hit Play. Two news anchors appeared on the screen after a fast forward through a car insurance commercial. She pressed fast forward once on the remote and scrutinized the screen as the images passed by. When she saw the object of her search, she hit the Play button.

* * *

Sarah toweled herself dry after her hot shower. She wrapped the damp towel around her hair and put on the matching taupe panties and bra. She looked at herself in the mirror, surprised at not seeing bags under her eyes. It had been a late night comforting her new friend after initially being distraught about failing to keep Miguel safe at the party. After arriving at her home, Mandy was filled with a strange sense of optimism that he would be alright.

Sarah smiled at her mirror reflection, thinking, *That girl certainly is the ultimate optimist. Gotta give her that.*

Mandy had been sound asleep when she had crept past her to the shower. She exited the bathroom, trying to be as silent as possible so as not to wake Mandy, and was surprised to find the bed empty.

A male voice was emanating from the living room. Sarah quickly realized the TV was on and moved to the doorway that separated the rooms. Mandy was faced away from her with the remote in her hand, watching the news.

A man with impeccably coiffed coal-black hair stood with a microphone in the middle of the screen. He was reporting on a house fire. In the background, over his right shoulder, were two exhausted fire fighters walking away from a home with charred siding and second-story windows clearly burned to the roofline. A white minivan was parked in the driveway to the left of the burned building. The banner at the bottom of the screen read "Bedford House Fire."

The reporter said, "The family's dog was the hero of the night. Its sharp bark heard at 2:00 a.m., alerting the family of four of the danger. A neighbor who lives next door said they had adopted the dog last year at a local rescue. The fire chief told me a short time ago they were fortunate to have had the warning from Alfredo, as the house did not have a functioning smoke alarm. He stated that the evidence suggested the fire began on the first floor. Had the dog not warned them, this may have had a very different ending. Fire fighters remain on the scene to put out hot spots. The house may be a total loss. This is Adam McAffrey, WMUR News, live in Bedford. Back to you in the studio, Bob."

The TV went black and silent. Mandy placed the remote on the coffee table with a soft thud, then slowly spun around. Tears were streaming down her face.

At first, Sarah thought something was wrong and closed the few steps between them. She gave her a hug. Mandy placed her hands on her own naked backside. They were ice cold.

Mandy let her friend give her a hug. The embrace was warm in contrast to the sudden chill she was experiencing in her extremities. She said, "He's alright."

"Who is, Mandy?"

She repeated, releasing herself from Sarah's hug, "He's alright! Miguel! He's okay."

"How do you know for sure?"

"The report on the news. The reporter was at a house fire! He wasn't covering a car crash. Isn't that great?" Mandy saw the look on Sarah's face. "Oh, sorry, but you know what I mean. Sarah, he's okay! My plan worked."

The evening before, as the trio of ladies plus one dog arrived at Mandy's home, she filled them in on her plan to save Miguel. If she wasn't able to prevent Miguel from leaving the party, her idea was to prevent the other vehicle from colliding with him. The idea came from Tennessee Williams' quote on the back of Sarah's phone: "Time is the longest distance between two places."

From her vision, she remembered the reporter stating the family was returning from food shopping a few miles from the crash scene. A Google search revealed only one grocery store that fit the description of being a few miles in the right direction. On her way home from work, she went to the store and met with the store manager, Emry. She arranged for him to award a five-hundred-dollar gift card to the family of four that would shop there within a certain time frame and fit the description she provided. However, to win it, they had to use it right then. This would increase the time on their end and make them return home later, disrupting the timeline by not being at the doomed intersection when Miguel was.

Mandy had explained she wasn't certain it would work for a few reasons. Miguel could be delayed, throwing her stall tactic in disarray. The store might not do what she had asked them to do. She wasn't even 100 percent sure the gift card would go to the correct people.

The text she had received while at the party was from Emry, confirming he had completed her request and awarded a family the five hundred dollars in food.

She had done all she could.

While Mandy was in the bathroom after relating her plan, Laurel and Sarah agreed it was a long shot. Sarah said she would stay with Mandy in the event her plan did not work, meaning Miguel had his accident. She had a flight out in the morning, but she would try to comfort Mandy, as she had done for her. Laurel went home with Ubu soon after, hoping for the best.

As Sarah stood nearly naked, hugging her new friend and telling her she should still confirm Miguel was okay, her own phone rang on the table where she had placed it the night before. She answered it, and after a lengthy discussion, she hit the End button rather forcefully with her finger.

Mandy perceived sadness from her and asked, "Is everything alright?"

"The man I'm filling in for is still sick, so now I have to do the afternoon return trip back here since we're low on staff." She placed the phone back down on the table, a little more forcibly than she had intended. "I better get dressed, and then I have to call my husband. Hopefully, he'll take it well. We were supposed to be going out to a nice dinner tonight."

"I'm sure he'll understand, and you're more than welcome to crash here."

"Oh, I couldn't impose. You've already been so kind and helpful." As Sarah was saying this, Autumn came into the room and brushed up against her bare legs.

Mandy smiled as her cat bumped and caressed her friend's legs, wrapping her tail around an ankle as she strutted around her. "You have to come back. You've made a new friend."

8

ACT OF CONTRITION

The morning burst of sunshine. Kourin's car was filled with the sweet fragrances of late spring, the fresh growth of trees and flowers creating an intoxicating aroma. New life had begun after the dead of winter. With a new love on her mind, Kourin's favorite time of year had blossomed.

Carlos was on duty as usual at the airport employee parking lot. As she walked toward him, he said, "I've called the tram for you, Kourin. He should be here shortly."

"Thank you, Carlos." She noted he hadn't made his usual morning banal witticism. Fortunately, she did not have to make small talk as several more vehicles pulled into the lot, keeping Carlos busy. Before long, Diric arrived with the tram to transport them the short distance to the employee entrance.

Once in the terminal, she noticed she could not smell the outside world. The ventilation system must be filtering the pollens. With the air conditioning on her mind, she was reminded that Phil was still in the hospital. She made a mental note to call Lindsay later in the morning to check on her husband.

Kourin stopped at the Coffee Bean and ordered her usual hot black tea with Eric. She marveled at how white and bright his teeth were. One of these days, she was going to ask him how he maintained them. As she rotated to depart after paying, with her mind wondering about bright white teeth, she bumped right into Harry.

Almost dropping her tea, which fortunately was covered, she recovered from her shock of being inches away from the man that had frightened the crap out of her two days before. She said, "Oh my, I'm so sorry." Kourin backed up a step and moved to walk around him.

Harry said, "Um, my fault entirely." He was about to reach out for her arm, but he could feel the heat radiating off of her body and stopped himself. "Kourin, do you have a moment?"

Kourin observed Harry stretch out toward her and instinctively shied away. She heard his question and froze, though not from fear. After spending time with him and Beth the previous night, as well as having Jack accompany her, she had become more comfortable around him.

She peeked at the clock prominently displayed on the wall and saw she had a few minutes to spare. She said, "Sure, Harry." There was an empty table just steps from where they stood. "Shall we?"

Kourin sat first. Harry seated himself opposite her, facing the rear of the store. Normally, he would not want this seat, but he made an exception this time. He could endure a few minutes of uneasiness to say what needed to be said.

Kourin waited for Harry to speak. She felt her insides warming from the anxiety of what Harry might say or possibly do. He had terrified her when he grabbed her arm two days earlier, but it was not because she feared the older man would indeed hurt her. It had triggered agonizing memories she had striven to bury, memories that eighteen years of therapy had worked to reframe so she could cope with her traumatic experience. The eventual comprehension of delivering a healthy baby girl into the world was the point of light she had fixated on for the last thirty plus years, keeping her on track and in control of her life. She kept placing one foot in front of the other every minute of every day with the hope her daughter had a childhood that she never had.

She sat silently, allowing Harry to find the words he wanted to say. This gave her time to reflect on how he had conducted himself at the party. He was subdued and not the same person he had been just the day before. She thought

Jack had spoken to him, but by the end of the evening, she realized it was Beth that had tempered him.

Harry said, "Kourin, I'm not sure how to put this, so I'm just going to say it." He glanced at her and then at his hands clasped on the table. "I want to apologize for my actions the other day. I don't know what came over me."

"Harry, I appreciate you apologizing, but there's no need." She paused for a moment, thinking how much she should say and a little apprehensive about uttering something that might set him off again. She was well aware of triggers from personal experience and tread lightly. "We've all been through a lot."

"That's no excuse for treating someone poorly." He looked up from his workingman's hands to the back of the café, seeing a few people enjoying their coffee. One was eating a muffin. Another young girl was tapping away on her smart phone. He came back to Kourin's face. "I can't explain what happened, but I just want you to know I . . ." he paused. "I know you had nothing to do with Jack and Kim. In fact, I'm happy to see he has found someone to be with."

"Harry, I'm happy to hear you say that." Kourin saw his eyes were normal and showed no sign of the malice they had Wednesday or even yesterday morning when she had picked up her tea. "Jack's a good man. I hope to see more of him in the future."

"Well, I hope things work out for the two of you. I should let you get to your shop." He moved to get up from the chair.

She reached out and touched the top of his hand. He froze in mid-stand. "Harry, if you need to talk, Jack, Laurel, and Mandy are all here for you, and I'm here as well."

At first Harry didn't respond. For several seconds, he did not even move. He pulled his hand from under Kourin's and said, "I appreciate that, but there are some things I need to do on my own." As Harry said that, he rose and gave Kourin one last glance. Without another word, he turned and walked out of the café.

Kourin watched Harry depart. He had spoken in a matter-of-fact manner. There was no malevolence in his voice, no threat of any kind. She knew Beth must have told Harry to apologize. Maybe she even went beyond that in making him understand Jack needed someone as well. Kourin still felt there was something more, though. Harry still wasn't a whole man. The death of a wife and child would do that.

* * *

Laurel completed the morning routine for her business and joined Eric at the counter as the rush would soon be upon them. Additional personnel would arrive shortly.

The evening before, she told Mandy to attend the meeting with John if she wanted, but there was sufficient staff scheduled to handle the day. Laurel felt Mandy should stay far away from the bench because of the trauma she went through. Her friend had been at her side many times over the years. This time, she needed to return the favor.

Laurel knew she herself would have insomnia, causing her to have an early start as usual. She was determined to get some answers from John. If she could go back to that fateful night, she could change the outcome and save her Army unit. Breck would be alive today.

As she arrived at the counter, she gave Ubu a smile. He had been snoozing in his spot behind the counter, content that Mom was safe in the back room. This morning he had no danger signals when at home, the drive in, or the last hour they were here. With a slight tail wag, he acknowledged Mom and lay his head back down to continue dreaming about chasing squirrels.

Laurel was amazed to see Kourin sitting with Harry at the first table. In between customers, she watched as they seemed to be in a serious conversation. She saw Harry rise, and Kourin reach out to him. The conversation ended thereafter.

Once there were no more customers at the counter, Laurel circled around to the front of Kourin's table and asked, "Are you okay?"

Kourin looked up to see Laurel standing where Harry had been several minutes before. Lost in her thoughts about Harry's words, she hadn't noticed Laurel come up. "Oh, hi, Laurel. Yes, I'm fine, I think." She looked out of the entrance in the direction that Harry had exited. "I just had the most interesting conversation with Harry."

"I saw him. He didn't threaten you again, did he?"

"Quite the opposite, actually. Please sit down."

Laurel checked back toward the counter. Eric was with one customer, with no one else waiting. She sat opposite Kourin.

Kourin said, "Harry apologized for his actions the other day. He said he was sorry. Not just that, he hoped things between Jack and me work out."

Laurel replied, "That's great. So, he seems to be back to his old self?" She studied Kourin's face and didn't see the relieved expression she expected. "Is there something you're not telling me?"

"I'm not sure. I assumed Jack, or maybe you, but mostly likely Beth, had talked to him, yet I'm now uncertain of what to think."

Laurel was puzzled. "Why do you say that? I mean I didn't talk to him about you and Jack. Things got a little crazy last night, and I never got the chance. Do you think he didn't mean what he said?"

"Oh, no. I think he truly is sorry for the way he acted. And honestly, I don't blame him with all he's been through." She shuddered a little, remembering Harry's story in Laurel's office the day before. "When he left, he said there were some things he needed to do alone. I'm not sure what that means, but it was more the way he said it. Know what I mean? He had a tone in his voice."

Laurel placed her hands on top of Kourin's that had been cradling her tea. "I'm sure he has things he's trying to deal with. Whether they're from the loss of his wife or the bench, that is something he needs to resolve in his mind."

Kourin looked into Laurel's eyes as she felt her touch her hands. "I suppose you're right." Kourin heard Eric call Laurel's name. She glanced over and saw several people in line. "I think Eric needs you."

After she heard her name called, Laurel gave Kourin's hands a slight squeeze and said, "We'll get through this." She left the table to assist the next customer.

Kourin watched Laurel walk away. The words to reassure her played again in her mind. Laurel said it was something that needed to be resolved in the mind. Kourin felt her heart race, not knowing if she was talking about herself, Harry, or the hidden truth Kourin had. All had tragic issues. All had them rekindled by the bench.

9

JACK

The clock read five forty-three. Jack realized he hadn't set a wake-up alarm. When he arrived home late last night, he undressed, lay down, and was asleep immediately. Thursday had worn him out completely.

Before rising, he thought about the previous night worrying about Miguel. There was the strange conversation with John. They lost Miguel. Mandy had a breakdown and a recovery. He danced with Kourin in his arms.

He checked his phone on the nightstand: no messages. He wasn't surprised he had not received an answer from Miguel, but it would have been an immense relief if he had.

Jack considered texting Kourin, but he realized it may be too early. He still had time before he had to be at the terminal for the soft opening. He turned on the TV while he went to the bathroom to get ready for the morning.

As the TV news changed from one topic to another, the name 'Benchmark' was mentioned. He watched the brief story about the terminal opening today. The newscaster said they would be live from the terminal later in the broadcast. Jack hadn't given the opening day much thought other than he had his target date to have the project completed, which was today. Since cameras would be at the terminal, he wore his good chinos and blue dress shirt. He contemplated wearing a tie, deciding against it. That wasn't who he was.

The story following the terminal opening was about a house fire. He watched the story to the end and was glad everyone made it out okay. He turned off the TV and went to the kitchen to start his day with a coffee and toast before heading to the terminal.

Despite his apprehension about Miguel and the bench, he had a spring in his step. The memory of having danced the night away with a beautiful woman will do that to a man.

***

Mandy showered and dressed. When she entered the living room, Sarah was sitting on the couch dressed in her pilot uniform having a coffee. She was watching the news on TV. The Benchmark story was playing. Mandy listened to it while she made herself a coffee. She joined Sarah on the couch and was about to ask her a question when the fire story came on again.

The story was similar to the first time she had heard it. It was still live with McAffrey reporting. This time, however, she noticed something she hadn't before. When the story ended, she grabbed the remote and hit the Back button to replay the last minute. She hit the Pause button when she saw what she had been searching for. A white minivan was parked in the driveway next to the burnt home. She turned toward Sarah. The remote, forgotten in her hand, fell to the floor.

Sarah watched Mandy replay what they had just watched and pause the image of the reporter commenting about the dog. The burnt home was visible in the background. She heard the remote drop, causing her to look at her friend. Mandy had a horrified expression, her eyes wide with shock. Sarah asked, "What is it? What's wrong?"

At first Mandy couldn't find the words. After several seconds, she said, "The minivan. The white minivan."

Sarah looked at the TV. "I see it. What's special about the van?"

"I didn't realize it before. Sarah, this is awful!"

"Mandy, what's up with the van?"

In a whisper, she answered, "That's the minivan I saw in my vision!"

* * *

Jack pulled into the employee parking lot. Carlos let him in, not questioning that technically he wasn't an employee. He asked the guard if he had a good time at the party. He said he did, but Jack got the impression it was a robotic answer. When Carlos asked if he wanted a tram ride, he told him no. He'd walk the short distance. It was a pleasant morning, and he had time to kill. It also gave him time to think about the bench and John.

* * *

Kourin remained seated at the Coffee Bean, lost in thought. She analyzed the outside of her tea. The words Harry had said, along with Laurel's comments, eddied in her mind. She thought of the vision she had two days past of the hospital and hearing her baby cry for the first time in over thirty years, the dark despair that had set in for many months after that, the time she spent with the therapist for many years more. Through all these thoughts, she kept coming back to the same question: *Why now? Why am I reliving those dark days all over again, for what purpose?*

While Kourin literally contemplated life, she had not noticed the man who spotted her sitting alone as he entered the café. The man purchased his coffee with a debit card. Not leaving a tip or a donation to Laurel's dog rescue, he walked over to Kourin's table, stopping where just a short time ago Laurel had stood. While she continued to scrutinize her tea, he said to her, "Good morning, Kourin."

Kourin heard a male voice beside her. Lost in thought, as with Laurel earlier, she hadn't noticed him beside her table. She looked up into piercing blue eyes.

Anders added, "I hope I'm not interrupting you."

It took her a moment to collect herself, having been a million miles away. "No, I'm just having my tea." She didn't offer the empty seat to him.

"May I join you?"

"I was just leaving to open my shop." She glanced at the clock on the wall and had a few minutes before she needed to go, but Anders didn't know that.

"I'll just take a moment of your time," he said, sitting opposite her.

Her first thought was, *Why don't you leave me alone?* Her second thought was, *I guess I should be civil for now.* She said, "You're here early."

"Well, truth be known, I was hoping to bump into you before the craziness of the day started." He smiled, flashing teeth that would rival Eric's smile. "I enjoyed our dance last night. I'm sorry we weren't able to have another." He let that statement hang without further comment.

"I'm sorry, but something came up with a friend and the night just got away from me. Before we knew it, it was time to leave."

"Understandable," he said, not revealing that he knew how Kourin had spent the evening. He had watched her every dance and every smile from afar. "Sometimes those corporate events can be overwhelming." He paused, but Kourin did not make an additional comment, so he continued with a wide smile. "And that's why I'd like to ask you, if you're free tonight, to a proper dinner and dancing if you'd like?"

* * *

Jack sauntered toward the new terminal, taking a moment to admire the work his crew had accomplished. From the outside, the terminal appeared similar to every other airport, albeit it was shiny and new. He saw two Benchmark planes parked along the side gates. A second plane must have arrived late last night or very early this morning. They were identical in their red, white, and blue coloring.

As he observed them, he wondered, *Which one did Sarah have her disturbance with*? He thought about the bench. *It must have been a trick of the light. She never even sat on the bench. But how do I explain the taste of strawberry daiquiri on my lips? I wasn't sitting on or even near the bench then, either. That must have been my imagination. But Kim felt so real. Her skin was warm against mine, the feel of her lips on mine, the softness of her ass cheeks in my hands as she . . .*

Jack stopped walking. *I need to stop thinking about this!* The face of Kourin came to him with her bright smile as he held her close while dancing. He held on to that image as he went through security and until he arrived at the Coffee Bean. Upon entering, he saw Kourin sitting at the first table across from a well-dressed man with blond hair. He heard him ask, "If you're free tonight, to a proper dinner and dancing if you'd like?" He was asking her out on a date!

* * *

Kourin was surprised by Anders' question and looked away from him, back to her tea. She didn't want to look into his eyes. She paused for several moments, not sure how to answer. Not wanting to be too abrupt with him, she needed to make it clear. She was with Jack now. Whatever Anders thought they had was in the past. She thought, *And it is not coming back.*

"I appreciate the offer, Anders," Kourin paused, trying to find the right words to dissuade him once and for all. It took her several seconds while he sat in anticipation. She continued, "But it's going to be a long day, and I'm not sure I'll be in any mood for dancing tonight. I'm sure it'll be an early evening for me."

Anders was disappointed by her answer after he at first thought she was going to say yes, but he wasn't ready to give up just yet. "That's a reasonable assumption. At six thirty in the morning, it's difficult to tell what you'll feel like at the end of the day." He smiled, flashing his pearly white teeth, and said, "I'll check back in with you later on."

Kourin glanced at the clock when he said the time. "I'm sorry, but I have to get my store open." She rose and picked up her cup. Anders remained where he was watching her. "All my staff will be arriving."

As she walked away from the table, he said, "No problem. I'll see you later."

* * *

Jack was mystified seeing Kourin having coffee with another man after they had spent a beautiful evening together. At least, he thought it had been. Maybe he had misjudged her feelings toward him.

He heard her reply, "I appreciate the offer, Anders." He turned around, a feeling of confusion and dismay washing over him as he left the café. His mind had already been struggling to make sense of the bench and what had befallen several people. Kim's smile and her wearing the red bikini appeared in his mind. He hurriedly replaced that with Kourin's smiling face from the night before. He knew he didn't want to go down the Kim rabbit hole again.

He found himself in the center of the garden with the bench feet away from him. He couldn't recall even walking up the path. *Why am I here?* he thought. *Why was Kourin having coffee with another man? Did I do something last night to offend her?*

Jack's mind was befuddled as he replayed the evening before, after the events with Miguel and Mandy. They had returned to the table and filled in Harry and Beth with what occurred. After discussing it for several minutes and futilely arriving at no plausible solutions, he sent Miguel a text message and eventually a phone call that went to voice mail. They arrived at no solutions to saving Miguel from himself.

After feeling failure, their spirits had been lifted when they received the texts from Laurel. Mandy had proactively done something that would alter Miguel's fate. All felt better, but all were uneasy about it as well.

Jack danced with Kourin many times through the next hour, relieving the tension they had felt earlier. Each time they returned to the table, Harry and Beth had been in close contact talking. Jack figured it was because the music was playing so loud. However, on two of the occasions, Beth had an odd expression Jack couldn't quite figure out. Harry seemed to be the same as he always had been, so he just let it go, presuming she was concerned about him with all that had occurred in recent days.

Jack looked around the garden and found he was now sitting on the bench. The rising sun was shining down at an angle into the garden and had not yet reached the center bench area. He did not recall walking to the bench, having been preoccupied thinking about Kourin and Anders.

Anders—Jack recognized him from the Benchmark entourage the day before. He hadn't spoken and had been at the back of the group for most of the walk-through until they came upon Kourin closing her store.

Jack recalled when John had told his entourage to go to the hotel to check in, one person was the last to turn and leave: Anders. There was no mistake in Jack's mind. He wasn't someone you could easily overlook. Anders stood taller than most of the others in the group. He had blond hair and wore a suit that was tailored to his athletic build. At the time, Jack had been focused on John and Peri. Now he recalled seeing Anders move to stand at the front of the group when John was speaking with Kourin.

Jack thought about Anders asking Kourin out and her reply, "*I appreciate the offer.*" He repeated it in his mind several times. *She appreciated the offer! She wants to go out with him?*

Jack replayed in his mind when they left the hall the night before. After retrieving Kourin's shawl from someone other than Chessa who was now covering the coat check room, he helped her into his truck, as he had done earlier. She smiled her dazzling smile at him as he closed her door for her. He then drove her home. *How could she now want to be with him? She invited me in, but again I declined because of the early morning we both had upcoming. Was she mad I didn't come in? Did I just fuck this up?*

* * *

Kourin exited the café, crossing the walkway to her store. Mary had already opened the gate and turned on the lights. She stood behind the counter and greeted Kourin. "Good morning. How are you today?"

"I'm well, Mary. Sorry I'm a bit late. I got tied up across the way. I'm sorry you weren't able to make it to the party last night."

"No prob. With the kids, it just wasn't in the cards."

"Understandable. Well, I'm going to put my stuff down in the back and be right up," said Kourin as she continued to the office. Her mind was thinking of what Anders had just asked her. *I thought I had made it clear to him weeks ago that we, us, he and I would have nothing more than a business relationship. I'm with Jack now. He's everything I ever desired: charming, thoughtful, handsome. So why do I feel like I just cheated on him?*

* * *

Anders watched Kourin exit the café. He was disappointed she hadn't readily said yes to his invitation. It was rare when he asked a woman out that she declined. In fact, he couldn't remember a recent memory when it had happened.

Kourin playing hard to get only increased his desire for her. It didn't matter several weeks ago, when assisting her with the store opening, she had rebuffed his advances. He had spent most of the daytime hours working side by side with her. At every opportunity, he complimented her and was as charming as ever. Every evening, he took her to dinner on Benchmark's dime. He had come so close, only to have her shut him out when he had to return to the home office.

He took a sip of his coffee and looked down the café at the other customers, enjoying their breakfast and coffee. Several women were sitting alone. He noticed at least two of them glancing his way. He knew he still had it. If he wanted to, he could find another date for tonight. Yet, he couldn't get Kourin off his mind. She continued to be a challenge. The pursuit made this even more exhilarating. The thrill of the chase would make holding her in his arms that much sweeter. Whatever it would take . . .

* * *

The bench felt comfortable under Jack. He argued with himself that last night he should have gone inside Kourin's home. Instead, he was, once again, being a gentleman and had told himself he didn't want to ruin this relationship by rushing it. *Did I screw this up by playing it too safe? I wanted the night to continue with her. But I also knew we had just been through hell with Miguel, so it wasn't a normal night by any stretch of the imagination. Maybe I should have gone in for at least one drink?*

Jack scanned the garden. He thought he had heard rustling in the leaves, but he saw nothing other than the sun shining down several yards away. *If I had gone in for that drink, more than likely I wouldn't have left. I think we both knew that. Maybe that's where I screwed up?*

* * *

Kourin should have been focused on her shop's opening day. Instead, her thoughts were of Jack. She knew he would stop in before Benchmark's soft opening event and looked forward to seeing him. She found herself craving his company, yearning to be near him, even if only for a few moments. The thought to text him occurred to her. She decided against it. This early in their relationship, she didn't know where their boundaries were. She thought, *Better to let him set some parameters for now.* She didn't want to smother him.

Her thoughts turned to the previous night. After hearing Miguel would be okay, both agreed to set aside any further discussion of the bench and just enjoy the party. They did. For a couple of hours, she savored the feel of Jack's arms around her as they swayed to the music. They had pleasant conversations in between dancing that had nothing to do with work, the terminal, or the bench. Moments at the table with Harry and Beth were, by anyone's standards, normal. There were no additional conversations with John or Vasud who had disappeared into the crowd. Thankfully, there was no second dance with Anders, and, as she gave it a thought, she did not see him for the rest of the evening. The night ended by holding Jack close to a slow romantic song she wished would never end.

This brought her to the goodnight kiss. When they arrived at her home, he helped her out of the truck. She could have completed it on her own, but still in her heels and a little tipsy from the drinks, she welcomed his gallantry. Hand in hand, they walked to her door. Once there, holding her in his arms, he gave her a passionate kiss, making her head swim.

When their lips separated, she invited him in. The only thing she wanted at that moment was to go on forever kissing him. In her state of mind, she would have surrendered to him if he desired.

Instead, he declined. At first, she was disappointed and momentarily thought she had done something to put him off. Two heartbeats later, she realized it was just Jack being Jack. On the drive home, both had said they had an exhausting day. She admitted to being surprised she hadn't collapsed from fatigue.

Jack whispered in her ear he had the next few days off after the soft opening and looked forward to spending time with her if she was up for it. She answered with an amorous kiss of her own.

Alone in her office, a smile came to her lips. She realized she loved Jack even more this morning than she had yesterday. He was everything she ever envisioned in a man. Astonishingly, he didn't even recognize how remarkable he truly was.

* * *

Jack thought about Kourin and her entrancing smile. As the minutes ticked by, he thought of Miguel and Mandy. He hoped both were alright. He checked his phone. Miguel had not responded to his texts or his voicemail. He would try calling him later. Mandy, he would see shortly at the meeting. He thought about Laurel. She had been through even more than he had. He hadn't noticed her at the café, but then again, he hadn't looked beyond Kourin's table.

Laurel seemed alright last night. All things considered. I guess, with all of us focused on Miguel, we had set aside the other issues with the bench. This bench. Jack looked down at the wood he sat upon. *What was it Laurel had said early in the evening?* Jack put his brain to work, trying to remember the comment his niece had made. It came to him. *When Harry was asking what the bench wanted from them, Laurel said she thought they were looking at it the wrong way. Before she could expand on her thought Miguel was back at the table and one thing led to another. What has she got on her mind? Earlier, she asked if she could bring something into a bench encounter. What is she hoping to accomplish? And what would the effect be if she changed something in the past?*

As Jack ran all these thoughts through his mind, repeating them several times, he didn't notice the increased rustling in the surrounding plants. The sun still shone down on the other side of the courtyard. As he focused on the light shafts hitting the leaves, his eyelids drooped and closed.

> Jack felt a change in the air. He opened his eyes upon Laurel's office, standing with his back against a wall. He saw her several feet away next to her desk. Beside her was Ubu. The dog was staring right at him. Beyond both of them stood someone Jack could not see fully behind Laurel. He watched as this person knelt down to pat Ubu. It was . . . him!
>
> The scene was suddenly familiar. This was yesterday morning when he visited Laurel, checking on her after her encounter with the bench. He watched himself walk over to where he stood. "Thursday" Jack scrutinized the area where he was standing. He was not seeing himself returning his gaze.
>
> Laurel asked "Thursday" Jack what he was doing.
>
> He responded Ubu was staring here, and perhaps there was a mouse. She jumped up and rushed over. She reached out her hand, positioning it into "Friday" Jack's stomach. The sight of his niece with her hand in his stomach from his angle was shocking.
>
> Laurel told "Thursday" Jack the area was ice cold, so he jabbed his hand into "Friday" Jack's stomach, confirming the coldness. He then moved his hand to the right and out of his stomach. The hand went back through "Friday" Jack as if cutting him in half and out the other side. "Thursday" Jack said the coldness was just where "Friday" Jack was standing.
>
> His niece plunged her hand back into "Friday" Jack and moved it right and left. She then went up and through his head. The arm then came back down through his head and down his body. When she got close

to "Friday" Jack's manhood, he closed his eyes tightly and flinched, not wanting his niece anywhere near his junk.

Jack felt a shift in the air and opened his eyes to find himself sitting on the bench as he had been earlier. He shivered, although not from the cold. He just experienced, by far, the weirdest occurrence of his life! What he and his niece had thought was a mouse not twenty-four hours before was, in fact, himself. Jack thought, *What the fuck just happened?*

10
SMITTEN

Kourin observed Mary and Tammy each assist a customer with a purchase. They offered extraordinary customer service, the kind that lingered in the minds of customers. Even with everything that had occurred since she began this journey, it was a promising start for her first official opening day.

As she watched Tammy assist another customer, she thought about the first meeting she had with John.

She was working the cosmetic counter of a large anchor store in the mall, waiting on two women who spoke with a haughty tone. After spending several minutes with them, she noticed a man several paces back watching her. She assumed he was with the two women and thought nothing more about it. When she made eye contact with him, she said hello, and he returned the gesture.

John observed Kourin with the two customers, pleased beyond his expectations at her level of service. The two customers were, as he would describe only to his wife when they were alone, complete bitches. They were obstinate, condescending, rude, full of self-importance, and entitled. John had run out of words to further describe them to his wife, but she got the picture. Through all of this, he observed Kourin never making them feel unwelcome, and she never seemed to be put off by their boorish behavior. Quite the opposite was true. John witnessed Kourin upsell them on several items that they had not intended to purchase. She had spent thirty minutes with the two ladies and processed a substantial purchase for them. They left happy.

When Kourin saw the man did not leave with them and instead approached the counter, she profusely apologized for keeping him waiting, explaining that she thought he was with the women who just left. He introduced himself and said he was interested in purchasing something for his wife.

Kourin worked her magic, asking questions to discern his wife's tastes and interests. He answered as best he could. After several minutes, Kourin suggested several items and presented them all to him. To his utter amazement, she offered several product options he knew she owned and used routinely. There were several additional items he thought she might like and purchased them.

While Kourin rang up the sale, John confessed who he was and why he was there. He was seeking talented individuals to open stores in his under-construction terminal.

Kourin accepted his card that first day. It took him another visit before she shared her contact information with him. They talked for an hour at the counter, concluding with her consent to meet with him when her shift was over so he could explain his entire proposal.

She was upfront and honest with him about her work experience. She had never run a business of her own beyond managing a store's cosmetic counters. He understood, offering his company's resources to help guide her and provide assistance from his operations department. When she had doubts, he recommended a specific individual from the department that could be most helpful, a man named Anders.

Hindsight being twenty-twenty, she wished she could have declined John's offer of Benchmark assistance or perhaps requested someone else. Anders had aided her in setting up her shop. He was organized and efficient, as John had told her. Unbeknownst to her, he had ulterior motives.

Initial phone calls quickly led to FaceTime calls after the first two days. Those became personal visits from Anders the following week. On his first two visits, he flew in, worked with her for several hours, and then flew out again. His third visit, which she knew would be a long day with ordering fixtures and detailed aspects of the shop, ended with Anders inviting her to dinner. She appreciated his help and hadn't thought it would be anything more than both of them having to eat.

By the end of their first dinner together, their working relationship had changed. She wasn't naïve and knew he desired more than just being business partners.

Until a decade ago, men were kept at arm's length. Since her world had been turned upside down as a teen, any relationship with a male had been difficult for her. After countless dates, in time, she slowly felt more comfortable being one on one with a man. Gradually, she reached a level that would be considered ordinary, with trivial things that most consider a given, like clasping hands and eventually kissing. However, as soon as the relationship grew more serious, she found a reason to end it. She occasionally had melancholy feelings for the life they could have had together if the circumstances had been different. She just wasn't ready.

Night after night, sitting across from Anders who showered her with compliments, she wondered, while mesmerized by his blue eyes, if she would ever be ready. She wanted to be ready. She desired to be touched and loved.

For a time, she thought, perhaps Anders was the one. His handsome face, along with being giddy with setting up her own shop, had clouded her normally rock-solid judgement. She thought she was falling in love with him.

Yet, something scratched at her brain, cautioning her to take it slow. Doubts about him echoed in her mind, and she could almost hear them nagging at her thoughts.

On the second-to-last night before he left town, they were having dinner at an Italian restaurant in Amherst. He was pouring it on thick, mostly talking about himself, when the conversation turned to Kourin's plan for hiring.

While they ate their salads, she explained her philosophy of achieving a cohesive and effective team. Her leadership style came from a manager she admired who had ambitious expectations and a strict code of standards. Even so, she was held in high esteem because of her even-handedness, willingness to perform the same tasks she asked of others, trustworthiness, and knack of never failing to fulfill a promise. She was refreshingly open and honest, while other managers in the department store thought nothing of bad-mouthing and back-stabbing in their attempts to climb the corporate ladder. Kourin ended her insights of the woman by stating that many had sought to work under her leadership.

Anders snorted and commented that such a person didn't exist.

Kourin ignored him and continued her narrative.

Hired as a part-time holiday employee, she was one of only two kept on after seasonal layoffs and was given full-time status in the cosmetics department. She had a lot to learn beyond selling skills, but the manager spent time with her training, coaching, and developing abilities she didn't know she possessed.

Three months later, two weeks prior to Easter, her mentor had a lasting effect on her when she received beneficial criticism on a project that had been incorrectly executed. Through questions and supportive guidance, the manager gave her encouragement. When the project was successfully completed later in the shift, the manager's farewell as they parted for the evening was accompanied by a "thank you" and a "job well done". The words were simple and sincere.

Those were her last words.

As the salads were finished, Kourin had tears welling up. With a trembling hand and her voice breaking, she placed her fork on the table and told Anders the woman had been tragically killed while driving home that night by someone who cut her off on the highway.

Anders nonchalantly took a sip of his wine and said the most egregious statement she had ever heard. He remarked that, for all the good the woman had done, in the end, it was not of any use to her.

Kourin stared at him with her mouth open. She couldn't believe that she heard what she did.

Without noticing or simply ignoring her expression, he explained to her how she should manage her store if she wanted to get ahead in the world. She needed to command their respect with an iron fist to keep the workers in line, or they would walk all over her. Make it clear from day one that they do what they were hired to do, or they would be on the outside looking in without a job.

Kourin was appalled by what she heard. When the entrée arrived, she was arguing with him how wrong literally everything he said was, but it fell on deaf ears.

Anders told her he didn't accept failure or excuses, only results. He had to tell more than one employee at his previous job not to let the door hit them on their way out.

From that moment on, she realized, beneath the ostentatious exterior that had enraptured her, there dwelt a wretched soul.

The next day, his final day to assist her, passed by slowly. His comments from the previous night echoed in her brain, causing anger to swell. A knot of tension churned in her gut, radiating a searing heat. Three times she had to go to the restroom to calm herself down before the day at long last came to an end.

As they were leaving, he told her he had planned a very special night for them before he flew out in the morning. She was dumbfounded that he was oblivious to how she felt about him after the previous night. In the nearly empty terminal outside her shop, she told him she did not want to see him anymore. She thanked him for his help and said she could handle it the rest of the way. Inside, her emotions were boiling. Outside, she fought to keep herself professional.

Fortunately, Phil appeared before she lost her restraint. He needed to discuss something with Anders. This allowed her a hasty exit out of the terminal. She was done with the egocentric jerk, or so she thought.

For days afterwards, he texted and called her. She ignored him. By the second week, the texts and calls had stopped. She placed it on the back burner to make John aware of his employee when she saw him in person. At the time, she thought that would be at the terminal's soft opening.

Anders had an unexpectedly profound impact on her. She used what she learned from him to hire her team. She hired staff that was virtuous on the inside and disregarded the mask they wore, no matter how pretty or blue eyed they were.

As she was putting her shop together and interviewing hundreds of applicants, she caught glimpses of a handsome man who seemed to be everywhere in the terminal. She most often saw him getting a coffee at the Coffee Bean across from her shop when they opened two months before the soft opening was scheduled. Although she had her own hot water and tea bags in her store for break time, it became a habit for her to visit the coffee shop for tea, hoping to run into the handsome man. She made friends with the manager who told her who he was, the owner of the construction company building the terminal, Jack Roberts.

That night she had a dream about Jack, a man she had yet to even meet up close. In the morning when she awoke, her sheets were wet from sweat. Her body must have been extremely warm as she slept and dreamed of the rugged construction worker.

The morning after her intense dream, Jack was in her shop to check on his team who were installing her display counters. John had arranged for Roberts Construction to do her store's fixture installation as part of her agreement to open the store. Three weeks at the terminal and enduring Anders during that time, this was the first time she met Jack face to face. His eyes were chestnut brown, but she perceived more depth in his eyes than she ever saw in Anders' striking blue ones. When Jack spoke to her, she felt her heart skip a beat and a warmth inside her. As he walked out of her shop, she admired his butt and felt her cheeks blush when she realized what she was doing. She felt a new level of desire for him that she had never experienced before. Later that day, she saw him across the walkway speaking with the person she now knew as Laurel. Just seeing him, even from a distance, caused a fire to burn brighter inside her.

The next morning, Bob from the construction company was working on her entrance door. She questioned him about Jack, and after some prodding, he told her all about him. His workmate, Miguel, added a few colorful stories that intrigued her even more. The crucial information she received was that he was divorced and not seeing anyone that they were aware of.

That afternoon, Harry installed her stockroom door. He was not as forthcoming as the others, but she learned more about the type of man Jack was. From that day forward, she was determined to get to know Jack Roberts.

Back in the present, she thought, *Is that a coincidence? Anders was—is a stuck-up dick. Is it fate that she would get together with Jack?* The bench came to her mind. *What the fuck is really going on in this place?*

Kourin greeted another person as they passed by her. She spotted Jack walking down from the garden area. He had a disconcerting expression. Her mind conjured up an image of Miguel in an accident. She rushed to him.

Jack saw Kourin a few steps away. He smiled, thinking to himself, *Well, she's alone.* She hugged him and asked if he was alright. He hugged her back, enjoying the curves he felt in his arms and against his body. They parted, but they continued to hold each other. Jack needed her closeness after what he had just experienced. With their lips just inches apart, she asked if Miguel was okay. He responded he hadn't heard from him yet. As he peered into her green eyes, he said, "We have a bigger problem with the bench than we thought."

11

LIVE FREE OR DIE

By the time Mandy arrived at the airport employee parking, the lot had many more vehicles than normal. The morning sun glinted off the windshields as she located an open spot a considerable distance from the entrance. As she walked with Sarah toward Carlos, she was apprehensive about what he might say to her after what had occurred at the party. He obviously had no idea what was happening with the bench or her vision involving Miguel. Fortunately, he was kind enough to ask if she was feeling better and engage her in polite conversation until the tram arrived.

The two ladies agreed to meet up at the café when Sarah returned from her round-trip flight. They went their separate ways after Sarah got a coffee and bagel to go at the café.

Before the pilot was even out of the coffee shop, Mandy texted Jack. Not having Miguel's cell number, she did the next best thing and texted Jack to see if he had heard from him. She placed her phone on vibrate and slid it into her back pocket.

The café was filled with the smell of freshly brewed coffee and the sound of customers chatting. After saying hello to everyone with a big Mandy smile, she retrieved her apron from a hook in the backroom. Upon returning to the front, she patted Ubu on the top of his head and received a tail wag in return. She jumped right in to help prepare customer orders.

In the thick of customers, she asked Laurel if she heard anything from Jack about Miguel. She had not and added that Kourin had been in earlier stating the same. Mandy remarked on the oddity of Jack not being there, while Kourin had already arrived. Laurel agreed, but she suggested perhaps her uncle had other business to attend to before the soft opening. Mandy didn't respond, not sure Jack would have had more pressing things on his mind than Kourin or the bench.

Twenty minutes later, with the customers caught up at the counter, Mandy grabbed a towel and wiped down the unoccupied tables. Most of the customers were thoughtful enough to have thrown away their trash. As she was wiping down the second table, Laurel approached her, holding two cups of coffee.

"How are you holding up this morning?" Her friend had a concerned expression and handed her a cup she was holding. "Any word about Miguel?"

Mandy stopped cleaning when Laurel handed over the drink. She faced her friend with no Mandy smile visible. "No. I texted Jack, hoping he'd have heard, but I haven't had a reply from him. I'm still hopeful he's okay."

"As are we all. I'm looking forward to hearing what John has to say. We need to get some answers."

"There is one other thing I need to tell you. Let's sit."

They sat at the table she had just cleaned off. Mandy relayed the story of what had befallen the family instead of the car accident. When she finished her story about the fire, she waited for a reaction.

Laurel sat silently for a moment, analyzing the curve of her cup for no apparent reason. After a few moments, she looked up at Mandy. "I'm not sure what to think of all that. Was it just a coincidence that something happened instead of what you saw?"

"I'm a little freaked out, to be honest with you. Maybe when we change the future, the alternative is just as bad?"

Laurel had a sip of coffee before answering. "Well, maybe it was fate that something tragic would happen to that family last night."

"Their destiny was that something bad was going to happen? Miguel's accident was the worst-case scenario, and this was . . . what, a better option?"

"Certainly, not a great option, to be sure, but it was better than the family dying." Laurel saw tears welling up in her friend's eyes. "I'm sorry. Maybe we should change the subject." Laurel put her hand across the table for Mandy to hold on to.

She reached out and held it. A tear trickled down her face. "I'm just glad they're all okay, considering. I just wish I knew if Miguel is alright."

* * *

Jack released Kourin from his embrace, but he held on to both her hands, not ready to lose the human touch. While still gazing into her mesmerizing eyes, he said, "Kori, I just had the weirdest thing happen."

Kourin replied without hesitation, "Jack, you didn't just sit on the bench, did you?" Without waiting for a reply, she added, "What were you thinking?"

He saw worry in her eyes and for a fleeting moment thought he saw the golden ring in her eye flare brighter. In his mind, he replayed the earlier café scene with her sitting with Anders. Jack never thought of himself as a jealous man, but with what occurred with his ex-wife, he reconsidered his stand on that over the last two years.

He said, "I was out of sorts and wound up in the garden." He continued holding her hands, but he loosened his grip, not wanting to seem distraught to her. "Um . . ." he paused, deciding he didn't want to discuss why she was sitting with Anders right now. "Why I was there isn't important. Look, can we sit somewhere and talk?" He looked around and spotted a traditional bench two storefronts down. Without waiting for a reply, he held on to her hand and led her to the bench. He held both her hands once again as they sat facing each other.

Kourin could sense he was acutely troubled. As he held her hands, she could feel a slight tremble through his welcome touch. She thought, *If he's this shook up, something terrible must have occurred.* She asked, "Jack, honey, what happened?"

He told her about his encounter on the bench. As he spoke, he intertwined his fingers with hers, never taking his eyes away from her. The bench experience was unnerving, but maintaining contact with her helped calm him down.

When Jack finished relating his story, Kourin felt the shakiness in his hands subside. As she peered into his eyes, she was met with a silent, desperate plea: *"Am I crazy?"* She thought, *Jack needs my understanding right now.* She released her hands from his and gave him a long tight hug.

As she pulled back, he said, "Thanks. I needed that." He continued to look into her eyes, his hands finding hers without looking down for them. "I'm not sure what to make of this."

"You're certain it wasn't just a dream? This sounds very different from anything that's happened before."

"That we know about. But yes, I'm pretty sure it wasn't a dream."

He glanced away from her eyes, his gaze settling on the store in front of him where tee shirts with the words "Live Free or Die" were on display in a kaleidoscope of colors. The next rack was filled with dark green tees, each with a bold outline of the state of New Hampshire printed on the front. Deep in thought, his mind wasn't registering what he was looking at.

"Like the other encounters or visions or whatever we're calling them, while I was in Laurel's office, I knew it was real, that it was actually happening." He looked back at Kourin's face. In his mind he was saying, *God, she's beautiful.* Out loud he said, "Somehow, I knew . . . I know it was real."

"But what does it mean? What was it all about?"

"Well, when I sat down, I was . . ." Jack paused, not wanting to say he was distressed about her and Anders. "I was thinking about Laurel and wondering if she was okay. With everything that's happened, I'm worried about her. She's more fragile than she lets on, I think. Anyway, my thoughts went to her, and the next thing I know, I'm in her office looking at her and me. That happened yesterday morning when Ubu seemed to react to something in the room's corner. From what I just went through, that something was me."

"Perhaps, or you're just thinking it was. With everything going on, maybe you just think you were there, and it was just a regular old dream."

Jack turned his attention to the tee shirts again, thinking about Kourin's comment for several seconds. He said, "Yeah, I guess you're right. It must have been a dream."

He thought about the event late yesterday when Harry was changing his clothes after somehow being drenched. In the same spot he was just talking about, he had felt someone unseen kiss him. That someone, he was certain, was Kourin. He was going to say as much to her when Mary from her shop approached them.

"I'm sorry to interrupt, Kourin," she said. "But we have an issue at the register we need help with."

Kourin looked at Jack who nodded that she needed to go. As they stood up, she said, "No prob, Mary. Jack, can we continue this in a little while?" She was still holding one of Jack's hands.

"Of course. Go do what you need to do." He gave her hand a little squeeze before he let it go. "Don't forget we have the meeting with John after the opening ceremony."

Kourin smiled at him and appreciated the hand squeeze. She leaned over and gave him a kiss on the cheek. "See ya' in a little bit." She turned and walked back to her store with Mary.

Jack watched them walk away to her store. He turned back to the display of tee shirts in front of him. Beside the "Live Free or Die" and state outline tees was a sweatshirt with a large orange-red leaf with "NH" in the center. Next to that was one with green pine trees with "New Hampshire" printed under it.

He thought of the cabin by the lake. He was brought back to the present by his phone vibrating in his pocket.

* * *

Mandy felt Ubu nudge her shin. She reached down to pet him after she wiped a tear from her cheek. She looked into Ubu's eyes and saw his gentle soul. Without turning away, she asked, "How does he know just the right moment to do what he does?"

Laurel, watching her dog interact with her best friend as he had done so many times before, replied, "I'm not sure how he knows, but he's been spot on every time. It's nice to see that he cares so much about you too."

Mandy continued to caress Ubu as she redirected her attention to Laurel. "He cares very much about you, as do I . . . as we all do." She paused, choosing her next words delicately. "My vision has come and passed. How are you doing dealing with yours?" She was uncertain about bringing this up, but she knew Laurel wasn't one to just let it go.

"I've given it a little thought." She turned away from her friend, believing a little white lie between friends was better than telling her she's been thinking about nothing else since it occurred. "I'm not sure what to make of it, but I look forward to whatever John has to say about the bench. Perhaps it'll give us more insight into what is going on."

"Possibly. Or maybe John doesn't actually know much about the bench, either."

Laurel looked up from the cup she hadn't realized she was staring at. "Why do you say that?"

"Well, I'm thinking John is a very smart man. He undoubtedly wants his airline and this terminal to do well. Why would he place such a dangerous item where it could actually ruin him? It makes little sense."

"I hadn't thought about that." Laurel glanced around the café, watching the customers sip their coffee and tea, laughing with one another as they nibbled on their bagels and muffins. "From the interactions I've had with John, even from last night, you're right. It makes little sense."

Before Mandy could answer, Jack entered the café. She called out to him. "Jack, over here!" A few eyes from surrounding tables looked away from their coffees to watch Jack's recognition of where he was called from and make a beeline to her. When he was a few feet away, Mandy asked, "Have you heard from Miguel?"

Without hesitation or a good morning greeting, he replied, "Great news! I just got off the phone with him. He's safe and sound." He sat next to Laurel before giving them a summarized version of his conversation with Miguel. "I got a text from him. He said he was okay. With circumstances being what they were from the previous night, I wanted to make sure everything was alright and called him. When he answered, he sounded groggy and said he had a super-sized hangover. Other than that, he was fine. I heard a female voice in the background. I can only assume it was Chessa, but I didn't ask as it isn't any of my business. He then apologized for how he had acted and hoped I wasn't mad at him. I assured him I wasn't and was glad he made it home safely. Before I disconnected the call, I told him to enjoy his vacation, and I'd see him in a little over a week."

The two ladies listened without interruption.

Laurel observed Mandy as her uncle spoke, wanting to make sure she handled the news well. She seemed to. As Jack concluded his update, Ubu calmly got up from beside Mandy and walked over to his usual spot sitting beside her.

That told Laurel all she needed to know.

12

SOFT OPENING

Harry plodded through the terminal after he left Kourin at the café. He stayed clear of the garden for now, not wanting to risk going near the bench until the meeting with John.

At the end of the terminal, Harry found a seat that faced out toward the tarmac. He watched planes on the far runway depart in a fairly consistent pattern.

He received and answered a text from Beth asking where he was. He thought about the conversations they had the night before. She had always been there for him and all the guys through the years. As another jet powered down the runway and left the ground, he knew what troubled him wasn't her fault. He also knew Jack wasn't to blame even though he had twisted it around and accused him two days ago. Another jet went airborne. The blame was his, but now he had a way to fix it—well, almost a way to fix it. He just needed to find the missing piece to get his Christine back.

As time passed and he watched the planes, a Benchmark plane taxied by and pulled into a gate two over from where he was seated. He hadn't noticed while he was watching the planes that a Benchmark employee had staffed the desk between that gate and the next one over. The employee was a young black woman who walked from her station over to the gate where the plane landed and opened the door. After several minutes, several passengers from the newly arrived plane walked into the terminal. With a broad smile, the Benchmark employee directed them to where baggage claim was. After a lull in traffic, the flight crew came through the door. They exchanged pleasantries. Harry could not hear what they said, but he got the impression they would be back on this plane soon for another flight. He glanced at the monitor. There were three flights for Benchmark Air scheduled to depart in the upcoming hours and displayed on the arrival side was the plane that just arrived and another one due in two hours. The terminal was in operation.

On his right side, he heard a familiar voice. "Hi, Harry. Mind if I join you?"

Harry looked up to see Beth smiling down at him.

* * *

As the eight o'clock hour approached, the walkway area in front of the Coffee Bean and garden area got very busy. Jack sat in a booth with a cup of coffee he nursed while watching the Benchmark team set up an area where speeches would be made. A camera crew from WMUR positioned themselves facing the area. He recognized the news reporter from the report she had done earlier in the morning.

After all was in place, the Benchmark team visited the Bean for pick-me-ups. Each said hello to Jack when they passed by his table to congregate at their own tables. Jack noted Anders was not with them. He was deep in thought about the blond man and Kourin when he saw the owner of Benchmark Air approach his table.

John said, "Good morning, Jack. May I join you?"

"Good morning! Yes, please. And where is your lovely wife this morning?"

John sat opposite Jack and laughed. "Oh, she's over at Kourin's shop. I knew she'd be there before any place else this morning."

"I'm sure Kori will take good care of her." Jack looked over at the cosmetic store. He could see some people moving around inside, but he could not make out Kourin or Peri.

"She's a special person, for sure. I'm glad you two found each other," said John, taking a sip of his coffee.

This made Jack turn away from the window. He wasn't sure how to take John's statement. "John, is there something you're not telling me?" When John didn't respond right away, he added, "For example, what you just said. There's been a few odd statements, and that's one of them. Until yesterday, maybe the day before, I wasn't even aware Kori and I would be together. Yet, I feel you already knew we would be."

John hesitated before speaking, taking a moment to look out at Kourin's store. He said, still viewing the storefront, "You two needed to meet and be together. If you hadn't . . ."

At that moment, the reporter appeared at the side of the table. "Good morning, John. I'm sorry to interrupt, but could we get started with setting up the shots? I'd like to ask you a few questions for the piece as well."

"Certainly." John turned to Jack. "We'll meet up afterwards. Perhaps things will be a little clearer. If you'll excuse me, we've got to get this terminal operational."

Jack's eyes followed John exiting the café with the reporter. Where John had been sitting, Laurel appeared asking, "Well, did he have anything more to say about the bench?"

He turned to his niece, answering, "I think John had his own horrifying visions he dealt with. We thought Mandy was the only one seeing the future? I think there's a lot more to the story than we thought. Somehow, the connection between Kori and me has something to do with it."

Ubu, who had been standing beside the table when Laurel sat down, closed the distance to Jack, laying his head on his thigh. Jack tenderly stroked Ubu's head, careful to avoid his injury.

Laurel watched her uncle interact with her dog. Ubu going to him at that moment confirmed to her what Jack was sensing—more was coming.

* * *

All the shop owners stood in an imprecise semicircle, facing the microphone situated with the garden entrance as the backdrop. Luca from the restaurant, Eloise from the electronics store, Laurel, Vasud with Niyati, Amir, Dafina, other Benchmark employees, and even Shannon from security were all intermixed in the area. Mandy wasn't attending, as the café was bustling with customers.

John stood at the microphone with Peri by his side. Several Benchmark vice presidents were positioned on either side. Jack noticed Anders standing at the very end of the semicircle next to the garden wall.

Jack held Kourin's hand. After the disturbing events he had earlier of Kourin sitting with Anders and then the bench vision in Laurel's office, he welcomed the warmth of her hand. Laurel was situated to his right and was unusually silent.

While they were patiently awaiting the start of the event, Jack studied Kourin's eyes. Illuminated by the skylights above, they appeared hazel with a touch of gold around the pupil. He said, "Your eyes look hazel."

"Yes," she said, somewhat mystified why he would bring that up at the moment.

"Sometimes they look green and not hazel at all."

"Yes."

"I don't understand. How can they be both?"

"Sometimes they're more one color than another. There's even gold in there as well."

To his right, he heard Laurel say, "You have beautiful eyes, Kourin. You're lucky. I have uninteresting brown eyes. Mandy has hazel eyes like you. Come to think of it, sometimes hers are more green than hazel, too."

Kourin said, with her gaze locked on Jack's brown eyes, "It's typically the lighting. What color eye shadow and liner you use makes a big difference in how they appear as well." She paused, placing her left hand on his cheek, and added, "But brown eyes are just as beautiful and sexy."

Jack thought he saw the golden flecks in her eyes become a little brighter as she spoke. He thought, *Maybe I'm just imagining that.*

The spell he was under gazing into her eyes was broken when John began speaking, bringing everyone's attention to the front.

The Benchmark Air owner's words filled the terminal as he spoke about the airline business and the potential for shop owners in New Hampshire. His voice was filled with excitement. The crowd erupted with applause several times in response to his words. Jack watched the camera crew record the speech and take shots of the crowd. He observed them capturing Laurel and Ubu who sat obediently by her side wearing his red service dog vest. With their past, he was certain they would be mentioned in the story: "Wounded vet opens new café," "Brave rescue dog by her side supporting her" . . . something on those lines. Additional coverage might bring more donations to her dog rescue charity.

He watched her face as she listened to John's words, wondering what was running through her mind. She had been through a lot and continued to deal with the aftermath. Her expression was not revealing what she was feeling or thinking. That worried him. The mention of Phil's name brought Jack back to the speech. As the night before, John wished him a quick recovery. For the interim, he was appointing a temporary manager of the terminal and introduced the tall blond with piercing blue eyes—Anders would manage the terminal until Phil's return.

Jack felt Kourin's sudden vice-like grip on his fingers when the announcement was made.

13

OPPOSING VIEW

Kourin released her grip on Jack's hand when she noticed the intensity of her grasp. She turned to him and whispered, "I'm sorry." She didn't say more.

"No prob," Jack answered back, rubbing his fingers with his other hand. However, he was thinking, *What is going on with this Anders guy?* Jack looked at Kourin's profile as she stared at the podium area. Her jaw moved back and forth, her expression a fierce mask as she ground her teeth together. He turned toward John's voice as he wrapped up his speech. Anders was staring back in his direction.

Kourin could not believe what she was hearing! *Anders was going to be working here?* she thought. *Are you fucking kidding me?* She watched as he walked up to stand next to John. Fortunately, he was not asked to speak. *Just look at how smug he looks. He must have known this was going to happen this morning when he asked me to dinner. Wait a minute! He doubtless knew last night. But he said nothing. What? Did he just think because he was back in town I'd just fall into his arms? Well, that's not going to happen.*

Anders was looking right at her. She would not be the first one to back down. *I don't know what game you're playing, but I will not be a part of it.*

John ended his speech, requiring Anders to turn and shake his hand, distracting him from his concentration on Kourin. She faced Jack who met her steely gaze with a worried expression.

She said, "Let's go." She pivoted toward her store without waiting.

Jack followed without comment and thought, *Definitely something going on here.*

* * *

Laurel entered her café with Ubu naturally by her side. The place was packed with several people in line and all the tables filled. Ubu trotted over to his usual spot behind the counter, walked in a circle twice, and lay down. Laurel jumped right in and helped process the incoming orders.

Mandy observed Laurel working. To everyone she interacted with while the rush was on, she presented a blasé character, displaying a non-emotional facade. When Eric asked her how the ribbon cutting went, she tersely answered it wasn't a ribbon cutting, which would be next month. As she turned away from him, she said the speech was fine.

Mandy noted it was a little out of character for her to be that matter-of-fact, especially with an employee. Whatever was bugging her wasn't something Ubu sensed. He remained snoozing on his mat.

When all the hustle and bustle of the restaurant had settled and the tables had been cleared and cleaned, Mandy asked if she could have a conversation with her in the office. Without comment, Laurel followed her to the back. Ubu saw them leave and remained where he was.

Four steps into the office, Mandy spun around to face her friend. She smiled and said, "Okay, out with it. What's got your panties in a bunch?"

At first, Laurel attempted to brush it off as being tired from the party and a lack of sleep. Mandy wasn't buying it. She knew her high school friend better than that and reached out, lightly touching her arm. "Lau, we've known each other for half as long as we've been alive. I can tell when something is bothering you. Now out with it."

Laurel's mind was troubled. She was aware she had to talk to someone. Who could she do it with if not her best friend? Mandy was the one person she had always been open with, and whatever was said between them remained that way.

It took Laurel over ten minutes to express all her thoughts. She began by recounting the terrifying bench vision, and then she discussed all of her ideas concerning the bench. If she could use the bench to go back to that night, she could alter the outcome with the new knowledge that there were two suicide bombers. She just needed to get there several minutes before they appeared. They would be stopped, and Breck would be saved so he could return home and marry Sarah.

As she revealed her most inner thoughts, Mandy listened. She didn't interrupt. She didn't dare bat an eye for fear that she would stop sharing. When Laurel finished, Mandy took a deep breath and gave her a hug.

Laurel asked, "And what's that for?"

"Because I know how it feels that something needs to be done and feeling powerless to do anything about it."

"But that's just it. I can do something about it! With all that's happened with me, you, and especially Harry, I can see we can alter the past. We have the ability to fix a mistake and make things right."

Mandy released her from her hug. Still cradling both her arms, she asked, "But should we?"

Astonished by the question, Laurel said, "You, of all people, should see the benefit of the bench, having just saved Miguel and a whole family, actually two families, from disaster!"

"You're right. But that was a future that had not yet happened. It's not the same thing."

Laurel's voice went several octaves higher as she responded, "Shouldn't I do everything I can to save a life? Is Breck's life worth less than Miguel's?"

Mandy remained calm, even though inside she was anything but. "Of course, his life is worth just as much as Miguel's. Every life is important." She paused, treading her words delicately. "That's not at all what I'm saying."

Laurel took a breath and asked, "Then what are you saying?"

"If you save Breck's life, what will that do to his future?"

"At least he'll have one. That's more than he had."

Mandy sensed Laurel going down her path of despair. She searched for the right words to ease the pain. "Yes. He'll have a future, but what does that mean for his girlfriend who had moved on? What happens to the life she made for herself?"

"Is there anything more important than marrying the love of her life? Another life would pale compared to being with the one you were meant to be with." Laurel felt she was on the verge of tears. She fought to hold them back. "I can bring them together. Shouldn't I?"

Mandy held her in another hug, tighter than the first.

Ubu appeared in the doorway and moved to them, placing his cranium against Mom and his body against Sister. He sensed a long day ahead for all of them.

* * *

Kourin led Jack all the way to her office. After they both entered, she closed the door, turned, and hugged him as closely as she could. In her mind, she was pissed. She was seething, but not at Jack. She was mad Anders had slithered his way back into her life.

Jack had followed Kourin to her office without saying a word. To say that he was confused was putting it mildly. He wasn't a complete idiot and knew there was something between Kourin and Anders. From the date offer this morning to her reaction of him being put in temporary charge of the terminal, she knew him more than just having met yesterday. What was that history, though? He had no clue. Once in her office, he didn't know what was coming and braced for whatever came his way. When she hugged him, he instinctively hugged her back. When she hugged him tighter, he knew she needed him more than ever before.

* * *

John completed his duties in front of the camera which took well over half an hour after his speech. He scanned the terminal from where he stood at the edge of the garden. Peri had disappeared visiting the various stores, spreading good will on his behalf. The Benchmark team had divided into small clusters and were exploring the terminal. All would board the ten o'clock flight back home, except one. He didn't know where Anders went, perhaps to the terminal manager's office to begin his new assignment. After the nine o'clock meeting, he would seek him out before heading back home. There were no words he could say that would prepare for what may be ahead of him.

He checked his watch. It was nearly nine. He spotted Jack and Kourin coming out of her shop. As they approached him, he asked if they were ready for their meeting. Both said yes.

* * *

When the reporter finished with John, she sought Laurel at the café counter. She did a brief interview with her at the café entrance. Ubu sat by her side the entire time. Laurel mentioned her charity several times, which she was grateful for. After the interview, the reporter ordered a coffee and made a donation into the box, all of it filmed. Mandy waited on her with Eric nearby. Laurel smiled, despite the inner turmoil she felt. With Mandy's and Eric's big smiles, you couldn't ask for a better representation of her brand.

Laurel reflected on the words she had said to Mandy earlier and the unexpected response. After thinking she had finally resolved a path to alter Breck's death, now she was conflicted if it was wise to do so. She unquestionably believed in her heart that it was. However, Mandy had planted a seed in her brain, causing contradiction. Was she saving Breck to save him or herself?

As the reporter and crew exited the café, Laurel saw John and Jack conversing near the garden. She let Mandy know they were ready and walked with the others up to the center courtyard.

When the small group arrived, they were surprised to see Harry and Beth were already there. They were standing near the opposite side entrance that came up the backside. Jack looked at Kourin. Both wondered how they knew the meeting would be held there.

John greeted them. "Good morning, Beth, Harry. I'm glad you two could make it this morning." In the center of the garden, standing within arm's reach of the bench, John stopped and turned to address the group. "Now, I understand you have a few questions for me."

14
SEEKING ANSWERS

Kourin asked the first question. "Okay, out with it. What the hell is going on with this bench?"

John kept his composure as always. He knew this was going to be a hard conversation, but he hadn't expected it to come from Kourin. He said, "Well, honestly, I'm not absolutely sure." John raised both of his arms to shoulder height and waved his hands, trying to block out the chorus of objections coming from the people standing in a semicircle ahead of him. "Just let me explain, please."

Peri arrived with Shannon from security as her husband settled the group. She stayed on the edge of the court with the security guard slightly behind her. John silently acknowledged them with eye contact and a nod.

John took an audible breath and told the group what he knew in a logical, step-by-step order. The backyard garden began many years ago. As it came near its completion, he had five of six benches in place per the plans. He and Peri had spent countless hours locating those from across the country. While searching for the last one, he was contacted by a friend of a friend of a friend about a special bench. In short order, the person agreed to sell him the bench at what seemed a too good to be true price. In reflection, the seller either had been directed to get the bench to him or had had enough of its strange nature.

Harry interrupted with a question. "Who would have directed him to get the bench to you?"

"That is a question I do not have an answer to. If you'll permit me, let me tell you what I know. Hopefully, I'll have answered at least some of your questions."

They all remained quiet for the duration as John told his tale.

The ancient bench arrived a few days after his conversation with the previous owner. As they had one open spot in the backyard, they placed it there. It fit in well with the other five and, with the backyard complete, didn't give it further thought. Months went by hosting several backyard parties, barbeques and get-togethers, as well as having their children and grandchildren visit.

"There was nothing out of the ordinary with this bench," John gestured to the bench behind him, "nor any of the others. Until one day, when I contemplated expanding Benchmark Air to go nationwide. Peri wanted me to retire so I could spend more time with the grandkids. I was on the fence, and she had me nearly convinced. As we were discussing this, Peri had a vision while sitting on the bench. When she awoke, she was more inclined for expansion. As the next few weeks and eventually months passed, I had visions while on the bench that led to the need for a terminal here in Manchester. Often, the visions were hard to understand, but as each one came, it added another piece to the puzzle. Even to this day, the puzzle is missing far more pieces than have been placed. There was even a vision my wife had that I did not. It involved aiding a business in Charleston."

Kourin interrupted and asked, "The dress shop?"

"Yes, Kourin. Without going into too much detail, Peri's vision was able to prevent the shop from experiencing something bad. Or rather, things went in a different direction, but ultimately all worked out well in the end. My wife still keeps tabs with the owner and, so far, so good. After this incident, I was convinced what I had been seeing was more than idle dreams. I was having them to serve a purpose."

John stopped here to gauge the group's reaction. They remained attentive but quiet. He continued telling them that often he would have dreams that were similar but had very different outcomes depending on differing factors within the dream. As more of these occurred, he worked out the path he needed to pursue: build the Manchester terminal and a garden that included the ancient bench. He told them he wasn't sure if he had done everything from his visions, but he believed he had. The garden was built. The well-worn bench was placed within it.

John's narrative concluded here, allowing the group a moment to comprehend what they had been told. Again, Kourin was the first to ask a question. "So, you brought this bench here knowing it was going to cause chaos? Why would you do that?"

"Well, if I hadn't, the alternatives were bad, very bad. Look, if any of you have sat on the bench, you must have seen various visions that had multiple conclusions, with 99 percent of them not ending well."

"Actually, we haven't," Jack said, looking around at the others in case anyone wanted to make an objection. "So far, the only person we know of having a future vision is Mandy. And that has come and passed already."

From behind the semicircle, they heard Peri ask, "Wait a minute, are you sayin' that none of y'all have had dreams on the bench?"

Everyone turned around, unaware they had Peri and Shannon behind them. Mandy spoke up this time. "I'm the only one that had a future vision, and I had only one. I didn't have alternative futures to see, but that could have been because I didn't want to sit on the bench again and stayed clear of it."

"I see," Peri said. "Then what occurred with the rest of you?"

Laurel answered, "Our past." She paused and looked at her uncle, then continued, "I was back in the desert when a suicide bomber attacked my unit." She reached down and pet Ubu. "But this time Ubu was there to save me, well, to at least help save me. He attacked my attacker, killing him, albeit he got injured."

"Ah, that explains it," John said. All eyes turned toward him.

"Explains what?" asked Laurel.

"In the visions, I could see that Ubu had an injury on his head, but I didn't know where it came from. I saw mostly events here in the terminal." He glanced at his wife and added, "Well, mostly here."

Jack asked, "You only saw the future? You never went into the past?"

John answered, as Peri came to stand next to him, "No. I only saw the future. I did not know the bench could also show the past."

"That's true," Peri added. "Although I only sat on the bench a couple of times, it was always a future look, never back."

"Well, that's fucking odd, isn't it?" Harry asked to no one in particular. "Doesn't anyone else think it's damn strange that all of us, except one encounter, were seeing the past?"

Mandy spoke up. "Except maybe one other time—Sarah. She saw a ghost plane when she arrived yesterday. That sounds more like the future to me."

Laurel countered, "She wasn't sitting on the bench. It could have been an illusion or something. She herself isn't sure what she saw."

"True. But with all the crazy stuff going on, it is strange," Mandy said.

John and Peri stood quietly, while the others bantered around theories and conjecture of what was going on around them.

Beth, staying next to Harry, watched him. Harry added a boisterous comment here and there. She remained quiet.

Shannon watched and listened. She made mental notes of each person's story as she could comprehend it.

As the talk slowed down, Jack watched Shannon listening at the edge of the courtyard, not moving from the initial spot she claimed upon arrival. He asked her, "Shannon, have you sat on the bench?"

All talk ceased when the others realized they hadn't heard Shannon's story or why she was there. She looked at Peri, John, and then across the faces of everyone present. "I haven't sat on the bench, nor do I plan to be any closer to it than I am now." She gave a sideways glance toward the bench that was near to where John was standing. "I reviewed the surveillance footage of the garden yesterday when Harry got wet and injured. This morning, I reviewed all the footage since the bench installation."

John asked, "And what did you see?"

Shannon answered, her eyes opening wide as she spoke, "This garden is alive!"

15

PLANTS

"What are you talking about?" John asked.

Scanning the area nervously, Shannon feared something could snatch her before she gave an answer. She took one step forward. "The plants move on their own." She glanced over at the foliage. "They're perhaps moving right now."

Harry was the first to speak. "Are you telling me these plants get up and walk around the garden? That's absurd."

"No, no, no, that's not what I mean."

Shannon described what she had observed when she watched Harry sitting on the bench. She then detailed what every other person did when on the bench. In nearly every instance, the same thing occurred. A person sat on the bench. They appeared to fall asleep. The recording became distorted. The picture resumed with the person waking up disoriented. In Harry's case, he was wet the last time, had an injury, and was not seated in the same spot as he had been. From what she observed, everyone else was.

Harry spoke up again. "How does that relate to the plants being alive?" He was curious if there was something he could use to once again see his Christine. Perhaps Shannon discovered an important clue.

"Well, it took me several reviews to figure that out," Shannon answered and again placed a wary eye on the plants near her. "At normal speed, everything seems okay. When you speed up the recording, though, every plant in here shakes, waves, moves, whatever you want to call it. They react. And don't tell me it's 'cuz of the air conditioning or any of that crap. I've already checked into that, and it ain't it."

"That's not a lot to go on," Harry said. Internally, he thought, *I think I've seen that! That explains the rustling sounds and the movement out of the corner of my eye.*

Shannon said, "I'll tell you what. If any of you want to check it out for yourselves, come down to the security office." With that, she said no more.

Jack spoke up. "Shannon, no one here doubts what you saw. I, for one, want to see what you've discovered." Jack thought about the incident in Laurel's office with a hand in his gut and when he sat in the terminal. "Have you noticed any other distortions in the recordings elsewhere in the terminal?"

John perked up now. "What are you suggesting, Jack?"

Not to raise any undo alarm, he said, "I'm just wondering if it's a system glitch."

"I only checked the other cameras surrounding the garden. All of them recorded normally," she answered. "No distortions and only recorded when there was movement to record. When I get back to the office, I'll review other cameras to verify everything is operating properly."

"I'll go with you," Jack said. He turned to Kourin. "Do you want to see this?"

"I have to get back to my shop. Why don't you check it out and let me—" Kourin glanced around at the others. "Let us know what you've found."

Laurel said, "That sounds like a good idea, Uncle Jack. Mandy and I should get back to the café as well." Mandy nodded in agreement. Laurel added, "John, thanks for letting us know about your experiences with the bench. I'm not sure how I feel about all of it yet."

"But we'll figure it out as best we can," Mandy finished Laurel's statement for her. With that, they both exited the courtyard, with Kourin behind them.

Jack said, "John, I don't know what to say."

"That's okay, Jack. I know this is a lot, but trust me when I say I did what I thought was best." John turned to Peri. "My dear, we need to go, or we'll miss our flight home." They exited the courtyard, leaving Jack, Harry, Beth, and Shannon.

"Harry, are you okay?" Jack asked.

"I am," he said. "Let's check out the recordings."

The four of them exited down the walkway together. Behind them, they didn't notice the plants throughout the courtyard moving up, down, and from side to side randomly. There was no breeze.

* * *

Minutes later, at the terminal security office, Shannon took her usual seat in front of the monitors, with Jack and Harry standing on either side of her. Beth sat in the only other seat in the small room. Shannon pulled up Harry's footage, playing all three encounters in order. She then played them again, sped up to eight times. All were stunned at what they saw. Indeed, the plant life seemed to be alive, moving randomly throughout the frame.

"Wow. That's unbelievable," said Jack. "I see your point. It doesn't appear to be caused by air flow. Let's check the other times people sat on the bench."

For the next hour, the trio observed Kourin, Laurel, Mandy, Beth, and Jack sitting on the bench. The results were similar to Harry, except after the distortion all were in the same spot or very close. There were three other people who sat on the bench yesterday, but no distortion occurred. From the camera view, it appeared as if nothing happened. One individual was Jimmy from the café. They didn't know the other two and were likely new employees from the terminal shops.

Harry said, "That's the kid from the café. He said nothing about the bench this morning when I got a coffee."

"It appears nothing happened to him," said Shannon.

Beth, who had been quiet throughout the review, asked, "So just because someone sits on the bench does not mean something automatically happens?"

"Apparently so," muttered Harry.

Beth said, "Shannon, go back to the second Harry encounter, please."

The guard hit a few buttons. They watched it again. She asked, "What are you looking for?"

"Play it again, but watch Ubu this time instead of Harry."

She did as she asked. "Wow," Shannon said, "I missed that before. I was concentrating on the bench and hadn't watched the dog."

The camera view showed Harry's backside and then Ubu, two paces behind, hesitantly walking into the frame. The dog stopped five feet away, watching Harry sit on the bench. When the distortion cleared, Ubu was two feet closer to the bench, upset and barking with hair down the spine of his back raised. After several seconds, he calmed down and resumed watching Harry. Moments later, he turned his head, wagged his tail, and bolted off screen in the direction he came from.

"That's when Laurel and I showed up," said Jack.

Beth said, "It appears Ubu moved during the distortion, which isn't odd as he had been standing, but something happened that riled him up."

"Yeah," Harry said. "He was in my bedroom, about to attack my father. Before he had a chance, we were both back on the bench in the garden."

"But you weren't. Well, you were, but Ubu wasn't. He wasn't ever close enough to be touching the bench."

Shannon looked at Beth, not comprehending.

"Look, with Laurel's encounter, Ubu was in contact with at least Laurel if not also the bench. In her vision, though, Ubu was not next to her on guard duty. He was at least several feet away, as he had to run and jump to protect Laurel. Here," Beth pointed to the paused image of Ubu turning to greet Laurel, "Ubu was at least five feet away from the bench. He doesn't appear to touch it.

The bench may be a common denominator where we all sat on it, but its radius of effectiveness goes beyond contact with it."

"What does that mean?" asked Shannon.

Jack answered for Beth. "Perhaps there is more to what Sarah saw than we at first thought."

16

LOCATION, LOCATION, LOCATION

Laurel and Mandy, with Ubu between them, returned to the Coffee Bean. The café was full of people, and the air was fragrant with the aroma of freshly brewed coffee. Mandy said she could handle it and jumped in to assist.

With her friend at the counter, Laurel continued on to her office with her four-legged friend close behind. There was an avalanche of paperwork growing from the café and the original shop downtown. She had fallen behind in her routine the last couple of days, distracted by the bench and the possibility of saving Breck.

Ubu circled and lay down in his favorite spot a few feet away. From his vantage point, he could keep an eye on both Mom and the doorway. At the moment, he didn't sense any problems.

Laurel got to work straightaway. Although she wanted to spend her time contemplating using the bench to save her unit from disaster over a decade in her past, she knew she needed to pay the bills as well. Her team wouldn't be happy if they didn't get paid. For the next two-plus hours, she buckled down and plowed through her work.

* * *

Upon entering her shop, Kourin searched for Mary to ask how everything was going. She reported the register was running with no further complications, and business had remained fairly consistent.

Over the next two hours, the two women worked side by side with the staff, providing on-the-job training and feedback on their performance. All were exceeding Kourin's expectations and reduced any anxiety she had had in the previous days. They were eager and enthusiastic to learn.

The positive reinforcement she provided made her think about the manager she once knew, her last words coming to her, "Good night, Kourin. Thank you for the great job you did tonight. See you tomorrow."

She was troubled by her sentiments. On one hand, she was proud to emulate the best manager she worked for. On the other, she was saddened by her sudden loss all those years ago and a tomorrow that never arrived.

She observed her team for several minutes. The atmosphere in the shop was one of joy and contentment, and the customers' smiles could be felt in the air. She beamed, cognizant of the fact that her manager would be proud of the progress she had made from a seasonal greenhorn worker to the proprietor of her own store.

Kourin decided her old boss would have said, "Thank you for the great job you did. I saw in your eyes you had it in you."

She watched another satisfied customer leave. Moments later, her elation faded when Anders passed through her shop's doorway.

* * *

Two knocks thumped on the office door. Before Laurel could reply, the door opened slowly. Immediately recognizing who it was, she said, "Hi, Uncle Jack."

"Hi, am I interrupting?"

"Not at all. Please come in."

Ubu lifted his head and gave his tail a happy wag as the visitor gave him a quick pet behind his uninjured ear. He settled back down as Jack sat in the chair opposite Mom's desk.

Jack asked, "How are you doing after this morning's meeting?" Concerned for his niece's state of mind, he was now also uneasy with her café being close to the bench.

"I'm holding up, all things considered. I've buried myself in paperwork to keep my mind occupied." She closed her laptop and focused her attention on her uncle. "I have to be honest. I'm more than a little worried about the bench. What if someone sits on it and it messes up the timeline?"

"Well, as you know, I just spent the last couple of hours with Shannon, Beth, and Harry reviewing the recordings of the garden. We even viewed footage elsewhere in the terminal. Um, some of it causes concern for sure, but one thing we discovered was several people sat on the bench and nothing happened."

"Really? That's a relief. I was worried people would sit on it all day long and have visions and what not. It's good to know that's not the case." She paused, noticing a look on her uncle's face, causing her to question her last statement. "Right? The bench isn't as bad a problem as we thought? Is it?"

Jack was hesitant to reveal too much to his niece. It wasn't because he didn't want to tell her. For one thing, all he had was questions with no answers. For another, and more importantly, he didn't want her to have a panic attack. He chose his words carefully and treaded lightly. "No. Not all were affected. Your Jimmy sat on the bench and nothing apparently happened. A few others did as well. So, what the catalyst is to have a reaction from the bench, I do not know."

"What things do concern you about the bench? Well, besides the fact it displays horrendous points in our lives?"

Jack looked away from Laurel and at Ubu as he replied, "It appears you don't have to be sitting on the bench to have something happen."

* * *

Kourin quelled her fury before she moved. She had spent the better part of two hours observing and coaching her crew. The unknowns of owning her own shop and having the proper staff in place were receding. Team chemistry was in the infant stage, needing time to nurture and develop. She wasn't about to blow it all up with an outburst at Anders in front of everyone.

The temporary terminal manager saw Kourin at the back of the store. He snaked his way around a customer shopping for eye shadow and thought, *I wouldn't have to go so far around you if you lost some weight.*

Kourin met him halfway.

"Nice to see your shop is busy." He glanced around. "I see all the displays we ordered came in. Looks nice all complete, but I would have set some of them up differently." He came back around to smile at her. "You look nice as well."

Kourin held her tongue, not uttering what was on her mind. "Can we have this conversation away from the sales floor?"

"Of course. Actually, that's why I'm here. How about an early lunch?"

Kourin wasn't hungry, but she needed to have a conversation with him. With no warmth in her voice, she said, "Sure. Let's go over to Luca's." Without waiting for a response, she headed for the doorway.

Anders was delighted she accepted his offer for lunch, and he had a suspicion she was just being coy. As she walked toward the exit, he was captivated by her curves. He thought, *I'm going to like this assignment very much!*

* * *

Laurel rose rapidly, causing Ubu to jump up. She caressed his head to reassure him, saying, "Sorry, boy, it's okay." He stayed on alert, just in case. She asked, scowling at her uncle, "What do you mean you don't have to be sitting on the bench to have something happen?"

"Well, remember in your bench encounter, Ubu ran toward you, jumping over you to bite your attacker? When you went into the vision and when you came out, he was in contact with you and perhaps the bench. Yet, in the vision, he was not near you." Jack paused so he could gauge his niece's reaction. He needed to make sure she stayed with him and didn't spiral downward.

"Yeah. I guess you're right. I hadn't thought about that."

"Right. During Harry's encounter in his childhood bedroom, Ubu was there and protected young Harry from his father."

"Yes, we heard him barking."

"Correct." Jack looked down at Ubu. "Yet, in Harry's case, Ubu was never closer than three feet away. In fact, it appears when Harry went into the vision, Ubu was at least five feet away."

"So, maybe there's some kind of halo or perimeter effect or something? Someone sits on the bench and the surrounding area is in the bubble or whatever."

"Perhaps."

"I can see on your face there's something more."

Jack hadn't wanted to bring this up, but he wanted Laurel aware of the danger she could be in. "Yesterday afternoon, when you found me sitting at the gate waiting for John, Ubu came within a few feet of me." He stopped there, thinking of the memory of Kim by the lake.

"Uncle Jack, what happened?"

Jack brought himself back from the lake scene. "I thought it was a dream. I was back at the lake cabin. You remember it, the one on Winnipesaukee?" He didn't wait for a reply. "It was many years ago. A night with Harry, Christine, and Kim." He paused. "Before we had kids." He paused a second time, realizing the awkwardness of saying his story out loud to his niece. "We were making love in an Adirondack chair and as we finished . . ." He did a shy quick glance toward his niece.

"It's okay, Uncle Jack. I'm not twelve."

"Yes, well, anyway, Kim was on top of me. She looked to her right and screamed. Just a few feet away was Ubu! There at the cabin!"

"Uncle, that's not possible. I had my eyes on him when he walked over to you. He was in the airport the whole time."

"That maybe so, but when I came out of the vision, Ubu was standing the same distance from Kim and I. And there's one more thing." He looked at his niece. "We were drinking Kim's favorite drink back then, strawberry daiquiris."

"So?"

"When I woke up, I could taste the strawberry in my mouth and on my lips. I'm sure of it. Laurel, Ubu was at my cabin over twenty years in the past!"

* * *

Wren greeted Kourin at Luca's entrance and asked if they wanted a table for two. She noted to herself she was with someone different from the day before.

Kourin answered in the affirmative.

Anders eyed the red-headed hostess, recognizing her from the party the night before.

Wren led the way, just a short distance from the entrance. Kourin followed with Anders behind her. Menus were placed in opposition to each other on the table. Kourin pulled the closest chair out and sat down, her back toward the entrance. Anders sat in the other.

Wren said with a smile, "Today's specials are clipped on the inside of the menu. Your waitress will be Sosie. She'll be right with you."

"Thank you," said Kourin when Anders did not.

Wren turned and walked away. Kourin noticed Anders' eyes watch her walk back to her station. She thought, *What did I ever see in him*?

Without preamble, Kourin asked, "When were you going to tell me you were going to be here awhile?"

Anders' eyes left Wren's butt and focused on Kourin before answering. "I thought it'd be a pleasurable surprise." He smiled, showing his perfectly aligned blindingly white teeth. When Kourin didn't respond, he continued, "I actually didn't find out until just before the party, after John visited Phil at the hospital. He asked if I could cover things until Phil was well enough to return or they found someone else. I'm not sure if this will be for a few days, weeks, or months."

Kourin watched Anders' eyes as he spoke. She felt something inside her, the same something that had let her guard down last time and led to disaster. She needed to take control of her emotions and the situation with him.

Anders continued, "So, naturally, I said yes, as this is a huge feather in my cap to have on my resume." He smiled again, adding, "Not to the mention the bonus of seeing you again, Kourin."

"When you were last here weeks ago, I told you, in no uncertain terms, that I never wanted to see you again."

Anders flashed a wider smile and said, "Yet, here we are. It's like fate has destined us to be together."

* * *

For the next fifteen minutes, Jack and Laurel went back and forth about what the bench could be. One thing they could agree on was that it wasn't just an antique wooden bench.

Midway through the conversation, Ubu lay back down. He perceived Mom was tense, so kept watch, but she was not overly upset or in danger.

Laurel said, in reply to her uncle's comment that it may be unsafe to work in close proximity to the bench, "Uncle, I am not closing or selling this café. You can just forget that idea. I think you may be overreacting a tad."

"I just want you to be safe."

She checked the time and wanted to change the subject. She said, "Uncle, it's nearly noon. How about I treat you to lunch?"

He glanced at the watch Kim had given him on their tenth anniversary and said, "That sounds great, but it's my treat. Do you mind if we invite Kourin?"

"I would have been surprised if you didn't."

They exited the office, with Ubu following Laurel. They asked Mandy if she'd like to join them, but she declined as she was covering her crew's lunch breaks. She told them to enjoy lunch without her.

While Jack went into the cosmetic shop to ask Kourin to lunch, Laurel waited outside with Ubu. She regarded the garden a short distance away with skylights cascading sunlight onto the short trees and plants below. She thought, *It seems so bright and peaceful.*

Jack exited Kourin's shop alone. "She's already gone to lunch."

"Oh, I'm sorry. I guess it's just you and me."

"And Ubu."

Wren met them at Luca's entrance. "Hi, Laurel. Two for lunch?"

"Yes, please, and one dog."

"Oh, yes, we can't forget Ubu, can we?" said Wren, smiling down at him. She picked up two menus from a shelf below a wipe-off map of the restaurant. "Right this way."

Laurel trailed Wren. Ubu kept pace beside his mom, with Jack following. A few steps into the restaurant, Jack saw Anders seated at a table. Two more steps in, he saw where Kourin was having lunch. He kept walking until he was near her table.

Anders looked up at him with a smug expression on his face.

Kourin sensed a person next to the table, thinking it was Sosie to take their order. As she glanced upwards, she was met with a sorrowful pair of brown eyes that made her heart ache.

17

HEARTBURN

Jack passed by Kourin's table. The atmosphere was tense and silent. He quickly glanced her way, mustering up a half-hearted smile before trailing Wren and Laurel to their table.

Laurel chose the closest chair. Jack sat opposite her, allowing for an unintentional view of Kourin, with Anders facing away from him.

He glimpsed Kourin looking over at him. He diverted his attention toward his niece.

* * *

Kourin was surprised when Jack passed by her table, so much so that she was tongue tied. Before she could utter a word, he moved on. When she looked his way across the room, he diverted his attention away from her. She decided to speak with him to clear up any misunderstanding he may have about the situation. As she was about to excuse herself, Sosie appeared to take their lunch order.

* * *

Laurel watched Jack sneak a third furtive look in Kourin's direction as the waitress took the other table's order. She finally said, "Uncle, go talk with her."

Jack's mind came back to the table. He said, "She's a grown woman and is welcome to have lunch with anyone she wants." He looked her way again. "I don't understand why she's having lunch with him. She told me she doesn't even like him. She made that abundantly clear before I came to see you."

"Well, maybe she has a good reason. Give her the benefit of the doubt here."

"You're right, of course." He thought, *This guy is trouble.* His thoughts were disrupted when Sosie came to take their lunch order.

* * *

Anders said, "So tell me about your shop, Kourin. Is it as wonderful as you hoped it would be?" He could tell something was on her mind. If it was the other guy, he needed to divert her attention away from him and on to more important matters—himself.

Kourin willed herself not to look in Jack's direction. She had a reason for coming here and needed to focus on that at the moment. "The shop is fine, and everything is as it should be. The staff is doing well. We even had more training just before you showed up."

He said, working to bring the conversation around to himself, "I'm glad I could help you with that. We made a great team getting it put together."

She glared at him. Her blood pressure rose, and it wasn't because of his chiseled face or blue eyes. "Look, I am grateful for the help John had you provide, but as I told you the last time we spoke, I've got it from here."

"I understand. You're a proud woman and want to make a go of it on your own."

Her hands were clasped together on the table, her knuckles white. He reached out and held her hand tightly, saying, "I'm willing to help you. As before, I'm here for you."

Kourin pulled her hand away from his. "I'm fine." She glanced toward Jack's table before catching herself. "I have everything under control."

Before she could add more or Anders replied, Sosie dropped off their drinks. Kourin had a sip of her ginger ale to give herself a moment to think and calm down.

A club soda with lemon bubbled in front of Anders. He ignored it. He cast an eye over Kourin's lips and her captivating green eyes with golden flecks. She had what he wanted, and he was done wasting time.

Confidently, he said, "We have something between us that few people have the chance to experience. Let's not squander that, Kourin."

She set her glass down with a thud. The gold in her eyes flared. She replied, "I told you last time, and I will tell you again. This time, listen and hear what I have to tell you."

She glared into the blue eyes that had fleetingly captivated her heart weeks ago until she fathomed what was underneath the false persona. Jack's visage came to her mind—cheerless brown eyes and sullen countenance as he passed by her table minutes ago. The time had come to end this once and for all. Heat rising inside her and her extremities turning cold, Kourin knew she had to say what was on her mind to save her heart.

She said, through clenched teeth, "Whatever you thought we had, we did not. As I told you before, going forward, we have a working relationship only. There is no 'us.' I have my shop to run. You have . . . temporarily have this terminal to manage. There is nothing between us."

Anders stared into her beautiful eyes and marveled at her passion as she spoke. Upon conclusion of her tirade, he opened his mouth to comment when she abruptly rose and stormed out of the restaurant.

He followed her, mesmerized by her curves until they were out of sight, listening to the sound of her footsteps echoing in the distance. By the time her last footfall was heard, her words had already been forgotten.

He thought, *God, she's hot! She's going to be my biggest challenge yet.* He had a sip of his club soda. *But she'll be worth it. I'm sure!*

* * *

Jack saw Kourin abruptly rise and rush out of the restaurant. He noted Anders just sitting there sipping his drink.

Laurel said, "Go after her, Uncle. I'll get our lunch to go."

"Thanks. I'll see you in a bit." He rushed after the woman he cared very much about.

Sosie came by with their drinks. Laurel asked her to change their order to go as something had just come up. She summarized what happened and also asked her if she could box up Kourin's and include it with her order.

The waitress glanced in Anders' direction who was sitting unaccompanied. Sosie told her Kourin had seemed agitated, but she didn't know the cause. She said changing the order to go wouldn't be a problem, and she'd be back shortly with everything.

When Sosie left, Laurel looked at Anders. A chill ran down her spine when his blue eyes returned her gaze. She averted her gaze to Ubu. His big brown eyes met hers, and his tail swished back and forth against the leg of Jack's empty chair. Even though Anders gave her the creeps, her dog brought a smile to her face.

* * *

Jack caught up with Kourin steps away from her shop. Upon hearing her name spoken behind her, she pivoted to face the voice she recognized. Tear lines were visible on her cheeks. He closed the few steps between them and hugged her.

She embraced him in return, her body trembling with a flood of emotion. Waves of heat pulsated from her body against his chest, while her hands on the lower part of his back felt like frigid blocks of ice against his flimsy shirt. After a few moments, he eased his hug, but he kept her within his arms.

With a deep and inquisitive gaze, he searched her green eyes for answers before she diverted them, and softly asked, "Are you okay?"

"It's been a rough day."

With a slight smile, he said, "It's only eleven thirty."

Kourin shifted her eyes to his. There was no malice in them, as there had been toward Anders. "Is that Jack Roberts trying to be funny?"

"I'm sorry."

Kourin allowed a hint of a smile to flicker across her sorrowful face. "No need to be sorry. You're not the one I'm pissed at."

"Well, that's a relief." Jack took the lightened mood as a sign she was feeling better. A small group of travelers passed by. "Kori, let's find someplace to sit."

He took her by the hand, which remained chilled, and led her past her store toward the garden. He felt resistance as he neared. "Don't worry. We're not going to the center." He proceeded to the bench on the left side. "Here, away from the traffic for a bit."

Before they sat down, she asked, "Jack, do you think this is safe?"

He knew what she was implying, and he hadn't yet told her the odd happenings in the garden may not be confined to the center bench. "I think so. We watched the garden video and nothing happened on the outer benches." To show his confidence, he sat down first.

She sat next to him after several seconds and nestled her body against his. She took his right hand in both of hers. "Jack, I need to tell you something."

The warmth of her hands had returned to a pleasant temperature, and he relished the pleasant tingling sensation from the contact. After seeing her with another man for the second time today, her touch had greater significance than even the day before. Was he jealous? Yes. He knew he shouldn't be, but he was in love with her. Insecurity and apprehension drove his thoughts of losing another wonderful woman in his life.

As Kourin tenderly held his hands, she summarized John's recruitment to open her own shop and her uncertainties about the entire process. He volunteered to provide her support through his operations team. With that commitment, along with a very favorable lease agreement, she became an entrepreneur.

She said, "The man you saw me with, Anders, is who John assigned to help me. For a short time, a very short time, we had a thing."

Jack kept quiet, uneasy about what she might say.

She avoided his gaze, her voice barely audible as she said, "It didn't get too serious. We had dinners together after work." She felt his hand tense and looked back into his brown eyes. "We didn't sleep together."

Jack blushed. "Kori, you don't have to—"

"I do, Jack. I need to be upfront with you." She realized, once again, she was squeezing his hands too tightly. "Sorry." She let them go.

"No worries. Kori, you're free to see who you like. You don't need to worry about me."

"That's just it, Jack. I do worry about you." A pleasant warmth spread through her body when she looked into his eyes. "Because I love you."

Her words swept the anxiety from his mind. Any doubts he had over the last few hours melted away in an instant. Without hesitation, he kissed her with an intensity that stirred her soul. Her fervor confirmed the love he held in his heart.

When they parted, she said, "You're twice the man he'll ever be. I just want you to know that." She took hold of both his hands again. "But I need to tell you. He still has a thing for me. I told him weeks ago to fuck off, but like a bad penny, he keeps turning up."

"I'll have a conversation with him."

"No. I know it's part of your DNA to come to my rescue, but I have this, Jack. Let me handle him. I just want you to know it is you I love. There isn't anything Anders or anyone else can do that will change that."

Jack hugged her. "I know you do, Kori. I know you do."

From several feet away, they heard, "So this is where you two lovebirds ran off to."

They both turned in the voice's direction. Laurel stood there with Ubu at her side and a plastic bag in both hands. "Anyone care for lunch?"

* * *

Anders ate his lunch in silence after Kourin walked out. He was in no hurry. He would speak with her later and convince her to go on a date. Smiling, he thought, *The chase was the fun part. Well, that's half the fun. Great sex is the other half!*

He leered at the brunette with short hair and trim athletic body as she lifted two bags of takeout food off her table. Her story was not known to him, but he knew her from the coffee place and always had the dog with her. It was a service dog, so something was up with that. She obviously knew the guy who was in the way of Kourin and him hooking up. He could be her father, or she just liked older men, which would benefit him.

As she passed by on her way out, she did not look his way. However, as she strode away, he watched her butt as he had Kourin's and added her to his short list.

When the waitress brought him his check, he noted only his lunch and drink were on the bill. Kourin's food never came to the table, and he assumed she must have canceled her order when she left. He paid with his Benchmark-issued debit card and added precisely 15 percent on the tip line.

On his way out the door, he stopped to chat with the cute hostess, Wren. He watched her at the party the night before and was enamored by her red hair and shapely body. Before he could say little more than hello, they were interrupted by a group of four travelers wanting to have lunch. He left her to her work, knowing he would be at the terminal for possibly several months and would definitely see her again. He put her on his short list to pursue as well.

He thought, *Not a bad lunch overall. It didn't go as planned with Kourin, but I will overcome any obstacles she has. I added two names to my list. Who knows how many others I'll have before the day is through?*

He checked his phone for the time and realized he should get back to work. He strolled through the terminal, observing the attractive female passengers, Benchmark gate personnel, and two stewardesses as he went. *Oh, flight attendants. Not stewardesses.* He had called an attractive brunette that once. She sternly corrected him to call her a flight attendant, and then she slapped him when he laughed at her. *She was a spitfire in the sack, though.* He smiled at the memory.

His mind came back to Kourin. *I bet she's a spitfire, too!*

18

PASSION

Beth and Harry watched Kourin and Anders arrive for lunch. It was clear Kourin was not in a good mood sitting across from the temporary terminal manager. Soon after those two arrived, Laurel walked in with Jack, occupying a table close by. Although the conversations could not be heard, Beth observed Jack catching glimpses of Kourin. She could tell he was agitated and not himself.

Sosie delivered Beth's and Harry's lunch. As they both poked at their food, Beth kept her eye on Jack while she and Harry talked about the bench. She sat on eggshells as she wasn't sure if Harry would spiral out of control as he had in the prior days. To his credit, he showed remarkable restraint, considering all he had been through.

She remained patient while he spoke, waiting for the best moment to bring up what needed to be discussed. She was certain it was a significant part of his undercurrent troubles. To this day, he acted as if it had never occurred.

As he was stating for the tenth time about needing to locate the mechanism to control the bench, Beth saw Kourin rise and walk out. Jack soon followed.

She said, "Well, that's odd."

"What's that?" asked Harry, looking up from his plate where he was pushing around what remained of his food.

Beth returned her attention to Harry. "Nothing, dear." She didn't want to mention Kourin's and Jack's names, possibly setting him off. Instead, she asked a question to deflect his attention. "Maybe the bench is showing you what you experienced for a particular reason?"

He looked at her without comment.

"Look, you saw Christine on vacation. You were back home as a child. You saved your grandfather. What do these all have in common?"

"The obvious answer is me. I've been down that road many times since yesterday. I don't see a correlation."

"True. You're a central part of each vision."

She analyzed his face. He seemed older than he had just a few days ago. She thought, *Probably not getting enough sleep. Maybe he's not getting any. Lord knows I haven't slept the last two nights.* She asked, "But what else is shared in all three?"

Harry set his fork down. He was done moving his lunch remains around on his plate. She could tell he was in thought, but he didn't speak what he was thinking. He was still holding back or denying the truth.

Harry's dour expression was unmistakable.

Her thoughts continued unspoken. *When you were down, I tried to cheer you up. I was stupid to have let it happen the way it did. I'm sorry, Harry.*

In a flash in her mind, she felt she had something. "Harry, I think I know what the common denominator is. It's not you, per se." She reached across the table. With both hands, she cradled one of his hands. She said, "It's emotions!"

"What?" Harry asked, finally turning his attention away from his uneaten lunch.

She saw the sparkle in his brown eyes. She smiled. "Emotion, my love. In all your visions, you had deep emotions, powerful feelings about what was happening . . . Christine, your father, your grandfather."

Beth continued to hold Harry's hand. He didn't pull them away.

He countered, "But I didn't know it was my grandfather until afterwards."

"True, but you saw a young boy in serious trouble and fought to save him. Your emotional reaction couldn't have been any higher!" She smiled and squeezed his hand.

Harry thought, *Could it have been that simple?* Out loud, he said, "But I didn't know about my grandfather and the storm. That makes little sense."

"That's not what brought you to him. When you sat on the bench, it was triggered by your love. You wanted to be with Christine."

"I don't get it."

Beth kept her patience. "Maybe the bench is triggered by the person's desires when they sit on it."

"But I wanted to see Christine. The damn thing didn't bring me to her."

"No, it did not. What I'm saying is, with everyone who has sat on the bench, the bench got activated by the person's emotions, a sort of fuel, if you will."

Harry seemed dubious about her theory.

"Let me put it another way. When I sat down on the bench, I was thinking . . ." she paused, debating whether to mention her next thought. She decided she couldn't avoid it. "I was thinking how happy I was for Jack being with Kourin. He's been sad for so long." She halted for a moment to gauge Harry's response. He seemed okay, so she went further. "And I was thinking about how I was lonely." She looked into Harry's eyes. "How I missed holding someone in my arms." She couldn't bring herself to say the next sentence.

Harry finished her line of thinking with what he thought she was going to say, "You missed Tom. That's understandable."

Beth squeezed Harry's hand, but she couldn't fully correct him out loud. *And I was terribly worried about you, my love!* She said, "Yes. I missed . . . I still miss my Tom." She looked away from his eyes. Her hands trembled.

He felt her hands shake and saw the pain in her eyes. *Just like that night.* He put that thought aside and fought to stay focused. He brought up his other hand and gently placed it over hers.

Beth glanced up when she felt the comforting weight of his hand on top of hers. The tear that had formed on the corner of her eye hung in place for a moment. She blinked, releasing it to carve a course down her cheek.

The emotional connection they shared revived the heartache from the past as he clasped her hand more firmly.

Harry gazed into Beth's eyes and saw a twinkle. He pressed his lips against hers. She felt the softness of his lips on hers as she slipped her tongue between them.

The sweat on his back cooled as he felt her desirable body beneath him, and the heat of the moment dissipated. His penis, still inside her warmth, felt a squeeze as she contracted her muscles, and its size decreased as his heartbeat slowed back to normal.

As their lips parted, she smiled and gave him a second squeeze. This caused him to be expelled from her. She laughed and said, "Oh, sorry."

The tear dropped from Beth's chin. Harry's eyes widened in shock as he gawked at her across the table. He released her hands and asked, "What the fuck just happened?"

* * *

Kourin nibbled at her mozzarella in carrozza sandwich, having been the special on Luca's lunch menu. She discovered she had no appetite.

Her bench mate had the same sandwich and had ordered it because the description resembled a traditional grilled cheese sandwich. To make it an authentic Italian experience, you could order it with anchovies. Jack skipped that, as had Kourin.

"This is fantastic," Jack said between mouthfuls. "I'm going to miss this restaurant."

Kourin set her sandwich down and wrapped it back up, saving it for later. "Well, you're in luck then. Sosie had stopped in my shop this morning before going to work. She told me Luca will be opening a second restaurant. It was part of the deal to have him open this one. Evidently, John is backing the second restaurant to get him started."

"Wow. That's a helluva deal. If Luca is doing a ground up, that could be very expensive," he said, putting the last bite of his sandwich into his mouth.

"I don't know the details."

"Before I leave, I'm gonna check in with Luca. Maybe he needs a contractor."

She used her napkin to wipe some cheese from the side of Jack's mouth. Laughing, she said, "Maybe you should clean up first."

"Um, thanks," he said. As she finished wiping, he took hold of her hand. "Kori, I need to tell you something. I'm very concerned about you." He held her hand a little tighter. "Your shop is very close to this garden, as is Laurel's. We don't know what's going on here."

"I appreciate you being worried about me, but I don't think my shop is in danger."

He raised a hand about to object.

Kourin continued before he could. "Please let me finish. Am I worried about what is going on here? Absolutely. I'm worried someone is going to sit on the bench, and history, as we now know it, will be utterly altered. There is much more we don't know than we do. However, when I am in my shop, I don't have any sensation of apprehension, fear, or anything that makes me afraid."

"But as you say, there's so much we don't know."

"Yes, but I think I need to be here and figure it out. I mean, so far, nothing horrible has actually happened. We've all had to relive our past, but that's all it's been. Right?"

"True. Painful as it's been, especially for Harry and you, it's akin to terrible dreams." He paused. "And Laurel—I'm concerned about her. She's putting on a brave face, but I'm not sure of what she's really feeling."

"Well, you surely know her better than I. I mean, she seems okay. She thought of us when we left Luca's and brought us our lunches. I think if she was a quote, unquote, mess, she wouldn't be doing something like that. She'd be trying to deal with her nightmare."

"Again, true, but something tells me she hasn't abandoned trying to alter what happened. She's never fully recovered."

"I don't think anyone would ever truly recover from a trauma like that." Kourin thought of her own vision. In her mind, she could hear her baby cry. "I know I wouldn't."

He saw a sorrowful look in her eyes, eyes that were now more green than hazel. He let go of her hand and gave her a hug. She reciprocated. In his arms, Kourin thought of the horrors she had faced. She didn't voice the thoughts she'd been having. *I can go into the past and stop my pain from having ever occurred. I can kill that bastard before . . .* she didn't finish her thought. Behind her, she heard a rustling in the Hosta plants. She opened her eyes. Before her, all the plants were moving randomly up, down, and side to side. *What the fuck?*

With a sudden rustling noise behind him, Jack released his hug. Both he and Kourin jumped to their feet, sending her sandwich bag to the ground. Fortunately, the contents did not spill out.

In silence, they watched the plants' movement die down and come to a stop. She asked, "What just happened?"

"I'll be damned if I know."

Kourin was a little less sure of herself now than she was moments ago. *Maybe we're not as safe in the shop as I had thought.*

* * *

Sosie stopped at Harry's table and asked, "Will there be anything else?"

Harry and Beth looked at each other. Neither spoke. She shook her head no.

"Okay. I hope you enjoyed your lunch. I'll leave this with you." Sosie set the check down on the table, leaving the two alone once again.

"Harry, did you just . . .? Did we just . . .?"

He searched her eyes. He studied her red lips, lips that moments ago he was kissing, or so it had seemed.

"I don't know what just happened." His gaze shifted from her lips back to her eyes, and he said, "How the fuck . . .?"

She knew what she felt, even though it was impossible. "Harry, we were just back on the night we . . . when we . . ." She broke her eye contact with him. "How can that be?"

He searched for answers, looking everywhere except back at her and not finding any in the nearly empty restaurant.

Sosie returned, and they settled their bill, leaving a considerable tip and now wanting to put some distance from the occurrence they just shared.

He said, "Let's get out of here. We need to get to the bottom of this."

Together, they exited the restaurant, silently and lost in thought.

She was recalling how wonderful that night had been until the consequences had driven a wedge between her and Harry.

He reflected on how he could manipulate his misery to go back to the time before the recent event took place. He was desperate to set things right and make amends for his most regrettable decision. It was the only way he could have Christine back!

19
DOG WHISPERER

Laurel brought the lunch that Sosie had packed for her uncle and Kourin to the garden. It took her a few moments to locate them, but there were only so many places they were likely to be. As she turned away from them, she thought, *They suit each other. I'm so happy for you, Uncle.*

Ubu trotted beside Mom. He was concerned when they had approached the garden, but Mom walked on the outside path for a short distance, coming to friends he knew. As quickly as they had arrived, they turned back and walked the short distance to the place he knew well. He followed Mom into the back and was ready for a nap. In this place, he could find some rest.

Laurel went to her office desk and flipped open her laptop. She recalled skimming many articles about time travel the previous day. With the new revelation of plants moving during the visions, something clicked in her mind. She needed to find a particular article.

Ubu lay down a couple feet away in his favorite spot, watching Mom and the door. He fell asleep within moments.

In her browser history, she went down the list. She had skimmed through so many online sources that she could not recollect where she had encountered it. There was a knock at the door. Mandy poked her head in to ask if everything was okay. After confirming with her all was well, she resumed her task.

Several minutes later, she found what she was searching for. On the floor, she heard Ubu making noise. His feet were moving like he was chasing something. She thought, *He's so cute when he does that.*

Ubu found himself in a place he did not recognize. He sniffed. He smelled trees, plants, and dirt. All were familiar smells yet not the ones he knew from being home or even in the new place where the scary man hurt Mom.

There were no paths to follow. He ducked under branches and jumped over plants. He was unsure of where he was going. His senses told him he was heading in the right direction. He wasn't with Mom and needed to find her to keep her safe. He thought, *I can't smell her. Maybe she's this way.* He trudged on, jumping over a downed tree.

Onward, Ubu trotted. He made solid forward progress in a place he did not know. He needed to find Mom.

He saw light ahead and redoubled his effort, coming upon a clearing where sunshine filled moss-covered earth. At the center of the opening were several boulders nestled together, with the highest one having a large flat surface.

That's a suitable spot to get a better look around. He jumped onto one of the lower rocks, using it as a stepping stone to the higher rock surface. He only saw trees several paces away in all directions. *No Mom,* he thought. *Where are you, Mom?*

An inner voice said, *Mom is not here, Ubu.*

Ubu could hear a voice in his head. He was confused as he hadn't heard it with his acute hearing. He peered through the trees in all directions, searching for the source of the voice. The hair on his back raised. He stood in his ready position, releasing a low growl.

Do not be alarmed, my friend. You are safe here.

Ubu realized he could understand what he was hearing. He barked.

You do not need to become alarmed. I need you to listen to what I have to tell you. It is important for saving your friends and your Mom.

Mom!

Yes, Ubu, Mom. Soon your Mom and her friends will be in great danger. You will need to protect Mom and the others. Do you understand?

Protect Mom.

Yes, Ubu, she will need your protection, as will your friend, your sister. Do you understand?

Sister! She was part of his pack, his sister. *Yes. Danger. But who are you? How do I know you are not the dark man who attacked Mom in that hot place?*

Ubu, there are forces far more dangerous to your Mom. I am a friend. I want to help you and your pack.

Why can't I see you?

You see me. I am standing right here in front of you.

Ubu used his keen eyesight to look closer at the trees in front of him. They were very large red cedar, but to him a tree was a tree. *All I see are trees.*

The tree branches of the largest cedar shook, as if hit by a strong breeze. The trees on either side remained motionless. *I am here, my friend. Save your pack when the time is right. I'll be there to guide you.*

Ubu awoke and lifted his head. Mom was looking down at him from her chair. *She's safe!* he thought. *Mom is safe.*

Laurel was startled by Ubu beside her. Minutes earlier, his legs had been moving as if he was chasing a squirrel. At one point, he growled and let out a short bark. He had become still for several minutes until waking and lifting his head, staring at her.

Laurel smiled down at him and asked, "Were you dreaming, sleepyhead?"

He stood up and closed the few steps between them. He placed his large head on her lap. *I'll protect you, Mom. I won't leave your side.*

As she read the headline of the article she had been searching for, her fingertips lightly grazed his head, avoiding the injured area: "Woman sees a tree move and hears voices in her head."

20

FORCE OF NATURE

Kourin stared at the foliage feet away and asked Jack, "We didn't just dream that, right? You saw it, too? All the plants were moving."

"Yes." He took hold of her hand. It was cold to the touch. He looked around to make sure there wasn't something, anything, in the area that could have caused it. "I don't know what to make of it."

"Why were they doing that?"

"Not sure, but . . ." He turned toward her, seeing her profile. She kept her eyes on the greenery. "Earlier we saw the plants moving a little when someone appeared to be having a vision. But it wasn't anything like this. I wonder if someone's on the center bench. I'll be right back." He released her hand and hurried up the path to the center.

"Be careful," she called to his back.

She returned to observing the plants. There was no movement. Out of the corner of her eye, she saw her lunch bag on the tiled floor and picked it up. For a moment, she contemplated sitting on the bench, but she opted not to have her back to the plants. They now felt unsettling to her.

Jack returned shortly after what felt like an eternity.

"No one," he said as he closed the space between them. "I didn't see anyone up there."

Kourin gave the Hosta near her a sideways look. "Let's get out of here. I feel creeped out."

"Sure." He held her hand again. Her hand was still cold, but it was warmer than moments ago. He paused before moving.

She looked at him and asked, "Are you okay?"

Jack peered into eyes of dark green with a golden ring around the pupil. No mistaking it—they were no longer hazel as they had been only a short time ago.

"Kori, your eyes."

She continued to return his gaze. "What about them?"

"They're green!"

"We've been through this before. Sometimes they appear green and sometimes hazel."

"No, Kori. I mean they're extraordinarily green." Jack took hold of her other hand and peered deeply into her eyes. "They're a dark green with a golden ring. It's like nothing I've ever seen." He released her hands to retrieve his cell phone and took her picture. He looked at the photo and then back at her. The vividness of the green was decreasing. The golden ring was quickly fading away and was already nearly imperceptible.

Kourin reached for his phone. He released it to her without saying a word.

She looked at her image and saw eyes she didn't recognize. She gasped. *What the hell?* "Jack, what the fuck is going on? Why do my eyes look like that?" She gaped at the photo.

He grabbed his trash off the bench, taking a moment to search for an answer to what was happening. He had nothing.

All he could think to say was, "Let's get out here."

He led her away from the garden.

* * *

When Mandy saw Laurel return from lunch, she checked in to see how she was doing. Her friend gave the impression of being in a healthier mental state than previously. Ubu was snoozing beside her as another indicator she was okay. As she closed the office door, she made a mental note to check back in with her later.

Back at the counter, she waited on a customer and refilled the bakery goods in the glass displays. When all was running well, she felt the need to relieve her bladder and took a bio break. She went to the employee bathroom in the back left corner next to the office. The single handicap toilet was plain and utilitarian, with a simple sink and mirror across the top.

As she was sitting on the toilet, she felt a chill creep up her arms and legs. She felt one hand with the other. They were ice cold. She wiped herself and rose, putting her clothing back into place. She rubbed her hands together. They remained cold. A burning sensation was deep in her innermost being. It made no sense. On the inside, she was burning up, yet on the outside, she was ice cold.

She turned on the faucet, using only hot water to warm herself. She kept her icy fingers beneath the hot water for a minute, feeling the warmth slowly trickle through her skin.

She could feel the heat inside her rising like a wave, threatening to overwhelm her.

To maintain her equilibrium, she clutched both sides of the sink and glanced in the mirror. She gasped at her reflection. Her eyes shone with a vivid emerald green luminescence. Around the pupil was an astounding sight – a shimmering golden ring. She blinked to make sure she wasn't seeing things. When she checked again, she saw eyes staring back at her she did not recognize.

Startled by the blonde in the mirror, aloud she said, "What the hell?"

* * *

Beth caught sight of Jack and Kourin coming toward them from the garden. She could tell, even from a distance, something was troubling them.

Internally, she did not feel well either. Her emotions were upside down. On one hand, she wanted to console Harry as a friend. On the other, she wanted to hold him close.

Harry walked beside her with a perceptible limp from his injury the previous day. Both of them were equally disturbed by the incident in the restaurant. She knew it was for very different reasons, though. Before she could even consider it further, they were face to face with her boss and his new girlfriend.

Harry said, "You two look like you've been through the haunted house at Canobie Lake." He paused, awaiting a response. When there wasn't one, he asked, "Did you sit on the bench?"

Both bore furrowed brows and tense lips.

Jack answered while peering into Kourin's eyes. They were more muted than they were moments ago. "We stayed on the outskirts." He turned away from Kourin's gaze. "I checked the center when . . . when something happened, but no one was there." He continued holding one of Kourin's hands and gave it a slight squeeze. "But we're okay now."

While he spoke, Beth observed Kourin who appeared to be having a hard time restraining her emotions. Beth said, "Maybe we should all sit down. We had something happen that . . . Well, it's hard to explain."

Jack looked up at the garden and said, "Let's put a little distance between us and the garden." He cast his eyes toward the Coffee Bean. "The café seems quiet now. Let's grab a table over there."

Kourin glanced at her shop, seeing Mary and the others inside with a few customers. All seemed well. She recognized she needed some time before going back there.

Without a word, all four walked the short distance across the terminal walkway, not daring to look in the garden's direction.

Most of the tables at the café were empty, but they bypassed several, choosing one as far away from the entrance and the garden as possible. Beth and Harry sat side by side, facing the entrance. Jack helped Kourin into a seat closest to the wall and sat next to her. He held her hand below the table. All were quiet for several moments.

Harry, being Harry, spoke up first. "Are we just gonna sit here like zombies, or are we gonna figure out what the fuck is going on?"

Beth reacted to him first. "Shh, Harry. There may be children around."

"I don't give a—" He saw her staring at him. "I don't care. There's something messed up here."

Jack looked at them and asked, "What happened? Where were you?"

Beth answered before Harry had a chance. "We were having lunch at Luca's."

Jack and Kourin shared a glance.

"Yes, we saw what happened," Beth said. "But that's not . . ." she paused, searching for the right words. With a smile, she said, "I have confidence you two will work it out."

Jack gave Kourin's hand a gentle squeeze, confirming to her he agreed with what was said. Her lips curved into a subtle yet sincere smile.

"Anyway," Beth continued, "we were almost ready to leave when something strange happened." She looked at Harry who remained quiet, allowing her to tell the story. "We both experienced the same dream while sitting in the restaurant. One moment we were talking, the next we were . . . someplace else, and then in a blink of the eye we were back in the restaurant. It was so real."

"Where did you go?" asked Jack.

Harry answered before she could figure out what to say. "That's not important." He glanced sideways at Beth and continued, "One moment we were at the restaurant. The next we were elsewhere. And then we were back at the restaurant like nothing had happened. But it did. We both felt it happen. It was as real as the times I had sat on the bench myself!"

Jack said, "Okay." He could see they had an experience they didn't want to disclose, for whatever reason, but he understood. The visions were personal when they occurred. "Can you at least tell us if it was the past or the future?"

Both Harry and Beth answered at the same time. "The past." They traded glances, yet neither said anything more.

Kourin sat quietly, watching the trio's discussion. She was still befuddled by the photo Jack had taken of her eyes. They had never been so vibrant. At times, they seemed more green than hazel, and occasionally she would see sparkles of gold mixed in. She had never seen a golden ring with dark green eyes.

When the conversation hit a silent moment, Kourin asked, "This just happened a short time ago? Say about twenty minutes ago?" She noted the dynamic had changed between the two from the night before. *I know what that something is*, she thought. *You both have a secret. That's obvious. Something just brought you to that secret, a shared event.*

"Yes," Beth answered. "Just before we got here about fifteen, twenty minutes ago. Why? What happened here?"

Jack recounted the events in the garden to them, excluding the part where Kourin's eyes shifted to a vibrant green.

As he finished his update, Ubu approached the table, followed seconds later by Laurel. "Hi, all. What brings you by? Can I get you something?"

All four exchanged glances. Jack answered, "Sweetie, you need to sit down for this."

Laurel scanned the faces at the table, taking in their expressions. *Oh, oh*, she thought. *What now?*

* * *

Mandy remained in the restroom for several minutes. Not removing her hands from the sides of the sink, she stared at her eyes in the mirror. When green eyes continued to return her gaze, she closed them tightly. Many minutes passed before she built up the courage to see her reflection again.

This time, her eyes were back to normal. They were still more on the green side, and she saw a touch of gold in them, which was odd. The striking emerald green had receded.

She exited the bathroom. There was no one in the hallway. She knocked on the office door, which was technically her office, as Laurel's office was back at the original café downtown. From the start, they shared the terminal office, but inside she knew Laurel sometimes needed solitude. She was more than willing to provide that for her friend.

No one answered her knock. She slowly opened the door to an empty room. She had expected to find Laurel at the desk with Ubu at her side. While she was in the restroom, she must have gone to the front. Mandy looked in that direction, and not seeing anyone, she felt her legs grow weak and decided she needed to sit down.

She sat in the same spot she had seen her friend a short time ago, propping her elbows on the table and cradling her head in her hands. She closed her eyes. An overwhelming sadness overcame her, and she wept.

* * *

Laurel grabbed a chair from the closest table and sat at the end to hear what had happened now. She listened with rapt attention as her uncle relayed a condensed version of what occurred on the outskirts of the garden and at the restaurant.

Kourin placed a hand over his as he spoke about the plants in the garden. He once more left out her eye color transformation.

As he finished, he heard Ubu whine below him. The dog was looking up at him.

Jack felt Kourin's hand tense up on his as he realized Ubu was looking past him at Kourin with an intense gaze. He shifted his eyes from the dog to her. Tears flowed down her cheeks. Her eyes were again a dark green with a faint golden ring.

> Kourin felt the pain. It was overwhelming. She took in her surroundings. She was in a bed, a hospital bed. Another pain shot through her body. She screamed. She could not contain herself.

Beside her, a woman in a crisp white nurse's uniform held her hand tightly. She was speaking, but Kourin wasn't comprehending what was being said. After a brief pause, the nurse's lips moved again, saying, "Breathe. Keep breathing, Kourin, in and out." Kourin started breathing. She hadn't realized she was holding her breath until then. "That's it," said the nurse. "In and out. Good. You're doing fine, dear."

Another wave of pain surged through her. Her hands clenched as she screamed. The pain grew more intense, coming in closer waves. As her thoughts cleared, she felt a wave of recognition instead of pain wash over her, knowing exactly where she was and what was happening. *My baby!*

She heard a male voice from the foot of the bed. "Your baby's coming. On the next one push. Okay, Kourin? Can you do that for me?"

She didn't answer. A sharp burst of pain surged through her body once more. The nurse told her to push. She did. Nature ran its course, and the baby entered the world.

Kourin let out a sigh of relief and felt her sweat-soaked hair brush against her neck as she turned her head to the side. Behind the nurse, on the other side of the small bright white room, she saw four people watching her: two males and two females. They bore astonished expressions. A black dog with a bright red vest stood confidently in front of them, his eyes fixed on her.

Kourin kept eye contact with Ubu. She suddenly realized he was standing between Jack and Laurel, sitting as they had been in the café. They were no longer in the hospital room. She looked at the faces staring back at her and felt water drip down her chin. With her left hand, she wiped it away. Her right hand was still holding Jack's. Moments ago, a nurse was holding it.

Harry was the first to speak. "What the fuck just happened?"

Beth, beside him, didn't correct or shush him this time. All she could say was, "Oh my."

Laurel sat dumfounded with her mouth open, no words coming out.

Jack placed his other hand on Kourin's. He squeezed it gently and asked, "Kori, was that . . .?" He didn't finish his sentence.

"Yes," she answered faintly. Her eyes welled up and tears flowed freely. "Yes. That was the birth of my daughter."

She freed her hand from his and picked up a paper napkin off the table. She wiped the tears from her face even as they were replaced by new ones. "My baby," she wept, her heart aching with sorrow. She looked up, her lips quivering, and softly uttered, "My baby."

His eyes met hers as he studied her gaze. They were once again vibrant dark green with a golden ring around the pupil.

* * *

Mandy wiped her face. She had been sobbing uncontrollably, with no sense of time passing. She had flashes of light in between her bouts of crying, but none of it made any sense. When the bright lights were gone and she opened her eyes, she saw the darkness of the office around her. Her cheeks were wet, and the desk below her had water stains from droplets of tears.

She grabbed a tissue from the decorative box at the edge of the desk. She cleaned herself and worked on getting her crying under control. After several more minutes, it abated. She grabbed another tissue after discarding the wet one in the trash can. Three more were required before she was adequately cleaned up.

Laurel had placed a handheld mirror in one of the desk drawers. They laughed about it for half an hour when she did it, making a joke that it was to make sure they didn't have a piece of spinach stuck between their teeth before they went back to work. She located it, bringing it up in front of her with the back facing her. She held the small mirror with both hands. Her hands trembled as she haltingly turned the reflective side toward her.

As her image appeared on the surface, she was transfixed by her own eyes. Two emerald green eyes peered back. A golden halo surrounded each pupil.

INTERLUDE

SALON-DE-PROVENCE, FRANCE 1548

Rain showered down, as it often did in Southern France. Michel trod along the cobblestone street, staying close to the stone building on his right to shelter himself from a light wind blowing between the long-standing buildings. He passed a sizeable stone vase half his height with small colorful blue flowers cascading down its side. Behind and to the right of this impressive planter was a bright red double door, starkly standing out against the monotonous beiges all around him. On the opposite side of the narrow pathway was a single doorway painted a deeper crimson, showing signs of time from the bright sun on its lower faded half. Next to the doorway stood a smaller taupe vase with a trellis covered with green vines and small white flowers rising from it. With no soul around, Michel picked a few of the blue and white flowers, cradling them in his palm. He continued onward in the rain.

Typically, he welcomed rain water splashing down on him when it came. After surviving through two horrendous outbreaks watching many of his friends perish before his eyes, his belief remained that the water washed away the filth and disease. Today it felt more of a nuisance as he walked the deserted streets to clear his mind.

At another doorway, he paused under the slight overhang to have a respite from the shower. The splashing water brought back the memory of his first wife, Henriette. It was a day similar to this one when he was out with his young family, and they were caught in a rainstorm. They were all soaked to the bone by the time they made it back to their home. Two months to the day after they warmed by the fire to chase away the chill, they were taken from him.

Fourteen years ago, a scar was left in his heart when he lost his wife and two young children. He had loved his family and labored tirelessly to make them and his neighbors healthy. The key to ending Le Charbon, the malady affecting many, he believed, was to improve their diets and hygiene. He even created a rosehips pill that had aided hundreds, saving entire villages.

Despite his efforts, he couldn't save his own family.

For his troubles, he was outcast as a charlatan for having been an apothecary. He knew in his heart and through his studies there was more that could have been done besides bloodletting and watching disease overcome the masses. Shortsightedness had doomed thousands, if not millions, to die a painful death. His lovely Henriette and children perished along with them.

The steady rain continued as he leaned against the stone wall, waiting for it to abate. His thoughts moved on to his travels through Italy, Greece, and Turkey in his younger days. He had left France when the inquisitors called upon him because of a remark he had made about a new statue in the churchyard. Excessive interest in him necessitated a sabbatical. Along the way, he learned new medicinal skills that some feared to even ponder.

Today, as the rain puddled around the potted plants, he wondered if it was the feebleminded fools who were afraid of what may lurk in the shadows or if it was those who have power and are afraid to lose what they have. Likely, it was both keeping advancement in science under their dimwitted thumbs.

Because of these unenlightened men, he recently traveled back to Italy where he privately met with others similar in thought as he. These were friends who were open to advancements in the medical field and were exploring innovations shunned by those in power. Michel felt he could prevent the black death from happening again and sought ways to combat it, besides through prayer. He remained Catholic, but he felt mankind needed to solve their own problems.

This trip would not have been possible if he had not won the heart of an attractive and wealthy woman, Anne. Although it took time for her to fall in love with him, he was smitten with her from the day they met. After Henriette, he did not think he would ever love again until he had met Anne.

While on their Italian trip, an old friend bestowed upon them a late wedding present. When the newlyweds brought this item home to Salon-de-Provence, they placed the wooden bench in a well-lit room where they could sit together. In front of the cedar bench, Michel placed a short table. Anne filled a brass bowl with herbs and water to create a pleasant scent in the room and added it to the table.

A thunderclap boom brought Michel back to the present. With an image in his mind of his lovely Anne awaiting his arrival, he left the safety of the doorway. The puddles of water on the cobblestones before him were lit up by lightning above. Thunder reverberated through the deserted streets, rattling his teeth.

Upon arriving home, he removed his jerkin, hanging it by the fireplace, but he kept his doublet on even though it was damp. Anne had a small fire glowing in the fireplace, and the room warmed Michel's chilled bones. He greeted his wife, kissing her cheek. He placed the fragile flowers he had collected into her delicate hand.

"And what is this for?" she asked.

"Because you bring a bright light to this dark day, my love." He scanned the room, remembering the bench in the adjacent room. "Let's sit on our new bench, shall we?"

He led her by the hand to the bench. The aroma from the herbs on the table added to the romantic mood he felt. They sat on the bench. Michel held her hand and leaned in for a kiss. She accepted his lips on hers.

For several minutes, they enjoyed their affection, embracing one another. When one kiss ended and before another began, Anne created several inches of space between them. She said to her husband, "If you keep this up, I'll not have dinner ready on time, my love."

"We can eat tomorrow."

"You say that now, but soon you will ask where your food is." Anne released him and stood, saying, "I'll make it up to you tonight." She smiled and left her husband alone in the room.

Michel watched his love leave his view into the next room. His attention focused on the bowl on the short table in front of him. He stared at the herbs as if analyzing them. His eyes became heavy.

Michel opened his eyes to a sunny cobblestone street. An old shepherd walked by him, heading up the hill holding the reins of a donkey as it struggled to pull the weighed-down cart. One wooden wheel was warped, turning unevenly as it struck the next cobblestone.

The man patted the donkey on his side, saying, "Get along, Munti. You can do it."

Michel turned in the other direction. Three children played a game. He didn't know their pastime, but they chased each other in a small circle. First, they playfully ran in one direction and then in the other. All the while, they laughed.

From behind him, he heard the cart continuing on its way up the incline. Clip-clop went the hooves of the donkey. Bam-bam-bam sounded the irregular wheel of the old cart.

Michel recognized the street. It was at least five streets over from his own new home. He looked around and saw his wife viewing the window display of a dress shop. She was on the opposite side of the street, the same as the children playing.

About to call out to her, he heard a loud crack from uphill behind him. He saw the cart that had passed him only moments ago coming down the hill backwards at a great rate of speed. The warped wheel caused the cart to veer to the other side of the road.

He called out to his wife, who turned and was clipped by the passing cart. The children playing turned toward him when he shouted his wife's name. Glass shattered as Anne was thrown into the dress display window.

In shock, Michel watched the cart continue several yards more, not slowing in the slightest from hitting his wife. With no time to react, the runaway cart crashed into the children, exploding to a stop against the wall behind them.

Michel raced across the cobblestones to his wife. She was face down. He delicately turned her over, seeing her vacant stare. She was gone from this world. He closed his eyes to cry.

Michel smelled the fire and his herbs in the water before he opened his eyes. He heard his wife's voice from the doorway say, "Dinner is almost ready, my love."

He saw her standing in the doorway, silhouetted by the fireplace beyond.

"Are you okay, dear?" she asked.

He hesitantly replied, "Yes." He scanned the room. All was as it had been. "I am fine. I will be in shortly."

After dinner, Michel pondered the dream he had. Unlike previous dreams, this one appeared to him as if he had been on the street and witnessed the old cart, the children playing, and his wife's . . . He couldn't bring himself to think about that. After the tragedy of losing his first wife and children, he could not survive another devastating loss.

He suffered a sleepless night.

The morning was filled with sunshine and a cloudless deep blue sky. After breakfast, Michel told his wife he was going for a walk.

She asked if she may join him.

He smiled and said, "Certainly, my love. You're always welcome to walk with me."

Together they strolled the streets of their village. With no agenda or destination, they walked up this street and down that one. Occasionally, Anne stopped to look at a window display, but Michel stayed by her side, the dream from the previous day still prominent in his mind.

They walked down yet another cobble street that looked the same as the others when he was approached by a man. Michel didn't know him well, but they had several cordial brief encounters in the last two months. The man knew Michel was a doctor and asked about a pain he was having in his stomach area.

As they spoke, Anne became bored with the conversation and crossed the street to view a beautiful white dress in a shop window.

In his conversation with the man, Michel failed to notice the cart with the askew wheel until it had rolled past him. He froze for a second, halting the conversation he was having. He saw children run around a corner, laughing. They played the odd game he had seen the day before in the dream.

He frantically searched for his wife, seeing her as she was in his dream in front of the dress shop. With no further thought, he sprung across the street. The gout in his leg flared up with each step, but he ignored it. He heard the now runaway cart on the cobblestone road to his right. Not needing to look and arriving at his wife's side moments before the cart, his momentum pushed her out of the way. He toppled on top of her to the cobblestones below. She banged her head, and his full weight landed on top of her, perhaps doing some damage as well. Fortunately, the cart missed both of them.

From his left, he heard blood-curdling screams followed by a deafening crash. What was an ideal morning moments ago was now a chaotic sight. An old man ran past him, stopping feet away. With his hands on his cheeks with a horrified expression, he wailed, "What have I done?"

Michel pulled himself off his wife, looking in the same direction as the old man. He saw a crashed cart against the wall and three bodies of small children lying lifeless on the cobblestones.

* * *

After the near catastrophe of losing his wife, Michel sat on the bench many times thereafter. The three deceased children weighed heavily on his heart. When visions were overwhelming and he contemplated never to sit on the bench again, he thought of those children. He had saved his wife, but he knew he could have done more if only he had acted faster.

He vowed not to let it happen again by sharing with the world what he was experiencing.

Michel's father, Pierre, had once told him every person was on this planet for a reason. Michel kept those words with him throughout his life, especially as he attempted to save lives through the waves of black death. It wasn't until he had his visions of the future while sitting on the bench that he felt he knew what his father had meant. He was on this earth for a reason. The visions were his to see, share, and save lives.

The bench showed him places, people, and events. In the beginning, they were of happenings that would unfold in the near future. As he shared these visions, some people shied away from him and his occult ways. Others, including King Henry and his queen, sought his counsel because of his skills.

Although some visions were fairly straightforward and readily understood, such as the king destined to die by a lance to the eye in his forty-first year, others were perplexing to him. Most times, he struggled to understand their meaning. Often, he had difficulty knowing what he was experiencing. The visions were strange and foreign to him. He had so many dreams he wrote them down.

Although painful to watch, as time went by, visions often repeated. With each one, he was better able to discern the meaning, at least from his point of view. Most were unmistakably from a far-off future. He saw people he didn't know dressed strangely and speaking languages he couldn't comprehend. Sometimes he would see wondrous flying machines and even boats that propelled under the sea. He also witnessed man's inhumanity through war, death, and destruction on a scale he thought was not possible. The black death was horrifying. What he witnessed was far beyond comprehension. Millions upon millions would perish.

The inquisitor and others were distrustful of things they didn't understand. Because of this, he wrote his visions in a poetic style. Fearful they would accuse him of heresy or, even worse, magic, he used Latin, Greek, Italian, and Provençal to obscure his writings and meanings. Many thought he had gone mad, having turned to the occult.

Two years after he sat with Anne on their wedding gift bench on a raw rainy afternoon, he published his first almanac using his Latin name—Nostradamus.

PART 2
PRESENT DAY

1

SHANNON

Minutes after Jack, Harry, and Beth exited the monitor office, Shannon radioed the officers on duty to ensure everything was running as it should be. There were no problems.

She sat back in her seat as the bank of monitors displayed various live views throughout the terminal. All seemed to be normal in every view, inside and out. She focused her attention on the garden monitor. Although there were several cameras in operation covering every pathway, the monitor only displayed one at a time. It was set on a ten second rotation, displaying each view before moving on to the next. The system recorded all cameras when there was movement detected whether or not the monitor displayed it.

After ensuring everything was running smoothly, Shannon brewed a cup of coffee at the station that had been set up the day they moved in. The last drip of coffee finished filtering through, and she lifted the mug with a smile, admiring the words inscribed on one side: "*Live Love Pray*." She knew what was on the other side by heart, not having to see them: "*Any Order As Long As You Do All Three.*"

She loved her Earl, even though they had their differences, as all married couples do. Underneath his bravado exterior, he was a loving man, a faithful man, a man of God. He had given her this mug a few years back on Mother's Day, accompanied by a beautiful bouquet. She smiled again. After twenty-eight years of marriage, it wasn't the gift that was important; it was the love behind it.

Whenever they had a spat, in time, one or the other would extend the proverbial olive branch, and all would be forgiven until the next spat. On and on it went as they raised their five children.

Thoughts of her children were ever present in her mind, with the second and third oldest post college working far away, one in New York and the other in Atlanta. Her fourth attended UNH, earning an educational degree to be a teacher. The youngest was a senior in high school with graduation coming up in a couple of weeks. She was looking forward to having all her babies together for the first time in two years.

She thought, *Well, almost all my babies.* Her eldest had taken a wrong turn years before ultimately quitting school and was estranged from the family shortly after reaching sixteen. She saw him once five years ago. It ended in a verbal fight. She left several messages in the subsequent months. No reply. She left messages on every holiday and birthday. No reply. He hadn't reached out to her since. To this day, she imagined he continued to make poor decisions. She prayed for him daily. *Lord, is my baby safe?* No reply. She blessed herself. *Please, Lord, keep my baby safe.*

Through the office window overlooking the terminal walkway, travelers passed by in both directions. As she blew on her coffee and took a sip, she watched a mother holding her son's hand as she had done with her own lost boy. She added a thought as she stared into the black liquid in her mug: *I hope you're safe, my son. I miss you.*

Back at the monitors, she settled onto her cushioned chair and continued her observation with additional attention each time the garden monitor changed scenes. All was as it should be.

Until it wasn't.

She observed Kourin and Jack sit on an outer bench. As the monitor cycled through the cameras several times, it eventually showed them standing and looking at the plants. She saw what they were seeing. This time, it was unmistakable. All the plants were moving.

Unable to leave her station, she watched the monitors. She hit a few buttons and kept the camera showing Jack and Kourin on her monitor. The plants came to a rest nearly as quickly as the commotion began.

She thought about them moving, deciding that wasn't the correct word to describe them. A thought came to her from something her mother had said one day after church services long ago.

When she was nine years old, walking between mother and father on the side of their dirt road in their Sunday best, she asked why some women sounded like they were squealing when the organ played in church.

Her father had let out a laugh he quickly stifled when mother gave him a sideways look.

Mother explained they were singing. It was just that some had a quaver in their voice when they sang.

Shannon didn't know what her mother meant and had to look up the word quaver in the dictionary at school the next day. She discovered another word that morning used to describe what a quaver was: tremulous. She had to look up that word as well: trembling, fearful.

The following week and every Sunday church service since, she watched the ladies with large colorful hats sing with quaver and tremulous in their voices and throughout their bodies as they warbled with powerful emotions.

That described what these plants were doing. They were shaking, quivering. As the ladies were moved at church, here too were the plants reacting with elation.

Motion on the monitor caught Shannon's eye as Jack exited up the pathway, leaving Kourin alone. She seemed troubled as she scanned the now still plant life and held herself tightly with both arms.

Jack returned less than two minutes later. She watched him look into Kourin's eyes, take out his phone, and hold it in front of her. They looked at the phone together and seemed surprised by something. They quickly left the area after gathering their lunch bags.

Shannon switched to other cameras to see the couple meet up with Harry and Beth. They walked over to the café where they stayed until joined by Laurel. She couldn't see much from the cameras as the angle only showed the inner part of the café from a distance.

She thought, *There's something odd going on here for sure.*

* * *

Mandy checked her reflection for the fourth time. Her eye color was now the usual hazel color. The white around her eye was streaked with red lines from crying. She placed the mirror back in the drawer where she had found it. She realized she had been away from the front for a very long time and went to the restroom to splash some water on her face. Refreshed, she returned to the front as if nothing had occurred. On the outside, she maintained a smile. On the inside, she was in turmoil.

* * *

Jack held Kourin's hand, watching her eyes change color from dark green to a lighter green. The golden ring subsided altogether. She wiped a tear away with a damp napkin before it could escape down her cheek. Her other hand trembled beneath his. She had no words to say and kept her eyes focused on a blank spot on the table.

Laurel asked, "Uncle Jack, what just happened?"

Her uncle redirected his eyes from Kourin's as they returned to normal to face his niece. He answered, "I think we all just shared a vision of Kourin giving birth to her daughter over thirty years ago."

"But how?" Laurel asked. "We aren't anywhere close to the bench." She looked at Harry and Beth who sat in stunned silence. "Not to mention, none of us even knew she had a daughter." Beth shook her head, acknowledging she hadn't known. Harry remained still. Laurel asked again, "How is this possible?"

Jack slowly shook his head. "I don't know." He glanced in Kourin's direction. She remained motionless. "Kori, may I tell them?"

At first, Kourin didn't respond. He squeezed her hand to get her attention. She looked up. Her eyes were more hazel now. She gave an almost imperceptible nod.

Jack told them she had a baby when she was a teenager and placed it up for adoption. Kourin stayed silent and added nothing to her story. The darkest part remained hidden in the past.

Beth was the first to speak. "Oh dear, that must have been so difficult for you. Do you know where she is today?"

Kourin's hand tightened under Jack's. She shook her head in response. She wiped away another tear.

"I'm so sorry," said Beth.

An uneasy stillness filled the table.

Harry broke the silence saying, "Emotion."

"What?" Laurel asked, turning toward him.

Harry said, "Emotion is the trigger. I don't know how, but what we just witnessed was Kourin's heartache about her daughter activating the vision. When I had my visions, I was . . . I was . . . I had powerful feelings about . . ."

Beth placed both hands on his as support and said, "You were hurting, dear."

He glanced sideways at her without comment.

Jack was surprised by the words and the tone Beth used. They seemed more intimate than how she ordinarily spoke to Harry.

"But we're not sitting on the bench," said Laurel, not noticing or not bringing attention to Beth's obvious affection for Harry.

Her uncle said, "You don't have to be. This is what I was afraid of after what occurred a little while ago, and now this. Somehow, just being in the vicinity is enough to make something happen. Earlier we saw on the video Ubu was in a vision when he was more than a yard away from the bench. Also, Sarah possibly had something happen when her plane taxied by outside." He paused, considering if he should say what happened with himself. He decided it was important enough to warrant it. "And yesterday, when I was waiting for John, I was back at the lake cabin."

Harry looked at Jack with raised eyebrows.

Laurel said, "Uncle, are you talking about when I saw you in the gate area?"

"Yes," he answered. He looked down at Ubu and pat behind his ear, the one not hurt two days earlier. "Ubu was there, which of course is impossible, but I know what I saw. I wasn't anywhere near the bench."

His niece said, "But I had my eye on him the entire time. Ubu was at my side and walked over to you. He paused about five feet away when you woke up."

"Yes, but in the vision, he was five feet away from me, standing exactly how he was when I saw you. I can't explain it, but he was there."

Harry said, "Maybe it has something to do with how strong the emotion is. You—" he paused and changed it to, "we all enjoyed going there." He hesitated again. "We all had a good time." He fell silent, lost in his own thoughts.

Beth, still holding his hand, squeezed it tenderly.

"Perhaps," Jack answered, looking at Kourin as she returned his gaze. "But I think there's more to it than just that." Her eyes remained more hazel than green. "I think something else is happening here."

A family of four sat at the next table. The two toddlers had small suitcases, one pink and one blue. They dragged them to the end of the table, abandoning them there, and scampered on to seats. The parents each had a black rolling carry-on they placed next to the smaller ones. The father retraced his steps back to the front counter, likely to order their food, while the mother spoke with the children about their upcoming trip to keep them occupied. For young children, they were well behaved and clearly excited about their trip.

Laurel said, "Maybe we should move this conversation to the office." All agreed. "But before we do that, I need to take Ubu outside."

of room to change in there."

After guiding her to where she could change, Mandy got two coffees and heated a cinnamon roll. By the time she was done, Sarah had returned.

"I hope it's okay that I left my bag back there for now?"

She led her dog along a narrow walkway behind the café. The unadorned passage for airport employees and an emergency exit ended where delivery trucks dropped their packages or, in Laurel's case, freshly made muffins, bagels, and other treats. The single female security guard, Delu, said hello and opened the door for them to exit to do his business. Delu chatted with her until Ubu was ready to come back a few moments later. As Laurel entered the building, she

EDD JORDAN

Declan retrieved the briefcase of the man who had fallen. He handed it to him. The man gave it a once-over, pointing to a spot on it. Declan shrugged his shoulders. The man tensed up, almost rising on the balls of his feet toward the guard. He then calmed back down when Declan didn't rise to his challenge. The man looked at the surrounding faces and saw no one paying attention to him. He looked one last time at the young man in front of him. After a three-second staring contest, he pivoted and strode off toward the gates. Shannon saw Declan shake his head as he walked away.

* * *

Jack knelt in front of Kourin with both hands gently but firmly clutching the side of each arm. He didn't shake her as he had done with Harry the day before. "Kori, are you okay?"

Kourin turned her head away from him toward an open space in the room and felt a wave of dizziness wash over her. In her mind, she saw green trees. The image of Jack's face came to her as she struggled to gain control of her increasing emotions. His mental picture with brown eyes morphed into Jack with dark green eyes. After several seconds, the odd sensation she had felt passed as quickly as it had come. Along with it, Jack's green-eyed image faded from her mind as well.

After several calming breaths, she answered Jack's question. "I don't know. I'm not sure what to think anymore."

"I'm here. We're all here for you, Kori," he said. "We'll find the answer together."

Kourin turned and saw the concern on his face, a face with brown eyes. She knew his words came from the heart. She whispered, "I don't understand what's happening. I was back at the hospital. How is that possible if we were in the café?"

Jack had no answer but noted that her eyes were more green now than they were moments ago. He was at a loss and needed help. He gazed at his niece on the other side of the desk.

2
GREEN-EYED LADY

"Hi, Sarah. Want a coffee before your next flight?" asked Mandy.

"Actually, there's been a slight change," she answered. "My second leg has been canceled because of the weather at the other end. Unexpected, but it cuts my extra day short." She saw something in Mandy's face. "I hope that's alright. If it's not, I can get a hotel room."

Mandy realized her innermost thoughts had been made visible on her face. "Oh no, no, no. I'm sorry. I've . . . I've been distracted lately." She gave her friend a smile. "Here, let me get you a coffee."

"No, you don't have to."

"Um," Mandy said, searching around her to see who was close by. "I need to talk to someone."

Sarah didn't like the sound of that. "Sure. In that case, I'll have one." She looked down at her flight bag she was toting behind her. "Do you mind if I change into something else first?"

"Oh, no. Go right ahead. Let me show you where the restroom is. Plenty of room to change in there."

After guiding her to where she could change, Mandy got two coffees and heated a cinnamon roll. By the time she was done, Sarah had returned.

"I hope it's okay that I left my bag back there for now?"

"Absolutely," Mandy replied. She led the way to an open table, setting down the tray. "I heated a cinnamon roll for you. Is there something else you'd rather have?"

"That's so sweet. Thank you," Sarah answered, sitting down. "I haven't had a cinnamon roll in ages." She picked it up from the tray, getting the sticky frosting on her fingers. After taking a bite, she said, "Mmm, this is delicious." She set it down and licked some frosting off her fingers and added, "Messy, though." She followed it up with a sip of coffee.

Mandy thanked her new friend with a nod of her head as she sat down. She took a sip of the coffee and traced the design on the cup with her finger.

Sarah studied her as she had another sip of her own coffee. She asked, "Did something happen to Miguel?"

Mandy looked up suddenly with alarm in her eyes, exclaiming, "Oh no!" She realized she shouted it, and customers sitting at the surrounding tables looked over at her. "Sorry, no, Miguel should be okay." She scrunched up her nose, thinking. "Actually, I don't know. Jack spoke with him this morning, and everything was okay then." She looked away from Sarah to her cup again. "As far as I know, he's alright."

Sarah sipped her coffee to give her time to study Mandy's face. She tilted her head slightly to one side and said, "Well, I think something is bothering you." She stopped to see if anyone was within earshot. The surrounding patrons were absorbed in their own conversations, so she continued in a lowered voice. "Has something more happened on the bench?"

Upon lifting her head away from the cup she was studying once more, Mandy spoke in a stilted manner, "Not exactly."

* * *

Laurel entered her office, and the sound of Ubu's claws tapping against the floor filled the room as he took his position next to the desk. Kourin sat in front of the desk, slightly to the right. Jack stood behind her, his hands providing a reassuring presence on her shoulders. Beth sat to the left. Harry retrieved the chair by the door he had used the day before and sat next to her.

With everyone present, Harry started off the conversation in his usual fashion. He said, turning to look at Kourin, "So, let's start with why the hell your eyes changed color when we went into your vision."

"Harry," Jack said, becoming defensive.

Laurel added, "Uncle Jack, he's right. I saw it, too. Kourin's eyes definitely changed color. When we were back from the . . . from the vision, her eyes were much darker than normal."

"Yes," Harry said. "And they had a gold ring. That was clear as day."

Laurel observed Kourin who was looking down at a nondescript spot on the desk. In a quieter voice than Harry, she said, "He's right. There appeared to be a ring, a bright ring, in your eye, Kourin. I've seen nothing like it."

Jack said, "Let's not gang up on her."

Kourin felt Jack's hand tense on her shoulder as he spoke. She placed her left hand on top of his and said, "It's okay, Jack. They want answers." She fixed her eyes on Laurel. "I want them, too."

* * *

Mandy spent the next ten minutes explaining what had happened to her in the bathroom and, subsequently, the office. When she was finished with her story, she kept silent and waited for a response.

Sarah listened without interruption, nibbling at her cinnamon roll and sipping her coffee. After a minute to ponder what she just heard, she said, "Mandy, I'm going to ask this because I have to. Please don't take offense."

Mandy nodded without a word.

"Are you certain you didn't imagine it? I mean you've been under a lot of stress with the Miguel and party issue. Is it possible you thought you saw something that wasn't there?"

Without answering, Mandy retrieved her phone from her apron pocket. She hit a couple of spots on the screen and held it up toward Sarah. A selfie of her face covered the entire screen. Her eyes were the focus of the shot.

When Sarah saw the photo, she said, "Holy shit!"

"Yeah, right? I took that after the second time it happened when I was in the office. I couldn't believe it either and wanted to make sure I wasn't just imagining it." She turned the phone back around so she could see the photo. "Kinda scary."

Sarah reached up to Mandy's hands and gently pushed them down so she couldn't continue to stare at the photo. She kept her hands resting on top of the ones clasping the phone, embracing them. "I don't know what to say to that." She resisted the urge to look into Mandy's eyes, but she couldn't help herself. They were the normal hazel color.

Mandy unconsciously shifted her gaze away.

Sarah said, "I'm sorry. I don't mean to make you uncomfortable." She gently squeezed her friend's hands. "They're not green now. No gold ring." She smiled and added, "They're the beautiful hazel they've always been."

"They've never been emerald green and certainly no gold ring. I don't understand what's happening to me."

Sarah glanced around and saw the café was filling up with customers. She said, "Hey, why don't we go for a walk? I find things become a little clearer when I go for a stroll."

They picked up their coffees. Mandy threw her nearly full cup of coffee into the trash receptacle near the entrance. She had no stomach for it right now. Sarah had finished her roll and threw her trash into the opening, keeping the half-full coffee with her.

Mandy led the way, turning right out of the café. Without hesitation or further thought, she felt drawn to the garden. Sarah had a larger stride and caught up to her.

Not saying a word, Mandy walked up the garden entrance toward the center. She entered the courtyard and strode directly to the bench, sitting down. She was cognizant of her surroundings and the anxiety the bench had caused. Despite this, she was irresistibly drawn to take a seat on the wooden bench, shutting her eyes in order to bask in the sun's warmth.

Sarah saw the center court was unoccupied. As the sunshine cascaded in through the skylights, the area was illuminated in a golden hue. She thought, *Not what I envisioned. This feels so warm and inviting.* She followed her friend to the well-worn bench and sat beside her. Slightly askew with her left butt cheek hanging off the edge, she wanted to keep an eye on her. She placed her coffee on the bench beside her and reached over to hold her hands as a sign of support. They felt like ice cubes.

Mandy experienced a peacefulness, like being in her mother's arms or feeling the warmth from a fireplace. She felt Sarah's hands holding hers. As she enjoyed the sunshine on her face, she sensed the warmth fading. She felt a chill run through her fingers and toes as a warmth emanated from her core.

The sunshine vanished, sending the courtyard into a shade similar to dusk, even though it was midday. The tranquility of the garden Sarah had experienced moments ago disappeared. She felt Mandy's hands trembling in hers, the muscles tensing and contracting.

Without opening her eyes, Mandy felt a consciousness flow through her. As opposed to the intense sorrow she had experienced earlier, this sensation was entirely different. She felt a powerful presence. It was as if another's thoughts touched hers. She saw a tall green tree and felt sadness, loneliness, fear, and hope. She turned toward Sarah, opening her eyes to see if her friend was having a similar reaction.

Mandy's body shuddered, and simultaneously, a moment of disorientation swept over Sarah. It vanished as quickly as it arrived. She observed her friend's face, and her blood ran cold. *Oh my God! Her eyes!*

* * *

Shannon continued watching the live monitor feeds throughout the terminal, and everything appeared to be normal. Travelers walked to or from their gate. Although the terminal was far busier than it had been in the previous days and weeks, having not been open to the public, it was still far from the capacity crowds that would eventually traverse the space.

She rose to stretch her legs and contemplated another coffee. She decided against it, having had more caffeine than she normally drank. Instead, she stood behind her chair, watching a family drag their carry-on as they maneuvered through the flow toward their gate. The little girl's case flipped sideways, causing her to release it. A man who had been trying to pass by the family tripped over it, losing his balance and crashing to the floor. His briefcase separated from his hand, sliding across the newly polished floor. It struck an older lady's cane, causing her to lose her balance. She fell onto one of the potted fern plants that lined the terminal every twenty feet. Her traveling companion rushed to her aid.

A woman who was nearby at the restaurant entrance rushed over to assist them. Shannon recognized her as Wren, the hostess at the restaurant. After a moment of speaking with the man kneeling beside the prone woman, she rushed back into the restaurant.

Shannon's phone buzzed.

"Hello, Shannon speaking."

"Hi, this is Wren, at Luca's restaurant." Shannon noted her voice was shaky. "We just had an accident on the walkway. A woman needs medical help. She hit her head."

"I'll call for help, Wren." She called the EMTs. After providing them the information they needed, she called Declan. He would be the closest guard to the restaurant. She directed him to respond to the incident immediately. The walkie broadcast would be heard by all the guards in the terminal, including the rookie, Brooks. He was paired with Declan and would respond without being directed to.

For the next several minutes, Shannon watched the area of the incident. As the chaos unfolded, the family with the two toddlers pulled in close together.

The mother held both of her children close, with a protective hand on each of their heads, as the daughter sobbed.

The father left his family to assist the man that had fallen. As he rose, he firmly shoved the father away, not wanting his help. The father backed off. Shannon saw him raise his arms slightly and thought of the words he was likely saying, probably something like, "No worries. I'm just trying to help."

The man who had fallen got into the father's face. Shannon had seen this before. The man who fell was embarrassed and was taking out his frustration at the presumed cause of his embarrassment.

Meanwhile, the older lady was to the right of them with her hand on her head where she had struck the edge of the planter. Wren returned at that moment with what appeared to be a towel or cloth napkin.

Declan arrived with Brooks a few steps behind. He observed two men about to fight and got between them. The man who had fallen faced Declan and threw a punch, not at the guard. He was trying to hit the father. Instead, it hit Declan in the jaw.

Fortunately, he could take the blow. To his credit, he did not return the punch. He grabbed the man's arms and quickly swung him around so he faced away from the guards and the father. He pushed the man away from everyone to the terminal wall on the other side of the planter. Shannon could not tell what was being said, but she assumed Declan was attempting to calm the man down.

Meanwhile, Brooks had ushered the father and family in the opposite direction. The daughter was still crying. The mother picked her up and held her close. Brooks retrieved the pink suitcase, handing it to the father. He escorted them away from the scene, presumably to their gate.

Shannon's attention returned to the lady who had been injured. She sat on the floor. Her husband knelt beside her, holding her hand. Within minutes, the EMTs arrived. They quickly checked her and helped her up onto a chair that Wren materialized with.

Declan retrieved the briefcase of the man who had fallen. He handed it to him. The man gave it a once-over, pointing to a spot on it. Declan shrugged his shoulders. The man tensed up, almost rising on the balls of his feet toward the guard. He then calmed back down when Declan didn't rise to his challenge. The man looked at the surrounding faces and saw no one paying attention to him. He looked one last time at the young man in front of him. After a three-second staring contest, he pivoted and strode off toward the gates. Shannon saw Declan shake his head as he walked away.

* * *

Jack knelt in front of Kourin with both hands gently but firmly clutching the side of each arm. He didn't shake her as he had done with Harry the day before. "Kori, are you okay?"

Kourin turned her head away from him toward an open space in the room and felt a wave of dizziness wash over her. In her mind, she saw green trees. The image of Jack's face came to her as she struggled to gain control of her increasing emotions. His mental picture with brown eyes morphed into Jack with dark green eyes. After several seconds, the odd sensation she had felt passed as quickly as it had come. Along with it, Jack's green-eyed image faded from her mind as well.

After several calming breaths, she answered Jack's question. "I don't know. I'm not sure what to think anymore."

"I'm here. We're all here for you, Kori," he said. "We'll find the answer together."

Kourin turned and saw the concern on his face, a face with brown eyes. She knew his words came from the heart. She whispered, "I don't understand what's happening. I was back at the hospital. How is that possible if we were in the café?"

Jack had no answer but noted that her eyes were more green now than they were moments ago. He was at a loss and needed help. He gazed at his niece on the other side of the desk.

Laurel knew her uncle well enough to know he was throwing out a lifeline to her. She could see the desperation in his expression. For the past day, she had been pondering various theories. Most of them were to figure out a way to go back to the desert early enough to prevent both suicide bombers from ever having the chance to detonate their bombs, saving Breckin and her team. The latest bench interaction was another monkey wrench into the theories she had formulated.

"This is new," Laurel said, not knowing what else to say. "How could we all be transported back to a time we never experienced?"

"We weren't transported," said Harry.

Everyone turned to him, including Kourin, whose emerald green eyes sparkled in the light.

Jack asked, "What do you mean? We all just witnessed the same thing."

Harry methodically looked from one person to the next before answering. Each waited to hear his response. The office was deathly quiet except for the murmured sounds from the café. "Unlike what we saw happen on the monitor in the security office where it appeared each person might have actually left the bench only to return, we were in the café and never actually left."

Beth asked, "But we were standing in the hospital room and saw . . ." She glanced at Kourin. "Sorry." She looked back at Harry. "We saw Kourin having a baby. We were there!"

Jack said, "I think I know what Harry is talking about. We weren't physically there this time like we were when we each had our experiences." He paused, deciding whether to say the next part. As he read Kourin's sad face, he decided everyone needed to have all the facts if they ever wanted to figure this out.

He told the others of his most recent bench encounter, going into the past and, in this case, the day before. With no explanation of how he ended up in Laurel's office, he said he had been feeling out of sorts while he was sitting on the bench. He remained tight-lipped about why.

After her uncle related his bizarre story, Laurel said, "I don't know what to say to that." She glanced into the office corner and back to her uncle. "Maybe you really just dreamed that happened this time. I mean, come on, how is that even possible?"

"I can't explain it. It was like how we felt after the visions. Even though it ended almost as quickly as it started, I felt . . . No, I knew I was back in that . . . in this office. I know it sounds incredible, but I know it happened."

"It fucking doesn't matter," Harry said. "If it happened, how does it help us control the bench and what is happening?"

Laurel and Jack looked at each other, but it was Kourin who spoke up. "If we can learn to control the visions, maybe we can figure out a way to stop them."

Intrigued because this was what Harry wanted most of all, he asked, "And how do you propose we do that?"

"We do what he just did. Go back to a specific time."

3

RING OF GOLD

"Mandy. Your eyes!" Sarah said, startled and releasing her friend's hands. Mandy observed her friend's wide-eyed surprise as she processed what she was seeing. Instantly, a long-forgotten memory of acrid laughter and taunting from three horrid girls on an autumn afternoon years ago filled her consciousness.

On a pleasant October afternoon, as a sophomore in high school, Mandy sat with her friend under an old oak tree as it shed shades of yellow and red leaves. Close to the tree was a green metal park bench, but the two decided it would be more enjoyable to sit on the newly fallen leaves. Her friend, Farashuu, a freshman black girl whose family had recently moved to New Hampshire, was telling her about the life she had left behind in Kenya. Mandy was appalled by the conditions she had endured as a child.

As she finished relating a description of the shack her family had lived in, three white female seniors from the varsity cheerleading squad passed by. As the girls giggled and walked past, one pointed at Fara. The taller brunette with her hair pulled back by a brightly colored scrunchie turned and said a nasty racial slur to Fara, picking on her braided hairstyle and laughing. The similarly dressed blonde and the other, with curly black hair, erupted into laughter. More high-pitched laughter ensued when the blonde added another cruel comment.

Mandy was livid and leapt to her feet, standing only a foot away from the callous threesome. She unleashed a tirade of words unlike anything she had ever said before, leaving them shocked by her capacity for fury. Horror-stricken, the three gaped at the young blonde as she vented her outrage at them.

As they backed away, they uttered some spiteful obscenities in her direction. The curly-haired girl tripped, falling behind the blonde who fell onto her. They scrambled off the lawn, rushing away with their bigoted hatred.

Mandy thought of Fara and the red oak leaves while she stared at Sarah. She hadn't thought about that afternoon in ages, and it was odd that it came to mind now.

Sarah held Mandy's shaking hands in hers. They were cool to the touch. "Are you okay? Should I call 911?"

Upon seeing the concern on her friend's face and in her blue eyes as they studied her own face, she answered, "No. I'm okay, I think." She looked away, picking a random plant across the courtyard to look at. "I'm okay," she repeated.

"Mandy, look at me."

Mandy turned her head toward her.

"Your eyes." Sarah tightened her grip on her friend's hands. "Mandy, your eye color changed to emerald green, and you had a golden ring around the center. They're not as green as they were, and the ring is almost gone now. I've never heard of anyone having eyes that could do that."

Mandy, again looking away to the courtyard floor, said, "Me neither. What's happening to me?"

Sarah studied her friend's profile. She seemed the same as she had been. As she observed her in that moment, a ray of sunshine splashed down from above onto them. The light felt like a warm blanket. She asked, "What did you experience when it was happening?"

She didn't ask if she had a vision like she had about Miguel, but Mandy knew that was what she meant. "I didn't go anywhere, if that's what you're asking." She reflected on the fall day she had defended Fara. "I had a memory come to me from long ago, someone I became close to, like a sister."

She thought more about the encounter now that it was fresh in her mind, as if it had just occurred. The faces of the three girls who had accosted Fara came into focus. *They had genuine fear on their faces as they stared at my face. No, not my face, my eyes! They were looking into my eyes!*

Sarah let her recover at her own pace. Not knowing what else to do, she gave her friend a hug.

Mandy felt her friend's embrace and welcomed it, along with the sunshine on her face. The three cheerleader faces remained on her mind. Fear was present in their eyes. At the time, she had thought it was because of the outburst she had released on them. Now she had other thoughts about it. Did her eyes change color all those years ago? She thought, *What the fuck is happening to me?*

* * *

Wren returned to the podium after having seated two middle-aged businessmen. Her mind was drawn to the construction workers who had been at Luca's the day before and the laughter they had shared at the party. They stood out in stark contrast to the two she just seated. The businessmen were tense, their faces contorted in grimaces and their eyes glued to their phones, barely uttering a word to her or to each other. Conversely, the construction workers were a jovial close-knit crew and certainly enjoyed each other's company.

As she returned to the podium, she thought, *I don't know what I want to do with my life, but I'd rather be like the gang last night. They all enjoyed themselves, and Joneal was so sweet.*

In front of her, she heard a familiar voice say, "Hi Wren."

The handsome face she was just thinking of beamed back at her. "Joneal! Why are you here?"

His smile becoming a concerned expression, he asked, "I hope it's okay? You mentioned last night you were getting off work at two, so I thought I'd surprise you."

With a cheek-to-cheek smile, she answered, "Yes!" As she glanced around, she realized she had spoken loudly. She saw Luca look up from the bar. She turned back to Joneal, in a quieter voice, "I still have a little while before I can leave."

Joneal replied, with a slight stammer, "That's okay. I can come back if that's alright with you?"

From behind her, Wren heard Luca's voice. "Is there a problem here?"

Wren went white, making her facial freckles stand out even more. She said, "Uh, no, sir . . ." When she turned, she saw Luca had a grin on his face.

"It's okay, Wren," he said, smiling. He turned to her friend. "Hi, Joneal. How are you today?"

He answered, "I'm well, sir, and how are you?" He reached out to shake Luca's hand.

Luca returned the handshake. "Wow, you have a grip there, my boy!" He turned to face Wren. "Wren, it's nearly two. I can take it from here if you want to go."

"Are you sure?"

"Certainly. You've done a great job today. I'm sure we're going to have some very busy days ahead, so you should take advantage of those times you get to sneak away. Go. Have fun! Don't worry about us. Maria will be in shortly to do the closing shift."

"Thanks!" Wren said, glancing at Joneal. "I guess I can go now. I'll be right back." She disappeared into the rear of the restaurant.

Joneal said, "Thanks for letting her go early, sir."

"No problem. And you don't have to call me sir. Everyone calls me Luca."

"Certainly, sir—I mean, Luca."

"She's a good kid. Take care of her."

"I will," he said as Wren reappeared.

"I'll see you tomorrow," she said to Luca. "And thanks again."

"Have fun, kids," he called after them. He thought, *Young love!*

After the young couple walked several paces from the restaurant, Wren asked, "Did you have work to do here today?"

"No, I came here to see you."

Wren stopped walking. Joneal halted next to her. "How did you get into the terminal?"

"That's a secret," he said. When he saw it would not be a sufficient answer from the look on her freckled face, he added, "Fortunately, I know all the guards here. I told Delu at the delivery entrance I left something I needed to pick up." Wren made a questioning face. "I didn't lie. She made an assumption it was tools or something. I came to pick you up!"

"That's so sweet," she said and started walking. "But that will not work a second time."

"No, it won't. But it was good enough for today."

"True. Hey, before we leave, do you mind if we do a detour?"

"No prob. Where do you want to go?"

"The garden," she answered. "I haven't seen it yet."

* * *

Kourin explained her idea to the group, doing what Jack had described. Instead of sitting on the bench, which she said she wasn't ready to try again any-time soon, she would do what he did at the gate area: think hard about some-thing important and concentrate on a particular point in time.

Jack immediately said he was against it, especially if she would be the one doing it. Beth said the same. Laurel said she would try, but Jack was even more opposed to that. Harry wanted Kourin to try, so he stayed quiet.

Ultimately, Kourin said she was the most suited and was adamant about attempting it. After fifteen minutes of back and forth, Jack realized she was going to do it no matter what. What finally convinced him was her need to discover what was happening to her. By her having control of the situation, she should be better able to handle it. At least that was her argument.

Before Kourin began, Laurel closed the office door. She thought about checking on the front, but she told herself Mandy was there so all should be fine. She was unaware Mandy was not in the café and was herself sitting on the bench.

Laurel returned to her seat, while Ubu verified all was well with a head lift and look about. He set his head back down, letting out a heavy breath as he settled in.

All sat quietly as Kourin closed her eyes, kept her breathing even, and thought about where and when she wanted to go to. She thought of the party the night before. She focused on the dance she had with Miguel, trying to be at the moment right before he walked away from her when she lost him.

Minutes passed with nothing happening. She began to think it was a waste of time. Her mind drifted to Anders arriving just after the time she was attempting to get to. This led to her thinking of Jack and how much she loved him. As she thought about his smile, his rugged good looks, and his sweet old-school nature, she felt a warmth overtake her body. She felt his kiss on her lips, the way it made her feel, unlike any she had experienced before.

Her mind traveled to the day before when they were in this very office after Harry had his vision and injured his leg. She recalled Jack telling her about how she kissed. She remembered his story of traveling back to this office himself. A burning warmth flowed through her body.

> Kourin opened her eyes, expecting to see Jack beside her. She did see Laurel's office around her, but she was no longer sitting down. She was standing in the corner where Jack said he had been when he had time traveled.
>
> She scanned the office. Jack and Harry were by the door talking. She called out to them. No response. However, Ubu, who had been lying by the desk, lifted his head in her direction.

He rose and looked directly at her. His tail wagged as he sauntered toward her. He sat on his haunches directly in front of her, lifting his right paw to her.

Kourin took Ubu's paw into her hand as she had done the day before. He wagged his tail vigorously, same as before. *Actually, that interaction happened several minutes after this.* She thought. *Boy, is this confusing!*

Her attention was caught by Jack standing up and walking toward her. When he was next to Ubu, he asked him what he was doing. She released his paw. Ubu's tail stopped wagging, and he turned toward Jack. Not receiving further commands, he resumed looking at Kourin and wagged his tail against the carpet. He lifted his paw to her again, so she obliged and held it for a moment, releasing it after a few seconds.

Kourin's focus was on him when she felt an odd sensation in her stomach area. She looked down in time to see Jack's hand pass through her body. He then looked in both directions. She was startled by his hand inside of her and moved several feet to her right, away from him and Ubu. She thought, *What the hell?*

Jack passed his hand through the same area he did previously, unbeknownst to him, the space Kourin had just vacated. He asked the dog what he saw.

Ubu ignored him. Now that Kourin was several steps away, he stood and walked back to his spot beside the desk and lay down. He kept his gaze on Jack and Kourin.

Kourin called out to Jack. He didn't respond. She needed to communicate with him. She moved closer to where Ubu had been standing. Directly in front of him, she placed her left hand on his chest. He didn't seem to notice it. She watched as he closed his eyes inches from her.

She reached her right hand up and placed it behind his head, concentrating on communicating with him. She moved in closer to give him a kiss and put all her love behind it.

He responded. She felt him kissing her back!

Jack turned away to look down at Ubu who had returned to his side wagging his tail. Simultaneously, she released from the kiss as he turned away from her. She backed up half a step, removing her hand from his neck.

There was a knock on the door. Across the room Harry said enter. Laurel came in, followed by herself! She was startled, and her heart raced when she saw her twin. She tightly shut her eyes to block out the disturbing image.

When she reopened her eyes, Jack was sitting next to her. Laurel was behind the desk. Harry and Beth sat an arm's length away.

She was back where she started.

Jack saw Kourin stir after being completely still for several minutes. When she opened her eyes and looked at him, he froze. For the third time today, her eyes were dark green with a bright golden ring around the pupil! *Oh my God! What is going on here?*

* * *

Shannon's shift ended at two. Her relief was punctual as usual, arriving with a lunchbox large enough to hold a dinner for four people. She filled him in on the events of the day, taking less than five minutes, as it was a relatively slow day. Most of the update was the incident in front of Luca's. No arrests were made, making it just a notation in the electronic log for the day. She kept everything about the garden and what she discovered on the monitors to herself. She knew if she started talking about tremulous plants beyond the circle of people she met within the garden, they'd take away her security clearance.

She had brought nothing with her to work, except her jacket. Without zipping it up, she wore it through the terminal so she wouldn't have to carry it.

As she approached Luca's, she was greeted by its namesake. "Welcome, Shannon. One for lunch today?"

"Perhaps tomorrow. I'm looking for Wren. I have a few questions about the incident earlier," Shannon said, looking past Luca into the elaborately decorated bar area.

"Ah, yes. That poor lady. Is she doing okay?" asked Luca, referring to the injured elderly traveler.

"As far as I know, yes, thanks to Wren's help. She aided her and her distraught husband until help arrived." Shannon looked around and asked, "Is she available?"

"Unfortunately, I let her off early just a little while ago, but I heard her mention the garden as they were leaving. Perhaps you can still catch them there."

"Them?"

"Yes, Joneal, from the construction company, showed up to take her home. I think he's smitten with her," Luca said with a wink.

"Okay. Thanks. I'll try to stop in tomorrow for a bite," Shannon said as she turned to go, heading to the one place she didn't want to go. *Why did she have to go there?* she thought. *Maybe I can catch them outside of it.*

* * *

Mandy knew she should return to the café since she was the manager and it was opening day for the terminal. She had faith in her people, but she knew she should be there with them. The closing shift supervisor would have arrived by now, and she took some solace in knowing Laurel was there, not realizing she was not.

Bewilderment swirled through her mind about what was happening to her. She needed to figure this out, at least enough to face people and be herself. Not being in control of her emotions frightened her.

Sarah released her hug, giving Mandy some distance between them. She saw the sadness on her face. *No, not sadness. Conflict.* Sarah kept her thoughts to herself for the moment, giving Mandy time to calm herself down.

After a couple of minutes of silence, Sarah asked, "Can I get you anything? Do you need a glass of water?"

"No. Thanks." Mandy stared at a plant across the courtyard.

"I have some coffee left if you'd like a sip. I hear it's the best in town." Sarah said it with a smile, trying to lighten the mood.

Mandy looked at her, ignoring the coffee comment. "Why do you think my eyes change color? Have you ever heard of that happening before?"

"No. Well, not like this anyway."

"What do you mean?" Mandy asked. She perked up a little.

"A few years back, during my yearly eye exam, I asked my optometrist if my eye color would fade as I get older. She gave me a noncommittal maybe. It had something to do with melatonin levels. No. That doesn't sound right; that makes you sleep. It's something like that. Melanon? Melanin? Anyway, eye color can change, but she said it was usually gradual, if at all. When I mentioned that some days my eyes seemed bluer, she said it was from the way light hit it. So, eye color can change." Sarah held Mandy's left hand in hers. "Eye color can change."

"Yes, but I'm not sure it is supposed to change from one color to a totally different color in seconds. And for no apparent reason," said Mandy, as she studied her friend's eyes. "Your blue eyes look the same right now as they did yesterday."

"And yours are back to hazel. May I ask you a question?"

"Sure."

"Did you feel your eye color changing?" Sarah cocked her head to one side. "I mean, did it feel like anything?"

Mandy turned away.

Sarah could tell she was thinking.

Mandy turned back to face her friend and placed her right hand on top of the Sarah's. Human contact made what was happening a little less surreal and distressing. "I felt powerful emotions. Yet they were different each time. There was overwhelming sadness, warmth like being in your favorite blanket, loneliness, fear, hope. No clue how they managed to come. They just did. The worst part was that I had no control over them."

"And that's when your eyes turned color?"

"Yes. When I looked in the mirror after it happened, my eyes were emerald green."

"And the gold ring? Was it there as well?"

"Yes." Mandy turned away, releasing the contact they had shared.

A memory came to her she hadn't thought of since Fara's high school graduation the year following hers. She had greeted her friend at a post grad party, giving her a big hug. Two months later would be the last time they saw each other and hugged one last time. Mandy was already attending UNH and worked long days to make ends meet all four years. Fara went to the University of Pennsylvania on a well-deserved full scholarship. Mandy smiled, recalling when Fara told her where she had been accepted. The whole weekend afterwards, Mandy had confused it with Penn State. They laughed until they cried when she realized her error.

Although they made plans to see each other during each summer break, something always came up, mostly because of internships each pursued. Neither had the money to plan a vacation together even if they had the time. The months passed, turning into years apart.

After obtaining her doctorate in education, Fara found herself back in Kenya making a difference there. They spoke several times on the phone over the years, but they never found the opportunity to visit one another. Fara's path was hard, but she was a determined woman. Mandy admired her courage and resolve.

Regret filled her heart at not making a greater effort to visit her friend.

The sight of the three cheerleaders from years before came to Mandy's mind again. She visualized their faces as she screamed at them for their bigotry. They were scared. After screaming at the trio, she had turned around to check on Fara after they scrambled to get away from her. Fara remained seated on the red leaves with her back against the mighty oak. She looked up at her with tears on her cheeks . . . and gasped.

Mandy had not recalled that until now. Her friend had definitely reacted when she had turned and looked at her. She helped her to her feet and hugged her, just like the last one she would give some four years later.

When they separated, Fara studied her face as if expecting something and now not seeing it. After a moment, she said thank you, and they gathered their backpacks to head home.

Sarah patiently sat in silence beside her friend, watching her intently as she was deep in thought. She glanced at her face several times, checking on her. In between those times, she finished her coffee and admired the plants surrounding the courtyard, wishing her backyard looked half as good as this place did.

Three times she thought she saw movement within the plants, but each time she tried to discern if there was anything there, she detected nothing.

While Sarah questioned if she was hallucinating, Mandy thought more about Fara and the afternoon that followed the cheerleader encounter. She recalled meeting Fara's mother for the first time, being invited for dinner because she stood up to the three girls on her daughter's behalf twice, and hearing stories of bigotry and hatred they endured through their lives.

Mandy realized that day had a profound effect on her life and how she conducted herself thereafter. Had she not stood up for her new friend twice that afternoon, she may have become a very different person.

As she sat on the bench staring at a red-colored plant, her extremities cooled. She could feel warmth deep inside at the memories of her friend and family.

She recalled the dinner they shared that evening. Her father arrived home from work with a bruise on his head, but he did not let it darken his infectious smile. Fara's younger brother, Zakia, otherwise known as Zak, joined them for dinner after having been sequestered in his room working on something.

Mandy remembered what it was: his first Halloween costume. He had gone trick-or-treating after dinner. They were a very happy family, indeed.

Sarah's attention was caught by the movement of a plant across the courtyard—definitely moving. She attempted to see what was causing it. There had to be a small animal underneath or behind it. She couldn't see one. Soon, plants on either side of it moved as well. She thought, *Is there a whole family of squirrels or something there? How did they get into the terminal?*

The plant Mandy stared at moved. She was drawn out of her thoughts about the past. At first, one leaf and then another moved slightly up and down. Several breaths later, the leaves moved faster with all the plants shaking.

Sarah turned toward Mandy to ask if she was seeing what she was and froze. She was staring straight ahead at the plants. Her concentration was undeniable. Sarah placed her hand on hers. It was cold, not just cool. It was almost too cold to hold. Frightened, she retrieved her hand but kept her attention on Mandy's profile. She called out to her friend, "Mandy!"

Mandy felt her body temperature surge. She felt the fury rising inside her as she thought about her friend and family having to endure such hatred. Her name being called out echoed in her ears. She turned to face the direction she heard it from.

Sarah let out an audible gasp of shock when Mandy looked her way. Emerald eyes returned her gaze. The world around the face staring back at her closed in as blackness overtook her vision. The last thing Sarah remembered before losing consciousness was seeing vibrant emerald eyes with a circle of golden fire around the pupil.

* * *

In a weak voice, Kourin said, "I did it, Jack. I went back to yesterday."

"But you never left," he replied. "I've been right here with you the whole time."

She peered into his chestnut-colored eyes and saw a faint reflection of herself. "I was in this office yesterday, over by the wall." She glanced at the space. "You came up to me, but you couldn't see me." She looked at the black dog snoozing next to the desk. "Ubu was there. And Harry." Her attention went to him. "It was when you were changing your clothes."

"You could have just thought you were there," said Laurel. "Like remembering a dream."

"I don't—" Kourin started.

Jack interrupted, "Sweetheart, you never left my sight here." He held her hands. They were ice cold. "I haven't let you go."

Kourin felt all four sets of eyes on her and the doubt behind them. "But I know what I saw, and felt. You put your hand into my stomach. I jumped back out of the way because it felt so . . ."

"Strange," Jack finished her sentence. He recalled when it happened to him.

Laurel said, "It still could have just been a dream. The mind can play strange tricks on you, making you think you see something when you don't." She was thinking about her own experience in the desert and the shadows she saw that night.

"You kissed me," Kourin said to Jack. "You even said afterwards, when you kissed me, you needed to see how I kissed."

"Again, your mind could have just filled in the blanks in a dream state, making it seem real," said Laurel.

Kourin looked at her. Laurel shied away as the green eyes caught her own. The vibrant color was disconcerting. She redirected her gaze from her to the dog and said, "Ubu gave me his paw. You never told me he did that."

"True, but he's done that with others. That's not absolute proof."

She answered, not averting her eyes from Ubu, "He came to me twice to do it while I was there. He did it twice."

Jack's mouth opened, but nothing came out.

"She's right," Harry said. "I saw the dog do it twice. Damnest thing I ever saw. He gave his paw to thin air two distinct times. No doubt about that." Harry was gaining excitement. They were getting close to controlling the time travel. Christine's image came into his mind. *I'm coming, Christine.*

Beth had been listening, but she kept quiet. All the talk about going back in time caused her to think about her late husband whom she had a vision about two days earlier. She could see her Tom's smile. She thought, *How I miss you, Tom!*

Laurel played the devil's advocate for Kourin's adventure. Not that she doubted Kourin had been back to yesterday. She needed her to say how she controlled going to when and where she wanted to. This was leading to how it would help her save Breckin!

Ubu felt Kourin's stare at him. He heard words he did not understand. He glanced at Mom. She was getting excited, but he didn't sense she needed him. It felt different. As the woman talking toward him finished, others spoke. He had given his paw to her the previous day several times, sensing she needed him similar to how Mom did. This was his way of letting her know he would safeguard her, like his Mom and Sister. He sensed she was in distress, stood, and walked over to her, resting his head on her thigh.

Jack watched Ubu as he placed his large cranium on Kourin's lap. He knew she had somehow experienced what he had earlier. His anxiety level went through the roof. *What the hell is going on?*

Kourin felt her heat rising. Jack still held her hands. She appreciated his touch, but she felt her temperature climbing. Her hands felt colder even with him holding them. The dog's head was resting in her lap. She could feel his heat adding to her own. An overwhelming emotion of rage overtook her. She didn't know where it was coming from. It built up deep inside of her until she felt she would explode. She nervously glanced at Jack, her heart pounding with fear.

Jack could feel the temperature of Kourin's hands drop as he held them while mesmerized by her glowing green eyes, with a brilliant ring of gold around the center. As he stared into the depths of the ring, he instinctively closed his eyes against the sudden, dazzling flare.

* * *

Joneal and Wren strolled side by side toward their destination. They were still in the unsure stage of their relationship, too early to even hold each other's hand. Along the way, Wren needed to use the restroom, so both made a pit stop.

As they passed the electronics store, Joneal asked Wren if she'd like something to drink. They stopped at the café. She ordered a strawberry peach smoothie. He opted for the mixed berry one. He was going to sit at a table in the café, but Wren said she wanted to drink it in the garden. They headed to the foliage, each sipping their drink on the way.

* * *

Shannon watched everyone as she hurried toward the garden. She didn't want to bypass Wren if she had already visited the garden and was leaving for the day.

Earlier, when the incident happened, Shannon had noticed some odd occurrences in the vicinity. She wanted to ask the restaurant hostess if she saw anything before the accident. Maybe it was nothing, but with the way the last two days had gone, everything was suspicious.

Luck was on her side. From a distance, she saw Wren exiting the café and turn toward the garden. She doubled her speed, which was to say she ambled along faster, but a young child on a tricycle could probably pass her. As Joneal and Wren came upon the first bench on the outer ring of the garden, she was close enough to call out to her.

From behind, Wren heard her name. When she turned around, she saw Shannon from security heading in her direction. Joneal stopped as well and waited for the guard, a woman in her fifties, to approach them.

Joneal said, "Oh, oh. She must have found out I'm not here for my tools."

"Don't worry," Wren said. "The worst they could do is arrest you for trespassing or possibly terrorism."

He had a panicked expression until he looked away from Shannon to Wren and saw her laughing. "Oh. Hilarious," he said and laughed along with her.

The guard reached them, and to Joneal's relief, she only wanted to speak to Wren about an incident that occurred earlier in the day outside the restaurant.

Shannon suggested they find a more secluded place to speak. They agreed and followed her around to the side where there was another bench similar but different from the one in the front. Joneal knew all of them as he had helped place them two days prior. The two ladies sat on the bench. He stood at the end near Wren.

For the next ten minutes, Wren was asked questions about the incident and was praised twice for readily assisting the elderly couple. Joneal listened intently. She hadn't mentioned the incident outside the restaurant, and he was impressed she had handled herself so well.

Wren was perplexed about the odd questions about the plants in the terminal and if she had observed anything out of the ordinary. She wasn't sure how this related to the accident, but she answered as best she could. Nothing strange was noticed, and she reacted as anyone would have if in the same situation. She had been a Girl Scout and maybe that helped her a little. What she most recalled from that experience was selling cookies every spring and the girls gossiping about how gross boys were.

She glanced at Joneal. He smiled at her. While Shannon was asking yet again about a plant next to the restaurant, she thought, *He has a sweet smile.* She ignored Shannon's question and thought about the woman from the cosmetics store from the day before, encouraging her to give him a chance and go on a date with him. Kourin had said she got a good vibe about him.

Shannon saw she would not get any more information from Wren than she already knew. She thanked both of them for their help, said her goodbyes, and walked to the garden exit, wanting to put some distance from the center bench.

The security guard had barely left when Wren got up. She asked Joneal, as she tilted her head toward the walkway leading to the center, "Shall we?"

With a few steps taken, the leaves in the garden rustled and, in the blink of an eye, their reality was upended.

4

HIGH SCHOOL

Before her, Mandy viewed a scene from her past. She stood under an oak tree on a bed of yellow-red leaves with the high school she attended looming to her left. Leaves rustled next to her, and she turned, expecting to see Sarah there. Shock registered in her brain as her high school friend Fara gazed up at her.

"Are you okay?" Fara asked. "That was unbelievable."

Mandy answered yes without looking at Fara directly. She glanced down at her body. She was not in the clothes she had on moments before. Her café apron was gone. Her fingers no longer had the red nail polish she had brushed on them on Sunday to prepare for the terminal party. She was dressed as a teenager. More specifically, she was dressed as she had been the day the cheerleaders assaulted Fara.

In the distance, she saw three girls in cheerleader outfits turning the corner onto an adjacent street. *That was them*, she thought. *I'm back in high school!*

Mandy turned around to speak to Fara, but her attention was caught by a movement on the other side of the tree. A bewildered Sarah sat on a green metal bench. She returned Mandy's gaze with her mouth agape.

* * *

Wren stumbled as she took another step. Joneal reached out, grasping her around the waist, preventing her from falling. As he did it, his smoothie slipped out of his hand, covering the sidewalk with its vibrant color. Unconsciously,

Wren held on to her cup. She felt the comforting embrace of Joneal's arms around her waist, helping her to regain her balance.

He released her from his grasp once he determined she was once again steady on her feet. The scene immediately in his vicinity was a tree-lined street ending on another street crossing its path. An imposing two-story red brick building stood across that street behind yellow and red-colored trees. Three girls turned the corner from that street, heading toward them, walking abreast, animatedly talking amongst themselves. They were dressed as cheerleaders in white and blue.

Joneal was extremely confused. After making sure Wren was okay at his side, he returned his gaze toward the cheerleaders in time to see them walking straight at them. He gently guided Wren to one side of the sidewalk out of the way. One girl, the blonde, said, "Watch where you're going!" The trio strutted by.

Wren let Joneal move her a couple of steps over as she watched the girls pass and continue down the sidewalk. She saw the trio split to two on one side and one on the other as they passed a stout black woman wearing a security guard uniform about ten feet away.

Shannon stood motionless, her gaze fixed on Wren and Joneal as three white girls sauntered past her. She thought, *Oh Lord, what have you gone and done?*

* * *

Mandy circled around the broad tree trunk to the bench in four long strides, leaving Fara sitting on the other side. As she approached the bench, her voice broke with emotion as she asked, "Sarah, are you okay?"

Sarah stared at the teenager and beyond to the black girl now standing by the tree. She returned to the blonde girl beside her, asking, "Mandy, is that you?" The teenager's head began nodding, but before she could answer, Sarah added, "You're so young! And your eyes, they're emerald green again."

Mandy sat on the bench and held the other's hands. She noticed how youthful her own hands were compared to the ones she grasped. They were warm to the touch. *Or are my hands cold?* Mandy asked herself before verbally asking, "Are you okay?"

"Me? What about you? You're . . . you're a fucking teenager!" said Sarah. "What . . .?" She looked around again and came back to Mandy's eyes. "What's going on? How is this possible? Where the fuck are we?"

"I don't know how this happened, but we're at my high school. I know this is going to sound crazy, but this is 2005."

From the tree area, they heard a voice say, "2006."

Mandy and Sarah turned toward the voice—Fara. She repeated, "Mandy, you know it's 2006." She looked at Sarah. "Who's your friend? Is this your mother?"

"Her mother?" asked a thunderstruck Sarah.

Mandy turned to her high school friend. "No, this is . . . someone I met yesterday. A good friend."

Fara answered, "I can't believe what you said to those girls. They're gonna be pissed." She walked closer to the bench. "What happened to your eyes? They're . . . I'm not sure what they are, but they're different."

Mandy became self-conscious and turned away from Fara.

Sarah reassured her, as they locked eyes for a moment, "They're already less green and the circle is not as bright." Not wanting to make her uncomfortable about her eye color, she diverted her own eyes and asked, "How did we get here? We were just in the garden."

"I don't know. I was just thinking about . . ." she paused. "Sarah, I was just thinking about this point in time when I felt an overwhelming rage about what happened here. The more I thought about it, the more intense it became. Three girls verbally taunted Fara. I told them—"

"You told those bitches off!" Fara said.

Both ladies on the bench turned toward her.

The black girl scrunched her eyes, peering at her friend, and said, "Your eyes are not like they were. They're almost . . . normal." She looked at Sarah, and with a smile, she said, "Hi, I'm Fara."

Sarah replied, "I'm Sarah. Pleasure to meet you." To Mandy, she asked, "How do we get back?"

"In my other vision, I returned without doing anything. One moment at my home, and the next, back on the bench. Maybe we'll just return once we see what we need to see here."

"But what are we supposed to see?" asked Sarah.

"I don't know. The last one was . . . not good," she said, releasing Sarah's hands. She scanned the area, thinking about what had occurred on this day many years before. She recalled telling off the cheerleaders when they insulted Fara. They hurried off, with two of them falling down. Afterwards, she went over to Fara's and had dinner with her family, meeting her parents for the first time. She remembered Fara was pretty shaken up by what the girls had said.

To her high school friend, she said, "Fara, I'm sorry. Are you okay? What those idiots said to you was appalling."

"I'm okay, I guess. I'm kinda used to it now." Fara's smile disappeared. "Since coming here, I've had to hear that and worse every day."

"We should tell their parents," Mandy said. "We need to stop this."

"No!" Fara said loudly and then softer. "No, if we do that, it'll only make them worse. It's best if we just ignore them."

Mandy gave Sarah an intense gaze.

"I don't know what they said," Sarah said, "but I can guess. I can't imagine what you're going through, but sometimes standing up for yourself does help."

"And sometimes standing up for yourself gets yourself killed," said the young black woman.

* * *

Jack opened his eyes. Kourin's attractive features met his gaze: red lips slightly parted, glimpses of pearl white teeth, rosy red cheeks, long full eyelashes. This brought his eyes to hers, bright green with a vivid golden ring circling the pupil staring at him. To his credit, he didn't shy away from the disconcerting eyes and continued holding her chilled hands. In his peripheral vision, he saw Ubu below him stir.

Ubu whined but kept his head in contact with Kourin's lap. He looked up at her face with only his eyebrows moving to do so.

Jack, who had been captivated by the woman he was growing to love, pulled his eyes away from her to take in the surrounding area. The office they had been sitting in was gone, replaced by a gently blowing breeze, rustling of leaves, and sunshine. He was seated on a simple park bench with Kourin and Ubu. A few feet away, Harry and Beth sat on a similar bench. In the opposite direction, he saw his niece on a matching bench about twenty feet away. Each of them looked around carefully. All appeared as confused as he was.

In usual fashion, Harry spoke first. "Where the hell are we?"

Jack answered, "I don't know. This place doesn't look familiar to me." He looked back into Kourin's eyes, which were now less green than moments ago. "Kori. Kori, do you know where we are?"

Kourin came back to herself as she heard Jack's voice. The rage she had felt had dissipated. Her internal temperature was returning to normal. She blinked. Her mouth was dry. She closed her lips and ran her tongue over them. It didn't help.

Jack was still holding her hands and had an obvious concern on his face. She blinked several more times and turned away from his gaze, self-conscious of her eyes not being normal. She thought, *What the fuck just happened? The anger I felt, but not my own.*

"Kori," Jack said again. "Kori, are you okay?" He delicately squeezed her hands. "Kori?"

Her gaze returned to Jack, answering, "I'm okay, I think. That feeling came over me again. Similar but different from when we . . . when we went back to the hospital."

Ubu adjusted his head and gave a nearly inaudible whine, continuing to look up.

She felt the dog below and moved her hand from under Jack's to pat Ubu's head between his ears. She felt his wound from the previous day and avoided it further. A slight smile curved at the edges of her lips as she stroked his fine hair.

Jack watched her interact with the dog, as he had seen Laurel do many times. He wondered *How does he know when to do what he does?*

From his right he heard Harry ask, "Why the fuck are we here? Does anyone want to tell me that?"

"Harry!" Beth said. He looked at her sideways without further comment. She remained quiet with a troubled expression.

Jack asked, "Kori, do you know where we are?"

She looked away from Ubu to the surrounding area. She answered, "No."

"No?" Harry yelled. "How the hell can you bring us here and not know where the fuck we are?"

"Harry, shouting will not help us figure this out," Jack chided him. "Kori, look around. Are you sure you don't this place?"

She peered around, coming back to him. She shook her head.

"That's just great," Harry said. "What do we do now?"

From the distance, Laurel spoke up. "Uncle Jack, I think I know where we are."

* * *

Fara said she needed to get home and invited Mandy and Sarah to come to her house for dinner. Sarah began to decline, but before she could, Mandy agreed. Fara said they always ate at five when Baba got home. Mandy assured her they would be there.

After Fara was out of earshot, Sarah asked the teenage version of Mandy why she agreed to go there for dinner. As they stood in front of the bench with the high school Mandy had attended at their backs, she explained she had dinner with Fara's family sixteen years ago after the incident with the cheerleaders. At that dinner, she met the rest of her family for the first time.

She looked around the area to see if there was anyone close by. There was not. She told Sarah she became good friends with Fara. Along with Laurel, they created a strong bond between them like they were sisters. With a sad face she confessed, in the years following graduation, the connection with Fara had waned. Today, she lived in Kenya with a family of her own.

As Mandy finished, Sarah said, "Oh my Jesus Christ!"

Mandy stopped talking and looked up.

"That is her . . . and him," Sarah said. "And her?"

Mandy saw what she was talking about. From around the corner the three racist cheerleaders had walked minutes ago came three people they recognized from 2022—Wren, Joneal, and Shannon.

"How the hell did they get here?" asked Sarah.

"I don't know," said teenage Mandy. "I don't know."

* * *

Shannon said hello to the teenager passing by her. The young black girl reminded her of herself at that age, weary of strangers but with a touch of kindness and humility.

The girl gave a half smile and said hello back, not slowing down as she continued on past.

Shannon thought of her teenage years. They were difficult, yet she made it through. She watched the girl continue down the sidewalk. She thought, *At least young black girls today have a chance of a better life than I had.*

Ahead of her, several steps away, were Wren and Joneal. They had stopped at the end of the street and were looking up and down the adjacent tree-lined street the cheerleaders had come from.

On one of the well-manicured lawns, Shannon saw a blue on white campaign sign reading "John Lynch Governor." *He's running again? He hasn't been governor for ten years.* On the opposite side of the street, a short distance further down, she saw a mother with her teenage daughter. The daughter was waving in her direction.

As Shannon caught up to the two young people, Wren asked, "Is she waving at us?"

Shannon looked behind them down the street in case the girl was waving to someone in that direction. No one was there. "Do either of you know that girl from school?"

Wren did not recognize the girl waving, but the woman looked familiar. She heard Shannon's question, but since she had no answer, she left it unanswered. Without waiting for her companions, she started walking toward the two, crossing the empty street to their side. In her peripheral vision, she saw Joneal follow beside her.

When she got within ten feet, she realized who the woman was. She thought, *I recognize her from the party last night. She was there with . . .* Wren stopped five feet away, looking closely at the teenager. She asked, "Mandy?"

Joneal stayed close to Wren as she crossed the street. She was headed to the two people under one of the oak trees. He thought, *She must know her. She looks kinda familiar.*

Shannon was two steps behind and caught up as Wren spoke up. She looked at the teen, confirming she looked like a younger version of the café manager. *A younger sister or cousin?*

Teenage Mandy replied, "Hi, Wren. I have some explaining to do. Joneal, Shannon, maybe you should sit down for this."

5

THE PARK

Laurel closed the gap to where the group was sitting so she didn't have to talk loudly. She said, "This is the park close to the high school I went to." She turned to her uncle. "We're at Piscataquog River Park. If we walk in that direction, a few blocks up, we'll find the high school." She pointed out the direction where a small bridge crossed a river.

"I think you're right," he said. "It looks familiar, but it was long ago when I was at that park. I mean this park."

"I'll check it out to make sure," she said and walked toward the bridge.

Ubu reacted to Mom moving, considered Kourin for a second, and bounded off quickly matching Mom's pace.

The others all rose in unison. Kourin was unsteady on her feet and immediately sat back down. Jack told Laurel they would wait where they were.

Beth said, "Harry, your leg is still hurting you. Let's wait here, too." Harry gave her an annoyed eye, but he sat back down without comment. Beth's and Jack's eyes connected, but neither was ready to say anymore. Right now, they all wanted to figure out how they got transported outside and tens of miles from where they had been a short time ago.

Laurel heard Ubu trotting up to her side. She glanced down at him and told him he was a good boy. He met her pace as he always did. From the landscape, it was obvious the time of year was autumn. Most of the trees had already turned from luscious green leaves to colorful yellows, reds, orange, and a dozen different shades of brown. A few trees were already bare. The air had a slight chill to it, but not so much that a jacket was needed. The sun filtered through the leaves remaining on the trees when not blocked by puffy clouds. *Cumulonimbus*, she thought. *Weird how I remember that.*

The cloud reminded her of the high school science class where two students sat side by side, becoming lab partners for the year. It was her first week at the new school. She watched the cloud above slowly swirl, ever changing its shape. *I had to memorize all the types of clouds for a test. That class was where I met Mandy on my first day. Junior year. I didn't give a shit about the clouds, but she made it into a game every time we were outside for the entire week.* Laurel smiled. *Doubtful I would have passed that class without her.*

From the first day in science class, they had kept a close friendship. Even when she joined the service, they stayed in contact. *Mandy never wavered in her encouragement that I was better than I thought I was,* Laurel finished the thought. *I hated having to move from Lincoln, leaving all my friends. She made the transition easier. When I thought I wasn't as pretty as the other girls, she helped me see past what I thought were flaws and accept me for who I am.* She looked down at Ubu who simply returned the look. *She hasn't changed since that first day we met.*

Laurel re-scanned where she was. Lost in her thoughts, she had walked halfway across the bridge with the Piscataquog River slowly passing by underneath. Three female cheerleaders walked past her, chatting amongst themselves. They ignored her, exiting the end of the bridge she had entered and walking past the others.

Over the well-worn wooden railing on the clear waters below, colorful leaves drifted down the gentle flow of the current disappearing under the bridge. She recalled dozens of times she had stood in this very spot the two years she went to high school nearby. She looked at the railing, recalling having visited this park with Ubu last summer. *Strange. This bridge is no longer wood.* Laurel remembered something about a severe storm. *It's metal now. We're in the past, but when? And how? Is this my vision? What the fuck is going on? Before last year,*

I hadn't been to this park since high school. She looked back at the others sitting and watching her. Beyond, she saw the cheerleaders stop at a bench about thirty feet farther down the path.

Her attention returned to the bridge, watching the gentle flow below. In the latter half of her senior year, she had crossed this bridge with Josh dozens, if not a hundred times, often observing the calming waters and almost always holding his hand. She had envisioned a life with him beyond their senior year, but that was not meant to be. They both joined the service, but their paths were eventually leading them in separate directions, losing touch with each other. This became clear months later when she was still recovering from her mental and physical wounds.

A habit she had since the attack, she absently touched the spot on her back. Although she couldn't feel the skin under her blouse, she thought, *One wound, I only have one wound now.* She continued watching the water flow under the bridge. The swirling current carried vibrant red and orange leaves toward a solitary branch poking up through the turbulent water. When the leaves reached that point, some were swept to the right and some to the left. Just beyond the obstruction, she watched a few of them meet up again while others continued to be carried downstream to some unknown destination. Watching the leaves float out of view, she wondered where Josh was today.

Ubu matched Mom's stride, sniffing the unfamiliar smells wafting by. He recognized where he was, having been here once before with Mom. Not understanding how he got here, he just accepted Mom needing his protection. All he knew was Mom and the other nice lady needed him. The strange voice had told him. From what he observed already today, he stood on guard.

Mom stopped, so he did as well, sitting by her side. He observed the squirrels on the river banks and in the trees. While watching a rather rambunctious one scurrying from one high up branch to another, he sensed tension from Mom. He looked up at her, seeing her touch her backside, a warning he had learned long ago that she was troubled. He whined and nuzzled his head against her shin.

Laurel was brought out of her funk, feeling Ubu bump her leg and hearing a soft whine from him. She looked down. He returned her gaze. She smiled and pet the top of his head. "Good boy, Ubu. I'm okay."

He stopped his whine and wagged his tail.

"You're such a good friend."

She thought of her other good friend, Mandy, and a friend from long ago, Fara. *We all walked over this bridge so many times. I wonder how she's doing.*

Laurel sensed movement to her right, taking her attention away from the swirling waters. A young black girl crossed the bridge toward her. As she closed the space between them, she realized who it was. *Oh my God, Fara!*

She faced the teenage girl crossing the bridge. They made eye contact. Laurel was certain it was Fara. There was no mistaking her.

They had met the same day she teamed up with Mandy in science class. The meeting was by chance when she was exiting the school and realized she had missed her bus. She had a slight panic attack as she tried to figure out how to get home. Her parents had only recently moved to the neighborhood, and she was unfamiliar with which direction she actually now lived. From behind her, she heard Mandy ask her if she was okay. She explained what had happened. Her new high school friend laughed, not in a mean-spirited way.

In the following years, Mandy's laugh was often what had grounded her when she strayed. Ubu was there now, having supplemented her friend's efforts.

Mandy explained her new home was the next street over from hers. It was an easy walk, no bus required. She added that Fara's home was three blocks beyond that, but it sounded more than it really was. The trio walked home together that day and nearly every day for the next two years. In her senior year, Josh had joined the trio.

Through this very park, Laurel thought as Fara walked closer. *Over this bridge.*

Laurel said hello when Fara was a few steps away. She said hello in reply, turning away and continuing her walk across the bridge.

At first, she was surprised Fara didn't recognize her. After a couple of thoughts, she realized the girl just didn't recognize her high school friend as an adult. She turned and watched her walk past the benches her uncle and the others occupied.

She needed to let the others know where—and when—they were. She hurried back to them, with Ubu at her side. As she approached where they sat, she saw movement farther down the path.

Laurel noticed Fara had moved to the far right of the path as she approached the bench where three cheerleaders were sitting. The three quickly rose and surrounded the black girl. She couldn't make out their words, but their body language conveyed a tense atmosphere.

With the four friends from the future watching her, waiting for her to clue them in on where they were, she instead yelled toward the commotion. "Hey!"

The girls ignored her.

She sprinted toward them and her teenage friend. As she did, one girl pushed Fara. She was caught off balance and fell to the ground. One girl kicked her in the side.

"Hey! Stop that!" Laurel yelled as she ran toward them.

Ubu stayed with Mom from the water to where they had been. He saw four people at a distance. Three were around the other. Mom took off running. He did as well.

Mom yelled something again, but it was not to him.

In his mind, he heard a voice say, "Ubu, protect," with a sense of urgency.

He looked up at Mom. She didn't seem to need protection. He was confused. He saw the girl in the middle fall.

In his head, Ubu heard a voice again telling him to protect the girl.

Without further thought, he charged toward the girls, his feet pounding the ground as he crossed the distance in seconds.

As Ubu came upon the girls, he did not attack them as he had the bad man that attacked Mom in that hot place. He bounded into the middle of them, taking up a protective position next to the girl on the ground. He growled as loud as he could at the three standing around her, baring his teeth and raising the hair on his back. They paused, unsure what to do. He barked at them.

When Ubu began barking, the trio of cheerleaders realized they were in way over their heads and ran away down the path away from the ferocious black dog. The blonde began crying. The curly-haired girl again tripped, this time over a rock. She fell, scraping her hands and receiving a cut on her right knee. The brunette led the flight away from the park.

When Ubu saw the girls were no longer a threat, he calmed down. He turned to the girl sitting on the path. She was holding her side and crying. Ubu did what he knew best to do. He whined, gave his tail a slight wag, and lay down next to her, placing his large head onto her thigh. In his head he heard the mysterious voice again, "Good boy, Ubu. Good boy."

* * *

Mandy explained to the three newcomers where and when they were. Wren and Joneal were completely in denial. Shannon, however, sat quietly, listening to the back and forth the young couple had with the teenager and woman. After several minutes, when all realized they were talking in circles, Shannon ended it by asking how were they going to get back. All looked at each other, not having an answer.

Sarah asked Mandy if they would return to their own time if she had dinner with Fara.

Mandy was about to answer when her facial expression dramatically changed to panic. The others, seeing her natural optimism cease, also panicked.

Mandy said, "Oh no! I was supposed to walk home with Fara!"

Sarah answered, "It's okay. We can still go there for dinner."

"No, you don't understand! After the cheerleader incident here, we ran into them in the park. They started picking on us, but I . . ." She frantically scanned the direction Fara had walked, the same direction Shannon and all had come from. "I need to go!" Without waiting for the others, she ran across the street in the direction the young black girl had gone.

The others stood with their mouths open, shocked she had run off. After a few moments of hesitation, they followed behind the running teen.

Shannon fell quickly behind, but she kept them in sight.

Mandy was yards ahead, and being much younger, she lengthened the distance between them.

Joneal stayed with Wren, matching her pace but keeping teen Mandy in sight. Sarah kept stride with them.

Fortunately, they saw her turn right onto a path shrouded in darkness by the tall trees surrounding it. When they arrived at the spot, they glimpsed her dashing across a wooden bridge in the distance.

Mandy's heart raced as she ran in a panic. The memory of her second encounter only just resurfaced in her mind. When time traveling back to this day from many years ahead, she had forgotten the consequences of her first encounter with the cheerleaders. She had accepted the dinner invitation from Fara and together they walked home, taking the shortcut through the park. On the way, they ran into the cheerleaders again. This time, they were more than verbally abusive. They had become physical.

The three ambushed them from behind, catching them off guard. The brunette had Mandy in a tight embrace. Fara was held by the blonde, and the curly-haired girl hit her in the face with a loud smack. She fell to the ground. Both girls delivered a swift kick to her ribs. Mandy felt the heat of her rage build as she fought to break free until she succeeded with a triumphant cry. With a sudden burst of energy, she lunged at the assailants. Her rage from earlier exploded into a physical assault, the sound of fists and slaps echoing in a whirlwind. The fight ended as quickly as it had begun. The girls fled and never threatened Fara again.

Seconds after the girls left, Mandy recovered from her rage and went to her friend lying on the ground. Fara gazed at her face with a startled expression and passed out. In that moment, she had connected her fear to the trauma of the attack.

Now, as she sped across the wooden bridge and spotted people in the distance, she pondered if Fara had noticed something in her eyes. She closed the gap to the group of people and feared she was too late to help her friend this time. Fara was lying on the ground. Next to her was a black dog she instantly recognized. She called out to him, her voice ringing clear, "Ubu!"

* * *

Jack, Kourin, Beth, and Harry arrived to where Laurel was aiding a teenage black girl lying on the ground. Ubu was next to her, his head on her lap. They were amazed by the dog's speed when they saw him sprint to her aid while the three girls were attacking her. Laurel had been seconds behind, but they had already made a hasty retreat from the ferocity of Ubu.

From behind, Jack heard a voice cry, "Ubu!" He turned to see a blonde teenager running at them. She exclaimed, "Ubu, it is you!"

All turned to the newcomer as she came to a sliding stop on the loose gravel steps behind the woman attending the young black girl. She asked, "Laurel?"

Her attention turned to the others in the group, and she asked, "Jack? Kourin? What are all of you doing here?"

The group looked at the young blonde addressing them. None spoke. Laurel broke the silence, asking, "Mandy?"

The others looked from Laurel, who was cradling Fara in her arms, to the person standing in front of them. It was a moment of sudden realization as they came to understand the situation.

"Oh my God, it is you!" Laurel said. With a nostalgic glance, she looked back at Fara, a friend from many years ago, yet they wouldn't meet until the following year, according to the correct timeline. Laurel asked her high school friend if she was okay and helped her to her feet. Fara clutched her side where a kick had been inflicted, yet she seemed to be unscathed.

Laurel scanned the others who remained in shock and unmoving. She said to the blonde teenager, "Mandy, I think I know what's happening, but maybe you should fill us in. But first, I think we need to get this girl to a doctor." She didn't call Fara by her name since she technically hadn't met her yet, although she knew everything about her.

"No, that's okay. I'll be alright," Fara said, holding her side a little tighter as she spoke. "I've had worse."

Mandy said, "I'll get her home. That's what happened—" She stopped herself, changing what she was about to say. "That's probably best." To Fara she said, "Fara, are you okay? Really, okay?"

Fara nodded her head. "I'm a little sore, but I think nothing is broken."

At this Beth, who had been silent nearly the entire time since arriving at the park, said, "Dear, you took a nasty hit. You might have internal damage. Let us take you to the hospital or call 911."

"No!" Fara said. "I mean, no." She gave a half smile. Laurel and Mandy involuntarily smiled with both recalling Fara's beautiful half smile from years before. She continued, "I'll be alright. I've had way worse growing up." She looked down at Ubu who sat silently at her side. "Thanks to this dog. Without her, I don't know what would have happened."

At the same time, Laurel and Mandy both said, "He," to Fara, signifying that Ubu is male. They both looked at each other and automatically said, "Jinx," and laughed.

Fara silently observed both of them, as did the gathering of adults.

Jack was about to utter a word when Harry spoke up, his voice ringing in the air. "What the hell are they doing here?"

All eyes turned to see Wren and Joneal with Sarah two steps behind, approaching them with a black female security guard a football field length farther back.

Harry said, “Houston, we have a problem.”

6

PIZZA

Mandy spoke before too much was said in front of Fara. "Fara, these are friends of mine from . . . out of town. Um," she glanced at Sarah, "how about we get you home?"

Sarah added, "Yes, that sounds like a good idea." She looked at the others to see if they had caught on. "We can get you safe at home and then discuss why we all got together today."

Jack picked up on what they were hinting at: *"Don't speak about time travel in front of Fara."* "Sounds good. Maybe there's someplace we can wait for you, or should we just wait here?" he asked no one in particular, having said it more toward teen Mandy and Sarah since they seemed to have a handle on what was going on.

It was Fara, though, who spoke up. "There's a sub shop on the corner of my street. It might be more comfortable than the park benches."

"The Oaks!" said both Laurel and teen Mandy in unison, adding, "Jinx."

Fara looked at them with a suspicious expression, but said, "Yes, the Oaks. It's not half bad, but it's too expensive for me."

Laurel and Mandy exchanged glances, remembering the hours they spent there years before, splitting the checks and never asking Fara to pay even when she insisted.

Teen Mandy said, "Sounds like a plan. Shall we?" She moved next to Fara. "Can I help you?"

"I can manage," Fara said. To the group, she said, "Thanks for helping me. I . . ." Ubu whined and bumped Fara's leg as she got teary-eyed. "I . . ." She reached down and pet Ubu's head.

Laurel spoke up. "No prob. I'm glad we were nearby to help."

Fara gave her a half smile, unable to articulate her heartfelt gratitude.

Mandy took hold of Fara's free hand and tugged gently. "Fara, let's get you home." She led her away, with the others following just as Shannon caught up with the group.

Shannon glared at everyone present. "Can someone please tell me what the hell is going on here?"

Laurel said, checking first to ensure Mandy had led Fara far enough away, "We're in 2006 at Piscataquog Park in Manchester." She gauged everyone's reaction before continuing. "The girl we saved is Fara. She was—is Mandy and my best friend in high school. Well, she will be my friend next year. I'm still living in Lincoln this year."

Half the group looked at each other with some understanding. The other half was in a dumbfounded state. Laurel said, "Maybe we should go to the sub shop first. I can fill you in there."

Harry asked, "Do you know why or how the hell we even got here?"

Laurel said, "Unfortunately, I'm as lost as you why we're all here or even how it happened." She looked in the direction her two high school friends and Sarah walked, seeing them a few hundred yards down the path. "Let's get to the sub shop. Maybe when Mandy and Sarah join us, we can find out why we're here."

* * *

Sarah followed a couple of steps behind the two teens. She thought, *Mandy is a teenager. What the hell is going on? Maybe this is just a dream.* She pinched herself, feeling her skin squeezed between her fingernails. *Well, if it is a dream, pinching yourself doesn't help.* She looked beyond Mandy. *I hope those three bitches aren't waiting to ambush us ahead. Doubtful. Laurel's dog terrified the shit out of them. I doubt they'll bother her again.*

She watched teen Mandy holding Fara as they walked in front and marveled at Mandy's kindness. *The other day when she helped me must just come naturally to her.*

Sarah's thoughts turned to when she was in high school. She thought of her high school sweetheart. *We were supposed to spend our lives together when I graduated, and you returned home.* She pictured his smile as he would forever appear in her mind and in her heart. For the rest of the walk to Fara's home, she thought about her high school sweetheart and how much she missed him, even all these years later. A tear escaped her eye. She wiped it away, thinking of her children instead, one child that wasn't much younger than the two girls walking ahead of her. *I'll get home to you, kids.*

* * *

Jack held the glass door open for the others to enter the sub shop, which was a small part of a larger convenience store. To the right were several narrow rows of typical neighborhood goods. He followed the others to the left where there were two small wooden tables with four mismatched chairs at each. Wren and Beth slid the tables together, forming a larger table capable of accommodating all seven of them and one dog.

Joneal said he'd place the order and asked what everyone wanted. Beth suggested a couple of pizzas to make it simple. They decided on one cheese and one pepperoni. None of them had an appetite. It was more to pass the time.

The young man ordered at the counter. He called back to everyone, asking what they wanted to drink. The man behind the counter, an older gentleman Joneal guessed was in his mid-sixties, suggested he could make it simple and ring up seven sodas. They could grab what they wanted from the three coolers lined up on the wall behind the tables. Joneal called back again, asking if they wanted any chips or anything to go with it. All passed on the chips. He ordered a large onion ring for the group to go with the pizzas. The man told him the price. He took out his debit card to pay, but it kept coming up as declined.

Joneal told the man to hold on for a minute. He went back to the tables and explained that his debit card was being declined. Harry told him the bank on the card probably doesn't exist yet. Jack took out his wallet, having remembered he put extra cash in it for the party the night before. He pulled out four twenty-dollar bills. He examined all of them and chose two, handing them to Joneal to cover the meal and a tip.

Laurel asked her uncle why he examined the bills before just giving two to Joneal. He explained by taking out his wallet and handing her one of the two twenties he didn't use. She looked at it, confused. He told her to look at the year on it: 2010. Her eyes lit up and her mouth opened as she realized why he did what he did. The bill she held in her hand hadn't been printed yet.

He told the group as quietly as he could but loud enough for all to hear that maybe it didn't matter. Someone noticing a date on a bill in with others was unlikely, but just by being in the sub shop having pizzas and soda could be problematic with the timeline.

Laurel asked, "What do you mean?"

"Do you remember the scene from Jurassic Park when the guy in the Jeep before the T-Rex arrived was talking about the butterfly effect?" Jack asked.

The others stared at him.

"Really? No one?"

More blank stares.

"Okay. Basically, if a butterfly flutters its wings in China, it rains in New York instead of having sunshine." He saw a blank stare. "Okay, I'm not saying this right." He picked up the salt shaker from the table. "This salt shaker is here for us to use. After we leave, an hour from now it will be there for another customer to use. With me so far?"

All eyes were on him. Wren nodded her head.

"Now, if I steal this salt shaker . . ." Jack hid it between his hands, "the next customer comes in doesn't have it to use. He sees one at the next table and gets up to get it. On his way, he twists his ankle, having to go to the emergency room to get it X-rayed. They put him in a cast. He misses the big high school football game where he would have caught the game-winning touchdown that a scout in the stands sees, leading to a scholarship to play at Boston College where he eventually gets picked in the second round of the NFL draft."

He saw more nods.

"So, whatever we do here right now could seriously affect our future or someone's future that we are totally unaware of."

"Or," Laurel added, "we can make a minor change that will alter a disastrous situation."

Jack took a breath before answering. "Laurel, sweetheart, I know what you're getting at, but we can't change the past."

"Why not? If we have the means to do it, shouldn't we if it's for the better?"

"But for the better of whom?" asked Jack. He saw her getting upset. Two women at the counter purchasing several bags of candy turned when Laurel's and Jack's voices grew louder. Ubu placed his head on her lap.

In a lower and calm voice, Jack said, "I'm not trying to be a pain in the ass. All I'm saying is we need to be very careful in our interactions with this timeline. For all we know, having a pepperoni pizza changes something down the road."

"What about helping Fara when she was attacked?" Laurel asked. "Should we have just stood by and let it happen?"

"No, of course not," Jack answered.

One woman peered in their direction as they exited the shop. Jack ignored her, searching the others for their reactions. They remained quiet. Both Harry and Shannon returned Jack's gaze. Beth had her head down and seemed lost in thought. Kourin had her arms wrapped around herself, staring down one of the store's aisles. Wren and Joneal exchanged glances.

When Jack saw his worker and the pretty redhead from the restaurant facing each other, he said, "I'm sorry. You two—" he looked at Shannon and added, "you three must be so confused right now. Maybe we should fill you in a little on what's going on."

Shannon answered for all three. "I'm not sure there's anythin' you can say that'll clear this confused mind."

"Well, let me try," Jack said.

While they waited for their pizzas and Mandy to return, he told them a condensed version of all the events that had happened since the bench had arrived in the terminal. By the time he got to the plants moving in the garden, the man behind the counter called to them that their order was ready.

* * *

The trio, comprising a disheveled Fara, teenage Mandy, and a woman old enough to be their mother, arrived at the black girl's home after passing the sub shop on the corner. The white duplex was two houses down the narrow street lined with nearly identical duplexes.

Fara went to the door on the left side. The exterior was in disrepair, with paint peeling in several places and one of the faded blue shutters hanging cock-eyed. On a second-floor window, one shutter was missing completely. To the left of the entry stairs, between the house and the sidewalk, was a small flower garden. Two Hosta plants had turned yellow as they neared the end of their cycle. In between these were the corpses of dead vegetable plants having given their lives for several salads and dinners.

As Mandy traversed the front steps, on the second well-worn wooden step was a medium-sized orange pumpkin. The stem was no longer attached. On the top step was a small yellow Hardy Mum plant. The orange pumpkin and yellow mum stood in stark contrast to the monotone colors of the entrance. Even the entrance door was a dull, washed-out blue.

Fara opened the door, allowing a bright, warm light to escape the confines of the home to spill onto the bleak porch. She entered, dropping her backpack onto the first step of the stairway on the right. Immediately to the left was a doorway leading to an empty living room. Instead of entering that room, she walked down the hall straight ahead toward the source of the light.

As Mandy entered the kitchen at the end of the hall, she was met by a cheerful black woman with graying hair, Fara's mother. Introductions were made, and in two shakes of a lamb's tail, they were sitting at a small round table sipping peach flavored Fresca.

Against Fara's wishes, teen Mandy told her mother about the two incidents that occurred with the cheerleaders. Sarah added a couple of comments but otherwise kept quiet. She felt she needed to stay in the background since, if time was repeating itself, she wasn't supposed to be here.

Fara's mother thanked them and insisted they stay for dinner. With everyone waiting at the sub shop a few doors down, Mandy said she had to run a quick errand first and would return shortly.

* * *

As Joneal retrieved the pizzas and rings, Beth got everyone a soda. Harry wanted a Moxie but there wasn't one, so he settled for an A&W Root Beer. The others had a Coke, Diet Coke, or Sprite.

Beth settled back down as the group dug into the pizzas. Although none of them had an appetite, the aroma from the pizzas was intoxicating. She asked, while watching another customer buy two bags of candy, "Why is everyone buying so much candy?"

Wren, who hadn't uttered two words since arriving, said, "It must be for Halloween."

As the group watched another person step up to the counter, the entrance door opened with a teenage blonde girl walking in with an older woman close behind.

* * *

Before exiting Fara's home, Mandy brought to mind the original version of the evening. She didn't want a repeat of missing a critical incident as she had done earlier in the park. Fortunately, Ubu had been there when she wasn't.

> Fara's mother hovered around her, peering over her shoulder to make sure she was alright as she sat at the kitchen table until Fara came back from freshening up.
>
> Soon after, Fara's brother appeared. A couple of years younger than his sister, he was what Mandy thought a brother would be if she had one. He made light fun of his sister and flirted with Mandy, as an eighth grader would do. She was charmed by his calm manner, especially after she learned of the horrors the family had escaped from Africa.
>
> The patriarch of the family came home just after five. He was quiet at first. Mandy noticed what appeared to be a welt on the side of his face and felt something had happened rattling him. After the first hour passed, he seemed to overcome whatever had troubled him. No one, at least in her presence, made a comment about his apparent injury.
>
> Through dinner and into the early evening, Mandy learned about life in Africa. Forevermore, she didn't take life for granted. If there was any pessimism in Mandy's body, she shed it for an optimistic view of the love she had found in that household, a view she held on to and vowed to share with others.

Mandy was quiet as she exited the front door behind Sarah. She took a moment on the porch, attempting to collect herself after reviewing what had occurred years before. The emotion of reliving this day was wearing on her effervescent optimism.

She surveyed the other homes, remembering some families living there. Two streets over, she lived a big part of her life, and being back felt like coming home.

After graduating high school, her mother moved to Newington while she attended UNH. Upon graduation, her mom stayed there since she had made many new friends and had a job she loved. She still lived in the same home.

The hardest decision she made to that point in her life was moving back to the Manchester area and leaving her mother. To this day, her mother reassured her it was the correct choice.

Mandy looked up and down the familiar street. Both sides had Halloween decorations on nearly every home, from simple like Fara's porch to more elaborate hanging ghosts, witches, and Jack-o'-lantern pumpkins. Two homes had orange lights wrapped around the porch railings.

Sarah hit the sidewalk and realized Mandy was not behind her. She looked back up at her on the porch, watching her look up and down the street. After a few moments of observing her new friend, who more closely resembled her eldest daughter than a peer, she asked if she felt different at all. She elaborated by explaining she meant being a teenager again.

Mandy replied that her youthful figure made her feel ancient in comparison. On her adult body, her boobs were not as pert as they once were and what her mother called smile lines were permanently etched on her face. Other than not feeling old, she felt physically the best she had been in years.

She added she wasn't sure mentally how she felt.

She traversed the steps to join her friend and said her mind was flooded from what she could recall. Memories long forgotten were resurfacing, yet in some respects, they didn't seem to be quite the same. She glanced back at the undecorated home without further comment on what she meant.

As they neared the sub shop, Sarah explained why she asked after giving Mandy time with her thoughts as they walked in silence. If they were now changing history, did she feel it altering her? Was she thinking or remembering things differently than she thought they had occurred before?

Mandy reassured her friend things were still the same as far as she could tell except for the incident with Fara. She still remembers walking her home and confronting the girls with Fara. There was no dog, no Laurel, or any of the others.

Outside the sub shop, before opening the door, she asked Sarah not to say anything about her eyes. Not sure what was happening, she wanted to keep that between them, at least for now.

As the blonde teenager opened the sub shop door, Sarah asked her if nothing was changing, then why were they here? Mandy thought about that as she held the door open for a customer exiting. As things had occurred for the last two hours, she hadn't stopped to analyze that maybe she was supposed to change something. Since arriving, she was reacting to events, same as she did sixteen years ago. Now she pondered, *Am I supposed to do something different?* The bench seemed purposeful the last time she experienced it. What was the message this time?

* * *

Teen Mandy and Sarah returned to the group. They both passed on a slice of pizza. Joneal grabbed a chair from a nearby table for Sarah. Mandy sat in the open one next to Ubu. She petted him and said hello as his tail wagged vigorously.

While the others anxiously awaited Mandy to enlighten them on why they were all present in her vision, Harry watched Ubu. The dog did not act differently toward teen Mandy than he had back at the terminal. Not that anyone doubted it, but this girl definitely was Mandy.

Laurel, Jack, and Shannon all asked a question at the same time. Although each phrased it differently, Mandy got the message asking what the hell was going on.

She said, "I'm a little confused why we're here just as you are. Sarah and I were sitting on the bench in the terminal, and the next thing we know we're here. Why the bench brought us here? I don't know."

She left out any reference to her eye color changing and the overwhelming emotions she endured. She gave an abbreviated version of what occurred in front of the high school and told them the original version of the day and how it had already been altered in the park.

Laurel and Jack looked at each other, keeping silent.

Harry watched as Mandy had stopped petting Ubu as she told her story, using her hands as she spoke. Ubu sat next to her, placing his head on her lap.

Wren asked, "What's today's date?"

"October 31, Halloween," Mandy answered. She looked at the clock on the wall.

Harry asked, "You got someplace to go?" Beth gave him a facial expression to be nice. He said to her gruffly, "What?" She just shook her head a little and took a sip of her Sprite.

"Actually, Harry, yes, I do. I need to get back to Fara's for dinner. The last time, I stayed there after walking her home. I think I'm supposed to be at her home for whatever reason that is." Mandy asked Sarah, "Can you come with me?"

Jack asked, "Won't that screw up what happens?"

Mandy answered, "I don't think so. It might look peculiar now if I left with Sarah and didn't come back with her. Honestly, I just would like her there for moral support and to watch what happens. Maybe an extra pair of eyes will catch something important." She got up to go.

Sarah rose without comment. She had no intention of allowing Mandy to leave without her, regardless of what anyone else said. She was glad it didn't come to that.

After spending a few minutes with everyone, she learned two things: *None of the others know why they are here, and Mandy clearly does not know why either.* The latter frightened her since she knew it was her that brought them back in time.

As the two women exited, Laurel said to no one in particular that Ubu probably needed to relieve himself. She rose, prompting Ubu to do the same. Jack asked if she'd like him to go with her. Before she could answer, Joneal said he needed to stretch his legs and would like a walk. Wren said she'd join as well. Laurel told Jack they'd be okay and wouldn't be too far. She said she'd take Ubu back to the park. The trio, plus one dog, exited.

Shortly after they left, a forty-something black man entered. He turned down the candy aisle as nearly every customer had before him. Randomly picking out two bags, he proceeded further down the aisle in search of additional items.

A woman at the counter finished paying, saying "Happy Halloween" as she departed the shop. As she arrived at the door, it opened. A costumed person held it open to allow her to exit first. She said thank you but received no response. The person, dressed as a clown, entered the shop looking at the seated group and turned to the right down an aisle.

Jack excused himself to use the restroom, leaving Kourin, Harry, Beth, and Shannon at the tables. The single restroom was in a nook to the far right of the counter.

The man buying candy came to the counter with an additional item: a can of cat food. He laid them on the counter.

The man behind the counter asked, "And how are you today, Tu?"

Tu answered with a heavy accent, "Same as yesterday, Everett. And the day before that. But I'll take that any day of the week, my friend."

"Same here. It's a beautiful day today. Should have a lot of trick-or-treaters out. Are you sure two bags will be enough?"

"It will have to do. Money is tight, but I don't want to disappoint the little ones."

"Will you be out with your children this year?"

"Fara is in high school now. Zakia will probably go. Who can resist free candy?" said Tu with a broad smile, revealing teeth that hadn't had proper dental treatment since they pushed out the baby ones.

Kourin heard the customer, Tu, speaking and the terminal tram operator came to mind. Diric's accent was similar, yet it was different. She watched him interact with Everett, which she now knew to be his name.

A person dressed in a clown costume approached from the aisle behind them, the left hand holding a bag of candy, the right hand beneath it.

Kourin thought, *That seems odd.*

7

THE CLOWN

Upon returning to Fara's home, teen Mandy and Sarah were startled when a ghost opened the door and said, "Boo!" The ghost had cutouts for the eyes. They were circled with black marker. Another dozen pair of black circles of similar size were drawn all over the white sheet.

"Wow, what a great costume, Zak," Mandy said.

"Aw, how d'ya' know it was me?"

"A lucky guess."

"Well, come on in. Baba's not home yet, but I'll tell Fa you're here." The ghost walked away toward the kitchen, the sheet billowing in his wake.

Sarah asked, "What kind of ghost is he supposed to be?"

Teen Mandy started laughing. "He's Charlie Brown."

"Ah, yes. Now I remember. Great pumpkin. All I got was rocks." They sat on the well-worn sofa. "I haven't seen that show in decades."

A voice from the kitchen hallway said, "It was on three nights ago. All Zak talked about since was being a Charlie Brown ghost." Zak's mother entered the room, adding, "Actually, he wanted to be Superman." She didn't explain that they barely had enough money for food; they certainly couldn't buy a costume that would be used once.

"Hello, Mrs. Otieno, I hope you don't mind Sarah joining us," said Mandy.

"Not at all, my dear. The more the merrier," Mrs. Otieno answered. "Sarah, you're welcome anytime. Would either of you like something to drink?" She looked out the window. "Tu should be along shortly. Hopefully, he remembered to stop by the market to pick up some candy to give out."

Both declined a drink. Fara entered the room, having cleaned up from the encounters and wearing matching fuchsia-colored sweats. She said hello and sat in a matching chair with sides worn the same as the couch. Mandy thought of her cat, Autumn, back in her apartment and sixteen years in the future. The telltale sign of a cat using the furniture as a scratching post was unmistakable. As if on cue, around the corner Fara had just passed came a tabby cat rubbing against the wood frame.

Mandy noticed Fara holding her side and asked, "Fara, are you sure you don't want to go to the hospital? You look like you're in pain."

She glanced at her mother before answering. "No. I'll be okay. I've had far worse than this." She caught her mother's eye before continuing. "I know, Mama. We don't talk about the past, but if we don't, how can we ever fix what is happening?"

Sarah and Mandy looked at each other. Sarah didn't know what was meant, but Mandy recalled being through this conversation before. She raised one hand slightly to let Sarah know to be quiet and let it play out.

Mrs. Otieno replied, "Fa, we left that life to provide an opportunity for you and your brother. We need to move on."

"But what of the others? We left shangazi, our mkoi, all the others," Fara said. She looked at Mandy. A tear escaped her eye, traveling between her cheek and nose to rest just above her lip.

Mandy looked from Fara to her mother and back before saying, "Why don't you tell us about your family back home? Maybe talking about it will help?"

Mandy saw a sullen expression on Mrs. Otieno, but she knew from having heard it all before: the family's healing would begin in the following two hours telling their life story. Teen Mandy also knew this would be the pivotal moment she became the person she would become, although she didn't know that then.

* * *

"That'll be nine forty-seven, Tu," Everett said. He glanced at the clown behind him.

Tu took out his wallet. "I should have just enough." He pulled out a five and several ones, counting them out on the counter and saying sorry to the clown behind him. He saw the bag of candy the clown was holding and added, "I see we all h'd the same idea. Gotta g't candy for the watoto. I'm sorry, I mean the children."

Tu saw the barrel of a gun under the candy. He looked up into the clown's eyes.

In a second, the peaceful sub shop erupted into chaos.

The clown threw the bag of candy that had been concealing his revolver to the floor and said, "Nob'y move!" He used his left hand to push Tu forward into the counter, while his right hand tightly gripped the gun, a finger resting on the trigger. He looked at the group sitting at the tables and waved his gun. "Don't move!" He barked at the man behind the counter, "Open the register and put the money in a bag!" Everett was frozen and didn't move. "Now, old man!"

When the clown had pushed Tu forward against the counter, his hand found the can of cat food. He wrapped his hand around it. Everett locked eyes with him and almost imperceptibly shook his head. Tu had dealt with clowns like this before, men who attacked with guns and machetes, indiscriminately killing only because they were of a different tribe.

The clown raised his weapon, pointing it at Everett. "Do as I say, and no one gets hurt. Come on, old man!"

Tu saw his opportunity as the clown spoke and waved his weapon away from him. He tightened his grip on the can of cat food. As quickly as he could, he spun around and swung the can at the clown's head.

As fast as he thought he was, and perhaps in his youth he would have succeeded, he was too slow. He placed a glancing blow against the clown's makeup, causing the white to smear with the red around the lips. He was able to hit his arm, causing the clown's aim to come off of Everett.

With a sudden clench of his right hand, the clown discharged his weapon, and the sound reverberated through the air. The contact from Tu was enough to cause the bullet to miss the clerk's head by several inches, lodging into the sub menu board on the wall.

All four people sitting down screamed when the shot rang out, but they were frozen in place as the gun swung back around.

Too close to point the gun at Tu, the clown used it to strike him on the side of the head. He fell back against the counter, stunned by the impact of the metal on his forehead.

Now, as the gun barrel was pointed right at his head, he wished he had taken the time to kiss his wife goodbye that morning.

* * *

Jack washed his hands, and as he opened the restroom door, the sharp sound of a gunshot echoed through the hall. In front of him, about four feet away, was the back of a person in a clown suit with a multicolored wig on. He recalled seeing the clown enter when he went to the bathroom.

He heard the clown tell someone, "You shouldn't have done that, ol' timer." Jack saw the clown's arm extend toward a man leaning on the counter, holding his head.

Shannon had training dealing with armed assailants. She could hold her own in the training she had received throughout her career in security. Until this moment, she had never been in an actual situation. She was also unarmed.

She thought of her Earl. What if the man who was now leaning against the counter was her husband? Wouldn't you want someone, anyone, to help him if they could? She stirred and rose slightly in her chair. *Yes. I would*, she thought.

The clown saw movement from the group seated at a table. One person, an older black lady, wore a uniform. He had observed from the aisle she was not a cop. She was a rent-a-cop, so no problem. Now she was stirring. He pointed his gun at her.

The group saw the gunman swing his arm toward them. Shannon froze partly off her chair. Kourin felt a wave of emotions swell inside her, and her chest was filled with an intense heat. Beth was like a statue, fear written all over her face. Harry had his eye on movement behind the clown.

Jack saw the clown's arm swing away from the black man against the counter. *Now or never*, he thought.

He rushed forward to the gunman, crashing into him. The gun discharged a second time. They both fell forward, a sudden rush of air leaving their lungs as they hit the cold hard floor.

Kourin screamed, "Jack!"

* * *

"Mandy. Mandy, can you hear me?"

Mandy opened her eyes to see Sarah two feet away from her, concern on her face.

"There you are," Sarah said. "You had me worried for a moment." She turned her head and added, "She's okay. She's coming to."

She moved closer to Mandy's ear so only she could hear. "You blacked out for a moment. We're still at Fara's house." She pulled away and looked into Mandy's eyes, returning next to her ear. "Your eyes are green, but they're already subsiding. You may want to avert them until it passes."

Mandy looked around Sarah to the room they were in. All appeared as it had, except Sarah stood before her. She heard Fara's voice. "Can I get you anything?"

Sarah answered for her. "I think a glass of water, please." She looked into Mandy's eyes and added quietly, "The gold ring is almost gone."

Mandy knew what she meant even though she did not know what was causing it. She thought about what they were talking about before it happened. Fara was talking about her village in Kenya and what life was like. She had been listening intently when she had a rush of emotions and blacked out.

Fara handed her a half-full glass of water. She took a sip. Without looking up, she said, "Thank you." She had another sip, adding, "I feel better now."

Fara's mother spoke from further away. "Fara, let's give Mandy a moment to recover. Can you help me in the kitchen?"

"Sure, Mama," Fara answered. She reached out, gently touching Mandy's arm and asked, "Are you sure you're okay?"

"Ya. I'm good. I just need a moment," Mandy replied.

Fara followed her mother out of the room, leaving Sarah with Mandy.

"Mandy, are you really okay?" Sarah asked. "Did something happen?"

"I don't know. The last thing I remember, I was thinking about Mr. Otieno. Fara was telling her story. I was recalling what had happened to him." She paused and gazed at Sarah, her face displaying sheer panic. "Oh my God! He died. Sarah, he died the night I went to Fara's for dinner!"

* * *

Laurel, with Ubu at her side, walked back the way they had come toward the park. The sun was going down, but the day had been unseasonably warm and continued to be so even with the setting sun. They still had plenty of light, as twilight was just beginning. The moon was waxing overhead, coming to full brightness in several days. Ubu paused several times to sniff an area and leave his scent.

Wren walked with Joneal to Laurel's left. They held hands. Laurel didn't comment on it, but she smiled.

Joneal asked, "Laurel, I have to admit I am completely confused about what is going on. It seems like science fiction. The bench I worked on has somehow teleported us here? We have to be dreaming or something."

"I know it seems crazy, but what Uncle Jack said is true. I had my experience, and now it seems we're all in one together." Laurel paused as Ubu found another telephone pole needing a message to be left. She looked at both of her walking mates. "Somehow, we'll get back. When this happened before, you were back on the bench as if you had never left."

"But we weren't sitting on the bench," Wren said. She squeezed Joneal's hand. "We were just walking by the garden."

"I know. I was in my office when—" She almost said "when Kourin's eyes changed," but she held back, not knowing what significance that may or may not have. Instead, she completed her sentence, "When we were all suddenly here."

Laurel entered the park via the dirt walkway off the street. "Don't worry. We'll return home."

She said the words, but she had doubts. Not knowing how they actually got here, she was uncertain how they would get home. For now, she would have to let the vision play out to whatever conclusion it had.

Ubu found a pine branch lying on the ground. He sniffed it, turned, and lifted his leg. *If I have to find my way back, I'll leave a trail.*

* * *

"Mandy, are you sure? Earlier, you said you ate dinner with the entire family. All of them, including the father." Sarah looked toward the kitchen to make sure no one was nearby. "Maybe it was just . . . I don't know, maybe just a weird vision, like what I had of the ghost plane. It wasn't real." Sarah thought of the vision she had when she landed the day before, taxiing by the Benchmark terminal. One of the glistening new planes at the gate morphed into an ugly, disturbing shadow of itself. She had felt an overwhelming dread as she passed it. Now, she shuddered just thinking about it.

"I don't know. It seems real. Both remembrances appear to be true. Both feel like they happened. How can that be?"

Sarah studied teen Mandy. The slight wrinkles that had been on her face when they met were gone. Her dimples were still noticeable, but the eventual laugh lines were smooth. A faint golden ring around green eyes faded to hazel. *Somehow, you're remembering two outcomes to today. I think we're at the point of the vision. Either Fara's dad lives or he dies.*

She said, "Whatever happens, I'm here for you."

* * *

Laurel stopped at the bridge. The water flowed unceasingly. Leaves continued to drift and swirl along with the current. The sky turned darker as the sunlit clouds faded. The moon appeared to be brighter, a trick of the eye as the amount of light never wavered, casting a luminous glow across the night sky. Whiteness amongst the passing leaves caught her eye as moonshine mirrored off the water. A cool breeze chilled her face.

"Maybe we should head back," she said to the other two. They were staring out at the passing water as well, still holding hands.

All turned away from the moonlit scene toward the way they had come. Ubu remained at Laurel's side. In the dusk, the three had not noticed Ubu's hair raise on his back and his ears perk up. He heard a voice that seemed to emanate from the depths of his own thoughts. *Soon, Ubu. Danger ahead.*

* * *

"Sarah, I have another memory. I think this is the original one, but now I'm not sure." Mandy moved to stand up.

Sarah saw her moving and automatically guided her even though she seemed herself. She glanced at the kitchen, saying, "What is it?"

"Several days after today, Fara's father was mugged on a walk in the park. He was killed. No one was ever charged." She looked at Sarah. Her eyes were green with a golden ring but not the intense green they had been when they arrived in this time period. It was a softer emerald and ring.

"You think that's what is supposed to happen? Are we here to prevent that?" Sarah asked, not expecting an answer.

"I don't know," Mandy answered anyway.

Sarah saw a far-off expression on her friend's face and remained silent, allowing her to work through whatever it was she was experiencing.

After several moments, Mandy said, "I can remember him coming here for dinner. He adds his stories to the rest of the family. I leave as kids come to the door for Halloween. About a week later, Mr. Otieno goes for a walk and is mugged. At least that's what the police say happened. He is killed. I go to the funeral. Some of the high school teachers are there." She pauses and looks at Sarah.

Sarah sees her eyes are vibrant emerald. The golden ring is more intense.

"Yet, a short time ago, I saw him getting shot at the sub shop. Now that memory is fading, kinda like when you wake up from a dream. You remember it. It feels real. Then it fades until it is only glimpses of what you saw, until it leaves your memory totally." She closed her eyes.

Sarah remained close to Mandy, uncertain if she would faint again, prepared for whatever might happen. She glanced toward the kitchen and saw Fara standing there.

Mandy opened her eyes. She looked right at Fara.

Fara held her gaze this time, not like she did under the oak tree what seemed like a lifetime ago.

"Fara, I . . ." Mandy started. She actually didn't know what to tell her.

"You don't need to explain. I know what you are," Fara said, turning to look back into the kitchen. "But you must not let Mama see!"

She closed the distance between them and gave teen Mandy a hug. "It is so nice to meet one of you." She looked at a perplexed Sarah and asked, "You do not know what she is?"

Sarah shook her head slowly.

Fara said, "She is a Wedeme."

* * *

Wren held Joneal's hand. The past few hours glided by like a dream. Although the cheese pizza certainly tasted real, she felt she would wake up at any moment and be in her bed in her own room. She turned to look at his profile. He walked with confidence. His hand was warm in hers, helping keep it warm as the late October chill chased away the warmth of the day. He turned and smiled at her. She returned his smile.

The shadows grew longer and deeper as they walked the path back to the sub shop. They turned on to the dirt path that led a hundred feet to the paved street. The sub shop was just two streets over from there.

Ubu was on full alert now. As he set a paw onto the dirt path, a voice in his head said, *Ubu. alert. Protect your mom and friends.*

On the right edge of the path, in deep shadows behind a bush, stood a deeper shadow. The shadow, remaining perfectly still, was angry his plans were ruined for an easy score. He rubbed the bump on the side of his face and thought, *I'll get even with you, old man! All you had to do was stand there while I cleaned out the register from the Halloween sales. It would have been nice and easy. Where did those people come from? I cased that place for two weeks. It should have been empty before the dinner rush. Ah, people coming. So, this isn't a total loss. I'll grab their cash and valuables. A disguise on Halloween makes this so easy!*

Mom continued walking a few steps behind the other two, but Ubu sensed there was something up ahead. He perceived danger close by even if the voice hadn't told him. He sniffed the air. The breeze was blowing from behind. No smell, yet something was in the shadow ahead behind some bushes.

Wren walked on Joneal's right, his warmth holding her hand. She thought, *If this is a dream, I don't mind spending it with him.* There was a sound to her right, off the trail. When she turned in that direction, she felt a forceful grip around her right arm. As she was pulled away from Joneal, she screamed.

* * *

Mr. Otieno opened the faded blue door. Fara turned from Mandy and Sarah, not explaining what a Wedeme was.

"Baba, you're home finally," Fara said. She turned back to Mandy with a finger to her lips. She whispered, "Say nothing."

Mrs. Otieno entered the room. "Welcome home, dear." She looked at her husband who was holding two bags of candy in one hand and a can in the other. "Oh my, what happened?"

Mr. Otieno turned toward the trio of females. A visible welt was on the side of his head. "There was some trouble at the sub shop."

Mrs. Otieno helped her husband into the kitchen, saying she would get some ice for his head.

Mandy and Sarah exchanged panicked looks, thinking of their friends they had left there until they returned. Fara saw their faces. She tilted her head without saying a word.

"Fara, we need to go," Mandy said. "We need to check on . . ."

Sarah completed the sentence for her, saying, "Our friends. They are waiting for us at the sub shop. We need to make sure they're okay."

"I'll go with you," Fara said.

Both Sarah and Mandy said, "No."

Mandy continued, "You need to stay here and look after your father. He needs you. Fara, I'm not a . . . whatever it is you said I was. I'm just a normal wom—girl, just a girl."

"Wedeme. I see it in your eyes. Of course, I've never seen one, but there are stories in my village about them." She looked at Sarah and back at Mandy. "Thank you for helping me today. I know you were sent to save me." Her mother called for her from the kitchen.

Sarah said, "Go to your mother. We'll check on our friends."

Mandy gave her high school friend a hug. She said, "Fara, it is good to see you again. I've missed you."

Fara gave her a silent inquisitive look, her head slightly cocked.

Sarah took hold of Mandy's hand and led her to the door. Mandy glanced back at her friend. They exchanged smiles.

8
WEDEME

Sarah interlocked her right arm into teen Mandy's left as they hurried back to the sub shop. To anyone watching them, they may have been mistaken for mother and daughter. Both ruminated on the potential danger their friends may be in. Neither spoke of what Fara had called Mandy, having set that aside for the moment.

Blue lights were visible in the dimming evening. There were streetlights on several telephone poles lining the sidewalk. With only half of them lit, the ones that were cast an eerie yellowish glow in the neighborhood. Sarah realized there wasn't anything wrong with the ones working. The light they cast was just what they were—a stark reminder they weren't in their own time with LED lighting the streets.

There was a small crowd of people on the sidewalk in front of the shop. Sarah had to release Mandy so they could maneuver their way through. Near the entrance, she spotted Harry sitting on the well-weathered bench just outside the entrance. Beth sat next to him. Shannon stood facing away from them. The others were not in sight.

Mandy panicked when she only saw half the group. She sprinted the last few steps, with Sarah trailing steps behind.

A male policeman who stood on the other side of the bench noticed the blonde teen and woman heading in his direction. He moved to intercept them from approaching closer, saying, "This is a crime scene, miss. I'm going to have to ask you to stay back."

Teen Mandy stopped several feet away and asked, "Harry, Beth, are you guys alright?"

Harry said, "She's with us."

At the same time Harry spoke, Beth added, "Officer, this is Mandy and Sarah. We told you about them. They're the ones we're waiting for."

The officer, appearing to be not much older than teen Mandy, waved them over without further comment.

Harry and Beth stood up. She placed her arm into his, aiding him. He appeared to be favoring the leg he injured the prior day.

Shannon, who had remained silent until now, said, "I'm glad you're back." Before she continued, she looked at the policeman who had turned the other way. In a lowered voice, she said, "Jack and Kourin went to find Laurel, Wren, and Joneal." When she saw Mandy's questioning look, she added, "We can talk on the way." Shannon said to the young officer, "We're going to find our friends." She said it as a statement of "this is what we're going to do." She wasn't asking permission to leave.

The officer said, "We have your statements. We'll be in touch if we have any more questions." He looked at them with concern on his face. "Be careful. He's still out there. You should go to your homes."

Shannon led the way up the street back toward the park. The way they had traveled earlier.

Once they were far enough away from the crowd, under the only yellow streetlight between the sub shop and the crossing street, Mandy asked, "Can you please tell me what's going on? Is Laurel okay?"

"I'm glad you're back," Shannon said to them. "Everyone's okay. There was an attempted holdup at the sub place. Jack ended up jumping the guy who took off before we could stop him. There were shots fired, but no one was injured."

"Except that customer," Beth added.

"Yes," Shannon said. "The perp had pistol whipped a customer, but Jack intervened before—"

Mandy finished the sentence, "Before the man was shot and killed."

* * *

After the bedlam at the sub shop, with the clown running off before Jack or Shannon could stop him and ensuring the injured customer was not seriously hurt, Jack told the group he had to locate Laurel. He was concerned for her safety with an armed clown on the loose.

Kourin said she would not let him go alone and insisted she was joining him. With the police on their way, Jack knew he didn't have time to argue and quickly conceded. He told the group to wait for Mandy and Sarah. He'd rejoin them shortly with the others.

The police arrived, preventing anyone from leaving. After what seemed like an eternity to Jack, the police took each of their statements.

Other than a few bruises, Jack was unharmed in his struggle with the clown. He was chided by the cop interviewing him for his brazen action, saying they could have been seriously injured. As much as Jack protested the clown was going to shoot the customer, the cop said that was doubtful. Jack silenced any other remarks, knowing he would not win the argument and his desire to exit the sub shop to locate Laurel as quickly as possible.

The injured customer refused medical treatment and was released to go home after providing a statement. Before leaving, he went to Jack to shake his hand and thank him for saving his life. Jack glanced at the cop beside him without comment.

After several minutes more, Jack and Kourin were finally released. They exited the sub shop and headed toward the park after telling the group they would be back shortly.

The evening was fully upon them. Kourin shuddered, though not from an autumn chill. She recalled being in the dark years ago. A memory she had buried long ago rearing its ugly head. She thought, *Keep it together, girl.*

Jack walked on the left side of the sidewalk toward the park with Kourin on his right. He kept himself between the traffic and her. Kourin thought, *He's a gentleman without even trying. With him with me, the demon of my past can't harm me anymore.*

Jack did not want to worry her, but he remained vigilant for the dangerous clown. The street was already dark where the yellow streetlights didn't shine. *He could lurk in the shadows.* His next thought was, *Why is it dark already? It's not even six yet.* He thought more on it and realized daylight savings time, or fall back as he remembered it, happened before Halloween years ago.

Kourin thought of teen Mandy and how, in some ways, she reminded her of herself at that age. Well, that was how she was until that terrifying day. She reached for Jack's hand, taking hold of it as they walked in search of Laurel and the others. *Maybe I should tell him what happened to me? He deserves to know.*

They crossed the perpendicular street to the sidewalk on the opposite side. There was a lone streetlight at the crosswalk. Several feet away was a bench, apparently a bus stop. She tugged gently on Jack's hand and said, "Jack, I need to tell you something."

Jack felt a tug and noticed Kourin looking at him with a curious expression. He answered, "Sure, Kori, I'm all ears."

Kourin looked away from Jack's gaze. She couldn't say what she needed to while looking into his brown eyes. No one was nearby as she scanned around them.

Jack saw the bench a short distance away and asked, "Do you want to sit down?"

"No," she answered, a little too briskly. In a softer voice, she added, "Sorry. No, I . . . I'd rather stand."

Jack knew what she meant. She'd rather stand than sit on a bench, even if was miles, and years, away from here.

For the next few minutes, as Jack held Kourin's hand, she related her traumatic story of what happened to her when she was fourteen and became pregnant. Midway through, Jack took Kourin's other hand into his for support. When Kourin finished, she had tears in her eyes. One welled up and forged a path around her cheekbone to her chin.

Jack embraced her when she finished her story. He felt there had to be a darker story behind Kourin's teenage pregnancy, but he never expected the brutality of it. He held her close and said, "Kori, I know how hard it was for you to tell me that. I'm here for you and always will be." He paused and looked around. There were shadows and shapes that appeared to be children on the sidewalk. He spied the bench nearby and asked again, "Do you want to sit down?"

"We need to find the others." She looked into his eyes, feeling tears on each of the bottom eyelids. "I just wanted you to know what . . ." she paused, unable to put the words together for a second time. "I just wanted you to know." She closed her eyes and looked away from him. The violation of what had happened to her all those years ago, even though none of it was her fault, tormented her still.

"Kori, I'll always be there to protect you. I promise," Jack assured her. He gave her a tight hug.

She held on to his embrace, wishing they were back home.

The tear that had clung to her chin dropped away to the ground. She felt secure in his arms and his words. She had lived by herself for many years, trapped in the horrors of that night. In every relationship, she eventually pushed the other person away, never revealing her secret—until now.

She loved Jack more than anyone except her baby. She felt a connection to him. In her heart, she knew he loved her, too. *That must be why I was able to tell you.*

As much as she did not want to, she pulled away from his embrace. She said, "We need to find the others."

Jack looked into her eyes, seeing sparkling emerald green but no golden ring. He didn't react to the difference in color from what they normally were and was getting used to how beautiful they made her look. He used both his thumbs to wipe the tears away and said, "Let's find my niece."

He led her toward the dirt pathway that went to the park. As he got closer to the path, he took out his cell phone and switched on the flashlight. It didn't illuminate far, but it showed the path ahead of them. As they walked deeper into the park, they heard a loud scream ahead of them. Jack's initial thought was Laurel!

* * *

The yellow streetlight cast an eerie glow as Shannon recounted the events that happened in the sub shop to Mandy and Sarah.

Mandy said she saw Mr. Otieno when he arrived home, and he seemed okay. She said she remembered him coming home that evening with a bump on his head. So overall, everything seemed to be as it was before. She did not tell them about experiencing the different timeline outcomes.

"Well, let's go find the others," Shannon said. The group retraced their steps to the park.

On the way, Harry mulled over Mandy's statements and felt she was holding something back. In the yellowish light, after crossing the street, he saw her and Sarah exchange looks several times as the conversation continued about the incident. If there was one thing he learned from his life experiences, when something seemed off, it probably was. He didn't know what was going on, but if he ever wanted to see his Christine again, he would have to understand how to manipulate time. Somehow Mandy did it with the bench, bringing them here for an unknown reason. How Kourin's eyes turning green fit into all of it, he couldn't surmise. There were still pieces missing to the puzzle.

Shannon saw the blue lights down the street they had just traversed go out. No police car came this direction, so she concluded they went the other way.

With the clown still on the loose, Shannon said, "Maybe we should wait here." She saw the bus stop bench several feet away.

Mandy wanted to find the rest of the group, but wandering through the park with a dangerous clown on the loose wasn't a good idea. She knew Laurel was probably safe with Ubu at her side.

When she heard what sounded like a gunshot echoing from the park, the hairs on the back of her neck stood up and she changed her mind.

* * *

Wren screamed at the sight of a clown with an eerie, twisted grin tugging her closer. She used her other hand to strike out against the attacker and connected with his throat with a strong jab. He released his hold on her. She stumbled backward away from him, colliding with Joneal.

As she was landing her punch, Ubu moved into action, lunging at the clown. He caught the arm that had been holding Wren, biting down hard as he had done saving Mom in that hot place. He landed on top of the attacker, and both rolled away from the others.

The clown had a stronghold of the girl. His plan was to hold his gun to her head while they handed over their cash and any valuables they had. He knew she would scream and was prepared for it. He wasn't prepared for her to fight back and punch him in his throat. Losing his grip on her, he was suddenly attacked by the mutt. Pain shot through his arm as he tried to bring his gun to shoot the wretched animal. The force from the dog pushed him over, causing him to lose his grip on his gun but not before his finger pulled the trigger. He rolled away from the dog, holding on to his weapon. The pain in his arm was excruciating. Whatever these people had, it wasn't worth this fight. As he had scrambled away in the sub shop, he did so here. From behind, he heard a female voice call the dog back to her. He would not take any chances of being bitten in the ass and ran as fast as his legs could carry him.

After the initial shock, Jack rushed toward the scream with Kourin right behind. Another scream, different from the first, echoed through the woods. It was a scream of pain, simultaneous with a gunshot. Panic ran through Jack's mind. *I'm coming, Laurel!*

As Jack rushed forward, a shadow came at him. With glimpses of white in his phone's flashlight, he realized it was the clown. He glimpsed a gun in his right hand. Without thinking, he turned to Kourin and heaved his body at her, causing both of them to tumble off the path, out of the way. His phone went flying several feet away.

After the clown had rushed past and continued running away from them, Jack helped Kourin to her feet. He apologized, but she told him to stop it. He did what needed to be done. She looked into his eyes. They reflected the waxing moon. She kissed him. He returned the kiss.

From behind, they heard a familiar voice. "Uncle Jack, is now really the best time for that?"

* * *

The clown saw two figures jump out of his way. He did not slow down, thinking the dog was behind him. He continued to the end of the path, staying in the shadows, and turned right, away from a group of people nearby on the sidewalk. Up ahead, he remembered a grove of pine trees he could hide in and still observe the street.

The clown watched the group under the streetlight. Three of them he recognized from the sub shop. He didn't see the one who had jumped him. When scrambling off the floor and out from under him, he caught his face. He wouldn't forget that face. Fortunately, his gun had fallen just a foot away and was easily recovered. He half thought about turning the gun on him then to pay for what he had done, but he knew if he was patient, he'd have another chance.

He noticed the police were gone. The sidewalks were filling up with costumed kids. All he had to do was wait a little longer, and he'd blend right in. His left arm hurt like hell from where the mutt had bitten him, but he couldn't do anything about that right now. He just needed a little more patience.

* * *

Laurel stood four feet away, but in the dimness, Jack wouldn't have known for sure it was her if she hadn't spoken. The giveaway was the dog scampering to Kourin. He sat in front of her, and her heart melted when she saw his paw extended toward her. She accepted it with a small shake. He put his paw down when released and sat facing her.

Jack was close enough to see her wonder at Ubu going to her again. He knew the dog was friendly, having shown his affection for others beside Laurel. Mandy came to mind immediately. At the moment, he couldn't recall anyone else besides those two that he reacted this way with. His experience with the dog was, if prompted for a paw, he would eventually comply. With Mandy, he did it often. Recently, he began doing the same with Kourin.

Laurel closed the few remaining steps to be nearer to her uncle. She asked, "Are you two alright?"

"I should ask you that!" Jack replied. He saw Wren and Joneal behind his niece. "I heard screaming and a gunshot. Everyone okay?"

"Thanks to the dog, we're good," Wren said. "The creep grabbed me, but Laurel's dog jumped at him. I don't know what would have happened if he wasn't there."

Joneal gave Wren a hug. Even in the darkness, all could tell she was still shaken.

"Let's get out of here," Jack said.

He saw his phone several feet away. Fortunately, it landed with the flashlight facing toward the sky. He retrieved it and used its limited distance to retrace their way back out of the park. He was extremely worried the clown was going to jump out of the shadows since he ran in this direction, but this was the way they had to go. When they safely reached the sidewalk, he felt some relief at seeing the others under the streetlight at the bus stop.

As the group moved closer to the light, Shannon met them halfway. She asked, "Everyone alright? We were worried sick when we heard what sounded like a gunshot."

"We're okay. The clown grabbed Wren, but Ubu saved the day again," Jack said. "He ran this way. Where are the cops?"

"The last of them left just before we heard the shot. We tried calling them back, but we don't have cell service." She saw Joneal holding Wren. To her she added, "Oh dear, you need to sit down."

"I think we should go back to the sub shop. It's well lit there," Jack said and looked over both shoulders. "And we don't know where the creep is."

"Good call," Shannon said.

"Wait a minute," Harry said. All turned to him. "Why the hell are we still here?" He looked at Mandy. "Haven't we done whatever the fuck we're supposed to do here so we can get back home?"

Beth gave Harry a disapproving glance for swearing out loud with costumed children not far away, but she said nothing. She also wanted to hear why they weren't back home yet.

Teen Mandy looked at Sarah and then at Laurel. She said, "I don't know. Things are like what I remember happening on this day." She thought before continuing. "I don't remember a clown, though. Mr. Otieno had a bruise, but I was never told how that happened." She looked at Sarah again.

Sarah took the hint. "Maybe we need to go back to Fara's." Four costumed children holding trick-or-treat bags passed by. "Perhaps there's more to the story." Mandy and Sarah knew what was implied. Both wanted to know what Wedeme meant.

"Do you think it is wise that we split up?" Harry asked. He wanted to learn how to control the bench. If Mandy was to learn something there, he may not know what it was.

"I don't think we have a choice," teen Mandy said.

They all crossed the street and went to the sub shop. Mandy and Sarah began walking further up the sidewalk and noticed Laurel and Ubu were with them. They stopped and turned to Laurel. She said, "Don't forget. I know Fara, too. Maybe I'll see something you're not."

Mandy and Sarah exchanged glances. "Okay," Mandy said. "But I'm not sure how she'll react if she finds out she's going to meet the teen you next year."

"Good point," Laurel said. They only had brief contact earlier in the day and had avoided that possibility. "Maybe we should not bring that up."

The trio and one dog continued to Fara's house as costumed children, many with a parent, walked by stopping at each home and saying, "Trick or treat!" A few of the parents wore costumes, most of them witch, pirate, and sports team variety. None of them were clowns. The trio was happy about that.

The group would have not been so at ease if they had seen the eyes watching them as they were highlighted in the yellow light. The clown tightened his grip on the handle of his gun, careful not to have his finger on the trigger. Three times he had pulled the trigger by accident. The next time, though, he wouldn't miss his target. As he crept through the brush and trees, he moved closer to the group, only to have them cross the street heading back toward the sub shop. He watched from a distance, keeping in the shadows. The group split up. The one he wanted went into the sub shop. *This time, you won't sneak up on me.*

All seven said hello to Everett when they entered. He was just finishing with a customer and asked them if he could get them something. He told them it was on the house for saving him earlier.

At first, they were going to decline but Wren needed some water, so they all got a water or a soda. Everett told them he'd make them a special pizza as a thank you. He set to work on that, while the others took seats to figure out what they were going to do.

Jack asked Wren and Joneal to tell them again about the encounter in the woods in case there were any clues they had missed. Without Laurel there, they didn't have a complete picture, but the details were the same as before. No additional news.

* * *

Teen Mandy knocked on Fara's door. They were greeted by her, holding a bowl of snack size candy. "Oh, hi," she said. "I didn't expect to see you again tonight." She looked behind her and turned back, saying, "Come in. Mama and Baba are in the kitchen."

Mandy and Sarah sat in the same seats they had before. Laurel took the matching chair with Ubu sitting beside her. He had his nose in the air, sniffing, but otherwise did not appear alarmed.

Laurel surveyed the room. Memories from many years ago came back to her. She had sat in the same chair many times over a two-year period. She recalled several hushed conversations about boys between Mandy, Fara, and herself. Mostly, though, they talked about the future. Laurel wanted to explore the world, which eventually meant joining the service. Mandy, unsure where her future was, hoped to discover her calling in college. Fara worked to improve herself in any way possible to return home to help those less fortunate than her. Laurel looked at Fara. *I shouldn't have lost contact with her. What little I have might have made a big difference where she came from. When I get back, I'm going to change that.*

Fara had to answer a knock on the door. A loud "Trick or treat" greeted her when she opened it. When she returned, she was without the bowl.

"I left the bowl at the door. I'm done answering it," she said. She looked at Ubu, hesitant to get too close. She asked, "Is he friendly?"

Laurel answered, "Absolutely. You're welcome to pet him if you'd like."

Fara slowly edged closer to the dog and held out her hand for the dog to sniff.

Ubu sniffed the girl's hand, already knowing she was not a threat. People thought putting their hand out for a dog to sniff made the interaction acceptable. If a dog had taken a dislike to you, you would have been aware of it far sooner. He allowed Fara to pet him.

Fara's hand lightly grazed Ubu's head. She had never petted a dog. The ones she knew back home weren't regarded as pets as they were in America. In her village, they would sniff the air in her direction but would never come within ten feet of her. The elders relied on them to help track and hunt in the wilderness. Although they did their job well, they were not friendly.

"I'm sorry if we're intruding, but we need to figure a few things out," teen Mandy said. She looked at Sarah who nodded. "We need to know what Wedeme is."

Laurel kept silent. She knew the black girl well, but she hoped she was keeping her own identity a secret. In her mind, she knew she had not met her until next year. In the following years, Fara never said she had met an older version of her on Halloween. *Come to think of it, Mandy had said nothing either. Is it possible what we're experiencing right now is the first time it is happening? Does that mean next year Fara actually will remember meeting an older version of me?* Laurel looked at the other three. *Are we changing the timeline like Uncle Jack and Mandy warned me about? But if it is for a good reason, shouldn't we?* She thought about Breckin. *Shouldn't I do everything I can to save him?*

Laurel came back to the conversation. Fara was telling the others about the dogs back in Africa. She said, "Ubu is much heavier than any dog I knew back home."

Laurel thought about how Fara phrased that sentence. *She still considers her African village her home.* She recalled more about her as she sat in the familiar living room.

In high school, the skinny black girl had studied diligently and made the honor roll consistently. With a strong will to make something of herself, she worked much harder than anyone else in all her tasks. Through it all, she often brought up her village and friends she had left behind. It was obvious that she was striving to be the best version of herself, intending to help her people back home.

Laurel thought, *I had forgotten about that. I was so caught up in my own life that I never realized how hard she fought for her village.* She looked at Fara in a new light. *She followed her dream and made a difference. I went off to discover the world, only to end up locked inside myself with pity and regret at failing in my duties to protect my unit.*

She heard Ubu whine and bump her leg. She petted his head to let him know she was okay. *How does he know when I'm thinking sad thoughts? He is an amazing dog, an amazing friend.*

The conversation occurring around her was Fara talking about her village. She spoke about the hunting the men in the village would do every day with their dogs. Often, they came home empty-handed. Occasionally, there would be one less man returning with them. Those who remained in the village tended to the needs of the huts and what passed as a garden. With little rain, the plants suffered through their life cycle.

One of Fara's mama mdogo, her mother's sister, often spoke of the Wedeme to her but only when her parents were not nearby. Fara learned at an early age her parents did not believe the ancient stories of the Wedeme.

One day, the sisters had an argument when they did not know Fara was close enough to hear. Her mama argued the Wedeme was a myth. She claimed it was a fable made up long ago to explain the growing seasons and the weather. Her mama mdogo, her aunt, said the Wedeme were tree spirits that aided their survival. Mama yelled back that next she'd be telling her a Kontomble was responsible for the river bed drying up. They argued back and forth for several minutes until Fara's mama had had enough and told her sister to never bring up the old superstitions again.

Fara related a story she had never revealed to anyone of when her mama mdogo was a little girl. Her aunt had seen a Wedeme when she had wandered away from the village. The woman had emerald green eyes that seemed to sparkle in the light and guided her in the right direction to find her home. When she arrived home, Fara's grandmother, her bibi, told her about the Wedeme tree spirits.

Laurel was studying Fara carefully, trying to figure out why Mandy had arrived in this timeline. When she heard the comment about green eyes, she perked up.

At that moment, Mrs. Otieno called for Fara. She needed her help in the kitchen. Fara paused her story and said she'd be right back.

Laurel looked at Sarah who also had been listening intently. Sarah must have felt eyes upon her because she turned toward Laurel and returned her gaze. *I never noticed how blue Sarah's eyes were. She reminds me of someone. It's like I've seen her eyes elsewhere, some place long ago, yet I just met her two days ago. Just can't put my finger on it.*

Laurel was brought out of her reminiscing by a whine from Ubu. She looked down at him again, telling him everything was okay.

Ubu was not looking at her.

She followed what Ubu was focused on—Mandy.

Laurel looked at her and gasped. *Oh my God! Her eyes are green like Kourin's!*

* * *

The group watched several patrons enter, purchase a few things, and leave. After the first few, they were more at ease and lost interest in the comings and goings through the sub shop door. They failed to notice a point where there were no patrons other than them and the owner in the building.

The special supreme pizza was delivered by Everett to the table as a gesture of thank you. The entire shop smelled of vegetables, meats, and cheese. All thanked the owner for his kindness. With their attention on the eight slices of deliciousness sitting in the middle of the table, no one noticed a lone figure enter the doorway, turn, and lock the door. Silently, he came up behind Everett.

The shop owner grunted and fell to the floor, unconscious.

All eyes immediately turned in his direction. Jack and Shannon rose. Jack made it all the way up but froze when he saw the gun pointed directly at his face. Shannon stopped midway when the clown told her to sit back down. The others were petrified in place.

Jack nervously positioned his hands halfway up in the air in response to the clown's intimidating gesture of pointing his gun at him and commanded him not to move a muscle. He remained perfectly still as he stared down the barrel of the handgun.

Beside Jack, Kourin felt her heart pounding in her chest. In a split second, her hands became ice cold. Her internal temperature deep within her boiled. Two and then three seconds ticked by. She could feel her internal heat radiating from her core, warming her skin and reaching out to her fingertips. Her hands were no longer cold. She felt like she was on fire and about to explode.

A gun was pointed at the man she loved. He was in danger. They all were.

She had not experienced this level of fear since . . . *since I was fourteen. Since I was . . .* Alarm, terror, panic swelled inside her. She felt her skin tingle as her temperature rose. Her chest tightened as her emotions surged like a tidal wave.

The clown said, "You fuckin' a'hole totally fucked up my night. I had this all planned out. Absolutely nothing could go wrong. Then you showed up. Mr. Hero. Well, how's it feel now, Mr. Hero? Huh? Still feel like a hero?"

Kourin stirred next to the clown, catching his attention. He glanced at her, momentarily taking his eyes off Jack.

Jack heard Kourin move slightly beside him. His first instinct was to look at her, but the barrel of the gun had his attention. He saw the clown's eyes move away from him for a moment. He thought, *It's now or never.*

The clown's eyes locked with Kourin's, and she felt an eerie chill run down her spine.

He was startled, seeing shimmering emerald green eyes with blazing golden rings glaring back at him. He was so taken aback that he stumbled back from her intense stare.

Jack lunged when the gunman flinched, grabbing the gun arm first and pushing it upward toward the ceiling. His body slammed into the clown for the second time today. The gun discharged for the fourth time, delivering the slug into the fluorescent light fixture above. The bulb shattered.

Kourin screamed, "Jack!"

A bright light flashed, but it was not from the fluorescent lighting above. A ripple in the air immediately followed by a wave of distortion extended outwards from Kourin.

All lost consciousness before the fragments from the light fixture above reached the space the group from the future had been occupying. Glass and dust fell to the floor, covering the unconscious sub shop owner and a confused clown pointing a gun at empty chairs.

* * *

Mandy listened to Fara's story about Africa. She recalled hearing how arduous life was there and understood why the Otienos felt moving to America would be an enormous improvement for their children. As Fara spoke about her past life, she sensed the teen preferred the life she had left behind. The three racist cheerleaders came to mind. *Maybe things here aren't better for some.* Fara began her telling of the Wedeme argument her mother and aunt had.

Teen Mandy began feeling a heat deep inside her as she recalled her interactions with the cheerleaders and listened to her friend's story.

Fara was called to the kitchen just as she was explaining why she called her a Wedeme.

Mandy had intense emotions wash over her as Fara exited the room: fear, alarm, terror, panic.

When Laurel saw her friend's eyes change color, she moved closer to hold her hand for support. They were cold to the touch. Ubu followed dutifully next to her and placed his cranium against Mandy's leg, giving her his support as well. She could feel her friend's touch on her hand and Ubu's on her leg. An instant later, the heat deep in her core expanded outward to her skin and her extremities.

Laurel felt her friend's hand go from ice cold to hot in a split second.

The emotions overtook teen Mandy. The last emotion she experienced was love, an overwhelming sensation of love. No, it was the sensation of fear of losing the one you love.

She heard Ubu whine next to her. She felt Laurel's reassuring touch. An image of the bench and garden at the terminal came to her as the heat escaped her body in a burst.

All lost their awareness of the world around them.

9

1990

Kourin's mind was muddled. Her body was on fire. Someone grabbed her left arm. She turned in that direction, thinking it was Jack. It wasn't him. Her eyes widened with shock and terror when she realized who had her, and a loud scream ripped from her throat as she struggled to free herself. She frantically scanned around her and spotted Jack in the distance. She screamed, "Jack! Help!"

Jack was disoriented. Rain drops landed on his face. He wiped them away and surveyed his surroundings. In the distance, he saw a white van. The side door was open. Beside the door was a medium-build man in a navy-blue jacket and matching baseball cap. A young girl with wet blonde hair wearing a pink jacket was next to him. He was holding her arm. His first thought was that it was teen Mandy.

Although the girl looked very much like her, he realized it was not when she turned and screamed his name. *Oh my God! Kourin!*

Jack realized what Kourin had told him only a short time ago was playing out in front of him. She was being abducted!

He sprinted toward her and was horrified to witness the man hit her. Her body went limp as he forced her through the van's side door. He glanced back at Jack.

Jack saw a man's face with a close-trimmed goatee beard. He was Caucasian, but he wasn't close enough to make out more details as the man turned and ran around the front of the van.

Moments later, as Jack neared the van, it drove off. The plate was New Hampshire. He only caught two numbers—"88"—before it was gone from sight.

Jack stopped running and looked around for help. There were no houses in either direction. He did not know where he was. Trees lined both sides with telephone poles on the right side every fifty feet in the direction the van traveled. In the other direction, he searched, seeing more of the same and what appeared to be people further down the road. He checked his cell phone. No cell service. No surprise, since it appeared he was back in 1990. The sky continued to sprinkle. He hurried toward the people in the distance in search of help.

He quickly realized the distant figures were Harry and Beth.

The sprinkles stopped. Fortunately, the air was on the warmer side with some humidity. A gentle breeze blew, releasing droplets of rain from the tree branches hanging over the road. His eyes scanned the trees, no longer seeing the brilliant colors of autumn that had been present before. They were vibrant shades of green, ranging from the softest mint to the richest emerald. A gray overcast sky made it difficult to tell what time of day it was.

"Where the hell are we now?" asked Harry.

Jack answered, "I think we're in 1990. We need to get to a phone and call the police." He saw a house tucked into the trees a hundred yards down the road. "I'll go call the police. You guys wait here," he told them.

"Why are we calling the police?" Beth asked.

"Kourin was just abducted," he said. "If we hurry, maybe we can stop it. And by the way, she is a teenager here. She looked a lot like Mandy does. I mean did." He looked around and realized she and the others were not with them. "You know like she did back at the park." He grew concerned for his niece. "And we're going to need to find the others. They must be close by."

Beth said, "Jack, I think we should stick together. We'll go to the house with you." She eyed him sideways. "I think there's more to this story you need to tell us."

Jack kept quiet, debating how much of what Kourin told him in confidence he should say.

"Jack, where are we?" Beth asked as she and Harry fought to keep up with Jack's quick pace. "It looks like late spring, maybe summer." She looked around. "I don't recognize this place."

"Me neither," he said. He explained the situation to them as they rushed toward the home. "All I know is that Kourin told me she was abducted as a teenager. I don't think she told me everything, but that is when she got pregnant."

"That's horrible!" Beth said. "I can't believe she's had to live with that her whole life. Did she tell you who kidnapped her?"

"Unfortunately, all she told me was it was someone she had trusted. I'm guessing that's why she was close to the van when he grabbed her."

They reached the house, a white garrison set back from the street. The lawn was neatly cut. The shrubs had stray weeds and a few small trees growing in them, but otherwise the home looked like an average New England home. There was a two-car garage with the doors closed. A silver BMW with New Hampshire plates sat in the driveway.

Although there was a main entrance door in the middle of the home, there was a side breezeway on the left. Jack surmised they likely used this as their main entrance. He pressed the lighted doorbell button.

When the door opened, a woman who Jack assumed to be in her late fifties stood in front of him, her hair graying at the temples. Jack quickly explained what had occurred and his need to call the police.

The woman stood in front of the door, nervously biting her lip as she contemplated letting Jack and the others in.

Jack saw her concern. Instead, he told her they would wait outside while she called 911. He told the woman to tell the police to look for a white van with New Hampshire plates having "88" in it.

The woman returned to the door a few long minutes later. She informed them the police were on their way. The woman's attention was drawn to Harry who was clasping the three-foot-high white plastic fence that divided the evergreen bushes near the house from the driveway. She eyed Beth, her hand clasped around his arm.

The woman said, "Why don't you wait in here?"

Jack figured, with the police on the way, the woman felt more secure with the strangers at her door. He said, "We don't want to impose. I'll wait out here for the police to arrive." In the distance, he could hear a siren. "Harry, Beth, why don't you wait inside? I'll talk to the police."

Beth realized what Jack was implying faster than Harry. One person talking with them would be better, since they didn't even know where they were. A kidnapping and three adults who didn't belong in the neighborhood would be difficult to explain.

"Harry, let me help you inside," she said.

Harry looked at Jack, finally getting the subtle hint. "Yeah. Okay." Beth and Harry followed the woman into the home.

"I'll be back shortly," Jack said. He turned and walked to the edge of the road. As he arrived, a dark blue, almost black, police car arrived, lights flashing. Jack finally learned what town they were in: Fairfield, New Hampshire.

* * *

Nearly an hour later, Jack returned to the garrison home. He was cordially greeted at the door by the homeowner and followed her to the dining room. A large gold chandelier hung over a mahogany table large enough to seat eight people. Jack pulled out a heavy matching chair opposite of where Harry and Beth sat.

The woman introduced herself to Jack as Carol. Jack reciprocated. She asked if he would like some tea. To be polite, he accepted, but he told her they would have to be leaving shortly.

When she was out of the room, even though he whispered, he was certain Carol would be listening from the adjoining kitchen. He told Harry and Beth the police were at the crime scene searching for clues. They instructed him to stay close because the FBI was on the way. They said it was their case. Harry asked how the FBI got involved so early since the abduction had just occurred. Jack slowly shook his head and answered he didn't know.

Jack looked toward the kitchen and in a nearly inaudible voice said, "The police are at the end of the driveway. They want to ensure we're not going anywhere. Somehow, we need to find the others. Who knows what could happen to them?"

Harry answered, "They can take care of themselves. Laurel is a trained fighter. Her dog certainly can defend them." He thought for a moment. "I'm not sure about Wren and Joneal, though. They're kinda young."

"Maybe they're all together," Beth stated.

"Perhaps," Harry answered. He didn't add more because of Carol arriving with Jack's tea.

After several minutes of small talk, Jack looked out the window as sunlight broke through the clouds. He said to Carol they appreciated her hospitality, but they needed to reconnect with the police. He added nothing about the FBI, but he was certain she knew everything they had discussed.

The trio walked to the end of the driveway where a Fairfield cop was leaning against his front fender. He was young. As Harry limped by, he thought he didn't look old enough to drive, let alone be a cop. The young man said hello but didn't move from where he was. Harry guessed he was the junior policeman and was told to position himself here and stay put.

A short distance up the road was a black SUV pulled in behind a police car. The FBI had arrived.

As they trekked to the FBI and where Jack last saw teen Kourin, he said, "Maybe if I acted sooner, I could have prevented it."

"Doubtful," Harry muttered.

"Why do you say that, Harry? If Jack had been closer, he could have stopped it before it happened," said Beth.

"Well, I'm thinking we're not meant to prevent what happened in the past. I think we're more like observers." He looked at the others. They stared back, waiting for him to explain. "I mean I think I saved my daideó, but I'm thinking maybe I did or maybe I didn't. Maybe he would have been saved whether or not I was there."

"So, what you're saying is Kourin was going to be abducted no matter what. Jack couldn't have prevented it?" Beth asked.

"I think so." He looked at Jack. "I think it was destined to happen. Our being here will not change what happens."

Jack said, "I don't believe that. Look, we just stopped the clown from hurting that customer and the sub shop owner. For all we know, he was supposed to kill them."

"No, he wasn't," Beth said. "Mandy told us she remembered her friend's father coming home with a bruise on his head. That's what happened. She mentioned nothing about someone being killed."

"She also said nothing about a clown, so she may not have had all the facts. You know how kids are. Remember, she was just a teenager," Jack said as they neared the crime scene.

He saw two men in dark suits and ties standing out amongst the police officers in their uniforms.

Quietly Jack said, "I think we need to be careful what we tell the FBI, or we're likely to be locked up for being lunatics. You guys saw nothing, so let me do the talking."

An overweight policeman waddled toward them.

Jack added before the cop reached them, "I think we can save Kourin from her horrifying nightmare."

Harry silently watched Jack speak with the policeman. They walked over to the spot Kourin was abducted and where the FBI was now standing.

He thought about how they got to be here. It couldn't be a coincidence that they went to a time Mandy was a teen and now to Kourin as a teen. There had to be a connection. He just didn't see it.

We need to find Mandy for some answers, Harry thought. *Wonder where they are?*

* * *

Mandy felt a hand on her shoulder, gently shaking her. She heard a familiar voice, Laurel's, ask her if she was okay. With eyes closed, she was apprehensive about what she might open them to. Her body temperature was returning to normal. The emotions that had overwhelmed her had vanished as if they were never there.

What she encountered moments before, fear of losing the one you love, consumed her thoughts. *Why did I feel that? Why was it so powerful?*

Yet, she knew the love and pain were not hers. She had experienced someone else's emotions, another's extraordinarily powerful emotions, unlike anything she had endured herself.

The foreign emotions brought to mind the few times in her life she had been in love. The first serious relationship was a sweet boy named Dillion she dated in college. She recalled his tears the night she kissed his cheek goodbye, his sad eyes when she said she hoped they could still be friends.

Three years after college was Blake. She had unequivocally ended that relationship when he cheated on her the week after they were engaged. The weekend after she threw his belongings from her window to the sidewalk below, he returned to her, tears streaming down his face, begging for forgiveness for his mistake. He promised to never do it again and his love for her hadn't changed.

All trust having evaporated out of their relationship, she sent him away and never saw him again. That one stung her for two years after it was over.

The third was Tyler. She thought they were in love. After Blake's infidelity, she eventually gave dating another shot and fell head over heels for Tyler. They hadn't been engaged, but she felt they were on the cusp of setting a date. Like in a romantic movie, he brought her to an expensive restaurant. As she sipped her wine, she felt a flutter of anticipation, expecting him to propose before dinner. Instead, the exact opposite happened.

He said he needed space.

Although it broke her heart to give him what he wanted, she acquiesced. As the heartrending conversation continued several more tearful minutes, he went beyond needing time away from the relationship to breaking up with her.

To this day, she wondered if there was anything she could have done differently, could have said more eloquently, or could have kept him from living his life without her.

After Tyler, she had not sought love again. She steeled her heart against the anguish it brought her.

Four years later, reliving an afternoon through the mystical powers of a bench, she had experienced an emotion that dwarfed all those feelings. The love she had just borne was deeper and more meaningful.

As she heard Laurel say her name again, she realized what she thought was love for Tyler wasn't that at all. She had been afraid of being alone after Blake hurt her. Now, as she reflected in hindsight, a new clarity dawned. The hurt she had caused Dillion was the most hurtful of all her relationships. He loved her with all his heart. She had strong feelings for him, but she wondered if there was someone else out there for her, the person she was destined to be with, her soulmate.

She had true love staring her right in the face and had cast it aside. In her mind's eye, she saw the tear traveling down Dillion's face as she kissed his cheek goodbye. In her heart, she realized she had made the biggest mistake of her life. She thought, *I'm sorry, Dillion. I didn't know.*

She felt her shoulder shake gently again. She heard her name called. Slowly, she opened her eyes, leery of what reality she was waking to.

A tear escaped her eye. For a love she had lost, a tear of regret slid down her face.

Before her stood Laurel returning her gaze. Beside her sat Ubu. He peered at her with his soulful eyes. She sensed someone sitting next to her and glanced over. Sarah sat unconscious with her head bent forward. Her chest rose and fell. Mandy looked beyond her at their surroundings. To her surprise and joy, she saw the terminal garden surrounding them.

Her eyes were brought back to her friend when she was asked, "Mandy, are you okay?"

"Yes," she replied groggily. She looked at the blonde next to her. "Is Sarah okay?"

As she asked this, Sarah stirred, showing signs of waking up.

"Mandy, look at me," said Laurel.

Mandy knew why she was asking. She complied.

"Your eyes are emerald green! And you have the golden ring!"

Mandy felt self-conscious and turned away. Laurel, using the hand she had on Mandy's shoulder, placed two fingers under her friend's chin and gently turned her head back toward her.

Laurel said, "Mandy, I think I've found the reason we're time traveling!"

From the other side of the courtyard, they heard Shannon. "There you are. Somehow, I knew you'd be sitting on that damn bench!"

Mandy looked away from Laurel and down at what she was sitting on—the bench. They were back where they had started, Sarah and her sitting on the center bench.

Beside Shannon were Wren and Joneal. They were holding hands. All walked toward the bench, but the guard stopped midway across the distance. "I'm not coming any closer."

Wren and Joneal stopped with her, not because of any fear they had. They looked at each other, not comprehending what Shannon was talking about, but also not taking any chances after the experience they just had.

Laurel straightened up, saying, "I'm not sure it matters how close you are to the bench, not if Mandy and Kourin are nearby."

All looked at Laurel, not comprehending.

Sarah became fully awake. She surveyed the area, her eyes eventually landing on Mandy. She said, "Oh crap, her eyes went green again, didn't they? When are we now?"

10

FAIRFIELD

Jack exited the FBI SUV and scanned for Harry and Beth. They were exiting the police car on his right. A short distance away, a large white sign with vertical red lettering and a rusted arrow at the bottom pointed in their direction. A vacancy sign hung below it. They were at a motel.

Special Agent Jenkins said, "This is where we've set up base camp. Fairfield doesn't have a police station." He gestured to the motel. "Hence, a room here. Not the Ritz, but it'll do."

They actually had two rooms, next to each other, with a connecting door. The rooms were typical two double beds with a hideous multicolored bed spread. There were several dark stains on the carpeted floor. A small wooden table with two chairs stood in front of the single large window that faced the parking lot. A well-worn air conditioner between the window and the floor ran the length of the window with water staining the carpet underneath that. Drab olive-colored drapes framed it all, currently pulled back as wide as they would go.

Jenkins stayed with them, while Special Agent Young returned from the adjacent room with two additional chairs. He placed them to the right of the table.

Jenkins said, "Now, you three are the only leads we have right now, so we're going to run through your statement one more time to be certain we missed nothing."

Harry spoke up before Jack could answer. He asked, "Why are you guys here? I mean wouldn't the state police be investigating a kidnapping here?"

Special Agent Young answered from behind Harry. "The staties are tied up with two high-profile murder investigations in Dover and Derry. We were brought in to assist them with this investigation."

Harry noted Jenkins gave a scowl toward his partner, silently suggesting he needed to stop providing any information to possible suspects. Young didn't say another word.

Jenkins told Jack again they were going to go through what they all witnessed one more time.

Jack said, "Only I saw what happened. Harry and Beth were further down the road. They didn't see the van."

"Well, we'll just cover everything again to be sure," Jenkins said. The other agent set a tape recorder on the table and hit the Record button. "Now, let's start at the top. Why were you on the road where the abduction took place, and how do you know the girl who was taken?"

Jack looked at Harry and Beth. This was going to be a tough interview. He asked if he could have a glass of water, stalling to get his thoughts in line. The best option was to be completely honest. He also knew, if he said they were from the future, they'd be locked up. Kourin would never be saved. He hoped he could be honest and not draw attention to himself or the others. Under no circumstances could he mention anything about the future.

As they gave their names and addresses, they used the address they had in 1990. Although it was thirty-two years in the past, at least the name would match if they did a casual search. Likely, the FBI would be far more thorough than that, but hopefully by the time they noticed a discrepancy, they would all be back in the correct timeline.

Jenkins interviewed Jack first. Before they got started, Jack asked what the progress was on locating the van and Kourin. Young said when there was any new information, they would let them know. Jack doubted they would be forthcoming about any information. Maybe he watched too many cop shows, but if he was in their shoes, all three of them were on a need-to-know basis, which was nothing. Worst-case scenario, they were suspects and possibly connected to the abduction.

Jack's questioning lasted over an hour. They asked the same questions at least four times, with slight variations. Harry and Beth were also questioned, but they could answer questions as a duo. The agents made an assumption they were a couple. No one said anything to change that opinion.

When the questioning was over, Harry used the restroom. While he was gone, Young asked how he had hurt his knee. Beth told him he stepped into a puddle that was deeper than he thought and fell, banging it against a rock.

Harry returned, and Beth went to use the restroom. Jack asked if he could use the one in the other room. They said yes, which surprised him, but he had to relieve himself. When he was returning, Jenkins was in the connecting room. Jack thought, *So, on some level, we are under suspicion if they thought I might flee.*

As Jack neared the connecting doors, he heard Harry talking about how he hurt his knee. Fortunately, he had the same story Beth had told. *Either they have some doubts about us, or they're just being thorough.*

When Jack returned, he asked Jenkins if they were free to go.

The two agents eyed each other, not speaking a word. Jenkins, who Jack had assumed was the senior agent for no other reason than he looked older, asked where they were staying.

Jack was caught off guard, as he hadn't thought ahead, thinking they'd be returning to their own timeline shortly. He replied they hadn't found a place yet. Young said he would reserve the next two rooms over for them. Again, he assumed Harry and Beth were together. Jack tried to decline, but Jenkins said he wanted them close by in case information came in about the teenager.

Jack almost asked what teenager but luckily caught himself when he realized they meant Kourin. He didn't voice an objection even though he knew they wanted them close by so they could monitor them.

He thanked him, thinking being polite was going to go further than being antagonistic. After several minutes, Young returned with two keys. He gave one to Harry and the other to Jack. He told them not to leave without letting them know.

These rooms were identical to the other two rooms, except there were no stains on the carpets. Jack opened the connecting doors so they could discuss what to do. They spoke in hushed voices, uncertain if the FBI here was like the FBI on TV. Harry asked if the room had surveillance devices. Jack assured him it was doubtful this room was bugged like that. They hadn't planned on needing these two rooms.

Jack sat on the edge of the bed, sinking in nearly a foot. Harry and Beth sat on chairs on either side of the small table. The drapes were open. The sun shined down brightly. All three gaped at each other, wondering what to do.

In the room next to them, the two special agents were quietly discussing the situation. They were highly suspicious of the three individuals next door. If nothing else, their story had notable gaps. Why were they walking on the road where the abduction took place? Why didn't they have any transportation close by since their addresses were over fifty miles away? It was raining when they were walking. Why were they walking in the rain with no jackets or umbrellas?

One crucial standout was, how did they know the teenage girl's name if they had never met her? Were they stalking her, too? How were they connected?

After several minutes, there was a knock on the door. Jack answered it. Jenkins said they were leaving for a while, but there would be an officer right outside if they needed anything. Jack asked if they were under arrest or something. Jenkins assured him they were not and reiterated the story line of wanting them close by so he could keep them informed.

The two agents left in the black SUV. The young Fairfield cop who had been sitting at the end of the driveway earlier was parked in the space in front of their rooms. Jack closed the door.

They were not under arrest, but they weren't free to leave either.

11

TERMINAL

Laurel answered Sarah's question of when in time they were. "I think we're back when and where we started. But to be sure, we should go check." She looked at Mandy and asked, "Are you okay to stand up?"

She replied by placing both hands on the bench and pushing her butt off it. Laurel held her right arm, just in case she needed help. She did not.

Mandy said, "It's good to be myself again." She looked down at herself, seeing she had on the clothes and work apron she had put on in the morning.

Sarah stood next to her. "It's good to have you back."

"I'm getting outta here while I can," Shannon said. She turned to exit down the path toward the terminal. "I need to get home to Earl. He must be worried sick of where I got off to."

Wren and Joneal followed. They continued holding hands. The others followed. When they reached the bottom of the walkway with the terminal before them, Wren turned and asked Mandy, "Did we all just have a dream?"

"No," she replied. "At least not in the sense that we were all asleep with what happened only in our heads." She looked at Laurel, but she had nothing to offer or didn't want to say what she thought out loud. "I think, somehow, we really did just go back in time to when I was in high school."

"Unbelievable," Wren said. She looked at Joneal, adding, "If Ubu hadn't been there, I don't know what would have happened." Joneal gave her a hug.

Laurel added, "Ubu is a wonderful protector." She reached down and gave him a pat. "He's always there for me." She fixed her gaze upon the others. "We were together at Fara's, so I think that's why we awoke together. You three were at the sub shop with Jack, Kourin, Harry, and Beth. Right?"

Shannon answered, having stopped next to Wren when she asked her question. "Yes. Then the clown showed up. He snuck up behind the owner and knocked him out. He blamed Jack for messing up his robbery and looked like he wanted to shoot him. Jack charged him. The gun went off, and next thing you know, we're all back here."

Joneal asked, "But where are they?"

Everyone looked at each other.

Laurel said, "Maybe they are back in the office where we started? I mean all of you kinda ended up where you started, except for me. Maybe I came back in the garden because I was with Mandy and Sarah at Fara's." She added nothing about her eye color changing. She looked at the Coffee Bean. "I'm gonna go check."

Without waiting for any replies, she walked to the café, Ubu diligently at her side. Two minutes later, she returned with Ubu. Her brow was lined with worry as she stated they were not there. "I asked everyone if they saw them, and they said they hadn't been in the café all afternoon. Where can they be?"

Mandy suggested, "Maybe they're at Kourin's?" She looked in the opposite direction of the café. All turned in that direction.

"I'll check it out," Wren offered. Joneal walked over with her, never letting go of her hand.

Sarah said, "I don't think those two will ever separate after what they've just been through."

"I think you're right," said Mandy.

"They make a cute couple," Laurel added.

Moments later, they too returned without the missing people.

Wren said, "The supervisor said she hadn't seen Kourin since before lunch."

"That's odd," Mandy said. "If we returned here, why didn't they? You don't think they got left behind?"

Laurel said, "I doubt it," in a lower voice so it wouldn't carry across the terminal even though music played and sounds of people in the distance made that all but impossible. "Somehow you have the power to travel through time and take whomever is in your vicinity with you. I have a theory I'm working on, but I'm pretty sure when you left, everyone else did as well."

"That's crazy," Mandy said, drawing her hands away from Laurel. "I have no way of doing that!"

Sarah, who had been quietly listening and piecing things together, said, "But you do, Mandy. And it's triggered by powerful emotion."

12
TERROR RELIVED

Kourin stirred from her unconsciousness on her back. The right side of her head was throbbing. She lifted her right hand to bring to the pained area. Instead, she felt cold metal against her wrist and the clang of handcuffs secured to the metal bed frame.

Frantically looking around, she saw to her horror where she was! *Oh no!* She yanked on the cuffs, somehow hoping it would magically become free. Not feeling it give even an inch, she looked down at herself. She was a teenager dressed in the tee shirt and shorts she had worn the day she was abducted. Her jacket was gone. *Fuck, fuck, fuck! This can't be happening!*

The room was nearly pitch black. She tried to calm herself down. She knew she had time. All those years ago, she wasn't raped on the first day. She had time.

This brought a new appalling thought to her. Her left hand was free. She inched it in the darkness to the blackness beyond.

She knew what she would find, yet somehow hoped she would be wrong. Her hand touched something next to her. She heard a slight moan.

Thirty-two years ago, she had screamed and cried for hours at this point. Now her older mature brain pushed the terror down. She knew the person next to her. Well, she had never really known her. They lived in the same town, but they had never met until this moment handcuffed to the same bed.

When the horrific experience ended, Kourin learned who she was from her obituary. She cried, reliving this experience and knowing the fate of the child next to her. She struggled to quell the tears. In the darkness, as tears flowed down her cheeks, with no one to bear witness, her eyes turned emerald green. Emotions clouded her reasoning—sadness, despair, anguish—not for her, for the twelve-year-old child lying next to her. In less than two hours, she would be raped again and strangled to death right next to her, the creature who abducted them replacing the child with a new girl.

The tears freely flowed, meandering down her temples into her ears as she peered up into the endless darkness above the bed. In between blinking away the tears and the sobs, Kourin found she could see shapes in the darkness. As she wiped away the tears again, she could make out the shape of the girl next to her. Several seconds later, she could see the child. Her vision was not her normal sight. There were no lights on. It was similar to what she had seen on TV when someone had used night vision googles. It wasn't quite that, as the shapes were not green. They were different shades of gray, no color. It was as if she was staring at a hazy gray-scale film playing on an old TV set with a dim light.

The child next to her was naked and curled up in a fetal position, her back was facing her. Kourin could see her light-colored hair. A memory came back to her. Their hair was nearly the same color at that age. She recalled overhearing adult conversations she wasn't meant to hear. The serial killer had sought young blonde girls. She had been the third abducted. The girl lying next to her was the second.

With a trembling hand, Kourin reached out to the girl once again. As before, she pulled it away when the girl made a slight whimpering sound and withdrew from her touch.

Kourin's whisper was like a gentle breeze in the room's stillness. "It's okay. I know you're scared, but we're going to get the hell out of here!"

Deep inside Kourin, her temperature rose and anger surged. She didn't black out as she had before, nor did she suddenly find herself elsewhere. She thought, *Why am I not waking up someplace else?*

She placed her hand gently upon the girl. *Maybe I need to be in contact with her.* Still, nothing happened. She could feel the anger within her. She felt the fire burning inside. Still, nothing changed.

The girl moaned, more awake now. She shied away from Kourin's touch. She wailed, "No more!"

In a quiet voice, trying to remain calm, Kourin said, "It's okay. I'm a prisoner, too." She wanted to hug the girl to reassure her, but from her own experience, she knew it would only panic her further. It had been a long process for herself to overcome her own fear of being touched.

Harry had unknowingly brought back that memory when he had grabbed her arm in her shop. She set the recent memory aside. It would not help her situation here. She needed to escape.

She said reassuringly to the scared young girl, "It's okay. My name is Kourin. I won't hurt you."

* * *

Jack couldn't sit in a depressing motel room, knowing Kourin was in danger. He had to do something.

Outside, the young cop was once again leaning against his car in the bright sunlight. He told Harry and Beth he was going to speak with him to see if there had been any news.

The cop straightened up as Jack approached.

Jack stopped several feet away. He didn't want the young man to feel threatened. He said, "Hi, Officer . . .?"

"Wright. Wesley Wright," said the officer. He had one hand close to his revolver.

Jack could see he was an inexperienced policeman. He didn't convey a strong sense of command of the situation. Yet, he could tell he seemed to be a very normal kid underneath and smiled. He thought of him as a kid. He probably wasn't much older than his own son, Brad.

"Officer Wright, have you heard anything about the abduction?"

"I'm not at liberty to say. Sorry. And please call me Wes."

"Wes," Jack began. He wanted to keep the conversation going. He was desperate to find out any information. "I'm curious why the FBI was so close by. Not that I'm complaining, but I wouldn't think they'd be located right here in this small town."

Wes debated for a moment if he should say more, but in the end, he decided it wasn't a secret why the FBI was there.

"It's because of the body found three days ago, a thirteen-year-old girl who went missing two weeks ago. A second girl went missing last week. At first, we thought—well, Mike did—but Dave eventually agreed with him they had been runaways. Upon finding the body of the first girl, buried in a shallow grave . . ." Unable to complete his thought, perhaps because of the trauma of remembering what he had seen, he momentarily turned his head away from Jack to compose himself.

After a few moments, he said, "It was a chance discovery by Mrs. Watkins out walking her dog who picked up a scent. The dog not . . ." He looked at Jack and continued, "It was a sickening scene. The poor girl was . . ." He trailed off again, clearly upset by what he had witnessed. "That was when the FBI got involved and moved in here since it's only me, Mike, and Dave. The staties have a couple guys working the case, but most of them are tied up with two other murders in Derry and Dover. One of them involved a teacher and some students. The media are all over that one."

Jack knew Dave was the overweight officer he spoke to earlier before the FBI arrived. He didn't know who Mike was. The murder he was talking about sounded familiar, but it was so long ago he couldn't recall what it was about.

"The staties are doing patrols, covering the schools, that sort of thing. We've been instructed to assist the FBI," said Wes. He looked at Jack and seemed dejected. Although it could be because of the missing girls, Jack didn't think so. He wasn't happy being told to stay out of the way.

"I see," Jack said as he looked around the motel parking lot. It was empty except for the police car and a silver Nissan Skyline near the motel entrance. "Do they have any leads?"

Jack didn't receive an answer because Wes' walkie talkie was going off.

"Wes, you there? Wes, where are you, boy?"

The officer retrieved his walkie. "I'm here, Dave."

"We have a report of a white van near to where you are. I want you to g't over there pronto. Don't engage. No siren. Just check it out. We're on our way." Dave gave him the address. "Just make sure it doesn't leave."

Into the walkie he said, "Shoot. That's just down the street. I'm on my way." He put away his walkie. "Please stay put. The FBI will have my ass if you're not here when they return."

Jack said, "Then take us with you! You can't lose us if we're with you!"

"I don't know," he said. He knew he had to make a quick decision. His boss would be mad he wasn't already on his way. "Okay. Let's go."

Jack waved to the others and yelled, "Come on!"

Harry and Beth had been watching and could hear the conversation through the open door. They rushed out. Jack was already getting into the shotgun seat. Wes eyed him, but he didn't object. Harry and Beth got in both sides of the rear.

Wes quickly backed out of the space and peeled out of the motel parking lot.

Jack thought, *Please be there, Kourin!*

* * *

Kourin looked around the room as best she could. Mostly, all she saw were shadows. Close by, there was nothing she could use to get the handcuffs off. *Damn! There has to be a way.*

The child next to her cried. Kourin wanted to comfort her. *Maybe if I get her talking, I can calm her down.* She asked, "You know my name. You can call me Kori. What's yours?" Kourin already knew her name, but she didn't want to take a chance of saying it without the girl telling her. She'd freak out if she thought Kourin was working with the creep.

"Jen. Jen Knowles" She didn't say more.

"Jen, we need to work together if we're going to get out of here."

She thought about what happened all those years ago when she had awakened to this scenario. She had cried for hours. Before that, not long after waking, the creep came into the room. It was dark. There was a sliver of light, but she couldn't see much, which was probably for the best. However, she had heard everything. That fateful day was forever etched into her memory. Not a day went by that she didn't think of the girl lying next to her being raped. The intensity of the devil in human form rose with every terrified scream. Repeated slaps were followed by the demon making vulgar statements. After what seemed an eternity, the girl became silent. Teen Kourin had no comprehension of what had occurred beside her.

After being rescued, she found out the girl had disappeared. Everyone assumed, especially from what Kourin could describe to the police, that she had been murdered and buried some place. Her body was never found.

"That will not happen!" Kourin said out loud.

"What?" Jen meekly asked.

"Jen, I will not let that creep touch you again. We need to find a way out of this. Are both your hands handcuffed?"

"Just . . . just my left one." She began crying harder. "He has my other one free so I can hold his . . ." Her crying became hysteria.

"Jen! Jen! Listen to me," Kourin nearly yelled. "I will not let him do that to you anymore."

"How . . . how can we stop him? I . . . I've tried fighting him. He only hurts me more." She continued crying, but the hysteria was gone.

"I'm—" Kourin stopped to listen. "Shh. Jen. Quiet!" Kourin realized she said it more forcefully than she meant to.

Jen quieted down, but she still sniffled and whimpered.

Kourin heard a vehicle pull up outside. She remembered this. It was the creep. He was about to enter the room. Kourin thought hard, trying to save the little girl next to her. She would learn in two days they were in a bedroom off the entrance to a ranch style home. She was finally saved when the police and FBI raided the home, saving her before she met the same fate of the two previous victims. One was Jen, the crying child constrained next to her.

She listened. The door to the home was unlocked. Boots walked on the linoleum floors.

Her mind was wild with thoughts. Could she hit him with something? Could she strangle him with her handcuffs? She tried it. *Not enough slack.*

The door to the bedroom creaked opened slowly. Rays of light burst through the darkness. Because of Kourin's sharpened eyesight, they appeared as bright as the full moon. She saw the silhouette of a person in the doorway—the demon!

Kourin panicked. She felt heat building inside her teenage body. Fear overtook her. She fought to control it. *Maybe I can get both of us out of here if I think hard enough.* She concentrated on being elsewhere, anywhere but in this room.

The man stepped into the room. He left the door open so he would have light to see his prizes on the bed. Slowly walking over to Jen's side of the bed, he stared at her.

She kept her head faced buried in the mattress and had balled herself up as small as she could make herself.

Kourin watched him. She could see him like a faded black-and-white photo. He had a goatee. Maybe thirty years old. Until this moment, she had blocked his face from her memory. It came back to her now. She had trusted him. All his victims had.

He reached out and ran the tip of two fingers of his left hand from Jen's shoulder down her side to her hip. She let out a whimper.

He said, "Now. Now. No need to cry, my little flower." He placed his full palm on her hip. His fingers grasping her tiny behind.

The child said, "No!"

"Now, now. I know you enjoy it as much as I do."

Kourin's fire burned intently. As much as she tried to whisk them away, she could not. *Maybe that's not how it works. Try, damn it!* She thought of Jack. She knew he was here in this timeline as well. *Where is he? Maybe I can go to where he is.* She was brought out of her thoughts to Jen screaming a foot away.

Kourin screamed, "Leave her alone!"

"Oh, so you are awake." He removed his hand from Jen. "You're just gonna have to wait your turn. I'm gonna have a little more fun with this one."

"How could you? You're supposed to—" Kourin was cut off by the creep telling her to shut up and a hand covering her mouth. She struggled against it, but she was only fourteen against an adult male.

He spoke in a harsh whisper, saying, "Shut your mouth right now." He clasped his hand against her mouth. "Be quiet and maybe I'll let you live."

Kourin remained silent, not out of obedience to the creep. She wanted to know why he wanted her to be quiet. She listened and heard a car coming up to the front of the house.

The creep left the bedside. She watched him go to a covered window and peek through the side. He mumbled, "Damn it. Why is Wes here?"

* * *

Jack held the handle on the door as Wes drove the winding roads like he was in a video game. Twice he thought they would not make a corner. As they presumably neared the address, they slowed. Jack could tell Wes was trying to figure out what to do.

The officer was in a quandary at the mailbox: drive past since he had confirmed the white van was in the driveway and wait for Dave and the FBI, or block the driveway to prevent the van from leaving.

Jack helped him decide. "That's the van! It has '88' on the license plate." He looked at Wes. "Wes, you can't let them get away. Kourin could be in serious trouble!"

At that moment, Wes resolved to block the van from escaping. He pulled in behind it. The front door opened as he was about to call Dave on the car's radio.

Wes did not want to be caught in his car by an assailant. He rapidly exited, drawing his weapon.

Jack also exited the car. He didn't have a weapon, so he used the car as a shield.

Harry tried to get out, but the door would not open. Beth tried her door—same result. They were locked in.

Jack was going to open Harry's door when he saw a thirty-year-old man with a goatee coming toward them.

The goatee man said, "Wes, what brings you here?"

"Mike, I'm surprised to see you here. Whose home is this?" Wes had his revolver in hand but pointed down.

Mike replied, with one hand behind his back, "This is my parents' home. This was left to me when my mother passed away last year. Who's your friend?" He eyed Jack.

"He's a witness to a kidnapping earlier today," said Wes, glancing at the van. "Aren't you supposed to be on patrol? What are you doing here?"

Mike observed Wes gazing at his van.

Jack asked, "Where's the girl? Where's Kourin?"

"I'm sorry. Who?"

Wes asked, "Mike, where did you get the van?"

At that moment, they heard a female childlike voice from inside the home. "Help! We're in here!"

Mike and Wes brought their weapons up at the same time. Mike was faster. He shot Wes, hitting him in the chest. The blow sent him reeling backwards.

The gunman turned toward Jack who was scrambling to duck behind the car. He didn't make it. He was hit and dropped to the ground.

Wes recovered from receiving a round into his bullet-proof vest and lined up a shot at Mike. Mike turned back toward Wes and rapidly fired twice as the younger officer squeezed off one shot. Mike's shots were six inches apart. One bullet missed, whizzing by his fellow cop's ear, hitting the patrol car. The second one was on target and impacted Wes in the face. He went down. The round Wes fired simultaneously struck Mike in the heart, instantly killing him.

Jack was bleeding, but he got to his feet. He had taken a bullet to the chest area. He stumbled and tripped, but he kept pushing forward, determined to save Kourin and get into the house.

Mike was lying dead near the home entrance. Blood pooled on the doorstep below him.

As Jack entered the house, he heard screams for help come from behind a door on his left. He pushed open the door and peered into a darkened room. His shoulder leaned against the threshold, keeping him upright. He felt around for a light switch and turned it on.

The sight he saw appalled him. Two teenage girls lay handcuffed to the bed. One was naked and badly bruised. The other was a teenaged Kourin!

He moved to take a step into the room and faltered, leaning back against the doorframe. He slid down to the floor. His vision became hazy. Each breath was harder to take in. He placed his hand on his chest and felt a warm liquid. As he removed his hand, he saw it was covered in red.

Teen Kourin called out, "Jack! No!"

A coughing fit overtook him. As it eased, he spat blood onto the floor. The bed, just feet away, became out of focus. Unable to stand and struggling to get to Kourin, he crawled the short distance. A trail of blood was left in his wake.

Kourin's temperature was rising. She could feel the anguish growing. The man she loved was wounded and badly bleeding.

Jack struggled, but he pulled himself up on Kourin's side of the bed. Blood smeared the mattress. His breathing was labored as he held his right hand to his wounded chest.

With his left hand, he brushed back the hair blocking one side of Kourin's teen face. He gazed at the young girl he never knew. His head rested on her belly. He coughed when he took another breath. Blood seeped from the side of his mouth.

"Kori . . . I . . . I'm sorry I didn't get here sooner." With all his effort, he lifted his head and gazed into her eyes. "Your eyes are green. They're beautiful. You're beautiful." He coughed again. Blood spat onto Kourin's tee shirt just below the letters "NKOTB." "Kori, I . . . I . . . love you."

He placed his head down on her, never removing his eye contact away from her emerald green eyes with shimmering golden rings. His labored breathing ceased. He lay motionless.

Kourin screamed, "No! Oh, no, no, no, no!" Tears fell as she tenderly stroked Jack's head with her shaking left hand as he lay on her teenage waist. She struggled to swing her other hand toward him. The handcuff held fast, cutting into her wrist. Her fervor was burning. The sound of her love's last breath echoed in her ears as she felt her heartache become unbearable. She cried out a second time with all the rage and sorrow she felt building inside.

The room spun, and there was a flash. She felt her arm released from the constraint. The horrific bedroom that had tormented her all her life disappeared in an instant. She opened her mouth to scream a third time. Nothing came out. Unable to vocalize her pain, she blacked out, freeing her from her anguish.

13

STORMS ARE BREWING IN YOUR EYES

"What are you talking about? I get upset and—poof—I'm somewhere else?" asked Mandy.

Sarah scanned the vicinity. "Maybe we should have this conversation someplace else."

Laurel suggested they go to Luca's and have a drink while they discuss it. Shannon said she wanted to know what was going on, but she needed to get home. Wren had enough excitement for the day and also would head home. Joneal, nodding his head, said, "I'm worried about Jack and Harry, though. Maybe we should stick around until we find them?"

Laurel retrieved her phone and hit the green button to call Jack—direct to voicemail. She left a message for him to call her. She tried Harry and Beth—same results.

"Give me your number," said Laurel. "I'll text you as soon as we learn anything." Joneal obliged. Shannon gave Laurel her number, too.

Mandy had kept her eye on Wren through the exchange. She took the three steps separating them and gave her a hug. Wren had to let go of Joneal's hand, for the first time since arriving back in the terminal, to embrace Mandy's show of empathy.

"I'm sorry to have dragged you into this," said Mandy.

Wren replied, "It's not your fault, I think. I don't know what craziness is going on here, but you're a good person. We're back to where we belong. No one got hurt."

Laurel and Sarah looked at each other. Neither said a word in contradiction.

Shannon cautioned the trio remaining behind to be safe. She advised them to stay away from the bench and let her know as soon as they located Jack and the others.

Laurel assured her they would.

As the guard walked away, she said she would say a prayer for them. The young couple followed, holding hands once again. They remained silent, trying to make sense of what had just transpired.

Sarah said to the two remaining ladies, "Let's go have a drink. I know I need one."

Mandy removed her apron and said she'd be right back. She went to the café and handed her apron to a young woman behind the counter. They chatted for a moment. She returned, saying, "I told them to have a good night and to call me if they see Jack or Harry."

On the way to the restaurant located midway through the terminal, the trio kept a watchful eye out for their missing friends to no avail.

Ubu padded along next to Laurel. He was happy to be back in a familiar place, but he remained on high alert. The voice had warned him of impending danger. He did not know what lay ahead and would be ready to protect his pack.

At Luca's, they asked for a booth and were led to one off to the side. Laurel thought about sitting at the bar so they could look out into the terminal in case they saw Jack or the others, but she changed her mind, knowing they needed to have a closed discussion.

She ordered a beer. Sarah ordered a Chablis. Mandy wasn't going to have anything, but Sarah ordered her what she was having.

While they waited for their drinks, Mandy asked Sarah what she thought was happening to her.

Sarah shared her thoughts about her eye color changing that coincided with her experiencing intense emotions in the restroom, on the bench, and at her friend's home. When they were together on the bench, she witnessed her new friend overcome with emotion. When they arrived in her past, it happened again when she confronted the cheerleaders and then at her friend's house. There was no doubt about it. Emotion had something to do with it.

"But why is it happening now?" Mandy asked. "I've had emotional things happen in the past and nothing ever happened. I certainly never friggin' time traveled!"

"The bench," Laurel said. "You sat on the bench and had the vision about Miguel."

Mandy wrung her hands together and said, "But others have sat on the bench, and nothing like this has happened to them."

"Well, that's not totally accurate," said Laurel.

The drinks arrived as she said that. The conversation paused until the waitress was several steps away. Laurel used that time to take a long sip of her beer. Sarah had a small taste of hers. Mandy didn't touch the glass in front of her. Instead, she held both her hands in a knot on the tabletop.

Laurel explained to her fidgeting friend. "At Fara's, when I saw your eyes change, we ended up back here. I saw Kourin's eyes turn emerald green, just as yours did when we time traveled to the birth of her child."

The two looked at her with open mouths.

She continued, "When we were in the café's office, for a minute we went back to when Kourin was at the hospital when she was a teenager. We witnessed her giving birth. In a New York second, we were back again."

Sarah looked at Mandy and said, "I think that's around the time your eyes turned green as well."

Mandy didn't reply.

After a few heartbeats, when Laurel saw her friend would say nothing, she said, "And Shannon just told us Jack rushed the clown at the sub shop, and the next thing she recalled was being back here." She placed her hands on top of her friend's clenched hands. "I would bet a million dollars Kourin's eyes turned emerald green the same time yours did at Fara's."

Sarah said, "You're saying they're connected?"

"I don't know how or why, but yes," Laurel answered. "Somehow, Kourin and Mandy are connected." She looked into Mandy's eyes. "They're linked to whatever power is controlling the bench." She squeezed her friend's hands. "And I think she's the answer to fix what happened to me."

Mandy finally spoke up. "Lau, we've been through this before." She looked at Sarah. "She wants to go back to—I'm sorry, Lau—she wants to stop the terrorist that killed her friend."

"Terrorists. There were two of them," Laurel said flatly. "At least there was when I was there with Ubu. The first time I only saw one, but I passed out."

"Yes, terrorists." Mandy unclenched her hands, pulled them out from under Laurel's, and placed them on top. "You can't change the past."

"But can't we?" asked Laurel, a little too loudly. "We've just been to your past. We definitely changed what had occurred. Fara's dad is okay. We stopped the clown from killing Everett."

"Did we?" Mandy asked. "Before all this time travel shit, Fara's dad got hit on the head. I remember that. He never said how it happened, at least to Fara and me. So maybe some details changed, but the outcome still seems to be the same. And you know as well as I, Everett owned the sub shop the whole time we were in high school."

Mandy didn't voice the visions she had of Fara's dad dying while they were there. Now that she was back in the present, the memory she had before time traveling seemed to be intact. Well, mostly it was. Fara's dad had died days later when he was mugged. Now she felt that the memory wasn't correct. She had a memory of him being at Fara's graduation with all of them posing for a group photo in front of the very oak tree she had defended her black friend against the racist bitches.

Her memories had changed.

Sarah asked, "So, did we just go into the past for no reason?"

Mandy kept quiet, trying to comprehend her new revelation.

Laurel attempted to determine when she should arrive in the desert to save her unit.

The blue-eyed blonde took a sip of her wine, waiting for one of her two new friends to answer her question. When none was forthcoming, she said, "Look, as I recall from the previous . . . visions you all had, there was a reason you went there. Mandy seeing Miguel's future so she could save him is one example. There was purpose." She looked at Laurel. "Mandy only told me you went back to a time when you served, a bomb went off, and . . ." she paused, not sure if she should continue, knowing Laurel had ongoing issues dealing with it. She decided there was too much at stake to hold back, but she treaded delicately. "Well, when the bomb went off, you held yourself responsible."

Ubu sat up and placed his head against Laurel's thigh. He felt something was not right with Mom.

"I was responsible. I was on guard duty. It was my job to protect my team," Laurel rebutted. She pulled her right hand out from under Mandy's and petted Ubu's head. "Now I can go back there and make things right."

Mandy spoke up. "Lau, we can't change history. It's wrong."

She screamed, "Why the hell not?"

Ubu whined and butted his head against her thigh, placing his jowls upon her lap.

In a lower voice, after inattentively petting Ubu, she added, "If I have the chance to go back and make things right, shouldn't I? Shouldn't I give Breck the chance to live his life the way he should have?"

Sarah was stunned by this statement. She interrupted and asked, "Breck? Breck Thompson?"

"Yes. Specialist Breckin Thompson was in my unit. He was the soldier killed because I didn't do my job."

Sarah went pale. Her hands trembled. She looked at Mandy and back to Laurel.

Mandy was afraid she was going to faint. She asked, "Sarah, are you okay?"

Laurel looked into Sarah's blue eyes, eyes that were tearing up. As before, in Fara's living room, she thought she had seen those eyes before. A faint memory came to her—a photo Breckin would show the entire world every chance he got. He had a smile from ear to ear when he spoke about her. The picture the unit playfully teased him about looking like Ken and Barbie. "Sarah. You're Breck's Sarah, his fiancé?"

Tears fell from Sarah's eyes. "Yes. We were to be married when he . . ." She couldn't finish the sentence. With a trembling hand, she picked up her wineglass and had a long drink from it. She placed it back on the table roughly.

Mandy reached over to take hold of her hand. "Oh, Sarah, I'm so sorry," she said. "I never thought . . ."

Laurel said, "I am so sorry for your loss. I . . ."

She looked at Mandy who shook her head a silent no.

Laurel looked back at Sarah, ignoring her best friend. "Sarah, we can bring him back. We can . . . I can make things right. I can correct my mistake."

Sarah stared up at her. At first, she was silent, unsure of what to say. She glanced at Mandy, still holding her hand. Finally, she heard Ubu whine. She looked at Laurel's lap. He kept his head on her, but he was looking at her. She gazed into his brown eyes. She saw sorrow in them.

The memory of Breck's face came to her: his brown eyes, chiseled features, strong arms holding her as she pulled her face away after a passionate kiss. She recalled the last time she saw his handsome face the day he left for his last tour of duty. When he was to return, they were to be married.

She never saw the love in his eyes again. She cried.

For a moment, she thought she could have her childhood friend and teenage sweetheart back. He could return home to her. They could wed and live their lives together.

She thought of her husband, Jerry. She thought of her children, two lovely daughters, Maddie and Chloe, she had with him. The man she fell in love with and married fourteen years ago after . . . after Breck died . . .

Mandy watched her friend who was clearly dealing with long dormant emotions. She wanted to give her a hug, but she knew Sarah had to deal with the remembrance of her lost love on her own for the moment. When she saw her friend's sobbing decline, she asked, "Is there anything I can do for you?"

Sarah was brought out of her despondency when she heard her friend's soft voice and looked away from the dog. She said, "I'm . . . I'm okay. It was just a shock to have those memories come back like that." With her free hand, she placed it on top of Mandy's as she held the other. "I'll be alright. When I lost Breck all those years ago, it hurt like hell. It still does. I'll always have a place in my heart for him, but I had to move on. I had to put his loss behind me. That is what he would have wanted. What he did for me . . . for anyone he knew . . . was to put their happiness ahead of his own, just as he did the day he died."

Laurel, who had been quiet coming to grips with whom she had been with for the last couple of days, came to life asking, "What do you mean? He was in the barracks asleep when the bomber struck."

Sarah shifted her gaze to Laurel. "Yes, he was. When the door opened, Breck was in the closest bunk. From what I was told at his funeral, he saw the intruder, and reacting as he had been trained to do, he jumped out of bed fighting with him. He put his own safety aside to protect those with him. He had forced the attacker back through the doorway when the bomb detonated. If it wasn't for him, many others may have died."

Tears flowed from Laurel's eyes.

Sarah continued, "Breck did what came natural to him. He wasn't trying to be a hero. In doing what he always did, he put the safety of others before his own."

Mandy now felt she had to give Sarah a hug and did. Tears flowed from all three ladies.

Laurel asked, "But shouldn't we do what we can to change that? We can make it so it doesn't even happen."

"And then what?" Sarah asked. "What if we do as you say? What if you go back and change what happens? As we saw happen in the sub shop, what if something changes and Breck doesn't push the attacker out the door? More people may die."

"But what if I go back with Ubu and we can stop both terrorists? We can prevent anyone from getting hurt," said Laurel. "We can stop them before they attack!"

Mandy said, "I don't think we can."

"*Why the hell not?*" Laurel asked, harsher than she meant to.

"As we saw in the park when Fara was attacked by the girls and then in the sub shop, the events are still going to happen. They may change a little from our interference, but the result may still be the same."

Mandy kept her new memory of the Otieno family to herself, not knowing what thoughts and memories were real. She looked at Sarah and said, "I not sure we can change what happened. I'm sorry."

Sarah contemplated her words and finally answered, "Even if we could change what happened, as painful as it is to say this, we can't."

Laurel was surprised by what she heard. "Why not?"

Sarah turned her sad eyes to her and replied, "Because if we changed what happened to Breck and somehow prevented the bombings, bringing him home to me . . ." she paused, gathering her strength to say the words out loud. "If Breck came home to me, we would have married. I never would have met Jerry. My two babies would not be born." She looked Laurel in the eye. "My daughters would cease to exist."

Laurel looked down at Ubu. She had been petting his head absently the entire time. She looked back to Sarah. "Maybe they would have been born with Breck being the father instead of Jerry."

Mandy looked at her as if to say, "Are you fucking crazy?"

Sarah became glummer than she had been. She used the napkin on the table to wipe her nose and dry her eyes. She felt two pairs of eyes on her awaiting a response.

"My dear Breck couldn't have been the father to my daughters." She paused, placing the balled-up napkin on the table before continuing. "When he was thirteen, there was an accident on the farm. He was with my younger brother saddling a horse when a snake slithered across the pasture, spooking the mare. Breck pushed my brother out of the way to safety. The mare kicked out her hind legs, striking Breck. He was hurt pretty badly and mostly healed, except for one thing." She paused again, thinking of Breck. She thought of her two daughters. "He could never father children of his own." A tear flowed down her cheek.

Mandy said, "Oh, Sarah." She hugged her.

Laurel said, "Sarah, I'm sorry. I thought . . ."

"I know," she said. "You mean well. I know your heart is in the right place, but know this." She looked Laurel in the eye again. "Breck died serving his country. He was proud of what he was doing. He knew the risks, as I'm sure you all did. His letters to me were often very vague. I think it was his way of protecting me from the horrors he endured. However, he mentioned a girl in his unit in his last three letters. He didn't reveal her by name. At first, I was jealous, but I trusted my Breck. Anyway, he had written that she felt like the sister he never had. He said they'd talk for hours about—"

Laurel interrupted, "The ocean."

"Yes," said Sarah. "Born and raised in Oklahoma, he had a fascination about the ocean. He wanted to join the Marines and then it was the Navy. They declined him because of his childhood injury. The Army was the only branch he was accepted into."

Laurel cried.

After a moment, Sarah said, "I miss my Breck dearly, but he lives on in my heart."

Sarah reached across the table to hold Laurel's hands into her own. "Laurel, it wasn't your fault. Breck died saving everyone else, probably thinking he was saving you as well." She smiled, a sad smile but a smile just the same. "He loved you in his own way as much as he loved me, but you have to let him go. He wouldn't want you to grieve for him wasting your life."

"But I can change what—" she began.

"No. He is gone. Gone from our sight, but he will live forever in our memories and in our hearts. His legacy will go on eternally."

Laurel cried harder.

Sarah released Laurel's hands, retrieving the napkin to wipe her nose. As she closed her eyes and wiped her face, she opened them to an empty booth.

In front of her was a single wineglass with one swallow remaining. She took a sip, dazed for a moment like she had been with someone, and then was suddenly alone. She tried to remember what she had just been thinking of—Breck. After all these years, he was on her mind. She finished the wine.

She needed to get to the hotel to rest for the morning flight back home. The receipt on the table told her the bill was paid. She glanced at her phone: no messages. She flipped it over and read the saying on the back of her phone: "Time is the longest distance between two places. Tennessee Williams."

She yearned to get back home to her husband, Jerry, and her daughters. As she stood, she reached for the handle of her bag. It was a two-hour direct flight to be back home. Unfortunately, she had to wait until her morning flight to get back to the ones she loved.

She paused for a moment. *Why do I feel like I just lost a friend?* She shook off the eerie sensation. *I just need some sleep. It's been a long day.*

As she walked past the bar area toward the exit, she heard a male voice call out. "Mandy!" She turned in his direction, not knowing why. Behind the counter, the brunette bartender in her mid-fifties answered him she'd be right over. *Why does that name ring a bell?*

On her way to the exit, she heard her name called out. "Sarah!"

She saw four people she had never met walking toward the restaurant. Three of them smiled as if seeing a long-lost friend. The statuesque blonde said, "Sarah, it is so good to see you! Are the others with you?"

Sarah stopped at the entrance, at first thinking perhaps they were speaking to someone behind her or at the bar with the same name. They were definitely looking at her, awaiting an answer.

When she didn't answer, the blonde said, "Sarah, it's me, Kourin. Please tell me Laurel and Mandy are with you!"

Sarah stood still. *That's the second time I've heard that name. Who are these people?* She responded, "I'm sorry. You must have me confused with someone else. If you'll excuse me, I need to get to my hotel."

She walked past them, rolling her flight bag behind her. *Why do these people look familiar?* She walked on, not looking back. *I should call Jerry when I get to the hotel.*

As she thought that, an image of Breck came to her mind as well as two faces she did not know: two women about her age, one with dark closely trimmed hair like she was in the military, the other a pretty blonde with dimples and striking emerald eyes. A black dog sat between them. *Ubu.*

She stopped walking. *How do I know his name?* In her mind, she saw the three of them. The dog lifted his paw to her, his sorrowful brown eyes penetrating her own. She thought, *What the fuck is happening?*

She considered going back to the bar to have another drink. *No. I have to fly first thing in the morning. I know I saw a pleasant garden near the café. It's on the way out. I'll go there for a stroll before I go over to my hotel. I need to clear my head.*

As Sarah neared the garden, she immediately walked to the center. It was unoccupied. An old bench was in the center. *Well, this seems like a peaceful place.* She thought she heard some rustling in the plants as she strolled to the bench. Not seeing anything, she rolled her flight bag next to the bench and sat down.

14

KOURIN'S NIGHTMARE

Kourin awoke in the garden and immediately saw Harry and Beth standing directly in front of her. They appeared to be normal, wearing the clothes she remembered from being in teen Mandy's sub shop and Laurel's office before that. Laurel's office seemed like a lifetime ago.

The garden surrounded them. The Hosta and other plants lay still. All appeared normal. There was no light from the skylights above. It was night time or at least evening.

She asked Harry, "Is Jack here?" She had just seen Jack take his last breath on her, but she hoped it did not truly happen. Perhaps it was just a warped vision caused by the bench. She kept calm by telling herself that, now they were back home, Jack would reappear from around a corner as if it had never happened.

"We haven't seen him yet," Beth answered, instead of Harry. When he didn't add a comment, she did. "We just awoke on the outer bench on the back-side of the garden. Not seeing you or Jack, we came up here and found you on the bench. After several minutes, you woke up." She paused. "We . . . we were afraid to disturb you."

Harry said, "Was Jack with you? We saw him go into the house. Shortly after that, we woke up on the bench. We thought he'd be here with you."

"He . . ." Kourin began and faltered, attempting to keep her emotions under control. She felt a burning sensation inside and forced it down. She took a long breath and spoke again. "He came into the bedroom where I was being held prisoner, where we were being held. There was a girl with me chained to the bed." She stopped speaking, emotions building inside her. After several more breaths to calm herself down, she told herself it was all in the past. It was a long time ago.

"But Jack was with you, right?" Harry asked again.

After a moment, Kourin said, "He was. He . . ." She couldn't complete her sentence.

"He got shot," Harry finished her sentence. "We saw him get shot beside the car."

Kourin looked at Harry with a confused expression.

"Maybe we should fill you in on what happened," Beth said. "But I don't think we should do it here." She peered around. "I'm not liking this place as much as I used to. Let's go someplace else. Maybe Jack is down at the main entrance on that bench."

Kourin agreed and stood up. She wasn't as wobbly as she had been on previous incidents. Maybe she was getting used to the aftereffects.

She stood and realized she wasn't dressed in the clothes she wore at the start of the day. As she looked down at herself, she was met with her cleavage strikingly displayed between a tightly fitting white blouse. Below that was a short black skirt dropping just below her knees, with a long slit up the side. She wore black open-toed three-inch heels. She said, "What the fuck?"

Harry said, "Well, that's a new look for you."

"Harry!" said Beth.

"What? All I'm sayin' is she looks very different from usual."

"Why am I different, but you two look the same?" asked Kourin. She thought for a moment. "If I'm different, what else has changed?" She looked at Beth and said, "We need to find Jack."

The three exited the garden. At the bottom of the main entrance, they were disappointed to not see Jack. What they saw was what was not there. The Coffee Bean sign was no longer above the café. The sign read "JaMocha Café."

Harry spoke up first. "Well, that can't be good."

"Where's the Coffee Bean?" asked Beth.

Kourin looked in the other direction, half expecting her shop to be different. It wasn't. Her sign still hung as it always had. From this distance, everything seemed as it was when she had left it earlier in the day. She told the others, "I'm going to check out my store. Maybe they've seen Jack."

Harry said, "Okay. We'll check the café to see what the hell happened."

He and Beth walked in that direction, leaving Kourin to survey the terminal for a moment. All the other stores appeared to be the same as they had been. In heels she was unaccustomed to, she walked over to her store.

The first thing she noticed out of place were the two young females working behind the counter. She didn't know who they were and observed them from several feet outside the entrance. They were dressed similar to her. Their makeup and hairstyles made them appear like models from a fashion magazine. There was something very wrong here. This was not her philosophy in the world of cosmetics. This was not the brand she was building.

A few steps into the entrance of her store, she noticed the display donating some of the profit to an African wildlife fund she had set up with Mary the day before wasn't there. She thought, *What is going on?*

The women behind the counter were each assisting a customer. *I know those girls! I passed on hiring them. Why are they here and not the women I hired? I need to find out what the fuck is going on!*

As she stepped further into the shop, one woman behind the counter greeted her. "You okay? You look a little troubled." She looked at the other woman. "I mean, not in a bad way. Um, you still look beautiful." The other woman didn't say a word. She let her counterpart dig her own hole deeper.

Kourin replied, "I'm okay." She looked around the store. Besides the wildlife display missing, several other ones were in different locations, while some she did not recognize at all. She asked, "Have you seen Jack?"

"Who?" the woman behind the counter asked. "Who is Jack?"

From behind her she heard a familiar voice ask, "Yes, my love, who is Jack?"

Kourin turned around to see Anders standing a foot away from her. He closed the distance and kissed her on her cheek, wrapping his hand around her backside and giving her a light goose on her butt.

He said to her as he pulled back, stopping inches from her, "I've been looking for you. Did you forget we were having dinner tonight to celebrate your store opening?"

"What?" That was all she could stammer out, having been caught totally off guard by his forwardness toward her.

"Dinner. You and me at Luca's," he said. "Come, my dear, there's still time before they close the kitchen." He took hold of her hand. "By the way, in case I didn't say so earlier, you look ravishing today." His eyes moved to her chest.

Kourin pulled her hand away from him. She said, "Um, I just need a minute to freshen up." She looked around, slightly panicking. "I'll be right back."

She passed by the counter and customers. The kiss she had given Jack in the very spot she was walking through came to her. She thought, *Where are you, Jack?*

In the mirror on the top of the wall at the rear of the store, she saw Anders' attention had turned to the two women behind the counter.

She made a beeline for the employee restroom in the backroom, trying to leave this nightmare behind her. She passed through the storeroom entrance doors where two days earlier Harry had grabbed her arm.

Upon entering the bathroom and turning on the light, she looked into the mirror. She gasped. A face she did not recognize was staring back at her. It resembled the two women at her front counter, but her makeup would put those two to shame: heavy eye shadow, dark eyeliner, blush, red lips. This was not her! She thought, *I look like a . . . like a . . . seductress! What the hell am I trying to sell?*

She turned away from her reflection and said to the empty room, "What the fuck is going on here? What has happened to me?"

Again, she turned her attention to her reflection. She peered into eyes she did not recognize. She saw green eyes staring back. The longer she looked, the greener they became. Golden rings formed around each pupil.

To the woman looking back at her, she said, "Where are you, Jack? I need you!"

* * *

Harry entered the café, checking each seating area for Jack. He knew it was a long shot of him being here, but they had to start somewhere. He also didn't see Mandy or Laurel. Beth was by his side as he went to the counter. The donation box built into the counter was not there.

He didn't know the person behind the counter, but there had been a lot of new hires for the terminal opening so he didn't give it much thought. The clerk asked him what he wanted. Instead of ordering something, he asked if Mandy or Laurel were there. The clerk said he didn't know who they were. When Harry explained Laurel owned the café and Mandy was the manager, the clerk said they weren't the ones in charge. He said a name of the owner, someone Harry didn't know. The clerk asked him again if he wanted to order something. A line formed behind them. Beth pulled Harry aside to let other people be waited on.

Outside the café, Beth asked, "What does this mean? Where are Laurel and Mandy?"

Harry looked across the terminal walkway at KCA, Kourin Cosmetics and Accessories. He said, "I think she holds all the answers we seek. When Jack went inside that house, something happened." He looked at Beth. "I think it was something really bad."

They walked across the terminal to Kourin's shop. Beth recognized Anders standing out front. They stopped next to him. He recognized both of them. Beth thought, *Well, that's a good sign, I guess.* She asked Anders, "Have you seen Laurel or Mandy around?"

"I'm sorry, who?"

"Laurel and Mandy. Owner and manager . . ." Harry said, trailing off. "Laurel, Jack's niece, travels with a dog. Her friend, Mandy, perpetual optimist."

"Sorry. I don't know who you mean. Jack, however, I know," he said. "But I haven't seen him today. The last time I saw him was when you two pulled the trailer out yesterday." He looked at Harry. "I bet you're both glad to have this project behind you."

"Yes, we are," Harry replied. He looked at Beth. "I just wish I knew where the hell he is."

* * *

In the bathroom, Kourin remembered she had her cell phone when she was last at Mandy's sub shop, even if it wasn't working then. Where it was at the moment, in the outfit she wore, she wasn't sure. She patted herself down around the waist and found a small pocket on the inside of the waist area. She thought, *That's a clever hiding place.*

She reached into the pocket and pulled out a phone she had never seen before. It was a compact flip phone. It wasn't the one she owned. She opened it. The screen folded out to a regular size phone and came to life asking for her finger print. She pressed her right-hand thumb on the image—no match. *Maybe it's not my phone.* She tried her right-hand index finger. The phone opened to a home screen. She stared at the photo it displayed—a smiling Anders. *Ugh. Are you kidding me!*

She scrolled through the contact entries. The first one she saw was Anders. *That's odd. I thought I had deleted his entry when I dumped his ass weeks ago.* She went to the Js. She looked under R for Roberts. No Jack. She scrolled through all the entries. Most of them were unknown to her. She noted there were many numbers absent from the phone that should have been there. Mary, her supervisor, was not listed, nor were the names of the employees she hired. She folded the phone and tucked it away into its hidden pocket.

She looked at her reflection again and wanted to wash off the makeup she wore. More than water was needed to remove the layers she had on. She left it as is, as much as it bothered her.

She thought, *I need to find Jack. I don't have time to worry about how I look.* She glared at her cleavage, adding to the thought, *But I'm changing my clothes the first chance I get.*

After exiting the restroom, she saw Anders speaking with Harry and Beth. As she approached, Anders said, "Ah, here she is at last." To Harry and Beth, he said, "If you two will excuse us, we are late for our dinner."

"Why don't you two join us?" Kourin asked. She saw Anders did not like what she asked. She did not want to be alone with him. "I have some things I'd like to discuss with you."

Harry looked at Anders who gave him a look saying "Don't you dare." He said, "Sure, we'd love to."

The four of them walked down the terminal to Luca's. Upon approaching the entrance, Kourin saw Sarah exiting. She was dressed in an airline uniform. She smiled, finally seeing someone she knew, and called out to her, "Sarah!"

Sarah didn't respond to her, but she followed up with, "Sarah. It is so good to see you. Are the others with you?" Sarah didn't respond and instead looked behind her before turning back. "Sarah, it's me Kourin. Please tell me Laurel and Mandy are with you!"

Sarah stood still and responded, "I'm sorry. You must have me confused with someone else. If you'll excuse me, I need to get to my hotel." She walked past them, not looking back.

Beth, Kourin, and Harry looked at each other, not knowing what to say. All three were certain that was Sarah, yet she didn't know who they were.

Anders interrupted their stupor and said, "Shall we sit down before they close for the night?"

Kourin considered going after Sarah, but she needed to speak with Harry and Beth about what occurred before they all found themselves here. This world was definitely not right. She answered Anders, "Sure."

They waited at the podium to be seated. Around the corner came Wren. She asked how many were in their party, retrieved four menus from a holder by the podium, and began leading them to their table. She acted as if nothing out of the ordinary had occurred.

As they were being seated, Kourin asked her, "How is Joneal?"

"Who?" she responded.

"Joneal. You went to the party with him last night."

"Sorry. I don't know what you're talking about. I didn't go to the party last night," said Wren. She had a somber face. "Your waitress will be right over to take your order." She turned and walked away.

Harry asked, "What the hell is going on?"

"I don't know," Kourin said. "But we need to figure this out."

Anders said he didn't have any idea what they were talking about and suggested they order. Everyone ordered drinks. Anders ordered the sampler appetizer as well. Other than him, none of them had an appetite. He ordered a main dish, while the others ordered a second round of drinks.

Anders talked about himself and how well the terminal ran on its first day of operation as he ate his entrée. The others picked at the sampler. When he finished eating, he received a phone call and said he had something to take care of but would be back shortly.

While he was gone, Harry and Beth filled Kourin in on what had occurred while she was abducted. When their story ended with Jack entering the house holding his chest, she told them the excruciating pain of seeing Jack crawl across the floor to her. She struggled to finish her story, but with great effort and a swallow finishing her drink, she said Jack died holding her.

Tears welled up in Kourin's eyes. Harry and Beth were on the verge of crying themselves. The only thing stopping them all from bawling their eyes out was Harry saying, "Your eyes are turning a brighter emerald green. I can see the gold ring."

Beth looked into Kourin's eyes and said, "They are!"

Kourin grabbed a napkin and wiped away her tears. She had felt the anguish growing in her as she told her side of the story. She tempered down her emotions. It was difficult, but she stopped thinking about Jack dying. She concentrated on where she would look to find him. As she calmed down, Anders returned to the table.

Anders paid the bill and whined the whole time about how much the drinks cost. Kourin stopped at the podium where Wren was standing. She wanted to speak with her, but Anders was insistent that they get home. Before Kourin could tell him to fuck off, Beth spoke up, saying they'd catch up with her. Kourin took the hint that Beth would question Wren while she got Anders out of the way.

As Kourin left Beth and Harry behind, she found out from Anders he had driven them both to the terminal that morning. Further, they were actually living together at her home. She didn't want to believe it and denied it to herself the entire time until she looked in the bedroom closet and saw his clothes hanging there. When Anders came out of the bathroom wearing just his boxer shorts, she knew this was a life she didn't want. She thought, *How the fuck did it all come to this?*

Anders came up behind her and wrapped his arms around her, kissing her in the space between her ear and her shoulder. She froze. He said, "Why don't you change and come to bed, dear?"

In the bathroom, Kourin took a long hot shower and washed away all the makeup from her face. For a moment, she thought of the clown that had attacked them. She had felt like a clown until now. As the sub shop clown had used his makeup to hide his identity, she realized in this reality she was doing the same thing. That was not who she was. Somehow, she had to make this right.

She looked for her typical sleepwear hung on the hook on the bathroom door. Her pajamas were not there. What was there was a nightie that was evidently made with as little material as possible. With nothing else to wear, she put it on. She looked in the mirror and thought, *Figures. It's a see-through. I wonder who bought this for me.* In the reflection, she could see her nipples under the fabric. She didn't see any underwear to put on, so she put the thong she had been wearing back on.

Anders was waiting for her in the bed under the covers. She could see his boxer shorts on the floor.

She thought, *Just fucking great. How am I going to get out of this?* Instead of getting into the bed, she said, "I have a slight headache. I'm going to sit in the living room for a bit."

Anders said, "Oh, I'm sorry to hear that."

Kourin thought, *Bet your ass you're sorry to hear that.*

He added, "I could give you a massage to make you feel better."

Kourin thought, *And I'm sure you think that's going to get you what you want tonight. I think not!* She said, "Thank you, but I just need a few minutes to relax." Without waiting for a reply, she grabbed a robe off a hook in the closet, put it on, and exited the bedroom.

She went to her desk downstairs and powered up her laptop. She began her search. First, she searched for Jack. Next was Laurel, Mandy, and the others that had time traveled. Several were dead ends. There was nothing on Mandy. She found Laurel, but all she found was an article on the suicide bomber. There was nothing after that. No mention of opening the Coffee Bean and donating money to save dogs or help vets. She even searched for Ubu. Nothing.

She pulled up today's *Union Leader* newspaper. The headline read of a horrible crash the evening before killing several people when a truck ran a stop sign plowing into a van carrying a family of four. She teared up and felt a burning inside as her emotions rose. She fought to keep them under control.

An idea came to her to check something in her bedroom. She really didn't want to go back in there with Anders waiting for her, but this was important.

As she stood at the bedroom doorway, she heard the rhythmic sound of his breathing. She thought, *Thank God he's asleep.* She tiptoed into the bedroom to the dresser. A lamp she did not recognize sat on the dresser. She turned it on and heard stirring on the bed. It was just Anders rolling over, away from the light.

She opened her jewelry box and searched for what she was looking for. It wasn't there. She emptied most of the contents quietly on to her dresser. It definitely wasn't there.

Tears welled in her eyes. After nearly a lifetime, her baby's locket was gone! She thought, *This is so wrong. I'm going to get some answers if I have to tear that fucking bench apart with my bare hands!*

Before turning off the light, she found black jeans and a white short-sleeve button-down blouse she could wear that didn't make her feel like a girl for hire. They were form fitting but better than the alternatives she saw readily available. She found a white bra and thong in the bureau. Further searching at the bottom of her closet resulted in a pair of white and black Hoka sneakers. They appeared to not have been worn.

She dressed quickly and silently. The bra was not the type she normally wore. Even with these new clothes, her chest was prominently displayed. Not looking at her eyes, she glanced in the mirror. She thought, *Either this or no bra at all.* She kept the bra on.

As she reached for the light switch, she took one last look at the bed. The sheet had ridden up, exposing Anders' butt. She thought, as she turned out the light, *I'm going to make this right if it's the last thing I do!*

With the room in darkness, she realized she could still see everything in gray tones. She heard the creak of the bed as Anders rolled onto his back. With her improved eyesight, she saw his fully exposed manscaped manhood. She turned and made a hasty exit. The sound of him snoring followed her out of the bedroom. As she raced down the stairs to get out of her own home, she thought, *Oh, I am definitely not going to live this life!*

* * *

Beth observed Kourin departing, accompanied by Anders. Kourin couldn't hide her disdain for him. Her demeanor differed from how she was with Jack. Add to that, she was not pleased with her appearance or attire. It wasn't Beth's taste either. However, she had to admit: Kourin was stunning and certainly stood out.

She turned her attention to Wren. The young woman seemed to be the same person she had spent time with for a large part of the day. Beth asked how her day had gone so far, hoping to get a little more information on what was taking place in this reality.

Wren responded things had been going well until the afternoon hostess didn't show, meaning she had to work a double.

Beth inquired if she knew who Jack was. She replied she didn't even after Harry explained he was the owner of the company who built the terminal. She still drew a blank, but she explained she literally had just started working at the restaurant yesterday when it opened.

Harry asked her if she remembered him eating lunch there yesterday with a few of the guys. She did. He probed if she remembered any of the guys or if any of them stood out to her. She admitted that a couple of them were cute, but nothing went beyond that.

He became frustrated, so Beth took over. She asked her why she hadn't gone to the terminal party the night before. Hesitant to answer a personal question to someone she didn't know, she finally replied after some additional prompting.

Her answer was simple. She didn't have a date and didn't want to show up alone, not knowing anyone since she had just started that day.

Harry thought of something and wanted to give it one more attempt. He asked her if she recalled a man with a blonde walking in as he and the guys left the restaurant the day before. She said she remembered him. Both Harry and Beth became excited when they heard that. He asked her who those two people were.

She answered. It was Kourin and Anders, the two they just had dinner with.

Beth and Harry had to admit defeat. Wren didn't know where Jack was. Based on her answers, everything she had experienced with them in Mandy's past was also not there. They said goodbye to her and wished her luck in her new job.

After their unsuccessful attempt to learn any useful information, they contemplated going home. Harry said there was nothing there for him. He was going to stay here and search for answers. He checked his phone: no messages or calls. Beth did likewise with the same result.

For the next hour, they walked the terminal checking every store, gate, and restroom for any sign of Jack. Eventually, they stood in front of the garden. With trepidation, they searched it thoroughly.

In the middle, Sarah, in her pilot attire, was discovered on the bench, asleep.

15

OKLAHOMA

Sarah had déjà vu as she relaxed on the antique bench. She thought, *I'm sure I've never been here. Why does it look so familiar?* She glanced to her left after hearing rustling in that direction. Not seeing anything, she scanned the area in a semicircle, left to right. Nothing. She was alone. She chuckled. *Well, as alone as is possible in a terminal full of people.*

Another thought popped into her head. *Why is it so quiet here? I don't even hear the music playing. Whoever built this place did a great job with soundproofing—Jack. Jack built this place.* She paused her thoughts and asked herself, *Jack? Who is Jack?* She gave it more thought. *Jack built this terminal. He and . . . Kourin are . . . Wait! The woman at the restaurant said her name was Kourin! Am I just putting random thoughts together?*

There was a rustle to her right. She focused in that direction. She saw nothing except a couple of leaves on a Hosta moving. *Must be a mouse or something.* She continued watching, but there was no further movement.

If she's Jack's Kourin, was the guy she was with Jack? No, that was not him. That guy looked stuck up.

She stopped to tell herself, *Jack isn't like that. And why do I think Jack, who I do not even know, is a really nice guy? He's . . . he's Laurel's uncle. Laurel—that was one name the blonde woman said. And the other was Mandy, another blonde, with emerald green eyes and . . . golden rings in her eyes? That can't be right. Yet, I feel it is.*

Movement again caught her eye to her right. She didn't turn her head, but she did a sideways glance in the direction. The plants were definitely moving: up and down, side to side. Not a lot, but they were moving. She couldn't see what was causing them to move. She kept her eye on them as a picture of a blonde woman with an infectious smile and dimples came into her mind. *Mandy.*

As her eyes closed, she saw a black dog next to Mandy, the same one she had in her mind a short time ago. He had a red vest on that identified him as a service dog. He looked at her and raised his paw.

Sarah opened her eyes.

Her parents' front yard filled her view. A fenced-in pasture with bur oak trees lined the area beginning on her right side and spanning the entire perimeter to the road in the distance. In the fall, the trees displayed a spectacular coloring of golden orange. Currently green, the gnarled branches provided much needed shade on the flat parched land below. The vast open area before her was mainly grassland. Two groves of hackberry trees provided shelter, their oblong crowns rustling in the breeze, where the farm's dairy cows rested while grazing the pasture. The area was currently unoccupied.

A well-compacted red dirt driveway to the right of the pasture followed the length of the white wooden fence, running beside the home and eventually ending at the sizable barn a short distance behind the homestead. At the opposite end of the driveway, a left onto the road in the distance brought you to the town's Main Street where everything was for a forty-mile radius, except the most important thing in her life that was in the other direction, just a short way away. Breck grew up at the next farm over.

A figure approached, taking advantage of the shade provided by the trees along the driveway.

While she waited for the distant figure to approach, she surveyed what was close to her. She rested on her momma's porch swing. A glass of iced tea with two tiny pieces of ice remaining sat on the small, weathered table next to her. The day was bright and hot, with the sun high overhead dominating a cloudless sky.

Yesterday, Breck called to say he would visit her today.

She wore his favorite white sundress with tiny red flowers decorating it every few inches throughout its short length. He would recite the same line every time she wore it. "That dress makes my heart think it's the Fourth of July."

Sarah smiled as she recalled why he said that. She was wearing the same dress on Independence Day two years earlier when they kissed for the first time, a proper kiss, an "I am in love with you" kiss.

A bead of sweat dripped from her hair line near her left ear down her neck, around the curve of her collarbone, and disappeared between her breasts. The simple white bra underneath was as wet as if she had been swimming in the creek.

She sipped her iced tea.

The figure striding up the driveway was still several hundred feet away.

No longer able to wait, in her bare feet, she abandoned the shade of the porch.

The sun beat down, intensifying her perspiration, but she ignored it. As she closed the distance to the man walking up her driveway, she felt more salty drips into her cleavage.

Fifty feet away, the man's smile was obvious. A tight green tee shirt, tucked into his Army fatigue pants, covered the muscles underneath his V-shape physique. Even from a distance, she saw him sweating from the summer sun.

Twenty feet apart, she closed the gap in a run, throwing herself at the man holding his arms open for her.

Sarah kissed his mouth with pent-up passion from months of longing for her man. He picked her up in his brawny arms, swinging her around and returning her kiss.

After several minutes of merging their sweat together, he set her down. From an arm's length away, he recited the line she knew he would. "That dress makes my heart think it's the Fourth of July!"

Together, they walked hand in hand back to the shade of the porch.

Sarah's joy at having her man home soon turned to disappointment when he told her he had to return for one more tour of duty. She had hoped he was returning for good so they could begin their life together as they had planned.

To hide her disappointment and with tears forming in her eyes, she left him waiting on the porch as she fetched a cold glass of iced tea. She used those few moments to recover herself back to a smile and to keep up her happy front for her man.

Her man.

They have known each other all their lives, growing up in dairy farms next door to each other. They played together every year since she could remember. She cried for hours when he was injured one summer, but he thankfully recovered, mostly recovered.

In the two years after the accident, their relationship changed from the friends they had been. He grew taller and stronger. She developed from a girl into a woman. They fell in love.

One aspect of him that never wavered was how he treated her. She was everything to him, and he was everything to her. Other than kissing and holding hands, they never moved beyond that even when she felt the burning desire for more. They agreed to wait until marriage.

For the last two years since that first kiss, she told herself they had their whole lives ahead of them. She could, would, had to, and did wait. Boys watched her when she walked past, but she never flirted with them. She never led them on. She waited for her man to come home.

She stopped in her tracks, holding his iced tea. In front of her, on her momma's porch, the man she loved was down on one knee. Slowly moving toward him, with trembling hands, she set the tea down next to hers.

Her blue eyes watched her love open a little box he had in one hand. He spoke the words she had dreamed about since she was a little girl: "I love you. When I return from my last tour, I want to marry you. Sarah, will you do me the honor of becoming my wife? Will you marry me?"

She immediately said yes, and they kissed again. He placed the small diamond ring on her left hand. They kissed again. He held her in his strong sweaty arms. Her dress was plastered to her from her own sweat. She didn't care. She was finally going to marry her childhood sweetheart. Once he returned from his final tour, they would have their whole lives to spend together.

As they hugged on her momma's sweltering porch, she knew nothing would take that away from them.

Until it did.

Sarah woke to two sets of eyes looking down at her from several feet away. She was sitting on the bench in the garden. Rivulets of perspiration streamed from the left side of her head, down her collarbone, and vanished beneath her uniform. When the heat that had been embracing her dissipated quickly, her skin was left with an icy coldness, resulting in an involuntary shudder. She focused on the two people staring at her. They were familiar. The female spoke.

"Sarah, are you okay?" She took a step forward. "Can I help you?" The man beside her did not move, nor did he speak.

"I'm okay," she answered. "I was just having a dream."

The man spoke up and asked, "Where did you go?"

Still a little groggy, she answered his question even though she didn't remember quite who these people were. Her mind was in disarray. "I was back home. My boyfriend proposed to me while he was home on leave."

"That must be a very happy memory for you," the woman said.

"It was," she answered. "It was until it wasn't."

"I don't understand," said the women who moved closer, leaving the man standing alone behind her. "What happened that made it unhappy?"

"He never returned to me." She cried. "My love never came back home to me!"

The woman closed the last two steps and sat down next to her. She put her arms around her and gave her a hug. "Tell me all about it."

She did.

Her dream had been confusing and very intense, unlike any she had before. She divulged things she had confided to no one, not even her own mother. She told of the dreams she had planned for her life with her fiancé. As they sat on that blistering hot porch on the Saturday afternoon he proposed, they discussed the life they would have together. Their farm would have dairy cows, of course, but he also wanted chickens, a few goats, maybe a pig or two. She wanted a horse—two horses so they could ride together. They couldn't have their own children, but they planned on adopting a boy and a girl to raise as their own. They'd get the children a dog.

She paused here. She said she didn't know why a black dog wearing a red vest came into her mind as she said that.

Her story continued about raising their kids and pushing them on a rope swing hanging from a hackberry tree. She told of her fiancé wanting to drive the tractor with his boy on his lap. She remembered punching his arm and adding the girl could do it, too. Together they laughed, saying their kids would be the happiest children in Oklahoma.

They spent the entire afternoon making their plans until it was time to help her momma get dinner on the table. After prayer, they announced their engagement. She laughed through her tears, remembering her daddy saying he already knew. Her love had asked for his permission to marry his daughter two months earlier in a clandestine phone call. Plus, in all the excitement, she still wore the ring he placed on her hand hours earlier. Her parents gave them both hugs and welcomed the young man from the dairy farm next door to the family. Even her brother was thrilled for them. Breck asked him to be his best man. She cried, unable to speak any further.

Beth did the only thing she could do. She hugged her until she was done crying the pain out of her system. She remembered the effect the bench had on her. After hearing the sad story, she fought back tears herself.

When Sarah had cried out as much as her body could, she sat back and apologized for being so hysterical. She wasn't normally like this.

Beth said she understood and told her the bench had a way of making someone react that way.

Sarah didn't know what she was talking about, but something in the back of her mind agreed with what she was saying.

The man who had been standing at a distance the entire time asked her, "What happened to your fiancé?"

"He was killed overseas on his last tour of duty," she answered. She looked from him to the woman sitting next to her and asked, "Who are you?"

Beth shifted her attention between Harry and Sarah. She said, "We need to tell you some things, and you may think we're crazy."

For the next half hour, she told her everything that had occurred over the last several days. Frequently, Harry interjected a comment. When Beth completed her story, she waited for Sarah to respond.

A familiar voice came from a short distance away before she could answer. "It's all true, Sarah, every word."

* * *

Kourin reached for the doorknob and changed her mind. Instead, she opened her closet door to her left, searching for a light jacket. The New England spring night would be cold, and the thin blouse would do little to cover the chill that would be evident on her chest.

She didn't find what she expected. None of the attire she knew should be there was in the small closet. Not wanting to wake the sleeping ego upstairs, she kept as silent as possible. She found one she could live with wearing and would cover her sufficiently.

She wondered, *Why has my taste in clothes changed so dramatically? What the fuck else has changed?*

She glanced up the stairway to where not-Prince Charming was sleeping. Just the night before, she had walked up those same stairs with Jack. Although it had ended in a heartrending episode with her crying on his shoulder, they had grown closer together. She pictured Jack in her mind and asked herself, *Where are you, Jack Roberts?*

Two sets of keys sat on the credenza against the wall. She grabbed the one Anders had not placed there earlier. She exited her own home, wanting to get as far as away from it as she could.

The keys were to a red BMW. *Figures*, she thought. *Has everything in my life changed?* She looked at her reflection in the rearview mirror. In the safety of her car, she said out loud, "What have you done, Kourin Sanders?" She looked away and started the car. She added, "And how do I make it right?"

There was only one destination in mind as she put distance between herself and a home she did not recognize. She had to return to the terminal. The answers had to be there.

Carlos was on duty at the airport employee parking area. *At least some things haven't changed.*

After some small talk about why she was there so late, she stood a few feet away from him, waiting for the tram. She felt she was being watched and glanced in his direction. He was looking back at her. She asked, "Is there something I can help you with?"

"I'm sorry, but you look so different from usual. I mean not in a bad way, but I don't think I've ever seen you looking . . . looking . . ." he struggled to find the right word.

Kourin finished the sentence for him. "Normal?" she asked.

"Yeah, I guess you could say that," he said as he looked up the road at the approaching tram. He added as she walked toward the slowing vehicle, "Have a good night."

Diric was operating the tram, another thing that hadn't changed. He greeted her in his usual warm Somalia accent. He made small talk, asking why she was there so late, if she thought the weather would turn warmer soon, and if she had a nice opening day. She answered she had some work to do in the store, the warm days would be on them before they knew it, and she wasn't sure about the day.

When the tram stopped near the employee entrance, he said he hoped she would find her happiness today. She thanked him and covered the short distance to the door, peering back toward the tram as she reached the building. Diric gave her a broad smile and a wave before he drove off. She thought, *Considerate of him to make sure I got into the building safely. Nice that some things haven't changed.*

After passing through security, she walked the empty terminal silently toward her store. Her footfalls were barely audible in sneakers, sneakers she had no memory of purchasing, as with the rest of the clothing she wore. Every business she passed had the gate down. The only lighting visible within each was the eerie glow from Fire Exit signs. The terminal was silent, with only the HVAC system humming overhead. Phil came to mind momentarily. She pushed that aside as she had larger worries right now.

She peered through the darkness beyond the gate of her shop. As she had enhanced eyesight earlier, she realized she did not have it now. Her emotions were in check. Although she was apprehensive about the unknown questions swirling through her head, she did not feel the burning in her core. She felt, for lack of a better term, normal as she had said to Carlos—normal yet living someone else's life. As she looked at the emptiness of her store, she thought, *The answers I seek are not in there.* She knew where she needed to go and turned toward the garden.

As she neared the center, she heard voices and stopped in the shadows a short distance away, listening to the conversation Sarah and Beth were having. Sarah was crying and talking about a day in the past when her fiancé proposed to her. By the end of the conversation, Kourin learned this Sarah was the same Sarah from Laurel's story.

Beth then gave her a summary of what she and Harry remembered as the past. She pointed out a few changes, such as the Coffee Bean and not being able to locate their friends. To Sarah's credit, she listened without interruption.

Kourin wondered if Sarah listened because she was interested or because the effect of the bench had not yet worn off. Either way, it felt good to her to hear that she wasn't crazy. Beth recited exactly what she knew to be the correct past. Whatever they were now living was anything but reality.

Beth waited for the blonde on the bench to say something after hearing her rendition of what the world should be.

Kourin interjected, "It's all true, Sarah, every word."

All three at the center bench turned toward her. She moved closer, coming out of the shadows to stand an arm's length from Harry. She added, "I know what you're hearing sounds fantastical, but it is all true."

Harry was the first to address her. "That's a refreshing look for you."

Kourin gazed at him. He seemed older to her and certainly not the crazy, scary person he was in the days before. "So I've heard," she said.

"That look suits you better," he said as he turned back to Sarah. "We need to figure out what the hell is going on here. I thought we all might wake up from this, but now I'm having my doubts."

Sarah sat silently. Her crying had long since ceased. She eyed the surrounding trio, trying to determine if they were insane, and she asked herself if she would wake up soon from this nightmare. When she glanced at her clothing, she noticed she had her flight suit on. She thought, *At least I'm not naked in this dream.*

Kourin asked Harry if he tried calling Jack again.

Harry took out his phone. The call went to voice mail. He shook his head.

She asked him for Jack's number.

They were surprised she didn't already have it. She explained her phone contacts had all changed, including Jack's not being there. She entered Jack's number into her phone. As she typed it, she knew it was the same number she had before but could not recall since, once entered, all she had to do was push a button to text or call him. She tried calling him. It went straight to voice mail, but it reconfirmed that it was his correct number.

Still trying to figure out how to get back to his Christine and looking for any answers he could get, Harry asked Kourin if she had any ideas on how to get back. He even asked her if she could do her magic thing with her eyes.

Kourin almost laughed, but she knew he was serious. She explained she didn't know why her eyes changed color or how to control it. However, she did say she had an idea and asked Sarah and Beth if she could sit on the bench. They obliged.

Sarah considered leaving when she stood up. She had a flight out in the morning, but she would be lying if she said she wasn't a little intrigued by what was happening with these three. She observed the woman she had seen outside the restaurant as she sat on the bench with her phone in hand. Earlier, she hadn't recognized the stunning blonde asking her questions. Now she appeared to be a different person without her makeup and fashionable clothes. In the half light of the garden, she was certain she knew her. She couldn't explain how or where she knew her from, but she knew her. A picture of Jack, whoever he was, came to her mind. She thought, *Maybe there is something to their wacky story.*

On the bench, Kourin closed her eyes, partly because she was self-conscious about them possibly turning emerald green, but also because she wanted to block out distractions. Her plan was to do what she had done before: go back a short time to when she could see Jack. She figured she could get to the time she had already been to in Laurel's office when she ghost kissed him. If she could see him there, maybe she could somehow warn him what was going to happen when they go back to Kourin's teen years or even before that, Mandy's teen years. As she thought about that, she realized, as a timeline it was backwards, but in relation to what they all experienced, it was chronologically correct.

Before she got herself confused, she concentrated on picturing Jack and Laurel's office. She pictured Ubu lifting his paw to her and concentrated on the details. She reasoned if she could visualize it in her head, she could somehow bring herself there.

The familiar heat built up inside her. Her hands went momentarily cold, but she felt them warm back up almost as quickly. She kept her eyes tightly closed and thought of Jack's kiss. Jack's dying image came to mind. She pushed it away and focused on his kiss. She focused on the love they shared, the love she held in her heart for him.

She sensed a noticeable shift in the air and opened her eyes.

In front of her, several feet away, she saw Jack. He was standing with Laurel near the corner of the office. She did it!

She called out to him. No response.

As she watched Jack and his niece, she realized she was in the timeline she knew, not the—whatever it was with the bozo back in her bed. This gave her confidence that whatever the hell was going on, the past, the true past she knew to be real, was still there. She just had to figure out how to make it come back.

The two were talking about a cold spot in the corner. She recalled Jack talking about this moment. This wasn't the time she had focused on, but it would do. This was when the bench sent him partially back in time, but he didn't fully materialize or interact in the timeline. He had been worried about Laurel and ended up here for a few minutes.

A similar thing happened to her when she attempted to manipulate the bench. She had interacted with him and Ubu. The dog had known she was there.

She searched for Ubu. He was sitting beside Laurel, but he was looking directly at where she stood now! She thought, *How does he know I'm here? If I can figure that out, maybe I can get Jack to understand me.*

She called out to Jack again. He didn't respond. She knew touching him wouldn't get the message to him she needed to. She needed to find another way.

It dawned on her that she was clenching her phone in her hand. Well, she held the flip phone from the alternate timeline, but she formed an idea. After flipping the phone open, she pressed the Call button for Jack. He didn't respond. She recalled he told her soon after this he had it on mute in the office.

When the voicemail prompt came up, she left a message. "Jack, it's me Kourin. Jack, something bad is going to happen tomorrow. Mandy and my eyes turn green. We go into the past, and reality is changed. You need to make sure that doesn't happen. Jack, everyone needs to stay away from the bench. I love you!" The phone connection was lost. Kourin watched Jack walk out of the office.

She blinked. In an instant, she saw Harry, Beth, and Sarah looking down at her.

"Well?" asked Harry. "Did it work?"

She answered after taking a moment to collect her thoughts. "Yes, and no. I was back in Laurel's office. The good news is it was the correct timeline, the one we remember. Jack was there with Laurel at the Coffee Bean."

She looked at Sarah and added, "Sorry, I know this is very confusing. I thought since I interacted with Jack before, I could do better this time and actually communicate with him."

"And, did you?" asked Harry.

"Not really. I was invisible to him. He couldn't hear me. I used my phone to call him, but from what I remember happening afterwards, the message he received was barely audible and not much more than static."

"So, it was a waste of time," Harry grumbled.

"No. No, it wasn't," Beth said. All eyes turned to her. She continued, "Look, you went back to an office that doesn't exist right now, right here. That means that reality still exists! If you could sort of be there, maybe there is a way to make things the way they were. We just have to figure out how."

There was silence for nearly a minute. Kourin spoke up. "There was something odd that occurred again this time, as it had the last time. Ubu could see me."

"Too bad you can't speak dog," Harry said.

Beth gave him an annoyed look.

He said, "What? I don't see how Ubu being able to see her helps."

"Unfortunately, I don't either, but it was still weird," said Kourin without adding more.

"Maybe he senses you're there?" Sarah finally added to the conversation. "I mean dogs are supposed to have far better senses than humans. Sight for sure, but they have an incredible sense of smell. Maybe he wasn't seeing you as much as he was smelling you."

"I suppose that is a possibility," Kourin said. "But he seemed to look right at me." She thought about it. "Maybe if I go back there again, I can figure it out."

"To what end?" Harry asked. "I don't see how interacting with the dog is going to prevent us from being here now."

"You're right, Harry. We have to think of another way to get back to where we were." Kourin asked Sarah, "Do you remember anything from before?"

"Before what?"

"True, your current timeline is your reality, but maybe that can help us."

"I don't follow," Sarah said. "I mean you three seem more familiar to me than us just meeting a short time ago, and—" she stopped mid-sentence.

"And what?" asked Harry.

She continued. "When you were just talking about the dog you interacted with, I pictured a black dog with a red service vest. Why does that come to my mind when I don't know what dog you're talking about?"

"That's Ubu!" Beth said. "That is Laurel's dog. Do you remember more about him? Do you remember Laurel or Mandy?"

"The name Mandy rings a bell. I don't know why." She paused, looking away from the others toward the garden. "All of this seems familiar, like a dream."

"Or a memory," said Kourin. "I think you have some memories of how things were. Maybe." She stopped to think. "Before we met you coming out of the restaurant, what were you doing? Were you with someone?"

"I had a glass of wine in front of me. I thought I had been speaking with someone." She thought, *Breck! I was speaking with someone about Breck. But why?*

The others watched her as they could tell she was thinking. Her expression changed to a melancholy one. Kourin rose off the bench. Beth moved closer to Sarah.

Beth said, "Perhaps you should sit down. You look as pale as a ghost." She guided Sarah to the bench and sat down with her. "You remember something, don't you?"

Sarah brought herself out of her memories to glance at Beth beside her. She said, "I remember speaking to someone or more than one . . . yes, two people. We were having a glass of wine. There was a dog . . . a black dog sitting by . . . Laurel. She just learned I am Sarah."

The three looked at each other. Kourin said, "But they already knew your name is Sarah."

"No," said Sarah. "We all just realized I am the Sarah from Laurel's past. I was engaged to Breck, the soldier who died when Laurel was on guard duty." Her expression transformed to one of wide-eyed wonder at the sudden epiphany. She said, "Oh my God! I remember sitting at Luca's with Mandy and Laurel. We were . . . We just came back from . . . from Mandy's past. She was a teenager." She paused for a breath. "We were talking about . . . Laurel wanted to go back and stop the bomber, but if she did—" Sarah stopped. A tear formed under her eye. She blinked, and it traveled down her cheek.

"If she did, what?" asked Harry.

Sad eyes looked up at him. "If she stopped the bomber and Breck came home to me as we had planned," she paused, taking a deep breath. Tears fell from both eyes. "If Breck and I married, I would not have met Jerry. We wouldn't have . . . My two daughters would cease to exist!"

Beth held her for support.

Sarah completed her memory and said, "If Laurel changes what happens, I lose my daughters!"

"Sarah, we won't let that happen," Kourin assured her. "Right now, we don't even know where Laurel is. She didn't open the Coffee Bean." She explained to the others. "I did an online search for her. All I found was an article about her returning home years ago after a suicide bombing incident. There was nothing more about her, no website for the Coffee Bean or anything about her charity for dog rescue and veterans. I also checked for Mandy and found nothing matching her bio. For reasons I can't explain, something is nagging at me about Laurel and especially Mandy. I know Jack is missing, but something tells me the key to this is those two."

Beth said, "When we were with teen Mandy, she said they met the year after we were there. What if they didn't meet? I know—" She looked at Harry and amended her statement, "We know Mandy is a big part of Laurel's life, especially when she came back from the service. Mandy was the friend she needed to get through serious bouts of depression. A couple years ago, Laurel got Ubu who helped bring her the rest of the way to where she is today or rather where she should be. Maybe something got messed up when we were in Mandy's past?"

All four sat quietly for a few moments. A sound came from the plants to Kourin's right. All heads turned in that direction. Plants could be seen moving slightly.

"Oh, oh," said Harry.

"No. I think we're on to something here," Kourin said. She looked at Harry and asked, "What color are my eyes?"

Harry looked into Kourin's eyes and said, "Emerald green."

"I thought so. I can feel emotions building inside of me. Each time that has happened we . . . Well, I'm not sure how to describe it. We went elsewhere." She paused, looking at Harry again, and asked, "You don't see the golden ring, do you?"

"No, just the green," he answered. "What are you getting at?" He was getting animated thinking this may be the breakthrough he had been searching for to get back to his Christine.

"I'm not 100 percent sure of this, but hear me out. Prior to us going back to . . . to when I was abducted, things were weird, but the timeline was still the one we all knew. Right?" Without waiting for an answer, she continued, "There were certainly odd things, but as far as we know, we had some visions from the past, Mandy saw a future vision, she saved Miguel, we all traveled back to my baby's birth for a moment, and then we all traveled to Mandy's teen years. Right after that, we traveled to my abduction."

Harry interrupted. "Not all of us."

"Right," Kourin agreed. "Us three and Jack went there." She asked Harry, "You never saw the others there, Shannon, Laurel, Mandy?"

"No, not them or Joneal and Wren." He looked at Beth. "But we didn't really have time to search for them, either. We don't know for sure they were not there. They could have been."

"We weren't," Sarah said.

All eyes turned toward her. She had calmed herself down and was listening to the conversation.

"You can remember?" Beth asked beside her.

"Sort of. I mean it all seems like a dream, but I recall sitting in someone's living room with . . . Mandy . . . and Laurel. Mandy's eyes turned . . ." She looked at Kourin. "Her eyes turned emerald green!"

Kourin nodded but didn't speak.

"And they had a golden ring. The dog placed his head on her lap. We . . . we . . . Next we were here! I was sitting here. Mandy was next to me. Laurel and Ubu, where you are." She indicated Kourin and Harry. "We didn't go wherever you are talking about. We came back here. Three others joined us, but then they left. We went to . . . Luca's to have a drink. We talked and . . . cried. Then I was alone."

16

CHOICES

Kourin said, "I think you returned with all the others when I went with Jack, Harry, and Beth to my past." She looked around the garden. "Somehow—and I don't know why—Mandy and I are connected in the same way. When Jack jumped on the clown and I got hysterical at the sub shop, it sounds like Mandy also got roused up. She brought you back home, while we went to my past."

"Why would some of us go with you and some with Mandy?" Harry asked. He saw the key to getting back to Christine was close at hand. "Why did Beth and I go with you instead of back here?"

Beth said, "Maybe because we were with her in Laurel's office when it originally happened?"

"What about Laurel and the dog?" asked Harry. "Why didn't they come with us instead of going back home?"

Sarah answered, "She and Ubu were with Mandy when her eyes changed. Laurel was holding Mandy's hand, and the dog had his head against her leg. Maybe being so close to her changed something?"

Harry said, "That has to be it. When the others went to Mandy's teen years, they weren't anywhere near Laurel's office. She must have brought them there somehow. When she had another . . . What do we call it, episode? Whatever it was. Her eyes changed color again and returned everyone to where they belonged. Laurel and Ubu went along for the ride. Beth, Jack, and I went elsewhere because . . .?"

Kourin finished his reasoning. "Because I was the one who brought you to Mandy's teen years. I don't know how or even why we would end up there, though. I certainly didn't know Mandy back then."

Beth said, "You didn't, but Laurel did. But she didn't know her until a year later. That makes little sense."

"Maybe it wasn't Laurel. Maybe I'm somehow connected to Mandy?" Kourin pondered.

"That's it!" said Sarah. "I remember something Laurel was saying when we . . . when I guess we were at Luca's. She said you two were connected. I don't know why she thought that, but she definitely said both your eyes turned the same color and then something would happen. She said it happened at the same time."

Harry asked, "What does all this mean? She's not here now, so if you need a connection to make it happen, we're screwed."

"There has to be something we're overlooking," said Kourin. "I refuse to accept the things as they are."

She looked at each person, her thoughts churning. *Beth and Harry were the same as they were when they started the day. They apparently had no change in their appearance nor what they remember. Sarah had changed completely—well, almost. She was dressed in her uniform, which she did not have on in teen Mandy's world. Her memory was changed. She still knew . . . her family was the same, but she didn't know Laurel or Mandy.*

Kourin knew she was on to something. She asked, "Sarah, what do you remember from the last few days? Not the fuzzy memories. What do you recall happening in this terminal?"

Harry said, "What are you thinking?"

Kourin answered Harry, but she kept her eye on Sarah. "I have an idea. Sarah?"

"Well, two days ago, I first visited the terminal to see what it looked like. I had some time between flights, so I went to the café for a coffee. After that, I flew out. I didn't return until . . . I returned to Manchester having to cover someone else's shift. This evening I must have come back to have dinner at Luca's."

Kourin asked, "Why did you come back?"

"I don't remember," she answered. "I guess I just must have been hungry and wanted to try the new restaurant."

Kourin said, "It's okay. That part isn't the important piece."

Beth asked, "What do you mean?"

Kourin didn't answer Beth. Instead, she asked Sarah, "When you went to the café, did you speak with anyone?"

"Um, I ordered my coffee, so I spoke to the guy who took my order."

"Anyone else?"

"No, I don't think so," she said. "I got my coffee, sat at a table for a while, and left to catch my flight."

Harry asked, "Kourin, what are you thinking? What does it matter if she spoke with anyone?"

She faced him and answered, "Because she never met Mandy. In the café two days ago, they met and became friends."

Harry could see her eyes, the green becoming more intense. Even from a distance, he could see a golden ring beginning to show around the pupil.

Kourin continued without interruption. "I've been so caught up in trying to find Jack, hoping what happened to him didn't really occur, that I've missed the biggest alteration that has happened, a change that I caused."

She turned away toward the plants. In the direction she gazed, first one plant moved, then another, and another. She spoke again. "Sarah said it. If Laurel went into the past and changed the outcome by stopping the bomber, Breck lives and returns home. They marry. Her two daughters cease to exist."

Within seconds, in a wave around them, all the plants swayed as if in a light wind.

"I altered the future."

Beth asked, as they remained wary of the surrounding plants, "What's changed, Kourin? We've been with you. What could you have done?"

Kourin turned to look at the others. Her eyes were brilliant emerald green. Vivid golden rings circled her pupils. She answered, "In trying to save Jen and Jack, I . . ." Tears trickled down her face. "I changed my past. I didn't mean to. It just happened when Jack went back with me. When you came back, it changed everything."

"What changed?" asked Harry.

Through teary eyes, she stated what she knew in her heart to be true. "I caused my daughter never to have been born!"

She broke down crying. Beth and Sarah rose off the bench and went to each side of her. The surrounding air seemed to shimmer from the immense heat radiating off her. They gently guided her to sit on the bench. Sarah stood off to the side.

Beth sat beside her. She kept hold of Kourin's right hand even though it felt hot to the touch. She asked, "What do you mean your daughter was never born? How do you know?"

Kourin wiped her runny nose and one side of her face in a very unladylike fashion. She used the sleeve of her jacket, but in her state, she didn't care. She looked at Beth, not with anger or any emotion she could quantify. Despite the overpowering sorrow, she felt a sense of numbness inside.

After several moments passed, she replied, "When Jack and you arrived at the house, it altered what happened. The asshole was killed before he . . ." She couldn't finish her sentence.

"It's okay. If it's too painful, you don't have to tell us," said Beth, attempting to console her.

Kourin looked into her eyes. Beth gasped even though she knew what was there. Up close, the vivid emerald eyes with golden rings were even more frightening than from several feet away.

"I have to say it out loud," Kourin said. She took a deep breath. "I need to keep control." She breathed again. "When we went back to when I was abducted, we changed what happened. The day you were there was the first day I was abducted. Jen was . . . She was raped beside me and strangled to death."

Kourin breathed for several seconds to regain her composure. "It wasn't until the next morning that I was raped."

She stopped and took deep breaths for over twenty seconds. "That afternoon, the police and FBI surrounded the house and eventually killed the guy and rescued me."

Unable to control herself any longer, she wept.

Beth instinctively gave her a hug. She could feel tremendous heat radiating off her. She said, "That was a long time ago. We're here for you now."

With tears in her eyes, Kourin pulled herself gently away from her. "But that's just it. It wasn't long ago. It was just a few hours ago, and now it has changed. The police arrived a day early and killed the asshole. The next thing I remember after Jack . . . died, I was back here. It's logical to assume they rescued me and Jen. I was never raped. I didn't get pregnant and have my daughter."

Harry said, "I don't see how that changed what's happened here?"

Kourin turned to Harry and said, "I never gave birth to my daughter. She never grew up to be in this world."

As Kourin spoke, Beth felt a chill come over her as the reality of her implication sunk in.

Harry saw astonishment on Beth's face and asked, "What the hell am I missing?"

Beth slowly said, pondering the words she spoke as she said them, "Harry, Kourin's baby was never born. She never met her best friend to help her through her troubles and with her business. The woman didn't meet a stranger and become friends. She didn't sit on this very bench and save another's life with a freakin' gift card." She gazed into Kourin's eyes, saying, "Mandy is Kourin's daughter!"

Harry's and Sarah's eyes widened, and their mouths hung open in amazement. Neither could speak to the revelation.

Kourin placed her hands on her face and sobbed.

After a minute, Harry asked, "How is that possible? Doesn't Mandy's mother live in Dover or Newmarket? Someplace up there?"

Beth said, "She does, but something few people know is Mandy was adopted. I only found about it after my Tom passed away. Her mother, Diane, came to the funeral with Mandy and Laurel. When the two of them were off on their own, Diane sat with me and Cathy, my friend from the hospital. We talked. The conversation turned to my three children and how they were holding up. I remember saying they were close and had each other."

She paused for a few moments before continuing, "Diane said it was hard on her when her husband passed. She only had Mandy, but together they got through. Fortunately, Mandy had Laurel and another girl from school. Now I think that must have been Fara. Anyway, in the conversation and consoling, she mentioned Mandy was adopted when she was a newborn. After her husband passed and she felt Mandy was old enough to understand, she confided the truth of her birth."

"How come I never heard of this before?" Harry asked.

"It seemed like a personal matter within their family. As far as anyone is concerned, Diane is Mandy's mother." Beth realized what she had just said and turned to Kourin. She said, "Oh, I'm sorry. I shouldn't have said that."

Kourin quietly replied, "It's okay. I'm happy my daughter grew up in such a wonderful home with a loving family. But now I've fucked it all up!" She wept again.

Harry gave Kourin a look, but he held his tongue. Instead, he asked Beth, "So, I'm guessing Laurel must know?"

"I'm sure she must, but she has never mentioned it," she answered. She looked at Kourin. "This must be very difficult for you, now knowing your daughter was here all the time."

Kourin returned her gaze.

Even though Kourin's eyes shined bright emerald green, Beth did not shy away from them this time.

"I wish I had known sooner," Kourin said, diverting her eyes from Beth and observing the plants beyond. They continued to sway and move. She looked down at the bench she sat upon, placing both her hands on the wood on either side of her, a revelation coming to her as she held her hands against the well-worn wood.

"I know what I need to do," she said with a newfound determination. "I'm going to go back there and reset the past to what originally happened." She beheld the shocked faces around her and said, "I have to become pregnant."

Beth suddenly rose off the bench and stood beside Harry. She told her how ridiculous and dangerous her idea was. Not only would she be subjecting herself to the horrors she had already faced once, there was no guarantee the outcome would be the same. There was a possibility the abductor would kill her.

Sarah watched Kourin's face as she heard Beth's words. She saw a determination there that read as a mind made up and thought of a different approach. She sat down beside the woman with green eyes.

When Beth exhausted herself while Harry stood beside her, Sarah saw an opening to voice her thoughts. She took hold of Kourin's right hand as she spoke. "Kourin, we've only just met, or we met a few days ago. Right now, I don't know, but I feel your pain in losing your daughter. Somewhere in my mind is a hurt I felt at realizing I could lose my two daughters if Breck came home when he was supposed to. Just thinking about it, even if it was just a shitty dream, makes me terrified. I would do anything to protect my children. I am sure that is what you feel right now. You want to protect Mandy."

She paused to separate her next statement from this truth. She said, "Have you considered what alternative path you just created?"

"What do you mean?" Kourin asked.

"Jen. You said it is likely she had been rescued with you. That would mean she lived her life, a life she otherwise didn't have." Sarah stopped to let Kourin ponder her words.

Several seconds later, Kourin said, "So, you're saying if I go back and change things to how they should have occurred, Jen doesn't have that life?"

Sarah nodded her head.

Kourin pulled out her phone. She tapped the screen and typed on the silent pad. She tapped some more.

Sarah saw a frustrated look on her face. From the plants around the bench, she heard rustling. She chanced a look at the garden beyond the woman sitting beside her and saw movement as if the plants were agitated as well. She returned to observe her searching for something on her phone.

Kourin silently read her screen, and then she abruptly closed her flip phone. The plants around the courtyard were all moving, but after several seconds, they calmed down. Yet, they never completely stopped.

Sarah asked, "Did you find something?"

"I searched for Jen Knowles," answered Kourin. "It took a while, but eventually I found her under a married name. Her Facebook page lists her as married with two children. There are many family photo posts."

Beth said, "We can't take that away from her."

Kourin looked up at Beth. At first, she was angry, but she calmed down, knowing Beth was right. She thought of the child that had lain next to her over thirty years earlier, the child that was raped and murdered as she did nothing but cry.

The plants in the area once again became agitated.

Kourin thought, *I cannot take those beautiful children away from someone who suffered so much. There has to be a way. How can I save Jen and her children and still bring back my daughter? If I go back and let things happen as they originally did, Jen dies and I suffer, but my daughter lives. There has to be something I—*

Kourin stopped in thought. She looked at the surrounding faces and thought of Jack resting his head on her teen body, his failed rescue attempt.

She continued her thought, *Maybe I alone can't change what happened, but with some help, we can change the outcome.*

To the group, she announced, "I have a new plan."

17

SACRIFICE

Kourin laid out her idea.

All three took turns providing a dozen significant and sound reasons it would fail.

Kourin was no fool and knew well the danger she was putting everyone in. As each spoke their piece, she listened, her eyes moving from one person to the next as she formulated her rebuttal. She needed their aid to improve the odds of success, but she was already determined to take this course of action, with or without them.

After going back and forth for several minutes, Harry was the first to cave in. In his mind, he saw this as a perfect test run for discovering a way to return to his wife.

Sarah next agreed to the plan and identified with Kourin's feelings about losing her daughter. As a mother, she would do anything to save her own two daughters. She accepted Kourin would stop at nothing to do the same. Provided with a path to save Mandy, she reasoned Kourin would risk herself no matter what the cost. Alone, her chances of success were slim, if not impossible.

Beth was the sole dissenter. Begrudgingly, she eventually agreed. The last reason presented to her and what ultimately changed her mind was Kourin flat out stating, if they did nothing, Mandy wasn't the only one no longer existing. Jack was also likely deceased, having died in the last episode. If he had survived, he should have reappeared in the terminal. Although Beth had hoped he was somewhere here, her intuition told her otherwise. There really was no alternative to not correcting the timeline.

With the quartet ready to enact Kourin's plan, she ran through it one last time. Beth objected, wanting to find another way. Harry assured her, if she ever wanted to see Jack and Mandy again, they had to follow Kourin's plan. As appalling as it was, it was what had to be done.

In the end, they all agreed. Each gave Kourin a hug.

Beth was the first and wished her Godspeed.

Sarah wished her luck.

Harry was hesitant to touch Kourin, but she went to him, wrapping her arms around him. He gently returned the hug. When she pulled back, he momentarily thought he saw an older version of Mandy in front of him. He said, "Take care of yourself. I promise I'll be there on time."

She whispered, "Thank you, Harry."

Kourin sat in the center of the bench alone, placing her hands on her lap. The others held hands directly in front of her, forming a semicircle with Beth in the middle. Harry and Sarah, on each end, held a corner of the bench. They were uncertain of how the bench operated and didn't want to risk Kourin going into the past without their planned support. They hoped having contact with the bench would improve the likelihood it would actually work.

Kourin closed her eyes. She thought of Jack, but she knew that wasn't where she needed to be right now. Instead, she thought of waking up on the bed with Jen in the dark next to her. If she could control her entry to the correct time, she could manipulate the outcome. It was imperative to her plan.

Heat roiled inside her. She felt the pain and anguish building as she thought back to that fateful time in her life. Her mind slipped to thinking of Jack. She forced herself to push that aside and concentrated on visualizing the dark bedroom she had seen with her enhanced eyesight. As her fear built, so did her determination to fix the timeline and save the people she loved.

As she built up her inner turmoil, the plants in the garden moved chaotically as if a tornado were at the center of the courtyard. The trio held hands and maintained contact with the bench. All three had their eyes closed, afraid of the unknown.

After several moments, Sarah and Harry had a lack of feeling the wooden bench in one hand while the other held Beth's. Harry opened his eyes. He was at the motel where the FBI had their room and pseudo field office. Still holding a hand, he turned toward Beth. She returned his gaze. Beyond her stood Sarah, a dazed expression on her face.

He surveyed the immediate area. Fortunately, they were alone, standing in a parking spot. Several steps away were the motel rooms. They all looked alike, and judging from the distance to the office to his left, they were in front of the room they had been brought to before.

He said, "We should find someplace to wait. We can't stand out here for an hour." A short distance away, he spied a small diner. "Let's go there. We should be able to keep an eye out for the FBI or police from there."

Still holding Beth's hand, he took a step, but he felt resistance. He stopped. She was watching Sarah. He said, "We need to go. If we're standing here and the FBI sees us, the timing will be off for Kourin's plan."

Beth said, still looking at Sarah and ignoring Harry, "Are you okay?" She still held Sarah's hand.

Sarah replied, as she pulled her hand from Beth's, "You guys talked about it, but I guess I thought it wasn't really going to happen. Where are we?"

Harry spoke up. "We're back when Kourin was a teen, and if we don't get out of here, we're going to screw up everything. Beth, we need to go."

He released Beth's hand and began walking toward the diner. Beth interlocked her right arm into Sarah's left to help guide her where they needed to go.

As they neared the diner entrance, a Fairfield police car drove down the street. They recognized the officer driving: Wes. He looked at them as he drove past, but he continued on down the street.

Once inside, they chose a table near the window with a clear view of the motel. After ordering two coffees and a tea, they checked the time. They had one hour before they had to alert the police to the location where Kourin should be.

Harry tapped his right-hand fingers, pinky to thumb, over and over on the table. It would have been an annoyance for the other two, but they had their own nervous actions they attended to. Beth stirred her tea every twenty seconds. Sarah tapped her right leg on the floor while she held on to her coffee mug with both hands as if someone were trying to steal it. All knew the importance of timing this correctly.

Their plan was to save Mandy and Jack. However, Kourin was very much putting her own life in jeopardy. There was a strong possibility all of them could cease to exist in what they knew as their timeline. All they could do was wait and try not to think about what was happening to Kourin.

* * *

Teen Kourin woke to the same scenario she had found herself in a short time ago and a very long time ago. Her right arm was handcuffed to the bed. She had on the NKOTB tee shirt and shorts. She checked next to her, seeing the silhouette of a body lying there: Jen. Her breathing was raspy, and she stirred slightly. Kourin's plan had a higher possibility of success if Jen would be asleep when the abductor came in.

Kourin thought, *Officer Mike Mersfelder, the asshole cop who was at every event held at the school. He even spoke at the assembly earlier in the year on Safety Day. No one suspected him. Everyone trusted him. Even I did the day he abducted me. When I was walking to school that misty morning, he stopped to offer me a ride. When I hesitated and distanced myself from him, he grabbed my arm and hit me on the side of my head.* Kourin felt the bump on her head with her left hand.

She heard Jen move and let out a slight groan. *Poor kid. She must have been fooled, just like I was. This time, though, things will be different. Hang in there, Jen. I will not let him hurt you anymore.*

As if on cue, Kourin heard a vehicle pull up outside the covered window. In the silence, the front door unlocked and opened. Muted footsteps could be heard. Silence. The sound of a flushing toilet. A minute later, the bedroom door creaked open, and a thin ray of light pierced the darkness.

Teen Kourin shuddered. Doubt entered her mind. She felt heat building inside her—despair, anger, fear. Kourin fought to overcome the emotions. Over and over, she told herself she needed to follow the plan, her plan. Lives depended on it. The life of her daughter depended on it.

With her enhanced vision, she saw a man enter the bedroom. He closed the door, but it didn't close all the way. A sliver of light shone through hitting the bed, cutting across Jen's legs and over Kourin's torso. She watched him remove his clothes.

When this happened thirty-two years ago, she couldn't see what she was witnessing now. Back then, she was crying and begging to be let go, not knowing it was Officer Mersfelder for certain until he told her to shut her mouth. She had recognized his voice.

When he had been at her school, some girls had made comments about how cute he was in his uniform with a goatee. No one knew the monster he truly was.

She thought, as she struggled to control her emotions, *Thirty years ago, in the next hour, Jen was raped and strangled to death next to me in total darkness while I lay next to her, helpless and crying.*

Kourin concentrated on what was taking place here and now. *This time it will be different. This time I save Jen.*

She watched the demon slowly step toward the bed. Her eyes shaped everything in shades of gray. His erection was clearly visible as he moved to Jen's side of the bed, reaching out to her.

She remembered this was when she cried out to be let go and he threatened her, confirming his identity. This time, she would take control of the situation.

In a shaky, barely audible voice, Jen told him to stop. She couldn't take anymore. In the twilight-like shadows, the demon replied that she'd be free after one more time.

Kourin had forgotten about that comment, her forty-six-year-old brain in a teen body now realizing what he meant by being free. A chill ran down her spine. She clamped down on her emotions. She had to maintain control.

Teen Kourin said, "Mike, why don't you leave Jen alone and come over here?" Her insides churned, but she had to go through with this.

He said, "Your time is coming, sweetie. I have some unfinished business I need to take care of."

"I'm sure you do, but I can show you a real good time." She saw him look over at her. She kept her head out of the ray of light, not wanting him to see the fear on her face.

He caressed Jen's side as she lay. She did her best to back away from him and cried out again that she couldn't take anymore.

Kourin had to convince him, as much as it sickened her to do so. "Leave her. I'm right here." She paused, not wanting to say the next line, but she had to keep him from hurting Jen. "I really want to make you happy. I'll do anything for you."

That got his attention.

He pulled away from Jen, but he wasn't convinced. He had his mind set on finishing the girl he had abducted days earlier before enjoying the new one, just as he had before.

Kourin almost had him and needed to convince him to leave Jen alone. Her life depended on it.

She observed him look back and forth at the outlines of the two girls on the bed. As much as it pained her to say, she added, "I need to feel you inside me." She paused, almost in tears, as the words came out. "Please. I've never been with a man."

The demon walked around the bed to her side. She was petrified. It took all her strength to control her emotions, with fear being at the top. Now would not be the time to suddenly find herself back on the bench.

The light shining through the bedroom door ran from her left hip across her right breast. She watched his hand glide over one breast to the other one. She shivered.

Fear dictated she back away as Jen had done and scream out for help. Instead, she bit the inside of her lip to stop herself from losing control.

She let him touch her. She needed him to. Her plan depended on him being interested in her instead of Jen. She just hoped the others would be on time to save them.

The demon ripped her tee shirt and bra off her body, tearing it away without having to remove the handcuffs. Kourin's plan had anticipated he would have to free her arm, allowing her to attack him afterwards. That part of the plan was already not going to happen.

She stifled a scream when rough fingers glided along her thigh. He pulled down her shorts and panties in one swift movement. She kept her legs together. He forced his hand between them, touching her. With panic raging inside her, she forced herself to let out a fake soft moan.

She needed this to happen as much as it repulsed and frightened her. Teen Kourin required becoming pregnant so her daughter could live. A tear escaped her eye as hands touched her. She bit the inside of her lip until she could taste blood. She told herself it would soon all be over. Tears escaped her emerald eyes.

* * *

A black SUV turned into the motel parking lot. Harry watched the special agents exit the vehicle and enter their room. He checked the time. He told the others it was time to go and paid the check with a twenty-dollar bill, leaving the difference for a sizable tip.

As they walked back to the motel, it occurred to Harry that he forgot to check the date on the bill he used. He glanced back at the diner and didn't see anyone chasing after him, so he figured it would be okay. He thought it would be ironic if, instead of rescuing Kourin, they all got arrested for forgery by the FBI.

As they neared the rear end of the black SUV, a Fairfield police car pulled into the motel lot and parked in the space on the other side. It was Wes, Officer Wright.

Beth said, "Hello, Officer."

"Good day, ma'am," he replied. "Is there something I can help you with?" He scrutinized each of them.

Beth glanced at Harry. He gave a slight nod. She said, "We have some information about the kidnapping. We were just going to tell the FBI." She looked at the motel door and back at Wes. "But we can tell you."

She told the officer the description of a suspicious van and where it was located, using the address from the last episode. A lot hinged on things being the same now as they were then. If not, Kourin was in huge trouble.

"We should tell the FBI," Officer Wright said.

Harry interrupted. "Yes, we should, but maybe you should check it out first to make sure the van is still there. You could then call for backup, making sure the van doesn't leave before the FBI arrives."

He looked at the motel door. "I suppose we should be sure. They got mad at me the other day when I thought I saw something that turned out to be nothing." He thought for a moment. "I think you're right." He turned to get into his car.

The others all opened doors to go with him.

Officer Wright asked, "What are you doing?"

Beth said, "You need us to identify the van. We won't be in your way."

He looked at Harry and Sarah, deciding she had a good point. They all got into the car. Harry rode in front, with the ladies in the back.

Wes drove the same roads as he did with Harry, Beth, and Jack. This time, he went at a slower but determined pace, which Harry appreciated.

By Harry's estimation, they were closing in on Kourin's timeline. He was relieved when Officer Wright showed up. One of the big caveats to Kourin's plan was convincing the FBI to drop everything and rush over to save her. Harry had argued with her about the possibility they would question Harry and the others for some time before acting, putting her in jeopardy. When Wes showed up, Harry recalled him wanting action and not just being a tool for the FBI to use at their whim. He played on that to get him to agree, keeping Kourin's timeline intact.

As they neared the address, Harry could see the van parked out front. He breathed a sigh of relief. If it wasn't there, they would have been screwed. Harry suggested blocking the exit with the police car, as Jack had suggested before.

Wes agreed. It would not be a good idea to let the van get away if it was part of the kidnapping.

Harry saw the license plate was the same as before. This time, however, it had no relevance in convincing Officer Wright this van had been used in an abduction. He needed to put the second part of Kourin's plan into motion. He looked back at Sarah. It was her turn.

Sarah said, "That's the van I saw."

Officer Wright asked, "What did you see?"

"Well, I wasn't certain, but I'm pretty sure I saw a man grab someone and throw them inside, slamming the door closed."

"Why didn't you call the police?" Officer Wright asked.

"I wasn't certain of what I saw, but now, I'm sure."

Harry could tell the cop wasn't convinced of that argument. He needed to do something. He said, "Maybe you should call it in. If you're right, you'll need backup."

"And if it's nothing, they'll have my ass in a sling," he replied. "I'm gonna check it out first." He got out of the car and walked over to the van. He circled it, looking inside and evidently seeing nothing useful.

Harry hadn't counted on this. The last time Wes confronted the abductor, he was shot. Harry had to think of something to get the officer to call for the FBI.

As if Beth was reading Harry's mind, she said, "The police need to get in the house and save Kourin. We're wasting time."

Harry opened his door and got out. Beth could not open hers, so he did. He went around and opened Sarah's side. As he did, Officer Wright had completed his circle of the van.

Harry walked over to him and said, "Maybe we should check inside." Harry wasn't the bravest man in the world, but he knew if they didn't get into the house to save Kourin, everything would go sideways.

"We can't go in," he said. "We don't have a search warrant."

* * *

Kourin had endured the most traumatic experience of her life for a second time. Through the pain, she kept her emotions in check. Twice she screamed he was hurting her. Both times, she received a whack on the left side of her head.

For the rest of the ordeal, she bit the inside of her lip, partly to keep from being struck again and partly because of knowing, if she let her emotions flare up too early, she wouldn't be impregnated before somehow being sent back to the bench and garden. Her plan depended on precise timing. Otherwise, all this agony would be for naught.

She felt the demon's penis rub against her thigh. Instead of screaming out and fighting her attacker as she had years ago, to no avail, she instead allowed him to violate her. Her emotions were tumultuous, yet the memory of Mandy's glowing face stayed at the forefront. She was determined to save her daughter.

After several horrifying minutes, the monster ejaculated inside her.

When the demon was finished molesting her, he rolled off her side of the bed and headed over to Jen. She didn't know what he intended to do and feared for her. He touched her naked side as he had before. She whimpered.

Teen Kourin cried out the only thing that came to mind. She pleaded with him to do her again.

He paused for a moment and told her they had plenty of time in the coming days for the fun he planned for her. Right now, he was going to finish what he had intended to do today with Jen and grabbed the child's right arm. She whimpered.

Kourin heard a car pull up out front. The cavalry had arrived!

The demon went to the darkened window, moving the blind slightly to peer out. He swore under his breath, "What the fuck is Wes doing here?"

She had to bite the inside of her lip again to keep from screaming for help. The metallic-tasting substance pooled in her mouth, causing her to swallow. She watched the devil pull on his pants, leaving his shirt hanging on the bedpost. He thankfully exited the room.

* * *

Harry looked back at Beth and Sarah from the side of the van. They stood on the passenger side of the police car, remembering what had occurred last time. Both had concerned expressions.

Harry said, "We can knock and see who answers. You don't need a search warrant just to ask a few questions." He knew who was likely to answer—the kidnapper.

The officer walked over to the front door. Harry, a step behind him, said, "We should be careful."

The cop turned to him and said, "You shouldn't be here at all." He looked to see where the two ladies were. They had ducked down behind the car. "Why don't you wait with them?"

As he said that, the door opened. A shirtless man with a goatee stood in the doorway.

"Mike, what are you doing here?" Officer Wright asked.

"This is my parents' place. They left it to me," he replied. "I know why I'm here. Why are you?"

Harry noted the man in the doorway had his right hand hidden behind the doorjamb. He knew from before he was holding a gun.

Harry slid over to Officer Wright's right so the officer was between the man and himself. He didn't have any intention of winding up like Jack.

Officer Wright said, "We had a report of a van used in a possible abduction." He looked back at the van, taking his eyes off his fellow officer. "I can see now there's been a mistake."

He turned back toward the shirtless man in the doorway, a gun pointed straight at him. Officer Wright had no choice but to hand over his own revolver to his fellow officer when requested.

The gun was waved threateningly toward the doorway. Mike escorted Wes and Harry inside. With the barrel of the gun used as a pointer toward handcuffs hanging on a coat hook by the door, he told Wes to handcuff himself to Harry.

Mike gave the outside a quick glance and shut the door. Once fully inside, he told his fellow officer to use his own set of handcuffs to secure themselves to the radiator inside the bedroom. Once completed, he searched Wes and removed his set of handcuff keys, placing them in his own front pants pocket.

18

FAIRFIELD'S FINEST: GOOD & EVIL

From behind the police car, out of sight, Sarah peeked around the corner and saw the cop and Harry at gunpoint. She pulled back, hiding herself. When she looked again, the door was closed.

They had to do something, or this would not end well. Kourin's plan had gone horribly wrong. Instead of the two girls inside being saved, two additional people were taken hostage, with Harry being one of them. Sarah assessed the situation. She knew how to defend herself, but the sight of an armed assailant made her realize that a frontal attack would be too risky.

Beth interrupted Sarah's thoughts, saying they needed to contact the FBI. With no cell phone service, she proposed using the police car radio to call for help. She opened the front passenger door. Wes had left the key in the ignition, providing power in the dashboard. Beth ignored all the extra buttons and concentrated on the radio area. Fortunately, it was rather intuitive. She placed a frantic call for help.

On the other end of the call was a very confused chief of police, Dave. He demanded to know where Officer Wright was.

Beth quickly told him he was taken captive by the kidnapper along with Harry, her friend. Dave began asking more questions, but Beth shut him down. She told him to get off his ass, contact the FBI at the motel, and get here now!

She gave him the address and told him she had to go as they were in danger where they were.

While Beth was in the car calling for help, Sarah watched the front door through the open door over the dashboard. She didn't see any movement. She glanced from Beth to the front door several times. The door remained closed.

Beth ended her call. Sarah retreated so she could depart the car and they could secure a safe haven while waiting for the FBI. As Beth clambered partially out of the car, Sarah's back was to the goateed man who had a gun trained on her.

The half-dressed man said, "And what do we have here?"

Sarah snapped her head around, seeing the revolver pointed in their direction. She fell back onto her butt. Beth stood up as she completed exiting the car.

With the gun pointed at Sarah, the man said, "Get up and keep your hands where I can see them."

She stood up and gave a brief thought of rushing the guy. If she had been alone, she would have tried it, but with Beth beside her, it was far too risky.

The man said, "Now, ladies, let's all go into the house, shall we?"

They looked at each other, trying to figure out another option.

The man said, "Move!"

Both ladies had their hands halfway raised as they walked to the front door. "Get inside," Mike commanded and added, "You didn't think to keep an eye on the back door, did ya'? Stupid bitches."

Beth, her heart racing, took the lead with Sarah trailing three steps behind. The memory of Jack and Wes being shot the last time they were here came to her. Even though they were stuck in the back of the cop car and couldn't do anything, she and Harry saw it all. It was shocking to see Jack being shot and not being able to help him. This time, she could move. She thought, *I have to do something!*

Sarah watched Beth walking slowly into the house, suspecting she was trying to come up with a way out of this situation the same as her. There was an open door to the left. It was dark inside, but she could hear whimpering emanating from within.

Mike directed them to enter the dark room.

Sarah felt the muzzle of the revolver against her back, putting the assailant within striking distance. In front of her, Beth moved to the left. Beyond her, Sarah could make out a bed with possibly two figures lying on it. She thought, *That must be Kourin on the bed.* Beth was to the left. On the right, she saw Harry and Wes standing handcuffed together. In the light from the doorway, she could see they were attached to another handcuff that was fastened to a large radiator. Sarah thought, *It's now or never.*

Kourin watched from the bed. She had difficulty seeing out of her left eye, having been struck near there twice while the demon brutally violated her. Even so, she had no trouble following what was happening in the dim light. Not wanting to antagonize the rapist, she kept silent while Jen sobbed next to her.

Sarah surveyed the room and suddenly spun herself around, grabbing the gunman's right arm and aiming the gun away from her. With her right hand, she jabbed him in the throat and pushed her weight against him, causing him to fall back against the door frame.

Beth screamed and ducked toward the bed area.

Mike brought the gun back around, being stronger than Sarah, and pulled the trigger. The gun went off, missing her.

The training she had undergone came back to her as she remembered how to successfully subdue a hijacker. She courageously fought to seize the weapon from him.

Unfortunately for her, Mike was a trained police officer and recognized what she was attempting to do. He forcefully pushed her away from him, making her stumble back.

She gripped his arms, pulling him with her away from the doorway and further to his right, close to where the two men were handcuffed.

He brought up his gun to shoot her and was grappled from behind by Wes, holding both his arms securely against his body. He attempted to do a reverse head butt, but he couldn't connect.

Wes was an ex-military police veteran. He had been surprised outside, but now he was ready for a fight, even being handcuffed by one hand.

Sarah looked for something to help her subdue Mike, and the glint of the metal lamp on the bureau caught her eye. She grabbed it and swung it at his head.

He managed to squeeze the trigger of the gun once more before the lamp struck him, but the shot flew past her. He went limp. His body slid to the floor.

Wes grabbed the revolver from his hand. He searched the unconscious man's pocket and found a set of keys. He unlocked the handcuff on his wrist, and then he unlocked Harry's without looking at him. In a kneeling posture, he rolled the unconscious man onto his stomach and bound his arms with the handcuffs. He then checked to see if his fellow officer still had a pulse. He did.

He saw a light switch by the doorway and flipped it up. Nothing happened, surmising the lamp the woman had used had been the light source. He moved over to the window, pushing open the drapes and allowing a flood of light to enter the room.

Wes turned to look at the bed. He saw two badly beaten nude teenage girls handcuffed to the metal headboard. The closest girl was not moving. He checked her for a pulse, and when he touched her, she moaned, "No more." He quickly unlocked her handcuff.

Kourin watched Wes open the blinds and check on Jen. After she moaned, teen Kourin said to Officer Wright, "She'll be okay. We're all going to be okay."

Just then she heard Beth scream, "Oh no, Harry!"

Beth recovered after throwing herself out of the way. She had hit her head on the bedpost, leaving herself momentarily dazed. After hearing two separate gunshots, she collected herself enough to see Wes handcuffing the lunatic on the floor.

She went to help Sarah who was standing over him with a lamp in one hand. Beth gently took hold of the lamp, but she refused to let it go. Sarah faced her and appeared to be in a state of shock. Beth hugged her and told her it was over. Everyone was safe. On her left, she heard a shuffle and saw Harry slide down to the floor, clutching his side. She screamed, "Oh no, Harry!"

Wes unlocked Kourin's handcuffs, freeing her. She was sore from the abuse she had just endured, but she was determined not to lose anyone like the previous time. She rushed her naked body over to where Harry was slumped on the floor. Arriving at the same time as Beth, it took her a moment to overcome her shock at seeing Harry had been shot.

Harry saw a young naked girl kneel beside him. He was going to say something, but he could not formulate the proper words to utter. He saw it was a teen blonde with a bruised left eye. What struck him was not the tangled mess of her hair, the bruise on her face, or even the nakedness of her body. What he saw foremost were emerald green eyes looking at him, eyes that burned with golden rings of fire.

Kourin checked Harry, pulling up his shirt. There was a lot of blood, but it appeared the wound was on the side and had a matching wound on his backside. She thought, *The bullet went right through. I don't know if that's a good thing or not, but there's an awful lot of blood.* She said, "We have to stop the bleeding." She turned to face Beth and Sarah. Their mouths opened when they looked at her.

Beth said, "Kourin, your eyes!"

Kourin repeated, "Beth, we need to stop the bleeding. Harry's been shot!"

Beth recovered enough to grab a shirt that was hanging on the bedpost, a Fairfield patrolman's shirt. She knelt beside teen Kourin and applied the shirt over the wound in front.

"The bullet went through Harry," Kourin said. "We need to get him to the hospital."

Beth, gawking at the naked teen, said, "Kourin, your eyes!" She tore her own eyes away from the sparking emeralds to glance at Harry and went back to teen Kourin, knowing she somehow held the key to what was required. "Harry needs to get home. We all need to go home right now!"

As a car could be heard pulling up outside, Kourin glanced at Sarah, standing two feet away. Behind her, on the bed, Officer Wright was doing his best to comfort Jen who was crying uncontrollably. Kourin brought the image of the terminal bench to her mind, trying to will them all back home. She heard a stirring beside her. Mike moved to get up. At the same time, in the outer doorway, she heard a male voice say, "What the hell is going on here? Wes, are you in there?"

The handcuffed man suddenly propelled himself towards Kourin, saying, "I'll kill you. You little bitch!"

Sarah caught sight of Kourin's horrified face and blazing emerald eyes facing her attacker. Still holding the metal lamp, she swung with all her might at the man's head. The crack of his skull echoed through the quietness of the bedroom.

Kourin screamed. Before her, the horrific bedroom vanished in a flash of light.

19

ALMOST HOME

Kourin found herself where she had envisioned herself to be—on the bench. She scanned the courtyard and found she was oddly alone.

Panic set in. She thought, *Oh, fuck! Where are the others? Did they get stuck in the past?*

She recalled she had been a naked teen just moments ago and lowered her eyes to check herself. She found her adult self fully clothed in the outfit she had originally put on for the terminal soft opening. It seemed like a lifetime ago.

Where is everyone? They should have been here with me.

She ran through the circumstances of the last transition. Harry had been shot. Sarah and Beth were within arm's reach. She saw the demon lunge at her. She screamed. Out of the corner of her eye, Sarah swung the lamp at his head. A flash of light occurred, returning her to the garden.

She pondered if she should try to return to her teen self to make sure they weren't still there. She shuddered. *No, I am never returning to that hell.*

I need to make sure I'm back to the correct reality. I have the right clothes on, so that's a good sign. On previous time jumps, people were close by, if not together. She recalled they had originally been in Laurel's office. *They must be there.*

She rushed down the garden walkway toward the shop area. On her right was her own store, dark and closed for the night. On her left was the Coffee

Bean. She had a spark of happiness it had returned to normal. The flicker darkened though, as the café was dark with the gate pulled down.

Not sure what to do, she walked over to the Bean's gate. She pulled up, hoping it would open. It did not. She peered in, but she did not see anyone.

A thought occurred to her, and she pulled out her cell phone. She smiled, recognizing her cell phone and not the flip cell phone she had used earlier in another life. She found what she wanted in contacts and hit the green Call button. It connected.

"Hi, Kori. Where are you?" asked Jack.

Kourin exclaimed, "Jack! You're okay! Oh my God. Where are you? I need to find Harry. He's been shot."

"We're at the Coffee Bean in the office. Harry's here. We just applied some emergency wraps on the wounds."

As he finished the last few words, Kourin saw light pierce the back of the café corridor leading to the office and a backlit figure within it. As the shape neared, she saw the rugged handsomeness she had fallen in love with.

Jack unlocked the gate, pulling it up high enough to walk through. Before he could let go of the gate's bottom, she wrapped him in her arms, kissing him.

As Kourin pulled away from her kiss, she said, "Jack, I'm so sorry. I thought I lost you."

"I'm here, Kori. We're all here."

Kourin paused, unsure of which reality Jack was referring to. She had a slight panic attack, wondering if everything truly was as the day had begun or if she was in a new, unknown existence.

Her fears were put at rest as the others walked toward her from the back room. Sarah and Beth were on either side of Harry, helping him walk. He appeared to be in better shape than Kourin would have thought, considering his potential blood loss. Behind them was Laurel, with Ubu at her side. Kourin didn't see the one other person she sought.

Without saying a word, Laurel walked past with Ubu out into the terminal.

Beth said, "I need to get him to the hospital. We've stopped the worst of it, but he's far from alright."

"I'll go with you," said Kourin.

"No, I think it's best if I take care of this," Beth answered back. "The hospital will be required to report a gunshot wound to the police. We obviously can't tell them where he got it. If just I go with him, we can say we were out for a walk and got mugged."

Sarah said, "Beth, you'll need help to get him there. I'll go with you. I can say I just happened along and provided help."

Kourin asked, "How will you explain being shot at the airport?"

"I'm going to tell them it happened by the Piscataquog River Park." Before the others could object, Beth added, "If Harry is under sedation and they ask him questions, he can honestly answer we were at the park today and there were gunshots, that it occurred ten or fifteen years ago . . ." Her voice trailed off; her statement left unfinished.

Harry slouched down. Sarah and Beth helped straighten him up.

"We need to go," Beth said and started walking him out with Sarah on the other side.

Laurel returned with an airport wheelchair, saying, "I remembered these were at each gate." She placed it behind Harry who was helped into it by the ladies on both sides of him. "Now go. I'll call Diric to meet you at the employee entrance to get you to your car faster."

"Thank you, Laurel," Harry said. He had been quiet until now. He looked at Ubu. Ubu briefly placed his head on Harry's lap. "Good dog," Harry said as he petted the top of his head. Ubu backed up as Sarah pushed the wheelchair away from the others. They disappeared down the terminal at a quick pace.

Jack saw the sad expression on Kourin's face and misinterpreted it. He said to her, "He should be okay. We stopped the bleeding."

She looked him in the eye. "It's not Harry I'm worried about."

He returned her gaze and saw hazel eyes looking back at him. "I don't understand. We've all made it back from the . . . from when you . . ." he trailed off, not knowing how to verbalize her pain.

She turned away from him, saying, "There's more to the story than you probably remember."

She turned to Laurel. "I'm glad you made it back. You and Ubu." The black dog closed the space between them, sat in front of Kourin, and offered her his paw. She bent over and took it in her right hand. She said to him, "It's good to see you, Ubu." After she released his paw, he retraced his steps to stand beside Laurel who was on the phone by the counter.

As the dog was offering his paw to Kourin, Jack said, "The last thing I remember was—" He stopped. "I think I was shot, too." He looked at Kourin. "I remember being shot, and a dark bedroom. It seems like a bad dream. The memory of it is already fading."

She said, "I can fill you in. There's something I need to tell you, both of you."

Laurel hung up the phone, having completed her call to airport transportation. Jack exchanged glances with her. He said, "Maybe we should sit down for this."

Kourin sat at the first table in the dim light. Jack and Laurel sat across from her. Ubu sat at the end of the table. Kourin studied the two across from her and wrung her hands, unsure of how to say what she needed to.

Jack perceived she was working something through her mind and said, "Whatever you have to say, you're with friends, Kori."

"I know," Kourin replied, looking into his brown eyes. "When we went back to . . . to when I was abducted, I lost you." She paused as tears swelled in her eyes.

He saw her eyes begin to water and change from hazel to green. To help reassure her, he reached over and covered her hands with his. He said, "Kori, you're never going to lose me."

She felt her insides warming and worked to control her emotions. She said, "You misunderstand me, Jack. You . . . you died. In trying to save me, you were shot and died." A tear fell from her eye as she recalled his bloody body beside her bed. "When we returned here, you did not."

Laurel spoke up. "Kourin, what happened?"

Kourin told them of the world she, Harry, and Beth returned to, the person she had become and did not recognize. She refrained from mentioning Anders, not wanting to relive that part of the nightmare. The terminal still existed, although some aspects of it had changed. The Coffee Bean was gone and, with it, Laurel. Jack was unreachable. Wren hadn't met Joneal. Sarah was there and could eventually recall glimpses of the true reality, the one they all knew. With Harry, Beth, and Sarah's help, they were able to go back to her teen years and correct the timeline.

She paused and gazed at the café behind Jack, not focusing on any one thing, although she could see almost as well as if the lights were on. She took a moment to collect herself and tamper down her emotions after assuming her eyes had turned green.

Try as she might to push specific thoughts to the side and bury them as she had all her life, she recounted to Jack and Laurel the pain she had endured.

She shuddered as she relived the abductor's hands on her teen body, being struck in the face when she screamed in pain, the violation of her childhood, and her innocence abruptly and brutally taken away. Her life forever ruptured.

Jack and Laurel sat in silence, witnessing the distress on Kourin's face. Tears welled in his eyes as he fought to be strong for the one he loved. Laurel let her tears flow as Kourin related the horrific nightmare she had endured over thirty years ago and again in the last hour.

In the darkness of the café hallway, a shadow listened and silently watched the trio at the table.

Although it was difficult, Kourin spoke of her plan to save Jen from her fate and the unforeseen fight that ensued in the bedroom. Harry had been taken prisoner along with Wes. A few minutes after that, Beth and Sarah were led into the bedroom where they had a heroic battle with the demon who had abducted her. Unfortunately, Harry was shot.

As she completed her tale, she admitted to being apprehensive that everything had indeed returned to the way it had been. She said, looking at Laurel, "One change affected so many lives. I think having the ability to go back in time is a curse that ought not to be done. Lives are altered in unforeseen ways."

Laurel did not respond. She thought of Breck and Sarah. She absently reached for Ubu who, as always, was by her side and petted his head on the side, avoiding the injured area.

When Kourin finished speaking, Jack asked, "Kori, what caused the change in your life? What is the curse you're speaking of?"

She shifted her gaze from Laurel to him, but she had to look away before answering. "In the timeline you remember, when you died, I was saved before my daughter was conceived. She was never born to grow up to be where she needed to be to touch so many lives." She said, looking at Laurel, "She wasn't there to become your best friend."

Laurel's mouth opened, unable to speak.

Jack's comprehension of Kourin's words took a little longer to fathom. He finally pieced it together and asked, "Mandy? Mandy is your daughter?"

Kourin pulled her eyes away from Laurel to him. "Yes. She is. That is why we are connected with . . . with whatever is happening here."

"That explains a lot," said Laurel. "I knew when I saw her eyes changing at Fara's that you two were linked. Now it makes perfect sense."

Jack said, "But I don't get why your personality changed because you didn't have her. How did not having a baby alter the woman you evolved into?"

Kourin answered, "I think because I didn't suffer the trauma of giving up my baby." After a few moments' thought, she added, "But also, I didn't experience the viciousness of the abduction. You stopped it by showing up a day early with the police. I was kidnapped, but other than a bump on my head, I was otherwise okay."

"Because you weren't . . ." Jack couldn't finish the sentence. Instead, he said, "So that means you just went back in time to allow yourself to be . . ." Again, he couldn't complete his thought.

"Yes," Kourin said with a despondent expression. "I had to. If I didn't become pregnant, Mandy would not have been born. Laurel would not have met her in high school, and she wouldn't have been there for her after Afghanistan."

Laurel spoke up. "You sacrificed yourself to improve my life?"

"Yes, but not just you," answered Kourin. Laurel's hands were on the top of the table. Kourin pulled hers out from under Jack's and held on to Laurel's. She continued. "I believe if Mandy had not come into this world, she wouldn't have been there for you when you needed her. You would never realize your potential and open a café. I don't know exactly what happened to you, but every fiber of my being said it was not good." She paused as an icy shiver ran down her back.

"And she wasn't there to save Miguel," Jack added. The two ladies looked at him. "If you never opened the café, she wasn't here to sit on the bench and save Miguel. Who knows what that change would lead to?"

Laurel thought for a moment and said, "Now I think I know why we all went back to Mandy's teen years." She placed one of her hands on top of Kourin's so they were intertwined. "While there, we were all seeking what Mandy needed to learn from going back to that time. We assumed the bench was showing something she needed to see. In fact, the bench was showing the rest of us what we needed to see. We needed to know how important she was—how important she is to all our lives." She paused and squeezed Kourin's hands, smiling. "Kourin, your daughter and my best friend, I don't know where I'd be without her. What you did . . . what you suffered . . ." Laurel couldn't say the words just as her uncle couldn't.

Kourin said, "I did what had to be done." She looked from Laurel to Jack. "My daughter is everything to me. I just wish I had been there for her growing up." Tears flowed from her eyes as Jack added his hands on top of theirs.

From the darkened shadow of the hallway leading to the office, they heard a female voice say to them, "You did what you had to do."

All three at the table turned toward the voice. Mandy stepped out of the shadows into the dim light from the terminal. Tears streamed down her cheeks. Her eyes were vivid green, and a bright golden circle was visible around her pupils.

Kourin released her hands from the others and rose to meet her halfway to the table. She enveloped her in a hug. They both cried onto each other's shoulders.

Jack and Laurel stood near the table, giving mother and daughter space to themselves. Neither noticed Ubu rise from where he had been sitting. He did not face Laurel and Jack. Nor did he face the two ladies sharing a long overdue hug. He was pointed toward the garden area where a glow emanated from the center in the darkened terminal.

The hair on Ubu's spine raised. He sniffed and watched the area beyond. Danger was lurking in the distance. He couldn't smell it or see it. He sensed it. Not like the dark man that had attacked his mom in that dark hot place—this was different. This was far more dangerous. Not knowing what else to do, he growled.

Mom was in danger. Sister was in danger. They were all in danger.

20

INFIDELITY

Harry was carted off immediately upon arrival at the reception desk in the emergency lobby. This was the second time in as many days for Harry and Beth to be there. After providing the nurse with Harry's information, which was all in the system from the day before, Sarah and she sat in the waiting area.

Fortunately, they could conceal the true discomfort Harry was in from Diric and the terminal security guards. On the drive to the hospital and while waiting for the police to arrive, the two ladies got their stories straight.

Beth and Harry were ambushed by a masked assailant dressed in black with a black ski mask. He held a gun that went off when he threatened them, striking Harry. That must have frightened him because he ran off into the night. From further down the path, Sarah appeared and helped them get to the hospital. They hadn't called an ambulance because they thought driving themselves would be faster.

Within twenty minutes, the police were taking their statements individually. They admonished both of them for not calling an ambulance, but it fit their narrative so the tongue lashing was worth it.

After the police left, Sarah sat beside Beth. Both were lost in their respective thoughts about the events of the day. They had just confronted a sadistic rapist and murderer. In worrying about Harry, they had set aside their anxiety of themselves coming close to death.

Beth had been shaken to her core, and now everything was catching up to her. She had never experienced having a gun pointed at her. Kourin's past had seemed surreal the first time and then the second until everything went sideways. She trembled at how close they came to disaster. She glanced down the corridor to bring herself back to what mattered at the moment. Still not having heard anything about Harry's condition, they had allowed a policeman in to speak with him, so she was optimistic he would be okay.

Sarah mulled over the revelation that Laurel was the same person Breck knew so long ago. She wasn't a believer in divine intervention, especially after losing Breck, yet something more than luck had taken her to the precise place she would cross paths with Mandy and Laurel.

She thought, *Not just meet them, but to be in the thick of it, whatever it was. Did we really just time travel?*

She glanced sideways at her companion who was deep in her own thoughts. Until yesterday, she had known none of these people. Today it seemed she had known them forever. She reached out and held Beth's hand.

Beth felt Sarah clasp her hand and turned to face her, placing her other hand over Sarah's. At first, she had trouble finding the words she wanted to say. A few finally came to her. "In all the commotion, I haven't said thank you for what you did. If you hadn't been there . . ." she trailed off, unable to speak the words.

Sarah placed her other hand on top of Beth's. "I did what I had to do." She glanced over at the nurse's station before turning back and continuing. "I'm just sorry Harry was injured. Perhaps I could have done something differently to avoid—"

Beth cut her off, saying, "As you said, you did what needed to be done. Poor Kourin and the other girl needed us, needed you to be strong. You saved them." She paused, putting her thoughts together before adding, "We all made it back. All of us, including Jack." She stopped again for several moments before continuing. "But I can't imagine the horrors Kourin had to endure to return everything to where it should be. Poor girl."

Sarah had tears in her eyes. "Yes. When I saw them lying on the bed, something just . . . something just told me I had to act. I had to save them."

Beth looked into her teary eyes, herself welling up, and said, "I imagine that's how Breck felt when he did what he did." After she said it, she was uncertain if she should have. She added, "I'm sorry. It's not my place to say."

Trails of tears trickled down Sarah's face. "Not a day goes by that I don't think of his smiling face. When I first learned of being able to alter the past, I was intrigued by trying to save him and to have what was taken from us. But then I looked at the picture on my phone—my two girls. As painful as it is to have lived without Breck, I couldn't imagine life without my little girls."

She wiped the tears from her face and continued. "And, of course, Jerry—he's such a great dad, and I truly love him very much."

After collecting her thoughts, she continued, "Lately, we've been having little spats, just tiny annoyances that really are nothing in the grand scheme of things. When I first met Mandy—oh my, that was yesterday! Wow, so much has happened. Anyway, when I met her, she made me realize what I had with my family, how much love there is with my kids, but also with Jerry. He really is a wonderful man and a loving father."

Beth listened. She let her speak without interruption, knowing she needed to air her thoughts. When she concluded, she tightened her hands upon Sarah's and said, "You need to make sure you tell him that the first chance you get. I know when I lost my Tom, I would have given anything to have just five more minutes with him. I guess now that may be possible."

Sarah had a stricken look when she looked up at Beth.

Beth quickly said, "No, although it may be possible, after seeing what happened with Kourin—after losing Jack and then Mandy—messing with the past is something not to be done." She thought of Harry, what they had shared and what had eaten away at him ever since.

Sarah studied her face, reading something there. She asked, "Beth, there's something more going on, isn't there? I know I shouldn't, but I'm going to say it anyway. In watching you and Harry last night and everything we just went through, there's something more between you. I can see it in your eyes that Harry is more than just a coworker to you."

Beth froze when Sarah said her words. She had promised Harry she wouldn't speak of what had happened. In the aftermath of all that she and Sarah had been through, and after carrying the weight of it for so long, she opened up to Sarah.

Beth told her everything.

On the fateful night of Christine's accident, Harry had been with her after work, having had a few beers together instead of going home to his wife. Earlier that day, when a disagreement with Christine left him feeling frustrated, he had no desire to rush back home. Their spat wasn't anything big, but when added with other minor issues over time, the mole hill became a mountain.

Once upon a time, they had an ideal marriage until tragedy struck. They lost their only child. Years later, it still haunted them. In retrospect, all their problems began after that. If they had sought counseling, they may have dealt with everything better. Minor fractures became chasms. Neither could find their way out of or a way to cross over.

After the third beer, Harry confided he and Christine had not been intimate for several years. He had tried to relight the spark, but every time he did, the evening ended in a squabble.

Beth told Sarah that Tom had died several years before, and she was lonely. She had her children, but she missed another's touch. As she consoled Harry, one thing led to another. They began kissing, and soon after, things got heated. They had sex. Neither had planned on it happening. It just did.

When they realized the mistake they had made and the line they had crossed, a rush of regret engulfed them both.

Harry was filled with remorse.

When he returned home that night, he confided his infidelity to Christine. She was hurt. Although she had some issues with him, she loved him very much, as he did her.

With tears in her eyes and her heart heavy with pain, she angrily stormed out of the house because of his unfaithfulness. She needed time to process what she had been told and drove around with no destination. Within sixty minutes, the car crash that rendered her comatose had occurred, and she succumbed to her injuries six weeks later.

Beth wiped her tears away. She said, "Harry blames himself for Christine's death. I blame me. I never should have let it happen. Harry was married and loved Christine. He was hurting as his marriage crumbled. I should have remained a friend to help him through it. If it wasn't for me . . ."

Sarah was at a loss for words. Not knowing what to say, she gave her a hug and thought, *Now I understand Harry's fascination with the bench. He wants to undo that night.*

As Sarah released Beth from the hug, they shared a knowing gaze. Without words spoken between them, both knew they had to keep Harry from changing the past. If Christine were to come back, what else in their timeline would change?

21

COMPREHENSION

Laurel noticed Ubu was not at her side. A few feet away, she spied him and followed his gaze outside the café. Her mouth opened as she gawked at what had caught her dog's attention. After a few moments, she uttered, "Uncle Jack, I think we have a problem."

Jack was observing Kourin reunite with her long-lost daughter when he heard his niece's voice next to him. He followed her gaze as she had done with her dog. "That can't be good," was all he could say.

Kourin hugged her daughter. Thirty-two years of anguish washed away in seconds. Words would not come to her, so she just held on, fearing she would wake from a dream holding nothing but her pillow.

Mandy returned the hug. She wasn't quite ready to call her mom. It wasn't out of disrespect, anger, or any of a dozen terms her psychology degree could expound upon. She had a mother living in Newmarket who had raised her as her own. To this day, even after being told about being adopted when she was a teenager, she was and always would be her mother. Ironically, she had been given this information at Thanksgiving dinner the month after the Halloween event she had just relived. In retrospect, the incident with Fara and the cheerleaders must have been in some way the catalyst for her mother to tell her. For the following two years, her thoughts were consumed by what her birth mother was like: where was she now and would she ever meet her? Fara and Laurel had been there to listen, providing her with a safe place to express her anxieties.

When she realized the woman who had given her love and raised her was her "mom", her uncertainties melted away. Through bouts of sickness, the woman cared for her. For years, entire weekends were devoted to driving across several states to compete at gymnastic events. When her first crush had broken her heart, the woman she had always called Mom was there, her gentle hand stroking her hair as she wept.

One question had remained since the day she learned she had been adopted. She still struggled with that one question to this day: why did her birth mother give her up?

She pulled back from Kourin's hug after several minutes. Usually, words came easily to her, words of encouragement, words of empathy. Not knowing what to say, she looked at the face of the cosmetics shop owner who had been buying tea from her for the last month.

Kourin gazed at her daughter's face, as if seeing her for the first time. She said, "I'm sorry I wasn't there for you."

Mandy didn't respond.

"I understand if you're angry with me, but with the circumstances . . ." said Kourin, trailing off.

When Mandy still didn't respond, Kourin took a deep breath and decided to put everything out in the open. Her daughter had a right to know the entire story.

"Before you were born, I thought I'd be able to raise you. As the months went by, my parents saw the emotional toll my . . ." Kourin paused, fighting for the strength to say what needed to be said. "I was not handling what had happened to me and Jen well. I was in therapy every day after school."

Kourin paused and clasped both of Mandy's hands. She continued, "I knew from the moment I was pregnant that I would have you. I thought I could raise you." She squeezed her daughter's hands. "My parents couldn't care for a baby. My pastor was the first to suggest I place you up for adoption. I was against it until three weeks before you were born. After extensive therapy sessions, my therapist advised me to consider adoption as an option. She knew I would be years away in my recovery from . . . from the rape and abuse I had endured."

Kourin locked eyes with Mandy as she said the rest. "They convinced me I would not have been able to care for you as you deserved. I was a mess for many years. Truthfully, I've never fully recovered."

She turned away toward the floor for several heartbeats before continuing. "With what happened to me, I realize now that they were right. Even with my thirty-plus years of having dealt with the emotional scars, I know I would not have been the stable mother you deserved. I wish it could have been different. I wish I could have been there for you."

She hesitated, her words heavy with regret as she said, "I'm sorry."

Mandy felt the distress expressed in the words, and the facial expressions revealed the sorrow created by the choices. She felt the deep sadness in Kourin's heart from the pain her father had caused her. As the reasons for adoption became clear, she felt a chill run through her body as she understood who her father was. He was a monster!

Kourin saw the troubled expression on her daughter's face and mistakenly attributed it to her failure as a mother. She said, "I understand if you hate me, but please know that I love you."

Mandy's heart sank as she looked at Kourin's furrowed brow. She was snapped out of her thoughts of her father and realized her mother was standing right in front of her, looking for forgiveness.

Finally, bringing coherent thoughts together, she said, "Kourin—" She stopped herself and started again in a gentle voice. "Mother, you did what you needed to do."

She beheld the same green eyes that she saw looking back at her in the mirror not too long ago. "You suffered a horrible ordeal. I can't even fathom . . ."

her voice broke as tears filled her eyes. She realized the words had to be spoken for the healing process to begin. "I can't imagine what my father did to you."

Kourin realized in an instant that the previous expression she had seen on her daughter's face wasn't for her. She hadn't thought of the ramifications of her daughter knowing who her father was.

She said, "Oh dear, your father . . . I was so worried about . . . Mandy, your father . . ." She struggled to find comforting words for her daughter. The father was a kidnapper, a rapist, and a cold-blooded murderer. He had killed two innocent girls before he was stopped but not before he impregnated her. "Mandy, I . . . I . . ."

A soft, whispered "Kourin" escaped Mandy's lips, followed by a stream of tears. "Mom, I'm going to need time to think this through. I am so happy to find you. Truly I am. There was a time I would daydream about what my mother was like, who she was and all that. I did the same with my father. Sometimes I imagined they were celebrities who had to hide a pregnancy or some other fantasy explaining why they couldn't keep me. I think I made up these dreams, deep down knowing the reality was far from my fantasy. It's just that . . . just that I never thought he would be . . ."

Kourin hugged her daughter, saying, "I know, dear. I know." She stepped back and looked into her daughter's vivid emerald green eyes, her voice a soft murmur as she said, "He was evil, but we have each other now."

* * *

As he watched the glow in the distance, Jack listened to the conversation between the mother and daughter behind him. He wasn't trying to eavesdrop. The circumstances of a silent terminal and the vicinity they all shared provided the acoustics to hear the heartfelt exchange. When Kourin called Mandy's father evil, he glanced at Laurel who returned his gaze, not realizing she had turned toward him. They remained silent, letting the two have their moment.

After several heartbeats, Jack sensed Kourin and Mandy moving to join them. Ubu was the first to look their way. He left Laurel's side to meet them halfway as they approached. He sat down and lifted his paw to them.

In the dim light of the café, with enhanced eyesight, Kourin could see Jack and Laurel a short distance away. Beyond and to the right, toward the garden, she saw a bright light glowing. In front of her, she saw Ubu sitting on his hind legs facing them with his paw raised, as he had done several times in the last two days.

Mandy remained next to her mother. She peered around the café, realizing she could see everything in a new light, so to speak. Somehow, the dimness of the dark terminal beyond was more like dusk. As she looked out to the terminal walkway, she saw a light to the right. She thought, *Perhaps it is more akin to dawn*. As she looked at her mother on her right, she added to her thought, *A dawning of a new day*.

With her enhanced eyesight making Ubu stand out before her, Mandy bent over to take his paw into her hand. She said, "Good boy, Ubu," releasing his paw and standing upright.

Ubu looked at Kourin and raised his paw a second time, awaiting a response from her. She repeated what Mandy had done. When she straightened up, the dog stood and returned to Laurel's side to observe the light beyond.

Mandy turned to Kourin, saying, "Ubu likes you."

"Yes, it seems so. Out of the blue, he started doing that yesterday in Laurel's office."

"Well, he is a very perceptive dog. Maybe he sensed something."

"Evidently. But at the moment, I think he senses something else."

She moved to be beside Jack. Mandy stood on her other side, staying close to her newfound mother. Kourin asked, looking toward the garden, "What's going on over there?"

Jack turned, fully facing Kourin and looking from her to the young woman beside her. The glow from the garden area lightened their faces enough for him to study their features side by side. He hadn't noticed before how the shape of their heads was similar and their height was nearly the same. In the half light, he realized the resemblance between the mother and the daughter. He thought, *Maybe I'm just seeing what isn't there, but God, they really look more alike than I had seen before. But their eyes! They have the same eyes.*

Aloud, he said, "I'm not sure, but you two may want to look in a mirror." They looked at him, somewhat perplexed. He continued. "Both of you have emerald eyes with the golden circle, a sparkling gold circle. I think maybe you're both connected to what's happening over there." He pointed to the garden with his thumb as if he was hitchhiking. He continued, "It can't be a coincidence there's a glow over there and in both your eyes."

Laurel added, facing the group, "I think it's more than that, Uncle." She paused, contemplating her next few words. "I think they're causing it."

"Why do you say that?" asked Jack.

Before Laurel could answer, Kourin did, "She's right. I can feel something." She paused, looking sideways at her daughter, and continued, "There's something. I can feel it."

"A presence," said Mandy. She looked into Kourin's eyes. "I can feel it, too. But there's something more."

"Yes," said Kourin. "There is." She reached out her hand toward her daughter. Mandy held it in hers. Kourin said, "We need to go there."

"No," Jack said firmly. "We don't know what we're dealing with. What if—" he stopped himself, unsure if he should say what came to his mind. He decided the necessity was there for him to let his fear be known. "We can't. You can't go near the bench. What if you go back and things change? There's no guarantee you'll be able to fix the timeline again. Hell, we're not even certain things are back to where they were."

Mother and daughter stood holding each other's hands, letting Jack say what was on his mind. Laurel and Ubu watched as well.

"What I mean is," Jack took hold of Kourin's free hand into both of his, "it's dangerous to go back in time. Events, even a small seemingly insignificant change, could have unknown ramifications to what we know is the true timeline. Kori," he paused and looked at her daughter, "Mandy. You've found each other. Let's leave it at that."

Kourin felt a warmth in her heart like she had never felt before. Literally, in one hand, she held her daughter's hand and, in the other, the man she loved held hers. A thought came to her. *Family.*

"Yes," Mandy said.

Laurel asked, "Yes, to which part, Mandy?"

Mandy looked at Kourin and said, "Family."

Kourin's mouth opened. She had only thought the word "family." She hadn't spoken it.

Laurel was puzzled and said, "I don't understand. Uncle Jack said we should leave things as is, and you said yes and family."

Mandy looked at Laurel. "Kourin—I mean Mom said family. I was just agreeing with her. It feels like family."

Jack looked from Kourin to Laurel to Mandy. He didn't say a word.

"No one said family," said Laurel.

Kourin, still looking at Mandy, said, "I only thought that. I didn't say it out loud."

Mandy's mouth opened. She said, "I felt a warm emotion inside, and I heard you say family." She looked at Jack and Laurel beyond. "Didn't I?"

All four stood silently for several heartbeats.

Jack felt Kourin's hand getting warmer. "Um, Kori, is it my imagination, or is your hand getting warmer?"

Kourin felt a warmth throughout her body. It was emanating from deep inside her. Just as she had felt the pain, anguish, and sorrow from the recent encounters, she felt an overwhelming sense of joy and love. She thought, *It's the warmth of my love for you, Jack.*

Mandy felt her body warming, but it differed from the previous episodes when she found herself back in high school and eventually back in the terminal. She held her mother's hand and felt the heat emanating from it, meeting her own. Kourin's voice was in her head, *It's the warmth of my love for you, Jack.* She thought, *You two make a great couple. I'm so happy for you!*

Kourin heard Mandy's voice in her head. She looked into her daughter's eyes and thought, *Can you hear me?*

Mandy returned her mother's gaze and heard her question in her mind. She answered in thought, *Yes, Mother. I hear you.*

22

UBU

Ubu had kept pace with Laurel throughout the traumatic time span since he had last been home. He was still in a state of bewilderment, unable to understand the events taking place. Until yesterday morning, his mom had been very predictable. They rose when it was still dark, ate kibbles, did a short walk for his constitutional, and either went to the new place that smelled good and where he got treats or to the smelly place where others ran in place or lifted things, getting more and more foul.

Today had started out normal but quickly went awry. He protected Mom, Sister, and the others several times. He did not have his usual nap times today, but he was fortunate to have slept enough to have remained alert for Mom.

Ubu did not like days that were not the same as every other day.

He was puzzled by how he went from the pleasant-smelling new spot where his mother, sister, and sister's friend were sitting to his mother's office where the group was earlier in the day. It was confusing, but he was with Mom. Mom being safe was all that mattered.

After waking up, he left the office with Mom and found the other nice lady. He knew from the day before she was important to Sister. He wasn't sure how, but he connected with her as he did with Sister. When he saw them together, he knew they were bonded as well. After giving each his paw gesture that they were under his protection, they accepted with their return sign to him.

Once they had accepted his protection, he returned to watch for threats from the area beyond. He sensed something from the area and could hear the voice telling him to bring Sister and her mother to him. Ubu at first was confused by the request until he realized the voice did not mean his mom. It was talking about Sister's mom. Now he understood. What he sensed in Sister and the other was their connection as mother and daughter. He would call her "Lady."

Ubu thought they were about to leave the nice-smelling place when he saw his pack sit down. Frustrated, he dutifully followed Mom and sat next to her.

The mysterious voice again told him to bring Sister and Lady to the garden.

23
THE BENCH

After the amazing realization that mother and daughter could perceive each other's thoughts and could carry out a dialogue via telepathy, all had to take a seat and deal with the reality.

The four sat at the first table in the café, with Kourin and Jack sitting next to each other. With Mandy and Laurel across from them, Jack tried to rationalize the telepathy as a coincidence. A quick test put that to rest when Kourin and Mandy proved they actually were communicating. Jack whispered things into Kourin's ear Mandy couldn't hear. Kourin thought about them, and Mandy said them out loud. Jack whispered a question about Laurel into Kourin's ear that she wouldn't know the answer to, but Mandy would. Sure enough, seconds later, Kourin gave the correct answer, having received it from Mandy across the table with no words spoken.

Laurel did the reverse, whispering into Mandy's ear. She asked, "What did Harry say to Kourin this morning sitting at this very table?"

Mandy answered, "He apologized for being a jerk and hoped Jack and I would be happy together. I mean Jack and Kourin, not me."

All sat stunned once they confirmed mother and daughter truly had a profound connection.

Jack finally broke the silence. He asked Laurel, "Earlier you said Kourin and Mandy were causing the light in the garden. They apparently have a link with each other. Why do you think they're causing whatever is going on with the bench?"

"I think they are connected not just with each other but also to the bench. As weird as it sounds, their eyes are glowing, and so is the bench. Well, at least from this distance, we can see a glow in the bench's area. I don't really know what's going on up there, but something certainly is. I think their emotions are causing the bench to react."

Kourin said, "There is something there. I can sense it, but I can't explain it." She looked at Mandy, who nodded her head. "I need to go there." She turned toward Jack. "Before you say no again, it is something that must be done. Whatever is happening, sitting here will not resolve it."

Kourin stood, as did Mandy.

Jack and Laurel rose. Ubu stayed where he was, but he kept his eye on his mom.

"Jack," said Kourin, looking at him and then Laurel, "I think it's best if you two stay here. I don't know what's going to happen, but I don't want to lose you again."

"Absolutely not," Laurel stated. "Whatever the hell is going on, we'll face it together."

Jack wanted to protest his niece going to the garden, but he knew if he protested her going, it would back up Kourin's claim of him also not going. Instead, he said, "We'll all go." He held Kourin's hand again. "Kori, I'm not letting you face this alone."

Kourin looked at her daughter and said, "I won't be." She added, as she turned back toward Jack, "But I know you, Jack Roberts. You're going to come no matter what I say. The chivalry in you knows no bounds."

It wasn't said in chastising Jack. Kourin knew his personality would not allow him not to come to her aid, whether or not she needed it. She only hoped the decision was not a mistake.

* * *

Ubu saw his pack finally stand. The voice had said nothing to him since earlier, telling him to bring Sister and Lady to the garden. He wasn't sure what he would do if Mom didn't also go, but he was relieved when everyone left the nice-smelling place and headed toward the garden. He waited beside Mom as she lowered and locked the gate. She hastened her pace to catch up with the others, so he matched her speed following behind them.

As they approached the center, he sensed something at the bench. It was much clearer now than ever before. When he had first entered the area with Mom yesterday, he was leery of what was unknown to him. He could sense it, but he could not see or smell it. That had unnerved him. That had not changed. He was filled with a sense of unease, unable to see or smell what he knew was there.

Light emanated around the bench, possibly from the wooden fixture. There was no one there, yet he definitely sensed a presence.

The voice in his head thanked him for bringing his sister and lady to him.

He answered he was not the one who brought them. He had simply followed along.

The voice thanked him all the same and told him to be ready. Soon they would meet. Soon, he would need to protect his pack.

* * *

Kourin had led the group up the walkway to the center of the garden. The bench seemed to glow. She looked up at the skylights and the darkness beyond. It was nighttime. The ambient light around the courtyard was drowned out by the brightness of the light radiating from the antique at the center.

Now that she was here, she paused. Fear creeped in as she recalled what had occurred in the last encounter.

Mandy felt her mother's distress growing as they stood side by side, staring toward the center. She reached out and held her mother's hand. It was trembling. She thought, *Mother, I'm here. I won't let anything happen to you.*

Kourin felt her daughter take her hand and heard her voice in her head. *I should be the one consoling you.* She turned and looked into her daughter's eyes. The golden ring in her emerald eyes returned her gaze. *We need to face this together. I don't know why, but something says we need to do this as one.*

Mandy gave her mother's hand a slight squeeze as acknowledgement. She thought, *As one.*

Jack said, "Now what do we do?"

Before anyone could answer, Ubu left Laurel's side, taking several steps closer to the bench. He had heard the voice in his head telling him to bring everyone to the bench. He said he didn't want to leave Mom's side, but the voice persisted. Finally, doing as the voice asked, he walked halfway.

He stopped. Without turning his body, he pivoted his head back toward the group, letting them know they needed to follow him. After several seconds, he proceeded closer to the bench, halting three feet away.

Although the voice assured him he was safe, he would not take any chances. From this distance, he could see around the entire bench area, just in case.

Laurel was surprised when Ubu left her side. She thought about calling him back, but she was curious why and what he was doing.

Kourin watched the dog turn to her and look her in the eye. She saw his gaze shift slightly to her right toward Mandy. She thought, *I think he's telling us to follow him.*

Mandy answered in thought, *I agree.*

They each took a step forward, followed by another, until they were crossing the distance to stand beside Ubu. They had not released the other's hand as they did so.

Jack came to stand next to Kourin, where he had been earlier. He repeated, "Now what do we do?"

Kourin answered, "We sit on the bench."

"Are you crazy?" asked Jack. "Kori, I'm begging you. Don't do that. You don't know what will happen."

"Jack," Kourin replied, "the only way we'll figure this out is to interact with it. We need to do this."

"I agree," said Mandy. "I can feel a presence, stronger than before. We need to . . ." she trailed off, thinking about what she was going to say. "We need to help . . ." she stopped and finally added, "help him."

"Yes," Kourin said. "But there's something else here, too."

Mandy thought about it. She closed her eyes. "His brother. There are two presences here."

"Perhaps we shouldn't be messing with this," said Jack.

Kourin said, "No, someone needs to help." As she stated that, she released her daughter's hand and moved forward to the bench. She rashly sat down.

The bench continued to radiate light, but nothing happened. There was no movement from the plants in the area, as had happened previously. She sat there, staring at the others looking back at her.

Mandy said, "Maybe it will take both of us." She joined her mother on the bench.

Again, nothing happened.

Laurel said, "Well, that was anticlimactic."

"I don't understand," said Kourin. "I can feel the intensity. It's like a fire burning inside."

"Yes, I feel it as well," Mandy said. She held her mother's hand again. She thought, *Maybe we need to be touching.*

Kourin thought back, *It has to be something more. When the bench activated before, only one of us was on it. We're missing something.*

Jack watched Kourin. He glanced over at Mandy and said, "If you two are conversing, maybe we can help."

Kourin looked at Jack and said, "I'm sorry. That's rude, isn't it?"

"I don't think Ms. Manners has a rule about telekinesis," said Jack.

"That's moving objects with your mind. You're thinking telepathy," Laurel said beside him. He looked at her. She added, "When I was doing research on the bench, those terms came up many times in the articles, along with teleportation." After a brief pause, she said, "Maybe it is all related somehow."

"Perhaps," Mandy said. "But we need to figure out how to make it work."

Laurel said, "When I saw your eyes turn color before, you were sitting in Fara's living room. We had just watched her father come home. Do you recall doing anything to make it happen?"

"No, I was just thinking about what Fara was telling us. She said I was a Wedeme. As she told us about her village and the argument between her mother and aunt, I began feeling intense fear and love. I don't know why. The next thing I know, we're back here," said Mandy.

"I don't think it was you that did it that time," Kourin said. "That was when Jack fought with the clown at the pizza place. I screamed and—"

"We found ourselves back in your teenage years," Jack said.

"And the next time was when you . . . when you died," Kourin said. She gazed at the man standing near her, happiness replacing the sorrow her heart briefly experienced.

"That's it!" Mandy exclaimed.

"I need to die?" asked Jack.

"No, no, no. It was the emotions in those moments that triggered it—intense, unbridled emotions. Just now, when Kour—when Mom was saying you died, I could feel her emotions rising. Sadness, love, and then joy. As her emotional state rose, mine did as well. When I was in Fara's living room and before that when I was in the bathroom, besides my eyes turning color, I experienced intense overwhelming emotions. I could literally feel the heat building inside me until I couldn't control it. My extremities were ice cold, but deep down, I was burning up. It has to be intense emotions that trigger it."

"But how does that help us now?" asked Jack. "I really don't want to die again."

Kourin quickly rose and gave Jack a hug. She said, whispering in his ear, "I'm never going to let that happen again." She held on to him tightly.

As she pulled back, their eyes met. Jack saw the golden ring burning brightly around her pupils. He could feel the heat radiating off her body.

Mandy thought, *Mom, I can feel your emotions building. This is the key. Your love for Jack can trigger the bench.*

Kourin answered back in thought, *How do we focus it to where we want to go?*

Kourin felt Ubu nudge her leg. She looked down at him. He was raising his paw to her. *This is going to sound crazy, but I think Ubu can hear us.*

Mandy watched Ubu go to her mother's side, sit, and raise his paw. She heard her mother's thoughts and pondered if what she was thinking was even possible. As Ubu nudged Kourin's leg, Mandy had a nudge in her mind. She knew they were all connected.

Mandy said aloud, "I think you're right. He can help us go where we want to go."

Jack looked past Kourin to Mandy. He said, "You two were talking to each other again, weren't you?"

Kourin told Jack to sit on the bench beside her, with Mandy still seated on her other side. She said, "Jack, I think we've figured this out. Well, at least somewhat. We need to do this, but I need you to trust me." Kourin took hold of both his hands in hers. She asked, "Do you trust me, Jack?"

He replied without hesitation, "As you wish."

Mandy sensed the intensity increase within her. She knew Kourin loved Jack. It was abundantly clear in the raw affection her mother felt and subsequently she experienced. Until that moment, she had no idea the depth of their love.

Years before, Mandy had been in love, but this was on a level she had yet to achieve. She loved her adoptive mother and her stray cat, Autumn. She loved Laurel and Ubu. Yet these bonds paled compared to what she was sensing from the two people sitting next to her.

In the middle of an airport terminal, sitting on a mysterious bench, the forever optimist who helped solve everyone else's problems realized why her past relationships had failed. It wasn't necessarily her partner's fault, as she had told herself over and over.

She thought she had been in love. She now held the truth that the fault was her own. Her heart had never reached the level of love her mother and Jack now clearly shared. She had affection for the partners she had been with—desire, infatuation, and even lust. When the truth dawned on her she had never truly been in love, a hollow feeling settled in her chest.

As she contemplated never having felt the same level of love and reverence she was now sensing, she was overcome with grief. She could hear her heart pounding in her ears as her internal temperature rose. Thoughts came to her that her father was a monster. Her mother had given her up for adoption. She thought, *How can I bring myself to love another when my conception was wrought with so much torment?*

Tears swelled in her eyes. She felt Ubu by her leg. He raised himself up, placing one leg onto hers and the other onto Kourin.

In her mind, she heard her mother say, *I'm fortunate to have found my love. Don't be sad, Mandy. You'll find true love when you least expect it.*

Laurel had been standing back from the bench, observing the occupants interacting. She could see from their eyes that something was happening as it had before. When she saw Ubu suddenly move forward and hop his front end onto their laps, she took a step closer.

Mandy saw Laurel move forward as she placed her right hand onto Ubu's left paw. She saw out of the corner of her eye her mother placing her own left hand onto Ubu's other paw.

With the physical and mental connections complete, Mandy felt Kourin's intense love swell and flow through her. She felt her own utter sadness meet that love like a window keeping the storm outside at bay.

Mandy heard her mother's voice once again in her mind. *Daughter, don't be sad. You are not your father's child. You are kind and giving—the antithesis of all he was. And know that you have always been in my heart. Although I have not been with you, I never stopped loving you.*

A new sensation arose in her, a resolute devotion to protect the pack along with unbridled love and adoration. She intuitively knew it was Ubu touching her soul.

Overwhelmed, the window that had blocked her mother's emotions burst open.

The world flashed in intense brightness.

24
THE FOREST

Kourin assumed Jack and her daughter would still be on either side of her. Still clutching his left hand with her right, Jack was there. He had not yet awakened. Ubu was not in front of her even though she had been holding his paw with her other hand.

On her left, she expected to see her newly found daughter. There was no sign of her! She frantically scoured the surroundings, hoping to catch sight of her a short distance away. She was nowhere in sight.

She thought, *Mandy, where are you?*

No reply.

In front of her, she saw a small pond with two-foot lily pads, their soft green color standing out against the shimmering surface of the water. Among them, cat-o'-nine-tails and other lush green plants filled the area with a vibrant life. The sun shone down from her right, illuminating the area. It was warm. She inhaled the fresh earthy scent of plants, moss, and trees. The aromas from the terminal garden were but a tease compared to the overwhelming fragrance here.

Jack stirred next to her, and she turned her attention to him.

He opened his eyes upon his beautiful Kourin who gazed back at him with her vivid green eyes. The brilliant golden rings had faded, now a gentle shimmering golden color. As he looked into her eyes, the golden halo around her pupils gradually faded away. He scanned the area as she had done and said, "Looks like we're not in Kansas anymore."

At first, Kourin was confused since they had been in New Hampshire, but she realized his reference and said, "At least we didn't kill a witch landing here."

He chuckled and said, "I don't see Laurel."

"Or Ubu and Mandy," she added.

"Do you recognize this place? Are we back in Fairfield?"

"Perhaps, but I don't think so. I get the sense that we're someplace else. Someplace . . ." she paused. She squeezed Jack's hand. "I think we're where we wanted to go. I feel the presence from the bench here." She paused again. "But I can't feel Mandy. I don't feel that connection."

Jack heard the concern in Kourin's voice and said, "Let's go find her and Laurel. Maybe they're together."

Both rose and realized they had been sitting on a flat raised rock. Kourin noticed a small dirt path a little more than a foot wide leading away from the water's edge. She said, "There's a path. Should we follow that?"

"It appears to be an animal path to the water, but it would be easier to traverse than going through the foliage," answered Jack.

The path was too narrow to walk side by side. Jack took the lead. She was going to object, but she realized he was just being Jack. She knew he'd say he wanted to make sure everything ahead was safe. It probably wouldn't occur to him she could be attacked from behind, but she let him have his chivalrous moment.

As they left the pond behind, a figure could be seen in the shadows ahead, emerging from the edge of the more densely wooded area. The darkness was moving toward them. Jack froze in place.

Kourin's keener sight revealed who was there. A sigh of relief came to her as she saw a black dog and woman walking toward them. She said, "At least we've found Laurel and Ubu."

He was about to ask how she knew it was them when they came into a ray of sunshine breaking through the overhead branches. He breathed a sigh of relief when he saw his niece was safe.

They met each other halfway. Ubu greeted Kourin with his paw. She accepted it.

Jack asked, "Are you okay? Is Mandy with you?"

Laurel replied, "I'm good. I thought she would be with you. We awoke a little way down the path. Ubu immediately set off in this direction, so I followed. He must have sensed you were here."

"No doubt," Jack said. "But where the hell is Mandy?"

"I don't know, and that is very concerning," said Kourin.

Laurel asked, "Is it possible she's still in the terminal on the bench?"

Kourin and Jack looked at each other. She answered, "I doubt it, but I guess it is possible. That would explain why I can't sense her here."

"Or she went someplace else," Jack said. He saw the concerned expression on Kourin's face and quickly added, "Or she's just too far away for you to . . . whatever it is you're doing with her."

"Uncle, you think there's a limit to their telepathy?" asked Laurel.

"Honestly, I have no idea, but I would think there would have to be. Just like when we talk, once you're too far away, you can't hear it. Perhaps it works something like that. We didn't test the range they had."

Kourin said, "True. That must be it."

Laurel and Jack shared a glance. They set that aside for now, as there was no way to prove or disprove it. A positive attitude was better than the alternative.

"Where to now?" asked Jack.

Kourin focused on the way Laurel had come and the dense dark woods beyond. She said, "That way, where Laurel had come from. I can sense that is where we want to go." She started walking in that direction, not waiting for the others. Ubu followed directly behind with Jack and Laurel.

Kourin walked with confidence several strides ahead of the others and felt she was headed in the correct direction. She reached out to Mandy several times, receiving no response. She sensed Ubu behind her and knew, without looking, Laurel and Jack would be there as well. What was ahead was what she focused on.

Jack kept pace with his niece. He was in good shape, but after walking up, over, and down several steep hills and mounds, he was becoming winded. He fell a few steps behind her.

After the last mound, Laurel had caught up with her dog who was pacing directly behind Kourin. Ahead, she could see a brightening through the trees.

As Kourin neared the sun lit area of the path ahead, she slowed her pace. She could sense the presence drawing ever nearer, and the hairs on her skin stood up. The confidence she had moments ago was waning. She took a moment to look back at Ubu. He was several feet back and slowing, with Laurel directly behind him. Jack was several feet further back. A random thought of wishing he was leading right now flashed through her mind. She pushed it aside and told herself to stop being a baby.

She faced forward again and walked to the edge of a thirty-foot vaguely oblong shaped clearing only twenty feet wide to the trees beyond. The path she had been following divided in either direction around the perimeter. The open area was covered with six-inch-high dried grass with yellow, purple, red, and white wildflowers scattered throughout. Small brambles, their thorns glistening in the sun, and miniature trees were scattered randomly.

What she did not see was what she was searching for. The clearing was unoccupied. She listened, but she heard nothing. In a forest such as this, the air should be alive with the chirping of birds and the rustling of small animals like chipmunks and squirrels. She eyed the tiny flowers close to her. There were no bees nor any insects flitting from flower to flower. The area was as much devoid of life as it was of sound.

She turned to Laurel as she came to her side with Ubu between them, saying, "Something's not right. I don't hear any life. No birds or insects. Nothing."

Laurel surveyed the area as she had, noting the same to herself.

Jack arrived on the other side of Kourin. He said, "Quiet, isn't it?"

"Yes," said Kourin. "But we're in the middle of the woods with plenty of plant life around. Where are the insects? No birds. No animal sounds." She scanned the area again, coming to rest her eyes on Jack. "There is something not right about this place."

Ubu let out a low growl. Both Laurel and Kourin immediately looked down at him. He was standing and facing the glade. The hairs on the back of his neck were standing up. His service vest covered the rest of his body. He glared intently.

Laurel followed his gaze and saw nothing except the open area and trees beyond. She peered into the darkness of the tree line beyond and still saw nothing.

Kourin surveyed where Ubu was facing, and even using her enhanced vision she could see the area was devoid of life. She saw nothing. After several seconds, she felt something. She could sense the presence in the area she was looking. A chill ran down her spine. She absently reached out with her right hand, taking Jack's left into hers.

Jack felt Kourin grasp his hand. At first, her fingers were deathly cold. After several moments, he could feel her warmth increasing. Her hand trembled. He braced himself for what was to come, having seen the same warning signs in recent events.

As her temperature rose, Kourin held Jack's hand for support. His closeness gave her reassurance and aided her in controlling her emotions. She feared if she lost control, they would end up in another place and time. She needed to be here. The bench needed to be stopped from destroying the reality they knew.

She heard, *That's correct, Kourin.*

She looked from her right at Jack to Laurel on her left. Both were facing forward, surveying the area. Neither one had spoken. She looked down at Ubu who was intently staring outward. She heard him let out a low growl.

The male sounding voice was heard in her head again. *I know you can hear me. I am here. No need to have fear.*

Kourin thought, *Who are you? Why are you changing time?*

The voice answered, *I am not changing time, but we'll get to that in a moment. Welcome to this world. I've been waiting a long time for this moment.*

Kourin smiled, realizing the irony of that sentence, but she let it pass. She answered, *How come we can't see you? Are you real?*

From across the clearing from behind a tree, a figure appeared: an adult male, mid-to-late thirties, with dark shoulder-length hair. He wore a dark purple toga, as the Greeks did long ago. He smiled and spoke. "I am here, Kourin."

Ubu's bark reverberated in the silence as the figure appeared, but he stood his ground, neither advancing nor cowering back. He growled and barked again as a warning not to advance.

Ubu heard in his head, *No need to bark at me, canine.*

Ubu ceased barking, but he did not lower his hairs. He stood at the ready in case Mom needed protection.

Laurel heard Ubu's low growl shortly before his barking began. She knew well that was his signal to her that danger was near. Others may have looked down at her excited dog as he became agitated. She knew from experience and her Army training to look outward at the danger the animal sensed. In that moment, she saw the person across the glade reveal himself from the shadows into the light. He looked like the Greek God Adonis. His smile melted her heart as her pulse raced.

Jack heard Ubu's warnings and turned in his direction. On the other side of Kourin, he could see Ubu snarling and barking toward the clearing. He brought his eyes up to Kourin who was intently observing the area beyond. He followed her gaze.

A man wearing a purple toga stood across from them. The man smiled and spoke to Kourin. He felt her squeeze his hand with all the strength she had.

The man standing twenty feet away was not what Kourin had envisioned. She didn't know what the presence was or what she had expected, but she didn't have a Greek God on her Bingo card.

A prickle teased the back of her neck. For a second, Anders' face flashed into her head. A fire burned deep inside her. It wasn't desire nor lust. She fought to control it, recalling the alternate reality of his nakedness in her bedroom. She squeezed the hand she was holding. Fervor built up inside her—abhorrence for the man with icy blue eyes.

In her mind, she named the emotions she was feeling: *anger* at being suckered in by Anders' fake fondness for her when all he was after was another conquest, *desire* for the smile and mesmerizing figure before her, *shame* for having that emotion when her love was standing next to her, *anxiety* about the whereabouts of her newly found daughter, and *anguish* for the torture she had endured at the hands of her daughter's father.

She drove all those down. They were overwhelming her senses and had her on the verge of losing control. She focused on love. *Love for the man whose hand I am holding.*

Kourin realized she was crushing Jack's hand. She shifted her gaze from the man in front of her to the one at her side and loosened the grip on his hand. She said to him, "Sorry."

Jack's hand was being squeezed so tightly he felt the pins and needles of blood loss. He knew Kourin was dealing with something in her mind, so he did his best to endure it. As the pain was beginning to almost be unbearable, she turned and spoke to him. He gazed into her eyes. They were vivid emerald with shimmering golden rings around the pupils. He saw the love she had for him within those eyes and felt the pressure on his hand subside. He could feel the heat radiating off her body and through her hand. She did not release his hand when she turned back toward the stranger.

The man in the purple toga spoke again. "I am glad you are here, Kourin, although I had not expected you to have brought friends along with you." He took two steps forward into the sunlight and continued. "Let me introduce myself. I am Artax, and I need your help." He smiled again.

25

ARTAX

Laurel smiled when Artax did. She couldn't help herself. The very appealing man wearing a toga in a dream setting made her think they were in a Hollywood movie or a romantic novel. Her body literally tingled, wanting to be close to him. As she took a step forward, she felt Ubu nudge her leg, snapping her out of the trance she was in. She shook her head and glanced down at him.

Ubu sensed danger. The man who suddenly appeared across from him was what he had sensed days earlier, before he found himself in that hot place where the dark man attacked Mom. He stayed on alert. As he watched the man, he felt Mom moving next to him. He feared for her safety and nudged her with his head. She stopped and looked his way. He nudged her again to tell her not to move, to stand her ground.

Artax smiled, knowing the effect his charisma was having on the humans. When he was unrestricted, he charmed many into his grasp, enjoying what they offered. That was so long ago.

The young one with short dark hair was intriguing to him, but he needed to stay focused. He had a job to do and needed the older blonde to help him. She was the key to his freedom.

When he had completed his task, he could celebrate. He eyed the dark-haired female. *It has been so long, but I can wait a little while longer.*

Artax said, "Friends, welcome to my world. I am certain you have many questions, but we have very little time. We are in danger here and must act quickly."

Laurel felt her inner desires wane slightly. She still craved the Adonis in the toga, but the overwhelming desire ebbed enough to regain control of herself.

Kourin spoke for the group. She said, "Artax, where are we?"

He answered, "We are in a realm that is not of your world. Here I exist, but I am not alone. There is another who seeks to destroy me and release destruction upon your world. I need your help to defeat him once and for all."

She looked away from him. Inside, she fought to keep her emotions in check. She could feel the person across the glade. He radiated magnetism. She sensed it. It was affecting her mind, her emotions. She felt his allure and fought to maintain her distance, having had fallen to something very similar in the near past. Blue eyes came to her mind, and she drove those thoughts out of her mind.

She asked, "What kind of help do you need from us?"

He took another step closer, smiling and showing perfectly white teeth. He said, "I need to tell you what has changed recently that has turned this world upside down, placing all of you in danger."

Jack sensed the woman next to him fighting to control her emotions. She squeezed his hand tighter as the robed figure smiled and moved a step closer. He thought of Eric with his bright white teeth and how he would envy this guy's chops. The sun's rays shining down on his sculptured face made them glisten.

Jack looked beyond Kourin to check on his niece. She was staring at the toga-covered man. He saw Ubu had moved ahead of her, his fur bristling as he barred her from going forward. Regardless of Artax's smile, Ubu was on alert.

Kourin once again realized she was squeezing Jack's hand tightly and eased up on it without looking his way. She kept her eyes on the figure across from her.

"There is danger in time traveling. Is that what you're talking about?" asked Kourin.

Artax took a step forward as he said, "That is a large part of it, but there is more to the danger. Hear my story. You need to know the whole of it if you're to help me."

Laurel felt herself lose concentration when Artax smiled again. She felt herself thinking of being with him, giving herself to him.

She sensed Ubu in front of her. Her mind came back to herself with his contact with her shin. She still had a desire for Artax, but Ubu had quelled it once again.

The robed man moved to the center of the glade. As the sun caught the golden specks within the robe, the fabric shimmered and glowed.

Jack softly said, "That's some plum-colored robe he's wearing."

Beside him Kourin said, "Midnight purple." She turned to him and smiled. "The color is midnight purple, not plum."

Jack thought back to the day before when he had entered her shop, seeing Kourin apply purple to a customer. He realized it was the same shade of the robe, midnight purple. He thought, *Is that just a coincidence?*

He saw Artax looking at him.

Crap. Can he read minds, too?

He saw Artax smile.

Kourin heard Jack's comment on the robe's color. Out of instinct, she corrected him. However, as Artax had moved closer, she took more interest in his eyes. Unlike the icy blue of Anders', these were blazing emerald green.

In her mind, she heard, *Yes, we have the same eyes, Kourin. We are very much alike.*

Artax said aloud to the group, "My story begins long ago in a land very similar to this one." He raised his hands, palms up and out to his sides. Jack couldn't help but perceive the resemblance of the robed man standing in front of him from a childhood memory. *Catechism was long ago too.*

Artax related his story to the trio.

"Hundreds of years ago, I became trapped. In this confinement, I have dwelled through the centuries, unable to escape. Prior to this, I had been free to live my life as my ancestors had for millennia and my kindred has, to this day, albeit sadly, in dwindling numbers. On a summer day, like the one you're experiencing here, I was in a battle with my brother, Cyrus, who sought to destroy me. We were locked in fierce combat when we became entrapped, neither of us able to escape the other. This is where we have remained since."

Artax paused. He studied the others, knowing they were captivated by his tale. Since the interaction with the blonde two days before, he had crafted his tale and her part in his plan. When she sat on the bench, he felt her power. She could transport herself to her younger self with only minimal aid from him. With all the others, he had to use his powers to transport them. They proved to be useless for his needs. He knew he could use the one who called herself Kourin to free himself permanently.

There was another who had sat on the bench who displayed similar power as her. His brother had transported her to the future to support his typical intrusion into these pitiful human lives. Surprisingly, she displayed her own substantial powers earlier today in unison with the older blonde. With the combined strength of the two, he could easily overpower his brother.

His plan began perfectly. He used his power to show his presence within the bench and used their own powers to lure them back, radiating visible light that they themselves created. It was delightful to behold.

Yet, for an unknown reason, the younger blonde had not appeared in the glade. He was perplexed by this, as they were side by side on the bench. She had simply vanished. Try as he might, he could not locate her in this realm.

He thought, *No matter. I can do this with just the older one. Although, I had plans for a celebration with the other one when I was freed.* He looked at each of the humans in front of him and thought, *Of course, I thought I was only going to convince the two human females who had the power to help me. These other two are no use to me, except . . . Well, I've been able to seduce multiple partners before. This is just a small wrinkle to my plan.*

Artax continued his tale. "I have been trapped here for a very long time. My brother recently escaped my hold on him. He is the one threatening your world. He seeks to eradicate it because humans destroyed his home and continue to annihilate his kindred."

When he paused, Kourin said, "You keep calling us humans. That implies you are not human." She inhaled deeply before continuing. Her nostrils were filled with intoxicating smells from the glade. She felt her fervor go up a notch. She asked, "What are you?"

Artax smiled and again he held his hands out, palms up, his robe once again sparkling in the sunlight. He said, "Kourin, my sweet Kourin, I am of the woods, a child of nature who desires nothing more than to live in harmony with all the world's creatures, human and otherwise."

Laurel thought of what Fara had said before they were suddenly whisked away from her home. She thought, *Wedeme.*

Artax turned to her and said aloud, "Wedeme is one name for us. We are called many names from your many cultures. Alas, through the ages, we have been seen in a different light as well."

Laurel's mouth opened. She had only thought about the word Fara had said. She looked into Artax's emerald eyes, finding it difficult to turn away.

Jack asked, "What is a Wedeme?"

Artax gave Laurel an extra second of their locked eyes. He broke the stare to look in Jack's direction and said, "My kindred in Africa are known as Wedeme, the keepers of the land. The water keepers are known as Kontomble. We have many names across every culture: Meliae, Dryads, Naiads, Nereids, Oreads."

Kourin said, "Dryads. I've heard that before someplace. Isn't that a fairy or something?"

Artax let out a maniacal laugh, echoing across the woods. He exclaimed, without the smile he had shown previously, "Fairies! Humans sought to diminish us to the likes of an insect or bug to be destroyed. We are not—" with hands clenched into fists, he stopped himself. He closed his eyes for a moment and unclenched his hands, bringing them together at his waist.

He continued in a calm voice, "Through the ages, our place in human history has transformed. Once we stood side by side, nurturing your ancestors to come down from the trees, to develop into beings such as ourselves, to become civilized, to . . ." he paused. He found he was once again clenching his hands. "Well, that is in the past. Today, we are the ones in hiding as our numbers diminish across the world. And that brings me back to my original statement. I need your help to stop my brother from seeking his revenge against your kind. Kourin, together we can stop him."

She said, "I don't understand. How can I help?"

Artax took another step forward. He was now past the center of the glade, less than ten feet away from the group. He answered with a smile, "You are a kindred spirit. Somewhere in your bloodline, your ancestor mated with my kind. Most, if not all humans, have traces of my kindred from interactions. However, in you is a uniqueness that is rare. I do not know why you exhibit a stronger bond with my people, but together we can defeat my brother."

"I will not kill someone, if that's what you're asking me to do."

"No, no, no," said Artax, taking two more steps toward the group. "I would never ask that of you. Together, we can trap him where he can cause no one any future problems forever."

When the robed figure moved closer, Ubu growled. His hair, which had relaxed, once again rose on his back.

Jack thought about the words Artax had spoken. He found it fantastical. Wedeme, dryads, fairies—none of this made any sense. There had to be a logical reason that wasn't something out of a fairy tale to explain where they were.

As Jack brought himself back from his thoughts, he found Artax staring at him. A chill ran down his spine even though the air was warm. In Artax's smile, there was no warmth.

Kourin was taken aback by Artax's claim that she was related to fantastical creatures from make-believe. She recalled reading children's books about fairies, princesses, and kingdoms where the charming prince saved the day and everyone lived happily ever after. She thought, *This must be a dream. It can't be real.*

In her mind, she heard Artax's voice. *But this is real, Kourin. Together, we can be as you read as a child. A terrible ogre threatens the kingdom. You have the power to stop it and save everyone.*

Kourin replied in thought, *How?*

Artax eyed Laurel and Jack before answering. After a moment, he smiled, saying, "Let's take a walk to discuss it in private." He moved another step closer. He was a little over two arms' length away.

Ubu let out a low growl.

Artax ignored the canine.

Jack said, "I think we should all stick together." He gripped Kourin's hand tighter.

Laurel looked down at Ubu when he growled. She was conflicted. In her mind, she agreed with Jack. In her heart, she wished she could take the walk with Artax. She felt Ubu nudge her leg with his body as he repositioned himself.

This cleared her head slightly as she sensed danger nearby. Her mind recalled the night of the suicide bomber. Although she stood in nearly the exact opposite conditions of that eventful night, she felt the icy chill as she had when she revisited that night two days ago. Her Army training told her something was off with the scenario playing out before her. She looked down at Ubu. He sensed something was wrong. She refrained from looking directly at Artax. Her mind cleared.

Kourin added to Jack's statement, "I agree. We stay together." She thought about her daughter, wondering where she was and not wanting to lose those with her, especially Jack.

Artax heard in his mind Kourin think about her daughter. He thought to himself, *So that is the connection! You are mother and daughter. I should have seen that. All the more the mystery of why she did not appear with you here in the glade. Since you won't leave your precious Jack behind, I will need to find another way to get him out of the way. The dark-haired girl is under my spell, but he is resisting. Humans these days are far more difficult to cajole than they used to be.*

Artax needed to stall for another few seconds so he could move closer and take Kourin away from the others. Once he had her in his grasp, he would have Kourin release them from the glade, sending them back to the outside world. To do that, he would need to persuade her it was best for their safety to do so. This was not his original plan, but it would work. Together, he and she could trap his brother out of the way. Once that was done, he would be free to take his revenge on the world that destroyed him.

He took two steps forward toward Kourin. In that instant, the peaceful glade exploded into chaos.

26
CONFRONTATION

Over Artax's left shoulder, Jack saw movement through the deep wood shadows. He could not make out what it was. It could have been a figure or several. It also could have been a large animal, although they had yet to see any other life near the glade. Perhaps there was more here than they had perceived.

Kourin sensed a presence beyond Artax. At first, she wasn't sure what she was feeling. As she told Artax her group would stay together and she thought of Mandy being lost, a wave of emotions overcame her.

In a surge, she felt her daughter's overwhelming love swell within her body as she had done to her earlier. She felt her daughter's emotions build within, spreading throughout her body, adding to her own. The vehemency was far more than she had ever experienced.

In the next moment, Artax sprang forward, his fingers grasping for her.

Laurel saw Artax close the last few steps between them. He was on a trajectory toward Kourin. With no thought to her own safety, she reacted to intercept him from possibly causing any harm to Kourin. As she leapt toward him, she felt her furry friend had anticipated the attack before she had.

Ubu sensed the other two individuals beyond in the woods. At first, he was growling because he did not know who they were. He was ready for an attack in case the dark man was back and wanted to injure Mom or his friends.

A breath later, he felt something he had not before in this place. He sensed Sister! His heart swelled with joy knowing Sister was safe and nearby. He still paused with caution because an unknown presence was with her. His hair stood on his back. The dark man?

In his mind, Ubu heard a familiar voice. *Ubu, it is I, your friend. I am here with Sister. Remember, I told you to be prepared to help save your mom and others. Now is the time, my friend. Now is the time to save us all!*

Ubu heard the voice and was uncertain. Yes, it was the voice he had heard before, but how could he know it was one he truly could trust? He hesitated. What should he do?

In his mind, he heard a familiar voice. It was Sister! *Trust him, Ubu. Save Laurel. Save my mom!*

In the next instant, Artax lunged forward. Ubu knew what he had to do. Without regard for his own safety, he launched himself at the man who had been speaking to them as he moved toward Lady.

He made contact and bit down as hard as he could. He heard a howl of pain before being swung off and beyond the figure.

Kourin saw Artax move toward her. She saw Ubu launch himself at him, biting down on the outstretched arm. The robed man screamed and swung his arm, causing Ubu to lose his grip and roll away on the glade.

Behind Ubu was Laurel. She too threw herself at the now unsmiling figure and hit him with the full force of her lean body, knocking him further off balance than the dog had. She rolled away with the man in the same direction as Ubu.

Kourin saw Mandy entering the glade several feet away. She was running as fast as she could toward her. By her side was a man who initially reminded her of Jack. It wasn't, but there were similarities. He appeared to be younger, with slightly graying temples, and he was extremely fit in a formfitting black tee shirt and blue jeans.

The new man raced to where Laurel had tumbled and joined the fracas. Ubu bounded back into the fight, snarling and biting the robed figure who screamed in pain. Kourin saw Laurel land several punches to the face of Artax.

Jack had seen Artax move forward. When he tried to move, he found himself frozen in place. He could watch, but he could not act. As he witnessed Ubu and Laurel's attack, Mandy came into the light of the glade with a stranger beside her. They sprinted to where Laurel was now punching Artax. With another blow to Artax's head, Jack had movement again and was able rush to where his niece was.

Before Jack could aid his niece, the new man had arrived and was holding Artax down on the ground. Artax was screaming in pain.

The new man looked at Ubu. Without a word spoken, Ubu ceased his attack and backed off, as did Laurel.

The man in the black tee shirt and jeans looked at Mandy and Kourin who were standing side by side. They held hands and appeared to be concentrating on something.

Jack saw their emerald eyes shine with shimmering golden rings. His eyes fell upon the man who was embracing Artax, and he saw his eyes were a striking emerald color and equally bright, with no golden ring.

A brilliant flash of light filled Jack's vision, temporarily blinding him. Artax's loud, desperate cry of "No!" pierced through the air.

27

RAPTURE

Jack faced Laurel's desk and was seated in her office where the day before they were discussing the possibilities of what the bench was, more specifically, what was controlling it.

He heard footsteps from the hallway behind him and turned in time to see Laurel enter the office with Ubu at her side.

His niece said, "Oh good, you're awake, Uncle." She walked to his side, gave him a hug, and said, "I woke a few minutes ago and checked to see if Kourin and Mandy were close by. They're not in the café. The terminal is dark. I came back to get you."

Jack knew what his niece meant by saying everything was dark. She was inferring there was no glow from the garden as before. "Well, let's find them," he said, rising from his chair. "Does it seem odd to you we're back in your office and not at the bench where we started?"

They exited the office as she answered, "I'm not sure what to think anymore. I mean what the hell just happened?"

They reached the closed gate. Laurel unlocked it. Her uncle pulled it up enough for them to go under it.

She asked, "Who was the guy with Mandy? Why did Artax attack Kourin?" Laurel relocked the gate.

He looked at the garden. The glow that had been visible earlier was gone, and the area had its normal dusk appearance for overnight. The only sounds he heard were a gentle thrumming of the HVAC system overhead and Ubu's nails tapping the terminal floor every time he moved a paw.

He said, "I don't know, but something seemed off about him, well, even more than him claiming he was a fairy."

"I don't think he enjoyed being called a fairy," Laurel said as she walked toward the garden. Ubu kept pace with her. "That was certainly the weirdest encounter we've had yet. Do you think it was real? Did we just imagine all that happening?"

He stopped. Laurel did as well when she saw her uncle pause. He said, "Let me see your hands."

She held them out for him. He examined them, palms down. They were bruised. "If it wasn't real, you beat the hell out of something."

Laurel looked at her hands, convinced now that what they experienced happened.

They walked the short distance to the center of the garden. Ubu stayed at Laurel's side the entire way, even as she approached the bench.

Jack said, "I thought they'd be here for sure."

"So did I. Where can they be?"

He took out his cell phone and hit the button for Kourin. It went to voicemail. She did the same for Mandy, with the same results. They pocketed their phones.

Jack said, "Well, do we wait here or at the café?"

She answered, "I think the café. At least we can have a cup of coffee. I'd guess it's been at least twenty-four hours since I woke up."

He looked at his niece, just realizing it had been one very long day. "Well, I will not sleep until the other two show up. A coffee right now sounds great."

They crossed the courtyard to the exit leading out. Laurel stopped when she realized Ubu was not with her. She turned and saw Ubu sitting facing the bench. He wasn't doing anything except sitting staring at the bench.

Jack halted when his niece had. He followed her gaze to where the dog was. He said, "That's new."

"Yes. Until now, he was hesitant to even get close to the bench. Whatever had spooked him before must no longer be there."

"I guess."

Laurel called to her dog. "Come, Ubu. Time to go."

Ubu heard Mom call to him. He sensed the danger that had been here before was gone and could feel the man that had been with Sister. Underneath, though, was the other. He was here, too.

Mom called out for him again. Time to go. He stood to leave.

As he turned, he heard the voice in his head. *Good boy, Ubu.*

* * *

At the café, Laurel made a fresh pot of coffee. She checked the time. It was nearly 4:00 a.m. The morning crew would come in soon. Although she had often gotten to work by now, her crew was not scheduled until 5:00 a.m. when the airport terminal opened. The baked goods would arrive shortly thereafter, and the day would begin. She wondered, as she walked two coffees to where her uncle was sitting, if the days would now be normal.

She smiled as she saw Ubu lying on the floor at the end of the table. His eyes were closed. He had protected her again, as well as Kourin. He truly was a remarkable dog.

Her uncle thanked her for the coffee as she set it down in front of him. He took a sip of the hot brew, keeping his hands on either side of the cup. He stared at the cup for no other reason than to calm his mind from the topsy-turvy twenty-four hours they had just endured.

"Uncle, do you think everything will be normal now?"

He thought for a moment. "I really don't know. I hope so, but until we find Kourin and Mandy, I don't know what to expect."

She took a sip of her coffee and jumped out of her seat when she heard the gate shake. She turned around quickly to see who was there and heard a familiar voice.

"Sorry, I forgot you keep the gate locked," Mandy said through the closed gate.

Ubu quickly stood and ran to the gate, wagging his tail as hard and fast as he could.

Laurel, with Jack right behind him, sprinted to the gate, opening it. Mandy and Kourin ducked under before Laurel let it come crashing down after they were through. The noise echoed throughout the silent terminal.

Laurel hugged Mandy, saying how worried she had been.

Ubu waited patiently for his turn to greet Sister, his tail wagging excitedly. Mandy pulled herself from her friend's arms to give Ubu a hug. He gave her lots of licks as she smiled and said, "There's my friend. Who's a good boy?"

Jack hugged Kourin tightly. Until this moment, he hadn't realized how worried he had been. Not wanting to voice or show it, adding to his niece's anxiety of the two missing ladies, he had bottled his own distress within him. He now released that tension in his hug.

After a minute, Kourin said, "Jack, you're crushing me."

He eased up his hug and said, "Sorry. I was so worried about you two." He moved back but still held her in his arms. "Where have you been? What happened to Artax?"

Laurel added her question. "Who was the other guy?"

Both were looking at Kourin. She answered, "I think it's best if Mandy tells the story."

Laurel grabbed Mandy's hand and led her over to their table. She said, "I want to hear all about it! Let me get two more coffees."

"Tea for me, please," said Kourin.

They sat down while Laurel returned with a coffee and a tea, sitting down next to Mandy.

Ubu sat at the end of the table between Mom and Kourin. He had his head on her lap as she petted him. His tail wagged slowly, coming to a halt as his eyes slowly closed.

Mandy said, "It's good to be back home."

Laurel said to her, "Well, spill the beans. Where were you while we were in the woods with Artax?"

Mandy looked at Kourin who smiled and gave a slight nod. She took a sip of her coffee and shared her story.

"I arrived in a sunny glade sitting on a rock in the center. Obviously, none of you were there. I panicked at first. I reached out with my mind to Kour— to Mom, but I couldn't connect with her. After several minutes, I realized I couldn't hear any sound. No birds. No insects. No wind. It was very unsettling."

She paused and sipped her coffee. The others gave her the time she needed to tell her story. Laurel placed her hand over hers and gave it a light squeeze for reassurance. Mandy returned her friend's thoughtfulness with a smile.

She resumed her story.

"I heard a male voice in my mind. He told me not to be frightened and that my mother was not far away. I asked him who he was. He explained he was trapped here with his brother for hundreds of years. He asked if it was alright to reveal himself to me."

Mandy looked at the others and then continued as her gaze fell upon her coffee cup. "I heard a male voice out loud behind me. I turned around and saw . . ."

All could see her blushing.

"I saw a very handsome man behind me." She paused again and sipped her coffee.

Laurel felt there was more to what she was saying and asked, "Mandy, is there something more about this man you're not saying?"

"Well, he at first appeared totally naked. I looked at him for a moment and turned away. His body was . . . was in very good shape." Her cheeks were flush.

Kourin and Laurel glanced at each other, a subtle smile playing on their lips.

Mandy continued, "He saw my embarrassment. After a moment, he told me it was okay to look again. When I did, he was wearing a black tee shirt and blue jeans. He apologized for upsetting me. I tried to play it cool and told him it was okay."

She paused again and looked at Laurel. "Lau, he appeared to me as the manager from the supermarket, except he was very naked."

She saw Jack looking at her and felt a need to explain further. She said, "When I bought the family a gift card at the supermarket to save Miguel, there was a handsome manager named Emry there who helped me."

Mandy took a sip of her coffee. "Anyway, here he was, standing in the glade with me. I asked him why he was here. He answered he wasn't Emry. He was just using his likeness to ease my mind. Honestly, I wish he had chosen some random guy I never met. Him being Emry was very disconcerting, especially seeing his . . . Well, anyway . . ." Mandy blushed again and had another sip of her coffee.

Kourin used the moment to interject. "When Artax first appeared to us, I thought he looked familiar. I realized when Mandy told me this earlier that I was seeing Anders but at a younger age. Evidently, they can mimic someone from our thoughts and, evidently, at any age. Artax thought he was using a persona that would ingratiate myself to him so he could manipulate me."

Jack gave Kourin a sideways glance, recalling Anders asking her out on a dinner date. That seemed so long ago. He did as Laurel had done to Mandy. He reached out and squeezed her hand.

She smiled back at him and said, "Don't worry, dear. He's not my type. By using Anders' likeness, after what I had just been through with the alternate reality, it had the opposite effect."

After her mother spoke, Mandy continued, "At first, I thought I was totally in a dream. However, the man assured me it was no dream. He told me to call him Cyrus and said we needed to hurry if we were going to save my mother and the others. That got my attention. I hadn't given it any thought that he referred to Kourin as my mother. I'm still uncertain if he had seen that in mind or knew some other way. We started off together to locate you. On the way, he told me he was blocking his brother from knowing where I was. He said in doing so he was also blocking my mother, but it could not be avoided. He told me his plan to surprise his brother at the right time so he could place him back under control."

Jack interrupted at this point and said, "That's like what Artax said, but he had it reversed."

Kourin added, "And I'm not so sure Artax just wanted to place his brother under control. I still think he wanted to kill him."

Mandy said, "I don't know. Cyrus said nothing about that while I was with him. However, they are brothers. He said as much in telling me about their past. They were having a fight one day long ago when their home was chopped down. Somehow, when they were entangled in their fight, they became bonded to what became their prison. They became trapped within the bench."

Laurel said, "Wait a fucking minute! Are you saying their home was a tree, and when it was made into a bench, it trapped them?"

"Yes," Kourin said. "On what we now know as the Azores, the brothers had trees in the same glade. One day, humans came to their glade and cut down all the cedar trees. The bench was made from their trees. One was the seat, and the other one was the back. The legs and armrests were made from parts of their trees and others."

Laurel asked, "Does that mean all the furniture we sit on has a fairy living in it?"

Mandy laughed and said, "I asked the same question! Cyrus said no. He believes it was just by chance they were caught when their tree was chopped down. Normally, his kind sees humans coming and leave their tree if they are in danger. Occasionally, some stay with the tree, and as far as he knows, they cease to exist when the tree is felled."

Mandy wiped a tear from her eye.

She continued, "I suppose it is possible those trees have their spirit within them. Cyrus said mankind has been wiping out their existence. Especially over the past few centuries, their kind is almost completely extinct."

Jack asked, "What are they?"

Kourin answered, "It's not just what they are." She placed both her hands on Jack's, squeezing them gently. "It's what we are. Mandy and I are directly related to them, as are both of you."

"How is that even possible?" asked Jack.

Kourin answered, "Their kind have been on Earth since the beginning. They evolved alongside our ancestors from the time all were living in trees. Our human ancestors came down from the trees to walk the forests. Their species evolved faster than ours, with branches of their kindred not only in trees, but also underground and in the water. As time passed, species intermingled. Evolution over time made humans more like them."

Laurel asked, "What about the water and earth lines? Do they still exist?"

Kourin answered, "He spoke little about them other than to say polluting the waterways and oceans was killing his kindred there as well."

Jack said, "I still don't get how they intermingled. How is it we don't know about this?"

"I think we do. We just choose not to believe it," said Kourin. "Humans don't want to believe they descended from anyone or anything different from what they are. In fact, we've evolved in the best possible way. We are part of the earth we live on."

Laurel said, "I find it hard to believe humans mating with a species outside their own."

Mandy spoke up. "Well, it was more the males of their species kept knocking up the females of the human species, thus altering their genes. The females of their species are more peculiar about who they mate with, so their lineage stayed intact through the millennia. However, he said there were exceptions in females seducing human males and where the legends of sirens, sylphs, dryads, mermaids, elves—you name it—came from. Their males, however, were constantly bedding females."

"And males," Kourin interjected. "Cyrus said their kind are bisexual. It's some kind of dominance thing. Although the males prefer the opposite sex, they will not pass up an opportunity for sex with either."

Laurel said, "Typical males."

Kourin and Mandy laughed.

Jack said, "You know I'm sitting right here and can hear you."

Kourin leaned over and gave Jack a kiss on his cheek. She said, "It's okay, dear. You can't help being who you are. Perhaps that is why human males have the drives they have. They got it from them."

Mandy added, "Eventually, humans evolved from where they were to where they are now. Cyrus' species guided humans to be better versions of themselves, most of the time."

Laurel asked, "What does that mean?"

Kourin answered, "As with humans, occasionally there are rotten apples in the basket. Cyrus said Artax is one of them, even though he is his brother. He always took every chance he had to seduce a human. That is eventually what led to their fight. Cyrus is more restrained in his sexual appetite. He puts his energy into improving humans to make the world a better place for all."

Mandy chimed in. "When Cyrus became trapped within the bench, he learned how to use his abilities for anyone who made contact with him when sitting on the bench. He could aid humans in selecting a better tomorrow by giving them foresight into possible futures dependent on the choices they make."

Kourin added, "But he did say he wasn't always successful. Often, people saw in the encounters of the future what they chose to see and still learned nothing to alter their decisions. Yet, he said he had many successful ones as well. Mandy's encounter with him was the example he used. He said she was the reason he guided John to build the terminal so she would alter Miguel's outcome at the party."

Jack asked, looking at Mandy, "We built the entire terminal just so you could do that?"

Mandy answered, "I guess so. Cyrus didn't expand on why Miguel was so important."

Laurel was confused and asked, "Why did we all have glimpses of past events if all that was supposed to happen was your encounter? Why torture us with the past?" She paused, glancing at Kourin and her uncle before finishing her question. "Sorry, but I have to ask. Why make us go through hell and possibly fucking up our reality? Why would Cyrus do that?"

Kourin answered, "It wasn't Cyrus. It was Artax. He escaped from his brother's hold on him when the bench was damaged at the terminal. He intended to wreak havoc on humans with the goal of destroying them for what they had done to him and his kind."

"So, they are good and evil," said Jack. "Wait, when was the bench damaged?"

"He didn't say," answered Kourin.

Mandy said, "I don't think they look at themselves as good or evil. They simply exist as part of nature, like a rabbit and the fox that chases them. Neither is good nor evil. They just do what they do. I guess from our viewpoint, them being humanoid casts them as good versus evil."

Jack and Laurel exchanged glances.

"What?" Mandy asked when she saw them look at each other.

Laurel said, "We had a conversation about this. I guess we weren't that far off."

Jack replied, "Not far off and not anywhere close at the same time. I didn't have tree elf on my radar at all. But I have a totally different question now. How do you have some of their abilities?"

Kourin answered, "Cyrus thinks one of his kind mated with one of my ancestors somewhere along my lineage. He said it used to be very common in our ancestors to have green eyes and enhanced abilities. It helped our species survive the harsh environment."

"Survival of the fittest," said Jack.

Kourin replied, "I guess something like that. Yes. He claimed it is extremely uncommon now, as there are far fewer of them in existence. He said he hadn't heard of humans having as much power as I do." She looked at Mandy and continued, "Or my daughter. He thinks it may have been my mother or grandmother that mated with one of his kind."

Jack said, "So it's possible your father was one of them? A fairy?"

"They don't like to be called that," Mandy said.

"Sorry. What is their species called? Artax said we had many names for them. What do they call themselves?"

Kourin said, "Ouga. They call us humans. They call themselves Ouga."

28

MANDY

The group gave each other hugs with a plan to regroup for dinner at seven that evening at the Bull and Bar after they all had time to sleep.

Beth called Jack to say Harry was patched up and would rest in the hospital for a few hours. She'd make sure he got home safely.

While they were speaking, Sarah texted Mandy to ask if she could crash at her place for a while. She was too tired to catch a flight back home. Mandy, of course, agreed. She kept the Ouga conversation out of the texts, telling the group she would fill Sarah in later.

As Mandy completed her texting with Sarah, she noticed she had a message from Emry.

She read it: *Hi. Hope everything worked out w/the gift card. Is it okay if I called you sometime? I'd like to see you again.*

She looked at the time stamp. It was sent twelve hours ago, last night. Unsure of how she felt about it, she put the phone in her pocket without answering the text. The vision of Cyrus appearing to her as Emry came to her. She felt her cheeks turning red.

The group all agreed to keep the existence of the Ouga limited to their small group. Jack said he would fill in Beth and Harry. He knew they'd keep it to themselves, not that anyone outside their group would even believe them. All felt fewer people knowing would be for the best. The threat of reality being changed had been averted, so they could all rest, knowing humanity was safe.

In their groggy state of mind, they forgot to discuss the other three in their adventures: Wren, Joneal, and Shannon.

Kourin thought of them as Jack walked with her to their vehicles. Even though they were exhausted, they enjoyed the early morning sunshine and cool, crisp New Hampshire spring air. She decided she'd fill them in when she saw them in the coming days.

With no one else on the walkway, Jack asked, "Kori, one thing I still don't understand. Why were the plants moving in the terminal garden?"

Kourin said, "I'm not 100 percent sure. The way Cyrus was explaining things about nature and all, I think somehow his species is connected to not just trees, but to nature as a whole."

"So, the plants moving coincided with his powers in the bench?"

"Seems so."

Jack chose not to pursue it further. His thoughts were on the plants not solely reacting to the bench. Kourin's state of mind seemed to have a lot to do with it as well. He glanced at her, and she returned his gaze with a broad smile. Her eyes were hazel. He thought, *Best to keep them hazel.*

Kourin thought about Jack's question. After the revelation of her heritage, she had a lot of questions. She knew she had enhanced eyesight. She thought, *What if I have other powers as well? What was it Cyrus said? He hadn't known other humans who had as much power as I did? And my daughter. Telepathy is one for sure.*

She felt Jack holding her hand. *Well, all that doesn't matter right now. I have you.* She squeezed his hand.

As she eyed a row of cedar trees lining the walkway, she amended her decision to tell Shannon, Wren, and Joneal the entire story. She decided to leave out the part of the Ouga and her heritage. *Maybe we should keep that a secret.*

In her fatigue, she thought she saw branches on one tree swaying even though there was no breeze. She decided she was seeing things and continued on, giving Jack's hand a little squeeze.

After they passed the trees, the trees gently swayed. There was no breeze.

They said hello to Carlos as they entered the employee parking lot. He made a quip of seeing them so early, but he kept further comments to himself, knowing both their cars had been in the lot since yesterday.

At Kourin's car, Jack gave her a kiss on her cheek as she stood in front of the open car door. When he pulled back, she placed her hand behind his neck and pulled him to her. She planted a big kiss on his lips. He returned it.

After several moments, she released him, saying, "After all we've been through, Jack, I don't want you to have any doubts about how I feel about you." Emerald eyes sparkled brightly in the morning sun.

Jack gazed into her mesmerizing eyes, witnessing the hazel color so easily replaced by emerald. He had his arms around her waist and said, "There are no doubts in my mind about you. I love you with all my heart."

"Shall we get out of here before something else happens?"

"As you wish," replied Jack.

They passionately kissed again.

Neither noticed the man who exited his Mercedes and strode to where Carlos stood near the gate. With his blue eyes glaring at the couple, he silently watched the pair kissing.

Carlos saw the man's jaw muscles flexing on his well-sculptured chin. For the first time in as long as he could recall, he kept his mouth shut and didn't crack a joke.

* * *

For a few minutes, Mandy and Laurel spoke with the café workers as they filed in for work. Fortunately, they had supervisor coverage for the weekend, so both were scheduled off and could head home for some much-needed rest.

As they walked down the terminal to the exit, Mandy asked Laurel if she was okay with Sarah and Breck. Laurel hesitated answering, but she acknowledged that attempting to change the past would be a mistake. Besides Sarah's children and husband, messing with the past would have far-reaching ramifications that could alter things well beyond one man's life.

Mandy was concerned she had erred in bringing up Breck, but she needed to be certain Laurel was in a fit state of mind after everything they went through. She was gratified her friend seemed to be content with the way things were. To change the subject from Breck, she asked, "What do you think will happen now with the bench?"

After several steps, Laurel said, "It seems to me the balance is restored in the bench to what it had been for centuries. Perhaps some people will sit on it and interact with Cyrus. I guess that's up to him."

Mandy said, "I suppose you're right."

Mandy thought about Artax and what Cyrus had said that neither Kourin nor she shared with the group.

After Artax was once again secured and the others had been returned home, Cyrus answered many of Kourin's and Mandy's questions. He also asked Kourin many, trying to determine who the father was and when the mating had occurred. He was surprised he had seen nothing about a mating of his species with her human ancestor. Someone might have been blocking him, as he had been doing to Artax.

Mandy recalled an offhand statement Cyrus made that, at the moment, didn't seem important. As she thought about it now, though, it seemed more ominous. Cyrus said he had his brother under control for the moment. He then changed the subject on to something else.

Mandy thought about his choice of words—under control for the moment. She didn't like the sound of that.

The two ladies reached the exit door and stepped out into the New England air. The slight chill felt good on Mandy's skin as her body temperature had been slowly rising while running Cyrus' words through her mind.

They rode the tram to the employee parking lot, with Ubu sitting between them on the floor. They exited as Anders stepped in. Neither made eye contact with him nor said hello, but they felt his stare as they walked off. As the tram pulled away, Laurel said, "One of these days he's going to get what Artax got from me."

They both laughed, relieving the tension both had felt.

Carlos greeted them at the entrance to the employee parking area. He asked Mandy how she was doing. His glib manner was more serious than usual, as he had been with them at the party when Miguel left. Mandy assured him she was fine and thanked him for asking.

Before the two ladies went to their respective vehicles, Mandy gave her friend a hug, asking one more time if she was okay. Laurel assured her she was and told her she would see her tonight at the restaurant.

Laurel opened her Jeep's door for Ubu, and he took his usual spot riding shotgun. Carlos opened the gate as she exited for home.

Mandy started her car and had to wait several moments for the morning dew to clear from her windshield even after running her wipers twice.

While she waited, she remembered the text Emry had sent her. She retrieved her phone and read it again. As with the feeling she had from Anders just moments ago, she felt something inside her warming. After having had this occur several times in the past twenty-four hours, she could feel the difference between the emotions Anders caused and the emotions stirring deep inside her core as she stared at Emry's text.

She looked at her reflection in her rearview mirror. Emerald eyes with a golden ring returned her stare. Emry came to her mind. She pictured his face, his body. A rosy red hue was visible on her cheeks in the reflection. She raised her gaze to look at her eyes. The golden ring grew brighter.

Her phone showed it was well before 6:00 a.m. She thought, *Well, he probably won't answer, but I'll leave a message telling him to call me if he still wanted to get together.*

She hit the green Call button. Prepared to leave a voicemail, she heard instead, "Hello, Mandy."

Her cheeks turned red as she floundered for the right words to say.

Emry asked, "Mandy? Are you there?"

She looked at her reflection in the mirror. Emerald eyes of her ancestors with golden rings like her mother's returned her gaze. She said, "Good morning, Emry. I'm sorry to call so early, but I just saw your text." She paused a heartbeat, still looking into her own eyes. She thought of her mother's courage and sacrifice to bring her into the world—twice!

If she can do that, I can certainly handle a get-together.

She said, "I'm seeing some friends tonight for dinner." She paused, questioning if she should call him a plus one. Her voice was soft and inviting as she said, "I'd love for you to be my date."

EPILOGUE

FRIDAY, JANUARY 20, 2073

The frigid mid-Atlantic breeze blew across the Capitol's West Front, bringing a tear to the president-elect's eye. Many wanted the event to be held indoors because of the harsh weather. Aleja had been unwavering that the swearing in should be conducted outdoors, as it had been traditionally done for many inaugurations, particularly given the chaos of the last two administrations. The country needed healing. As had occurred when she was a child, the Constitution was put to the test. Fortunately, it held.

Her candidacy ran on the platform of unity, inclusion, and, of course, prosperity. Without the third promised and delivered, she would not have the resources and the political backing to put her agenda into law.

The country had made strides since the late 1900s to early 2000s in equality and diversity. The decades of turmoil that followed came to a head in the administration eight years before. Her predecessor was a humble man with an honest upbringing and good intentions. However, he surrounded himself with individuals who caused discord, as most of them had personal agendas that were not in line with his. His administration failed to deliver on the promises made, as most of the time was spent arguing in-house. No progress was made in healing the country.

As Aleja observed the crowd stretched out before her down the promenade as far as the eye could see through the falling snow, she marveled that so many had endured the harsh temperatures and gently falling snow. As a New Englander, she was used to the stinging cold of winter. The day felt like home.

Her husband of twenty-one happily married years stood behind her along with her children, two girls from her first marriage and the third and only child, a boy, from her current. The girls were joined by their respective spouses, one male and one female. Her youngest child stood alone next to her husband. He was in between relationships.

Behind them, her father stood proudly. He was in frail health, but he insisted on being there for his daughter. The chilly wind would not be good for him. She had given her aides strict orders to bring him in from the frigid weather once her speech was finished.

The address had been amended to one of the shortest speeches ever spoken at an inauguration. The brevity of the oration would not diminish the profound words spoken to begin the recovery process. In Aleja's time in office, she found speeches that were succinct and direct were more impactful than lengthy, flowery, and insincere ones. Her directness and integrity were qualities that endeared her to the troubling nation.

The road to today had not been an easy one. She had humble roots as her parents' second daughter, and her journey in politics began when a kindhearted woman she had met at an airport terminal sat down beside her during her work break. They spoke about her past and the present. Her mother had passed away six months earlier, and she was trying to determine where she fit in, having had several run-ins with racist bullies at her high school. Life had quickly taken a downward turn, and she had not been coping well. She even considered ending it all.

The part-time job at the electronics store in the airport terminal had been a temporary distraction, yet she had not created many acquaintances, being an introverted person. The exception was the lady she had met who shared similarities with her own high school experience. In time, this woman had become a close friend, and as the years passed, they became closer still. She had become her surrogate mother.

Alie, as her friend fondly called her, was overwhelmed with gratitude for her friend's unwavering support through the years. As she watched the crowd cheering her name and waving banners, she thought of how close she had come to not having a life at all.

From that chance encounter, her life had changed. Her friend had given her purpose and guidance. At first, she worked to make her school a better place, an inclusive place where kids would not live in fear. She was bullied and chastised, but she never gave up hope. Every taunting she received strengthened her until she graduated in the top 10 percent of her class. She went to college, graduating summa cum laude.

She began her humble political start on the school committee. From there, she advanced on her platform of ending racism once and for all. It was challenging every step of the way. Strides were made, and as often as one step was made forward, incidents throughout the country caused steps backwards. Eventually, new ground was forged. In time, she was elected to the US Senate, filing and passing several landmark bills.

This day, she was moments away from swearing the oath of office as the fifty-fifth President of the United States.

As she reflected on her teen years at the airport just under forty years ago, she had a moment of disbelief that this was actually happening. She took a moment to observe the organized chaos, the sound of people talking in excited whispers as they arranged themselves into position. Steps away, the chief justice held Lincoln's burgundy Bible, having chosen it as a symbol of humankind's universal rights to equality.

Aleja searched for her lifelong friend. She had extended the invitation and wasn't sure if she would attend because of the inclement weather and her advanced age. After several seconds of searching, she could not locate her. She was saddened, but there was no time to dwell on it. The time had come for her to be sworn in.

As she approached the spot next to her husband, the wind died down. Snow lightly fell onto hands holding the Bible. The chief justice protected the artifact with one hand, covering the delicate book. Snow melted as it fell onto her hand.

Aleja reached out to place her hand upon the Bible and raised her other. As she did so, a ray of sunshine broke through the cloud cover and shined upon the attendees. The light reflected off the falling snow, making the scene surreal as it sparkled from the falling ice crystals.

She glanced to her right through the crowd of family, friends, high-ranking politicians, and invited guests. At the rear of the gathering, she saw a familiar-colored jacket with the hood pulled up tightly against the bitter cold. The figure had a matching scarf concealing most of her face, but she peered out under her coverings to watch her friend take her oath.

There was no mistaking who the person was. Her emerald green eyes sparkled in the clear, crisp Washington air. Aleja smiled toward her, a silent acknowledgement for years of friendship.

Mandy smiled beneath her scarf. Her dimples were not visible to those sharing the stage with her. Emotions of serenity and elation warmed her from the inside out. Long since having mastered control of her powers, she returned Alie's gaze, knowing the bench's legacy had been fulfilled at last.

From beneath layers of clothing, the figure with emerald eyes watched as the woman, first made known to her fifty years before, began to take her oath. The president-elect had been shepherded by the steady hand of fate to arrive at this specific point in time. As a child, the same woman was saved by a mysterious bench and a five-hundred-dollar supermarket gift card. The bundled-up lady's emerald eyes brightened and her golden rings shimmered with a warm glow as she remembered one spring morning when Alfredo, a scruffy little rescue dog, had bravely saved Alie and her family from a house fire.

"I, Alejandra Francieli Baro Domingo, do solemnly swear that I will faithfully execute the Office of President of the United States and will to the best of my ability, preserve, protect, and defend the Constitution of the United States."

The vast crowd around her was full of excitement, their hands clapping and voices cheering as the fifty-four states were united in optimism—all thanks to that little rescue dog who continued to live on in the memories of the elderly green-eyed lady and her friend, the president of the United States.

If you or someone you know is in crisis, call **988** to reach the

Suicide and Crisis Lifeline 800-273-TALK (8255) or

Text HOME to 741741 (U.S.); 686868 (Canada); 85258 (UK).

Visit **SpeakingOfSuicide.com/resources** for additional information and resources.

The Benchmark Legacy Series will continue with Book 3 of the Relic saga!

RELIC REALM

The sweet freshness of the morning air filled Mandy's senses, a sign the dawn was upon her. The melodic sound of sparrows and chickadees singing filled the open bedroom window. With her eyes still closed, she listened to the gentle, sweet birdsong.

Two months had passed since the incident with the bench. Subsequent to that day, the beauty of the world – its sights, sounds, and emotions – was observed and experienced with a newfound appreciation. The morning brought the joyous trill of a male sparrow, and then a gentle, almost whispering reply from a female, filling her ears. She heard tones of joy in their sounds and felt their optimism in the air – wishing each other a good morning, praising the beauty of the day, reassuring one another there was no danger near, and reminders to bring back food for the chicks.

Mandy's lips curved into a full smile that was accompanied by a soft giggle. They were not precisely conveying that to each other. She was inferring based on the distinct sound of each bird's vocalization. It was apparent to her they were delighted with their situation and what the new sunrise had brought. Perhaps one day she would comprehend the melodious chirping, but not today.

She opened her eyes. In the far-off distance, the sun lit up the sky with its warm, orange glow. A gentle breeze rustled the leaves as the upper branches of the distant trees were touched by golden light. With her eyes automatically adjusting, she felt no need to reach for the nightstand lamp. These days, the only time she turned on the lights was when she had guests. Even in the dead of night, the details of her home were all in shades of gray monochrome.

Mandy had not been so calm in the beginning. In the first few days, she would panic after turning out the lights to sleep. Whenever her eyes opened, her bedroom was in view. Even though the room was dark to normal humans, she could see her furniture, the doorway, and Autumn, her cat, curled up in her favorite spot next to her.

Upon the completion of the initial week, she became accustomed to not using electric lighting to bridge the divide between day and night. In the weeks that followed, her brain had adapted to her new vision. In the daylight, throughout her day, she felt the same as she had before the bench encounter. Conversely, when the sun set and night fell, her home and the world around her lit up with a special magic. Gradually, she grew accustomed to it. Now, it was a seamless part of her.

However, her cat, Autumn, continued to be an enigma with bright and inquisitive eyes. In the beginning, she often would sit nearby and stare at her for hours while her tail twitched back and forth. It was disconcerting, but as the days went by, she did it less often.

Mandy felt a glimmer of hope with her cat on a dreary Sunday afternoon in May as a Hallmark movie hummed in the background and rain pattered against her window. The cat lay at a distance, quietly staring at her with wide eyes, while its tail remained still.

On this lazy day during a commercial while looking into the cat's yellow eyes, Mandy felt she had a telepathic connection with her. She was certain she heard a voice speaking in her thoughts, expressing *love.*

After a moment, though, the reality of the situation became apparent, and it was not what she had expected. Autumn contorted her body, extending one leg up and licking her backside. Mandy's deep laughter caused the cat to pause, her tongue hanging out of her mouth as she glared in her direction. She laughed harder still, thinking that nothing says I love you like a good butt licking.

At the memory of that day, she smiled down at her curled-up cat beside her as she extricated herself from under her sheet and rotated her legs to the side of the bed, careful not to disturb the sleeping feline. With just a nightshirt on and the windows wide open, she had not slept well. When she went to sleep the night before, the temperature had been close to eighty degrees, an uncommonly warm evening for June in New Hampshire. The morning had ushered in more seasonable temperatures. As she stood next to her bed, she felt her skin tingle as the cool air blew against her bare legs.

She placed her palms down onto the windowsill, observing nature at dawn. A solitary ray of sunshine broke through the trees' leafy cover and arrived at her window where she was standing. She relished the sun's warmth on her skin as she watched the tiny birds flit through the tree branches.

She thought about what lay ahead for her today. Her friend Sarah and her family would arrive in New Hampshire for their family vacation. This would be the first time meeting her husband and two daughters, but she felt a part of the family already from all the warm conversations she had with Sarah. As she observed another sparrow flying off from its nest, she looked forward to spending time with her friend's daughters. If they were anything like their mother, she would enjoy their company.

It had been Laurel's idea to invite Sarah and her family to vacation in New Hampshire. Since discovering she was the Sarah from Breck's past, the three of them spent time together when the airline pilot had a layover in Manchester. The underutilized extra bedroom had been converted to a true bedroom Sarah used whenever she was in town.

In the beginning, Sarah insisted on paying a rental fee, which Mandy steadfastly refused. Eventually, Mandy admitted that she had hidden intentions for her friend's stay and couldn't accept any payment with a clear conscience.

The first was Laurel's mental health. After the revelation of Sarah's identity, Laurel worked to cast aside the pain of her past and move on with her life. With the unwavering support of her friends, family and trusty service dog, Ubu, she had made notable strides. She came to accept that although Breck had died, he likely saved others. Furthermore, any alteration to the past would have disastrous consequences for Sarah's family. Laurel's focus was now on the present and the future. As she spent more time with Sarah, it helped her keep the past at bay and the future ahead.

The second reason Mandy wanted Sarah to stay with her was to have someone to talk to about her own problems. After discovering the truth about her hybrid identity, she needed help to understand what it meant to be both human and Ouga. Laurel, her confidant and closest friend, had her own issues to take care of. She didn't want to burden her with new ones. The comfort of hearing Sarah's voice on the phone nearly every day and having her there once or twice a week normalized her life. Many supportive conversations had helped her maintain her own emotional composure.

Mandy's attention was grabbed by a sparrow darting away. She thought. *At least no one has been mysteriously transported to a different timeline because of me.* She watched another one fly off after the first and added. *Well, as far as I know.*

Her attention turned to the thought of the other person flying in today, bringing a smile to her face. As soon as the extraordinary bench events were behind her, she had wasted no time in reaching out to her high school friend. After several FaceTime calls, on a whim three weeks ago, she asked her friend to visit New Hampshire. To her surprise, the invitation was accepted without hesitation, and today was the day her flight was scheduled to land a few minutes after six. With Sarah and her family staying at a hotel for the night, this friend would have the guest bedroom. Tomorrow, everyone would be at Jack's cabin by the lake for a weeklong stay.

Mandy left the window and stepped into her bathroom. Her gaze fell upon her reflection in the mirror above the sink. She ignored her bird's nest hair and focused on her eyes. It had become a routine for her to pause and peer at her eyes on any reflective surface she came across. The day she found out about her birth mother coincided with the last time her eyes were in their original hazel color. After returning from the last bench encounter with Kourin, her eyes had remained emerald green. At first, she had feared the alien emerald green eyes staring back at her. As the weeks passed, she grew accustomed to them.

The golden ring, however, was disconcerting, shining brightly during the bench encounters. Although she hoped it was gone forever, her newfound ancestry was unlikely to be easily dismissed. As a precaution, she remained guarded and kept her emotions in check as best she could. As she stared into the depths of her pupils, she thought. *There is still much to be fearful of.*

She ran through the memories of the past two months, feeling the emotions that had come with each step of her journey.

* * *

Immediately following the Artax encounter, she felt like a leaf in the wind. After it was confirmed reality was back to normal, she had difficulty keeping her emotions in check, especially when she was in proximity to her birth mother, Kourin. The intensity of her mother's emotions caused her to have unrestrained responses to them. As the days passed with Kourin stopping by the café for a snack or a cup of tea, they became better at controlling their emotions between them.

Twice, though, Mandy's emotions threatened to overpower her. The first was when she went to Newmarket to visit her adoptive mother to tell her she had located her birth mother. It had been an emotional afternoon, and she had felt herself being overwhelmed by those emotions. Prior to arriving, she had the foresight to wear lightly tinted sunglasses that concealed her emerald eyes. She kept what happened in the prior days to herself. Someday, she would open up and tell her everything, but until she could understand and accept herself, she would wait to share her true ancestry.

The second time, two weeks after the incident in the bench realm, she could barely keep her emotions in check on a date with Emry. Their first date at the Bull and Bar had gone well. After learning of her mother's identity and the extraordinary abilities they shared, she was able to set all that aside for a few hours and focused on the night out with her friends. The entire time her gaze had lingered on the man she had met the day before. Emry was an absolute dream come true. He was kind, caring, and had a delightful personality, plus he revealed a bit of a playful side, which she found endearing. The night was over before they knew it, and they both agreed it had been enjoyable.

The next day, Emry called her at midday. After talking on the phone for nearly an hour, they set up a date, just the two of them, for the following Friday night.

After the traumatic Sunday visit with her adoptive mother, the week flew by as she worked on controlling her emotions with her birth mother. Several times each day, her mind wandered to Emry's smile, and twice she caught herself with Cyrus' image of Emry. Luckily, she had been alone each time, so no one witnessed her flushed cheeks and asked questions.

The second date with Emry was dinner and a movie. Mandy spent part of that Friday afternoon at the cosmetic counter at her mother's insistence. Properly applied makeup accentuated the green in her eyes. When Kourin had finished with the makeover, Mandy looked in the mirror and felt like a beautiful princess.

When she returned to the café, every head turned in her direction. It was not her imagination. Not only seeing it, she could sense it. She rushed straight to the office to get her friend's opinion. Laurel proclaimed Emry would be enchanted when he saw her.

Since it was late in the afternoon, Laurel told her to take off early to get ready. They embraced tightly. The joy radiating off both their faces. Laurel felt a great sense of gratification when her friend expressed a newfound sense of love after the devastation of her ex-fiancé's cheating years before. Mandy's stomach was filled with butterflies as she contemplated what was to come with a mix of eagerness and apprehension.

Upon reaching home, Mandy took the risk of showering below her shoulders, something she had never done before. She did not want to undo her mother's hard work. She chose to wear a black dress, and when she put it on, she realized it was the same one she had been intending to wear at the terminal party the previous week. That seemed like a lifetime ago. The dry cleaner had made it look like new. This time, she made sure Autumn didn't get near it.

Emry's eyes lit up when he saw her, commenting on how stunning she was. Her cheeks reddened as she thanked and complimented him on his handsome appearance. As they drove to the restaurant he had chosen, she reflected on how much she appreciated his attention. The week before, she had glanced in the mirror, brush in hand, and declared that she was content with her reflection as is. She glanced at his profile as they drove. She thought. *Maybe a little extra now and again isn't such a bad thing after all.*

After devouring a tasty Italian dinner, they hopped in the car and drove to the movie theater. She felt a tingle of excitement as Emry took her hand for the first time, walking across the parking lot until they reached the theater entrance. As the movie played, Mandy's heart fluttered each time she peeked in his direction. With her enhanced vision, his features were clearly visible to her in the darkness, and with each glance, she grew more enamored. She yearned to feel his touch and reached out to him, holding his warm hand tenderly until the credits rolled.

When he walked her to her condo door, she tilted her head back and looked up at him with a playful sparkle in her eye, inviting him in for a drink. He said he would like to, but as it was already well past eleven, he had to be at work for six. With her heart fluttering with exhilaration, she clasped both his hands and said the night had been wonderful. He agreed with a smile, saying he looked forward to repeating the experience. Without hesitation, she proposed they should go out again the following night. His face beamed with joy, and he promised to call her after lunch. He hugged her close and planted a tender kiss on her cheek before stepping away and walking back to his car.

As the car drove away, she could feel the disappointment weighing on her, wondering why he had only kissed her on the cheek and not on the lips. She kept tossing and turning that night, wondering if it meant he wasn't as into her as she was into him.

When Kourin visited the café for her tea the following morning, she was eager for an update on how the date went. She had sensed her daughter's distress through the night and asked her to sit with her at a table. Mandy recounted the date, the previous night's kiss, and her feelings of trepidation. She finished by looking up at her mother, her voice trembling as she asked if she had done something wrong.

Her mother gave her a comforting smile while she shared the story of her and Jack. She stated they were similar. In the beginning, Jack expressed affection in the same tentative way as Emry. They both demonstrated gentlemanly behavior. She admitted it could be nerve-wracking, but they had good intentions. Whether it was their demeanor, or the way they treated others. They were who they were and that would not change.

Mandy experienced a wave of calm as her mother shared her thoughts about Emry. She realized that her worries about him had been created by her own assumptions. As she was listening to her mother, memories of earlier unsuccessful relationships floated into her thoughts, which she quickly pushed away to concentrate on the present instead. She had to shake off the feeling of regret that the past had brought her and accept the unknown future with courage.

As Mandy's anxiety mounted, Kourin's emerald eyes met hers, conveying understanding. Her mother gave her a loving smile and thought. *Control what you can control. The here and now.*

She nodded in agreement, her lips curling into a smile as she thought to her mother that they had another date that night.

Kourin assured her that if Emry wasn't interested, he wouldn't be spending time with her again so soon. Mandy agreed, displaying her dimpled smile. Without words spoken, both felt the previous anxiety lift away. Mandy rose, went to the other side of the table, and gave her mother a heartfelt hug.

As they embraced, neither was aware of the delicate motion of the plants in the nearby garden, as if a gentle breeze had brushed them.

* * *

After a hot shower and meticulously blow drying her hair, Mandy did her own makeup for this date, having learned the techniques from her mother the day before. She gazed at her work and thought. *Not as good as Mom did, but not too bad.*

She delicately donned the red dress she had worn at the terminal party, being careful not to smudge her makeup. When she had first thought about wearing the red dress, she was hesitant, as the last time she had worn it, things had not gone as planned. In the end, she wore it since that was also the day she had first met Emry.

She cast a critical eye over her figure in the full-length mirror on the back of her bedroom door. The dress hugged her body in all the right places. Her face lit up with a devilish grin as she looked at her legs in the reflection. Had she been looking at her eyes in that moment, she would have seen the golden ring flare around her pupils. By the time her eyes had risen to her head, the ring had diminished, showing off the emerald hue she was becoming familiar with.

* * *

After their dinner at a renowned restaurant in downtown Manchester, Mandy and Emry needed to do some physical activity to balance out the delicious yet hefty meal. Connected to the restaurant was a nightclub, with the same owners styling it to match the energy of New York and Los Angeles. Two burly bouncers were positioned at the entrance with their arms crossed across their chests. Because Mandy and Emry had already dined at the restaurant attached to the venue, they were given preferential treatment and entry.

The subdued, colorful lighting was carefully chosen to create an inviting atmosphere inside the venue, just enough to see without running into anything. Mandy used her enhanced vision to guide them to an unoccupied table in the distance, her fingers intertwined with Emry's as they went. The venue was filling up, and the atmosphere was alive with conversation and laughter. Mandy had been to this club before with Laurel and knew the floor would soon be packed with people.

A waitress, who was a few years younger than Mandy, delivered their drinks several minutes after ordering. As they enjoyed their cocktails, lively music filled the air while their eyes followed the energetic movements on the dance floor. When the opening chords of a song Mandy liked filled the air, she quickly drained her drink and grabbed Emry's hand, letting the rhythm take control as she tugged him to the dance floor.

After two strenuous songs that Emry found challenging to keep up with, a slower song gave them the chance to draw close and take a breath. In the middle of the song, as they were pressed together, Mandy looked up into his eyes and was overcome with a powerful longing to kiss him. She placed her lips against his as if nothing else in the world mattered in that moment.

His soft lips returned her kiss with a fiery passion that made her heart race.

As the song ended and their lips parted, she felt a rush of emotions overwhelming her. With her eyes closed, she could feel the warmth of an internal fire radiating through her body. She inhaled a deep breath and opened her eyes. The dancefloor and patrons lit up with a shimmering brilliance as if the lights had come on.

As they made their way back to the table, she could feel the electricity between their hands as she excused herself to go to the restroom. Her heart felt like it was going to burst out of her chest. She felt her emotions bubbling up, threatening to spill over and take control.

When she entered the ladies' room, the aroma of perfume wafted in the air from two women in their twenties talking by the sinks. She averted her gaze and went into the nearest stall. She closed her eyes and breathed in and out with measured breaths. After a few moments, she heard the door close as the two women departed. With no other sound, she cracked open the stall to peek out. The restroom was silent, so she walked to the sink across from her and met her gaze in the mirror.

Her eyes were sparkling emerald green. The pupils were framed with a hint of gold, but the ring was muted compared to the interactions with the bench. She continued to take slow, steady breaths and gradually felt her emotions calming. She felt better.

The restroom door opened. She nervously peered at the reflection of the person entering and was taken aback to see her mother! She spun towards her.

Before she could open her mouth, Kourin said, "Don't worry. I'm not stalking you. Jack and I are on a date and noticed you dancing with Emry. When I saw you go to the restroom, I deliberated going to you."

"What made you decide to?"

Kourin paused before answering. She peered into her daughter's eyes. "I could sense your intense emotions. You really like Emry."

"Yes, I do."

"No, Mandy. You... really like him. It's all right to have feelings for him."

Mandy was filled with an unexpected emotion as she grasped the significance of her mother's words. Their mother-daughter special connection made it impossible for her to camouflage her feelings. Emry was stealing her heart.

She looked into her own mirrored reflection, her voice trembling. "What if he doesn't feel the same about me?"

When their emerald eyes met in the mirror, her mother's words were a comforting whisper. "I am certain neither of us will have any difficulty comprehending the emotions of a person close to us." When she saw the perplexed expression on her daughter's face, she reached out to take both her hands into hers. She mentally addressed her daughter without vocalizing. *You know in your heart that he cares about you. You can feel it. Don't be afraid to open up to him.*

Mandy thought back. *What if it doesn't work out?*

Kourin gave her daughter a hug and thought. *If you keep your heart sheltered, it will never break, but you also can never feel the delicate embrace of love. Give him a chance.*

Kourin released her. Her own eyes blazed with an emerald sheen and a golden halo. She said, "Besides, if he breaks your heart, he's going to face the wrath of mama bear!"

They shared a laugh, and then a gentle hug. The restroom door opened with three women entering. Mother and daughter exited, walking back towards Mandy's table. Halfway there, Mandy thought. *Mom, can you and Jack join us?*

I don't want to intrude on your night out.

Um, I'm not sure I can control my emotions. She stopped walking. In the distance, she could see where Emry was sitting by himself. *I can already feel my heart pounding.*

Yes. I can feel it, too. Kourin glanced towards Emry and then in the direction she knew Jack was sitting, but there were too many people in the way to see him. *Let's stop by your table. If it's okay with Emry, I'll go get Jack and come right back.*

Thanks, Mom. Mandy realized two things. One, the passion she had for Emry was undeniable, and she had to learn to control it. Two, she felt her mother's love radiating towards her, filling her with joy when she was invited to be a part of her daughter's life.

As they walked towards Emry, Kourin thought. *We're going to have to figure out how to block each other's thoughts, or this could become awkward.*

Emry watched Mandy come near, and his heart swelled and his face lit up with a beaming smile.

His emotions reached out to Mandy, washing over her with warmth and love. The nude, well-endowed image of Emry, as Cyrus had appeared to her in the forest, came to Mandy's mind and was reflected in Kourin's.

Kourin thought. *Oh, my! He has a remarkable... smile.* As they approached Emry's table, they could not contain their laughter.

* * *

Her mother and she eventually mastered the technique of blocking each other's thoughts. Fortunately, they worked across from each other in the terminal, giving them plenty of time to practice. At the outset, it was hard, yet as the weeks went by, they grew more adept at concealing specific thoughts. They soon realized they could conceal particular information by shielding the thought within their mind. It wasn't safeguarded for very long. In the beginning, it was for a few seconds. With practice the time increased. Eventually, they shielded themselves from each other without having to focus on it. Unless there was an unexpected emotional outburst.

This revelation happened one afternoon when Mandy burned her finger in the café. Kourin was at home when she sensed her daughter's pain, and even though it wasn't a serious injury, she picked up on it right away. In an instant, she made a telepathic connection, reaching out without thinking. Mandy reassured she was alright. It wasn't until later on that day Kourin shared with her daughter she had been over ten miles away when the accident occurred. They were astounded by how far they could connect.

Since that day, the farthest apart they had established a mental connection was forty miles. This occurred on a warm June Sunday when Kourin and Jack were at Rye Beach. Soon after arriving, he removed his shirt, and she felt the heat radiating from his skin as she spread suntan lotion across his back. The smell of salt and sand mixed with coconut filled the air as Kourin moved her hands over his toned shoulders. With the sound of waves crashing onto the beach in the background, she felt a rush of energy flare within her, radiating outwards from her core. Her mind wandered. She envisioned Jack's embrace, his soft kisses on her neck, and the tickle of his breath on her skin. She imagined the warmth of his manhood pulsating against her.

Lost in her thoughts, she was jolted back to reality by a familiar voice ringing inside her mind. *Mother!*

The melodic sound of Kourin's laughter echoed behind Jack. He turned towards her. "What's so funny, dear?"

She felt her cheeks flush as she sought to skirt her awkward answer, but Jack's gaze changed her mind. She leaned in to his ear. "I was just thinking about how much I'd love to be somewhere else with you right now."

Her daughter's voice reverberated in her mind. *Get a room, Mom!*

Before Jack could open his mouth, she added. "And my daughter heard me."

Kourin pressed her lips to his, and they kissed passionately as the sound of seagulls echoed close by in the salty breeze. She felt a pleasant tingling sensation that spread from within her, accompanied by a familiar voice in her head. *You really should get a room!* A burst of laughter echoed through her mind before she blocked her daughter.

* * *

Mandy came back to the present and peeled off her nightshirt. The cool air on her skin felt invigorating. She had gone to bed without panties and now was standing naked in front of the mirror. Her blond hair was tangled and unruly, so she ran a brush through it to make it easier to wash. She avoided looking at her eyes again as she brushed out her hair. Her eyes wandered down to her chest in the mirror. Not that long ago, she had been pondering in this very spot if she was growing old.

Her gaze lifted towards her face. Despite her breasts appearing to be the same as before, she felt her face had taken on a more youthful visage. She scrutinized the faint wrinkles at the corner of her eyes. She thought. *Must just be my imagination.* Her mind meandered to Emry's smile. *Or maybe I'm just feeling better about myself.*

Her thoughts turned to her biological mother having found true love. A smile spread across her face. She eyed her reflection. The wrinkles had become more pronounced. Two small dimples were now visible on her cheeks. Her mother's face came to mind. *There's no hint of dimples when she smiles.* She looked into her own eyes, seeing the flecks of gold shimmering in their depths. *But I certainly have her eyes.*

She recalled the memory of her mother kissing Jack on the beach. If she was asked a few months back what love was, she wouldn't have been able to respond. The passion behind her mother's kiss with Jack had provided her the answer. *I'm glad you two found each other!*

She pictured Emry and felt the same warmth in her heart. Since their second date, they had spent many evenings together. Whenever they had the same day off, they spent it together. So far, they had not been intimate.

Not that she didn't want to. She did. She dreamed of having sex with him. Often, she awoke from a very steamy dream aroused. It was during those times that she was fearful. What would happen if she lost control of her emotions during sex?

The intense fear she felt created an invisible wall that prevented her relationship from advancing. She required a sense of mastery and control over her own emotions. The image of Cyrus as naked Emry came to her. She felt her face flush and her emotions rising.

In her mind, she heard her mother's familiar voice. *Get a room!* Followed by laughter.

As she turned on the shower, she thought to herself. *Come hell or high water, this week I'm going to learn how to control myself.*

She heard her mother's voice. *Have faith in yourself, my dear. I'm certain you can succeed.*

As the hot water splashed on her breasts, she heard her mother add. *After all, you didn't hear me last night, did you, dear?*

Oh gross, Mom! TMI, Mom. TMI.

ABOUT THE AUTHOR

Ed, together with his wife Angela, is based in Westford, Massachusetts, surrounded by their two sons, grandchildren, and a cherished rescue dog, Molly. With an illustrious career spanning over forty years in retail management, Ed's philosophy has always been rooted in kindness, respect, and the golden rule. Known for his dry humor, he spent a significant part of his career as Santa's helper at a leading toy store, creating joyous memories for two generations of children.

Now, entering a new phase in his life, Ed is channeling these decades of wisdom into his writings, particularly in the Benchmark Legacy Series. His engaging, thought-provoking tales unravel the consequences of life's choices, encouraging readers to reflect on their own journey. Ed's stories serve as an inspiration to create a positive influence and strive for a better future.